Donna Alward lives on Canada's east coast with her family, which includes a husband, a couple of kids, a senior dog and two crazy cats. Her heart-warming stories of love, hope and homecoming have been translated into several languages, hit bestseller lists and won awards, but her favourite thing is hearing from readers! When she's not writing she enjoys reading—of course!—knitting, gardening, cooking...and she's a *Masterpiece Theater* addict. You can visit her on the web at DonnaAlward.com, and join her mailing list at DonnaAlward.com/newsletter

USA TODAY bestselling and RITA® Award-winning author **Marie Ferrarella** has written more than 250 books for Mills & Boon, some under the name Marie Nicole. Her romances are beloved by fans worldwide. Visit her website, marieferrarella.com

D0550952

Discover more at millsandboon.co.uk

THE BILLIONAIRE'S ISLAND BRIDE

DONNA ALWARD

COMING TO A CROSSROADS

MARIE FERRARELLA

MILLS & BOON

First Published in Great Britain 2020
by Mills & Boon, an imprint of HarperCollinsPublishers,
1 London Bridge Street, London, SE1 9GF

The Billionaire's Island Bride © 2020 Donna Alward
Coming to a Crossroads © 2020 Marie Rydzynski-Ferrarella

ISBN: 978-0-263-27883-5

0620

MIX
Paper from
responsible sources
FSC
www.fsc.org
FSC™ C007454

This book is produced from independently certified FSC™
paper to ensure responsible forest management.

For more information visit: www.harpercollins.co.uk/green

Printed and bound in Spain
by CPI, Barcelona

THE BILLIONAIRE'S ISLAND BRIDE

DONNA ALWARD

To Dreamer, the best dog.

CHAPTER ONE

BROOKLYN GRAVES HEARD the *whomp-whomp-whomp* of helicopter rotors and rolled her eyes, then let out a long breath as she turned her back on the cliff and followed its progress.

The wind off the ocean whipped her hair around her face and she shoved it back with a hand, tucking it behind her ears, where it stayed for all of about ten seconds before it was loose and blowing around again. She shaded her eyes and stared at the red-and-white chopper as it arced over her corner of the island and then headed toward the grand house and the helipad there.

She'd known this day was coming. Ernest Chetwynd had finally sold the island, and an American had bought it. If the ostentatious aerial arrival was anything to go by, Cole Abbott was going to be a real piece of work. Money to throw around on private islands, and an ego to match.

The sound faded, muffled by the rhythmic roar of the waves crashing on the rocks below. Ernest, who had been the one to build the landing pad, had occasionally had a helicopter chartered. He'd taken her up once, on her birthday, and given her a tour of the Nova Scotia south shore. It had been so different seeing it from the air, all the rugged rocks and islands and sandy beaches. And utterly harmless, since Ernest had been at least seventy-five at that time. He was lonely, and she and Ernest had been friends of a sort. There'd certainly been mutual respect, making her presence on the island quite secure.

His big mansion had once housed him and his wife, and then quite often their children and grandchildren. After Marietta's death, everything had changed. Ernest went to see his kids instead. The house—all twelve thousand square feet of it—was too much for an aging bachelor, even though he'd hired Brooklyn to care for the grounds and he had a housekeeper come over from the mainland once a week.

As long as Ernest had owned the island, Brooklyn had been safe. She owned the southeast corner, a wonderful acreage passed down by her great-grandparents, and which provided her with solitude and peace and an amazing atmosphere to make a living. Her little boat ensured that she could get back and forth to the mainland whenever she wanted. And she did, often. For supplies and visits with friends. But always, Bellwether Island had been there for her to retreat to. Her safe haven.

Which was now spoiled by the new owner, who was ostentatiously arriving by chopper, now that crews had ferried his things from the mainland to the island and delivered them to the grand house on the bluff. She'd started calling him Mr. Fancy Man in her head.

In short, she was not happy about this new development, even though she'd known it was bound to happen. Ernest couldn't hold on forever, and she'd hoped one of his kids would take it over. But none of them wanted it—not the isolation of being the only occupants of the island, nor the upkeep. Just some American billionaire who wanted to add it to his list of... well, whatever. Accomplishments? Possessions? It didn't matter.

She let out another breath and started the walk back to the house. The sound of the waves faded, though the wind still tossed her hair around. She stopped at the vegetable garden behind the century-old house. The garden was nearly done now, in mid-September. It had been a good summer, a little dry, perhaps, but with enough rain to fill Brooklyn's water tanks for when Mother Nature needed a little help. She'd spent every summer here as a kid, running over the island, swimming on the beach and helping her grandmother with gardening and canning while her grandfather fished. There'd been a hammock between two spruce trees, and she'd spent hours there curled up with a book. Almost every good memory she had of her childhood was tied to this island. It was why, when everything in her life fell horrifically apart, she'd come back. To the place where she'd last felt safe and happy. And here she'd stayed.

Now that peaceful existence was threatened. Because exactly one week ago, on the day that Cole Abbott took possession of Bellwether Island, she'd received an offer from his attorney, attempting to buy her out.

One she'd rejected immediately. The truth was, despite the gorgeous mansion and spectacular setting, living here wasn't always easy. Popping to the store for a last-minute item couldn't happen. Going out to dinner took planning, taking the weather and tides into account. And in the winter, it was downright isolating. She'd bet a hundred bucks that Abbott would be gone once he'd sat through his first January northeaster. And then she wouldn't have to worry about him, except for maybe a few months of the year. The shine would certainly wear off his new toy.

She just had to do what she always did: persevere.

Cole hopped out of the helicopter and reached back for his duffel bag. With a wave to the pilot, he ran from the helipad toward the house. He was nearly to the back garden when the chopper lifted off again and started back toward mainland Nova Scotia.

He was finally here.

In a few days, work crews would ferry over and begin the renovations he had planned, and in early October, his first corporate retreat was booked, from one of his own companies. The executives were scheduled to stay four days, for rest, rejuvenation and an informal sharing of ideas while they unplugged.

During this event, there would be no Wi-Fi provided. His team would enjoy top-notch dining, an on-site gym, the hot tub, and the sound of the ocean. An antidote to the high-pressure lives they led and a way to keep them from burning out and to remind them of why they loved their careers.

He wished he'd had such a thing not so long ago.

The keys to his house were in his pocket, but he put his bag by the door and then ventured down to the beach. It wasn't large—maybe two hundred feet of sandy shoreline that gave way to rocks, but it was enough. The September day was warm, and he took off his shoes and socks and rolled up the cuffs of his jeans, letting his toes squidge in the sand. Wind blew the short strands of his hair off his face, and he drew the salt air into his lungs. Ten extra steps led him to the water, where the cold Atlantic fizzed over his toes. The breakers washed over his ankles, splashing a little and dampening his jeans. But he didn't care.

Having his Realtor best friend, Jeremy, find this place was the answer to a prayer.

Cole let out a breath and pulled in another. And another. A year ago he'd found himself on a dangerous path. One that mimicked his father's, including a cardiac episode that had scared him to death. He didn't want to end like his dad, dead at fifty-one—or thirty-five—from a heart attack because he'd been a workaholic.

Work hard, play hard. That was what Jeremy and Bran had always said about him. He never did anything halfway. Maybe not. He did tend to commit fully to something when he took it on. But in this case, it wasn't about achieving. It was about living.

He dawdled in the water for nearly an hour, before heading back to the house and finally going inside.

It was a cavernous edifice for one person: twelve thousand square feet of understated luxury. There was a not-too-big garage, but it was enough to house a golf cart for getting around the island, and maintenance machinery, like the small tractor for mowing the grass and various garden implements. And a snow blower. He shivered, thinking about how bleak it would be here in the middle of a winter storm. And yet…there was something comforting about being snug inside while the outside was wild and untamed. He certainly couldn't live here year round. He still had responsibilities. At thirty-five, retirement wasn't an option. He still ran his father's empire of manufacturing companies, and he needed that challenge. But he was less hands-on than he used to be, delegating far more responsibility. His hope was to spend maybe a third of the year here, overseeing the corporate retreat business, and two thirds back in Manhattan, home of the headquarters of Abbott Industries.

His things were already in the room he'd chosen for himself, a large suite facing southeast, with windows overlooking the beach and down the island, where the roof of the farmhouse was just visible among the trees. He put down his duffel and went to the window. Brooklyn Graves. That was the name of the woman who lived there, the one who refused to sell her parcel of land. It complicated things, in his mind. They shared access to the dock, which wasn't really sufficient to his needs, and she owned the boathouse at the tip of the island. He'd hired a husband and wife to be caretakers here, and right now they had to be housed in the apartment above the garage. It would be far better if they could live in the farmhouse and have their own real home.

If only stubborn Ms. Graves would sell. What on earth was a single woman doing living on an island twelve months of the year, anyway?

He knew little about her, except that she ran some sort of cottage industry—had Jeremy mentioned knitting or something?—from her home and that her family had lived on the island for generations. He would have to put on the charm and visit, make her come around. She sounded like the type to offer him tea and scones. Knitting? She was probably someone's reclusive aunt, too stubborn to move. It might take all his powers of persuasion.

He didn't really want to, but he figured he should introduce himself as soon as possible. The longer he put it off, the more awkward it was bound to become. Chances were his reception would be chilly, anyway.

With a last look out the window, he turned away and went back downstairs, and out the front door this time.

He'd just walk down to meet her and break the ice. He wouldn't even mention selling. Not yet.

The front gardens were beautiful. The grass was neatly trimmed, and there were still flowers, yellow and red and rusty-colored ones, brightening the beds. Further along, past the manicured lawns, the landscape was wilder. One either side of the lane was waving grass and thick bunches of goldenrod and light purple wild asters. Most of the trees were evergreens, with very little hardwood, but here and there he saw birches and maples. The leaves on the birches were starting to yellow, but the maples were still green and vibrant. The walk took maybe only ten, fifteen minutes, tops, but it was a beautiful one.

The farmhouse came into view and he stopped for a moment, struck by the sight of it. It was old and rambling, but well kept, with freshly painted spindles on the veranda and potted flowers on the stained steps. There was nothing special about it really; the outside was white, with no fancy trim or shutters, but it was charming and cozy and like something he expected to see on an old-time greeting card. All that was missing was—

A bark sounded and a retriever bounded from around the corner of the house, straight toward him. Apparently a dog *wasn't* missing from the picture, and he resisted the urge to roll his eyes at the homey scene. Eyes bright and tongue lolling happily, the dog ran up to him and immediately rubbed against his legs, looking for pats.

Cole couldn't help obliging. He loved dogs. Not that he'd ever had one growing up.

"Who's a good boy?" He rubbed the dog's head and then laughed when the dog dropped to the grass and rolled over, showing his belly. Cole willingly knelt down and gave him a belly rub, chuckling at the obvious enjoyment of the pooch as he rolled his back this way and that, legs in the air. Dogs were just so pure in everything they did. No agendas. Unlike himself...

"Marvin, come."

The female voice jolted him from his thoughts and he stood, leaving Marvin on his back with his paws up. A clap from the owner of the voice had the dog jumping up and shaking all over, then trotting back to his human's side.

Cole's brain momentarily emptied. All the opening lines he'd imagined flew straight out of his head and away on the ocean breeze. He'd expected someone middle-aged or older. A...spinster. Not a thirtyish woman with hair the color of peanut butter, wearing skinny jeans, boots, and a sweater that nipped in at her waist and hugged her hips.

This was Brooklyn Graves?

"You're Mr. Abbott."

He realized he'd been standing there for long seconds and saying absolutely nothing. He nodded, then moved forward and held out his hand. "Yes, Cole Abbott. It's good to finally meet."

More than good. Wow.

She didn't smile as she shook his hand. As he got closer he noticed that a few freckles dotted her nose, and her eyes were a clear, clear blue. Her hand was warm and strong, and he felt a few rough spots at the base of her fingers. Calluses? Interesting.

She dropped his hand and stepped back. "What can I do for you, Mr. Abbott?"

"Please, call me Cole." He tried a warm smile, but it didn't appear to be getting him anywhere. "We're neighbors, after all."

She gave a shrug with one shoulder. "Well, I know you'd like to change that, so I'll be as clear as I can. I'm not interested in selling my house or acreage."

Cole took a few moments to gather himself before responding. In the end, he tried a small smile. "I got your reply, Ms. Graves. I truly did just come down to say hello. The island will be pretty small if we aren't on speaking terms."

"Tell me you don't want to buy me out and we can be the best of friends." She put her hands on her hips, and Marvin the dog sat at her feet, the soul of loyalty and obedience.

He couldn't lie to her. For one, he got the sneaky suspicion she'd see right through it. For another, lying always came back to bite him in the butt.

Instead he put away his "let's be friends" face, choosing instead a more businesslike manner. "I'll be honest. I would like to buy your property." He figured it wouldn't hurt to sweeten the pot. "What I'm prepared to offer can set you up somewhere very nicely."

His initial offer had been for three hundred and fifty thousand dollars. The house would likely need renovations and the dock definitely needed work. It had been…reasonable.

"Would you pay me a million dollars?"

Her gaze was sharp and pinned him in place, but he'd been in business a long time. He knew how to hide his reactions, and right now he wanted to chuckle a little bit. He'd paid seven million for the rest of the land and house and considered it a steal. Her property accounted for maybe, at best, a sixth of the island. A million wasn't that outrageous, really. Not considering the buildings on the property and the dock access.

"Yes." Heck, if all it took was a million bucks to get

her to sign away the deed, he'd do it happily. Jeremy had been the one to recommend lowballing. Cole didn't mind upping the ante. "Yes, I'm prepared to offer you a million."

She started at him a long moment and then turned away. "I don't think so," she said and started walking toward the house. "Come, Marvin."

The dog jumped up and trotted at her heels. Meanwhile, Cole stood flummoxed on her front path, staring at her as she went in through the screen door, took Marvin with her and let the door fall shut with a loud snap behind them.

Huh. So, round one and two to Ms. Graves. But Cole wasn't done yet. He had a history of getting what he wanted, and this was nothing more than a challenge.

CHAPTER TWO

BROOKLYN SAT IN her favorite chair, yarn trailing perfectly from her yarn bowl to the needles, and adjusted the weight of the shawl she was knitting. It was a simple pattern but incredibly lovely, both stylish and warm, and this was one item she was knitting for herself and not to sell.

The click of the needles in the silence gave her comfort, which was good. She'd come inside yesterday after talking to Cole Abbott and had shaken for a good thirty minutes. Confrontation was not her thing. She knew how to be strong but it had cost her, stealing her energy, prompting a near panic attack.

Marvin had stayed close all evening, soothing her and being steady and reliable with his company. At one point her therapist had asked if she wanted to get a service dog, but Brooklyn had declined. She had Marvin. And she'd come a very long way since she'd started counseling. She'd come to the island to escape and heal, but she'd stayed because she'd built a life she truly loved. And if she was occasionally lonely…oh, well. She'd learned that there were worse things in life than loneliness. She had everything just the way she wanted it here. No surprises.

Her needles slowed. Still, she'd coexisted with Ernest

and his extended family without any trouble, and she'd admit—only to herself—that just knowing someone else was on the island had been a comfort. She wasn't sure she could say the same about Cole Abbott. His very presence threatened the life she'd built for herself.

Maybe she should head over to the mainland tomorrow and get out for a bit. Pick up a few groceries, perhaps go for a coffee with Delilah or Jen, the sisters who ran the yarn and craft store in Liverpool. Hadn't she just told herself that she needed to be patient? Mr. Fancy Man wouldn't be on the island forever. It would be another plaything he'd tire of and move on. But her life… it would remain unchanged. Just the way she wanted it.

The morning dawned foggy, but by ten it had burned off and the mellow September sun had warmed the air. Brooklyn carried a large handbag over her shoulder, which contained fabric shopping bags, her wallet, her phone, and a leash for Marvin, who always joined her on her trips to town. In her hands were five small shipping boxes containing orders ready to be shipped to customers of her online store. She turned the corner toward the dock and stopped short. There was a second boat anchored there, and Cole stood on the dock while another man moved around, taking pictures with his phone.

What the heck were they doing? It wasn't as if Cole didn't have a reason to be there. He did. Their access to the dock was shared.

The sight of him, though, was unexpected. And she couldn't deny that she rather enjoyed seeing him in faded jeans and a dark blue windbreaker. He looked… normal. Not like some rich tycoon, which he most certainly must be.

He caught sight of her and smiled, then waved. "Ms. Graves. Good morning."

"Good morning," she replied and wished she'd put Marvin on his leash, because at the friendly sound of Cole's voice, the dog trotted off for more pats and head rubs.

Traitor.

"Marvin, come," she called. But Marvin was too busy having his ears rubbed to pay much attention. Brooklyn sighed and went toward the two men, both to get Marvin and to satisfy her curiosity about what was going on.

"I'd say you're spoiling him, but I'm not sure it's possible to spoil a dog with pats," she said, trying to be friendly. Things had been tense during their earlier conversation. Establishing a little peace didn't mean she'd changed her mind.

"He's hard to resist. What a friendly guy." Cole's tone left a hint of insinuation, perhaps that her dog was more amiable than she was. Which was true.

"Is there a problem or something?" She stared pointedly at the other man, who was now at the end of the dock, writing something on a clipboard.

"Oh, Mike. Hey, Mike, come meet Brooklyn Graves. We share docking privileges."

Mike came over and held out his hand. "Nice to meet you, Brooklyn."

Cole turned to her. "Mike's going to make some repairs and mods to the dock. It doesn't quite suit my needs."

Her heart stuttered. Sure, the dock was old but it was sturdy and sound. She adjusted her packages and briefly shook Mike's hand. "What sort of needs?"

Cole answered. "Your boat's small, but I need to be

able to accommodate bigger vessels. I've hired Mike to expand it and also make any repairs necessary."

She wanted to be angry, and she would be later, but right now all she felt was shock and amazement at his audacity. "Um, you do remember that we share the dock, right?"

He bestowed another one of those charming smiles on her. "Well, of course. I'm sure Mike will have no trouble splitting the invoice between us."

Another layer of shock rippled through her. Share the cost? How was she supposed to pay for that? A hole opened up in her middle, the place where worry and panic seemed to live. The hole was soon filled with indignation.

"You can't do that without consulting me first."

At her sharp tone, Marvin moved away from Cole and went to sit at her heel. Mike discreetly left the conversation and continued on with his assessment.

"Oh. Well, I could just foot the bill, if…"

Her mouth tightened as she finally let the anger in. "If I sell to you, right? That's what this is all about? I won't sell so you're going to bankrupt me with foolish repairs?" She mentally calculated her equity between the house, business and her savings account, and lifted her chin. "Do I need to consult my lawyer on this, Mr. Abbott?"

She was reasonably sure that he couldn't just do repairs without getting her to sign off on them. But he'd make sure she spent legal fees to guarantee it, wouldn't he? Fire burned in her veins. Why did successful, rich people always have to get their own way and swing their power around like a mace?

"Now, Ms. Graves…"

She stepped back. "Don't you dare *Ms. Graves* me,

especially in that patronizing tone. At this rate, *Mister*
Abbott…" she paused and let the emphasis on the word
ring in the air. "… I would not sell to you for a million
dollars. Or two million. My great-grandparents were the
first people to live on this island. My great-grandfather
was a fisherman, like his father before him. My grandparents lived here and brought up five children. I spent
every summer as a kid here and I know each square foot
of it better in my sleep than you ever will. Maybe our
family doesn't own the entire island anymore, but my
corner of it is still mine. And I am not for sale."

Her hands were shaking, so she clutched the boxes
tighter as she stared at him.

"Noted," he said quietly.

"Now, if you will excuse me, I am going to get on
my boat and pilot it to the mainland. Marvin, come."

This time Marvin obeyed immediately, falling in
at her heel without need of a leash or a second urging.

She made it to the boat with sure steps, got them
both aboard and stowed her bag and parcels. It wasn't
until she'd untied from the dock and steered away that
she relaxed her shoulders and tried to suck in big, calming gulps of air.

She was okay. This was not the same as…that other
time. He did not have a weapon and she was not in
danger. Her body response had been triggered but she
worked her way through the reaction until she wasn't
shaking any longer. She looked over her shoulder and
couldn't see the dock anymore, or Cole and Mike. It
was almost as if it had never happened.

No, Cole Abbott hadn't threatened her person. Instead, he had threatened her security and the life she'd
built for herself. Maybe it wasn't as frightening as an

assault on a visceral level, but the idea of change was terrifying to her.

How many times was someone supposed to start over? Maybe in the past she'd given up too easily. Well, not this time. This time she would fight tooth and nail to preserve what was important to her. And if that meant dipping into her very small savings account for a visit to the lawyer, then that was what she'd do.

Cole had messed up again. He'd planned on the conversation with Brooklyn going differently. The idea had been for him to do the dock repairs as a gesture of goodwill. But he'd teased, and she'd taken him seriously, bringing legal advice into it. He'd miscalculated.

Now he too was on the mainland, sitting in his best friend, Jeremy Fisher's rather large kitchen, drinking coffee and feeling grouchy about it all. His other pal, Branson Black, was back in New York, dealing with getting his brownstone ready to sell. While Jeremy was settled with his new wife and baby, Branson's love life was up in the air since the departure of artist Jessica Blundon, who had spent the summer on the south shore.

Cole's love life was nonexistent, and he was okay with that. For now, anyway. He had too much going on to devote much time to a relationship. Even a casual one. And he wasn't sure he was capable of any other kind. It wasn't like he'd had a stellar example growing up.

"So she threatened to go to her lawyer?" Jeremy re-entered the kitchen, his baby daughter on his arm. She'd just awakened from a nap, and Jeremy's wife, Tori, was running errands. It was still an adjustment, seeing his friend so settled into domestic life.

"I know. I meant to tell her that I would cover the cost since I was the one needing the modifications, but she got the jump on me and I took the bait. She's very prickly about the fact I made her an offer." He took a sip of his coffee. "This morning she told me she wouldn't sell for two million dollars."

Jeremy laughed. "Well, it's her home. And clearly she's attached to it. What's the big deal, anyway? It's not like there isn't enough room for the two of you. You're not even going to be there all year round."

Cole thought about it. "I'll be honest. Some of it is ego. I mean, I don't like being told no and I look at it as an extra challenge to get my way."

Jeremy met his gaze, his eyes alight with humor. "How very self-aware of you. But gee, Cole, you were never competitive in school."

"I see you haven't lost your talent for sarcasm," Cole answered. "And hey, I know that trait can be a strength or a weakness, depending on the situation. She's not what I expected."

"How so?"

"You said she ran some sort of business from her home, knitting or some such. I was expecting someone…hell, someone not young and pretty and…"

His voice trailed off. The truth was, as infuriating as their two conversations had been, he had found them invigorating.

Jeremy's laughter drew him back to the moment. He held Rose in one arm as he prepped a bottle with his free hand. "So she's pretty."

Cole sighed. "To be honest? Stunning. Beautiful hair, big eyes, nice body. But it's more than that. She's a strong woman, Jer. She's got to be, to live out there by herself. It's not far offshore but it's cut off from everything, especially in bad weather. She hopped on that boat today and steered away the way we'd get in a car and drive to the store."

"Ah. A woman who is capable and doesn't need rescuing. Interesting."

"Shut up." He took a long drink of coffee and grinned behind the rim. A bit of ribbing from his best friend made the world seem all right after all.

Rose was grumbling, so Jeremy tested the bottle and then began to feed her, standing right there in the kitchen. Cole was not good with babies. Not even a little. But even he had to admit that Rose was cute. There'd been a recent health scare as she'd contracted measles, but she seemed completely recovered now.

"So what's your game plan now?" Jeremy asked, perching on a bar stool across the counter from Cole.

"I don't know. She'd see right through flowers or some sort of gift. Maybe I should just apologize and do a better job of explaining."

Jeremy looked at him for a long moment. "Cake. Take her cake. Or a bottle of wine or something. Just don't go empty-handed. And yeah, maybe explain that you got off on the wrong foot."

Cole considered for a minute. "Good suggestions. Or at least half of a good suggestion. I have an idea for the other."

"You sure you're not interested in her?" Jeremy asked, removing the bottle and wiping Rose's chin before giving her the bottle again. "When was the last time you went on a date?"

Cole's smile slipped away. The last time had been over a year ago, just before his world had come crashing down.

Not that anyone really knew anything about that. He'd been able to hide it really well. Faking his way through stuff was his specialty. Even Bran and Jeremy didn't know the true extent of what had happened.

"It's been a long time. But no, that would just get messy, wouldn't it? Besides, as you say, I'm only planning to be here part of the year. I do still have Abbott to run."

And that required him to be in New York. Not on an island in the Atlantic off the coast of Nova Scotia. The island was to be his retreat. And hopefully he could offer the same to his own executives.

The hum of the garage door opener interrupted the silence. "Tori's home. Are you staying for dinner?"

Cole looked at his watch and then shook his head. "Naw, but thanks. I have those errands to run and then pick up the boat. I'm leaving the car at the marina garage." He looked up as Tori came inside, a bag of produce in her hands. "Hello, gorgeous."

"Hey, Cole. How are things on the island?"

Jeremy jumped in. "The farmhouse owner is a hottie."

"Of course she is. Brooklyn has a really neat business, too. She runs an online store and ships all over. Knitted items but she also dyes her own yarn and sells it. And her big thing is patterns. She develops patterns and sells them. One was even picked up by some big magazine last year. She's wicked smart. Her overhead is really low and she doesn't have a mortgage since she inherited the house from her grandparents."

Cole stared at her. "You knew?"

Tori laughed and started taking vegetables out of the bag. "Of course I knew. This is a small town and I've lived in the area my whole life."

"You didn't say anything in the summer, when we went over there."

"Why should I? You were buying the rest of the land, not hers." Her brows pulled together in confusion. "Why? What happened?"

Jeremy put the bottle down and put Rose up on his shoulder as he patted her back. "Cole offered to buy her out, and made her pretty angry from the sounds of it. She threatened to lawyer up."

Tori nodded. "Good for her. That place means a lot to her."

"It does?"

Tori seemed to hesitate, her hand resting on a large bundle of leeks. "It's been in her family a long time," she finally said. "And Brooklyn moved there permanently a few years ago."

Cole thought about it. The only reason he could see for moving somewhere so isolated was if someone was running from something. He certainly was, or at least using it to shape his life differently. But what could someone like Brooklyn be running from?

"I'd better go. Thanks for the coffee, bro. I'll be in touch soon."

"Good luck. And stop in any time."

"Let me know when Branson is back. I'm kinda worried about the guy."

"Me, too."

Cole stopped and gave Tori a kiss on the cheek, then made his way to the front door and put on his shoes.

Maybe he'd messed up the first two times he'd encountered Ms. Graves, but the third time could be the charm. And he knew just what he had to do to get past her thorny exterior.

CHAPTER THREE

THE DAY AWAY hadn't settled Brooklyn's thoughts, so she spent the next morning cooking. She did this every few weeks, making large quantities and then freezing in portion-size dishes. Cooking for one could be a lonely enterprise, but spending a day in the kitchen fed her soul as well as her body.

Today it was her grandmother's baked beans, done in her slow cooker, and fish cakes. She'd do them up and freeze them, and then fry a few off for tonight's dinner. Combined with the chow she'd just made this summer—a Maritime recipe of pickled green tomatoes—and she'd have the perfect dinner.

She was also making four small pans of lasagna, and a curried squash soup from the butternut squash in her garden.

As she put the squash in the pot, she figured she must be out of sorts indeed. This was enough food to feed her for weeks.

Her kitchen was a mess but the lasagnas were baking in the oven, the beans were bubbling, and it all smelled delicious. Two loaves of fresh bread were on the counter; mixing and kneading had helped her work out some of her frustration.

It was only eleven thirty when there was a knock

and Marvin leaped up from his doggie bed, rushing to the door and barking the whole time.

It had to be Cole. There was literally no one else it could be.

She steeled herself, wiped her hands on her apron and went to the door. There was no sense pretending she wasn't home. Besides, she'd popped in to her lawyer's yesterday for a quick chat. She was going to look into the legalities and get back to Brooklyn in a few days. Even if Cole had the dock assessed, any work wouldn't start for a while.

She opened the door and tried to look polite.

"Hi," he said. "I come in peace."

She lifted an eyebrow. She couldn't escape the notion that there was always something behind his charm. "Oh?"

He held out his hands. One held a paper bag that she recognized from the baker in town. The other was from a pet store in Mahone Bay.

"Wine and cake for you, and something for Marvin, because he's a very good boy."

Okay, so charm aside, complimenting Marvin was the same as telling a mother her kid was great. It was the easiest way to get in her good graces. "I suppose you should come in, then." She stood aside.

Cole entered while Marvin danced in circles around him. She wished her dog didn't seem to like the guy so much. At first glance, Cole seemed to be dressed normally. Casually. Until she looked at the fine wool of his sweater and the rich leather of his shoes. There was no forgetting how stupid rich he had to be. After all, he'd bought most of the island and hadn't batted an eye at the idea of giving her a million dollars for her small corner of it.

"My God, it smells heavenly in here." He handed her the bag and then courteously removed his shoes and left them on the mat. "I heard you were a knitter. But apparently you're a cook, too."

She would not be charmed. She would not.

"It's messy at the moment. I tend to cook in batches and freeze it."

She put the bag on an empty space of counter and removed the wine and cake. A lovely crisp white, and a small but gorgeous lemon cream cake. She did love lemon.

"Thank you," she said, putting the wine in the fridge. "It wasn't necessary."

"But it was." He put his hands in his pockets. "Ms. Graves, we got off on the wrong foot, and that's my fault. What I should have said yesterday was that I would foot the bill for any changes to the dock. I'm the one who wants them, and it wouldn't be fair for me to ask you to pay half of that." He took a small step forward. "I know you aren't happy about me being here. But I promise, I'm not out to do you harm."

She wasn't sure what to say. He seemed very genuine and contrite.

"The previous owners and I got along very well," she admitted. "Before that, my grandparents owned the whole island. But then my grandfather got sick and needed a lot of care. Care he couldn't get here on the island, of course, and it put a financial strain on them. Ernest bought it, minus this parcel of land, and rented this house for two years before he built the grand house on the bluff. He set up the conditions for the shared dock and made sure we were taken care of. I understand why he sold. But it was a good relationship built on trust." She met his gaze evenly. "You haven't built up that trust."

"Yet," he said, and didn't smile. He seemed to be taking everything she said very seriously. "Maybe if I tell you my plans for the property, it'll put your mind at ease."

The squash was nearly done, so she motioned toward the table and chairs. "I've got to finish this up, but please have a seat. Would you like a coffee?" There was still half a pot left.

"I'd like that a lot. Just black for me."

She poured him a cup and put it before him, and then went to test the squash and add the remainder of the ingredients. She tried to ignore how he was watching her as she poured the mixture over into her food processor and whizzed it until it was velvety smooth, and then poured it back over into the pot.

"What is that?" he asked. "It smells amazing."

"Curried squash soup. Do you cook, Mr. Abbott?"

He sighed. "Can we maybe forgo the formalities? Just call me Cole."

"All right." She didn't extend the offer to use her first name, though she suspected he would, eventually, anyway. She didn't want to be friends with him, but he had brought a peace offering and she appreciated his putting her mind at ease about the dock. Maybe, just maybe, she'd been a little hyper-defensive.

"Anyway," he continued, "I cook a little. But I'm better at buying stuff that's already prepped. I, uh, didn't really have to cook for myself growing up."

She snorted. "I kind of figured that about you. Let me guess. Private school? Trust fund baby?"

"Something like that." He shrugged. "But just to clarify, I've had to work my way to where I am. I absolutely had advantages because of family money. Hopefully I didn't waste any of them."

She turned around to look at him. There was something in the set of his jaw and behind his eyes that spoke of a deeper story. She wondered what it was. She should not dismiss him as an idle rich jerk. Everyone had their own story, didn't they?

"So buying this island…it isn't a whim or a toy for you?"

He shook his head. "No, it's not. I bought it for a few reasons. I'll tell you if you're interested in hearing about them."

He took a long drink of his coffee and Brooklyn looked at the clock. It was just shy of noon.

"I guess I'd better spoon up some of this soup then, shouldn't I?"

She reached into the cupboard for two bowls and wondered if hearing him out was the right thing to do. Because right now it felt a bit dangerous.

Cole wasn't sure why he was ready to confide in Brooklyn or why he felt this pressing need to have her understand or think well of him. They'd got off to a rocky start and she certainly wasn't a friend or even someone he could really trust.

But he wanted to tell her, to disabuse the notion that he hadn't just bought the island as a toy or new thing on an acquisitions list. Besides, he was looking forward to hosting his first retreat in a few weeks, just a small gathering of executives from his own companies. Nothing formal, just four days of unplugging, sea air, good food. A time to slow down.

Brooklyn put a bowl of the delicious-smelling soup in front of him, and then went to the kitchen island and grabbed a loaf of fresh bread, a cutting board and a knife. She sliced it right there at the table, handed him a slice and put a crock of butter beside him.

The bread was still slightly warm and smelled like heaven.

"So. You have plans for the property. Do tell."

She got a second bowl and joined him at the table.

Cole went to work spreading butter on his bread. "A while ago I had a bit of a…well, I don't want to say a breakdown. It was more burnout, I guess. I'd been working sixty hour weeks for as long as I could remember, and then my social life… Well, I don't do anything half way. I'm not a partier or anything, but I'd do dinners and events and just… I never took any downtime." He broke off a piece of bread and popped it into his mouth. Amazing. A quick glance told him that Brooklyn was watching him intently, her eyes focused on his and her brow slightly furrowed as if she were trying to puzzle him out.

"Burning the candle at both ends," she said.

"Exactly. Until the flame got snuffed out. I was exhausted. Then one morning I woke up and I had chest pains. It scared the hell out of me."

She had picked up her spoon but now she put it down again. "Did you have a heart attack? But you're only what, thirty-five? Forty?"

He grinned. "Thirty-five, if you must know, and no, thankfully it wasn't a heart attack. It was a panic attack."

"Thank goodness," she said and picked up her spoon again.

He did the same and tasted the soup. It was velvety smooth and divine. He'd eaten in Michelin-starred restaurants and this simple soup could stand with the best of them. "This is amazing."

"It's the coconut milk. I stir a little in at the end, too, and it makes it pop." She looked at him over her spoon. "So, you had a panic attack."

"It wasn't an isolated thing. My friend Branson said that it was my body's way of telling me I needed to slow down and I needed to listen. I didn't have any choice. I could hardly get out of bed in the morning. I was tired all the time. I didn't believe him, you know? I thought I had some horrible disease. Turns out it was workaholism."

"So you bought the house."

"I'm getting there." He spooned up more of the soup like it was a tonic, which maybe it was. Simple, wholesome nourishment. Perfection. "It took me a long time to recover. Thankfully, I had strong executives in place, but the whole thing could have been avoided if I'd done a better job at balancing my workload. I didn't take time off until my own body forced me to. So I bought the house for a few reasons. One, it's a getaway for me, and one that is close to my two best friends, who bought places on the south shore. The other reason is that I don't want what happened to me to happen to other executives. I'm going to hold corporate retreats. First for my own people, and then for other companies."

He didn't mention how dark a place his burnout had been, though. How he'd felt so alone and questioned his existence. Wondering if anyone would miss him because other than Branson and Jeremy, he hadn't nurtured any relationships in his life. Especially romantic ones. His parents had put on a brilliant public face but in private they were strangers. If that was marriage, he didn't want any part of it.

Brooklyn frowned. "It's a neat idea, for sure. I'm going to be honest, though. It makes me uncomfortable thinking about strangers roaming about the island all the time." She stirred her soup as if deliberating something, then looked up again. "You're creating an oasis for people, which is admirable. But in doing so, you're threatening mine. It's a hard pill to swallow."

He hadn't thought of it that way. But of course. Every time he held a retreat, there would be strangers on the beaches, walking the island, on the boat launch. He could understand how that made her uneasy. Maybe it would convince her to sell to him after all?

And yet, the thought of her not being here, in this house, in this kitchen, suddenly seemed wrong.

"I'm sorry about that. It's definitely an unintended consequence. I guess it must seem as if I'm invading your home. That's not my intention at all. I hope you believe that."

She nodded but didn't meet his eyes. Instead she sliced him more bread. He got the feeling that it was more to keep her hands busy than anything.

He reached over and put his hand over hers.

She stopped breathing.

Something changed in that moment, in that small but intimate physical touch. He felt it in his solar plexus, reaching in to grab him and hold him captive. It had been meant to reassure. But as her gaze darted to his, the energy between them became something bigger. Something unexpected.

She slipped her hand away from his. "Would you like more soup?"

It had rattled her, too. Cole cleared his throat and knew he'd better get out of there before he started sharing other things or, worse, inviting her to share. The idea was to convince her to sell. Not get himself tangled up in her.

"I should get back. I really just came with the peace offering."

Brooklyn gathered up their bowls and took them to

the sink. "Thank you. And I appreciate the clarification on the dock maintenance."

Cole stood and brushed a few breadcrumbs off his pants. "I want us to deal fairly with each other. It's not my intention to cause you financial hardship."

She spun around and pinned him with a stare. "Don't worry about my financial situation. I'm doing just fine."

Dammit, he'd stepped in it again. Just when he'd let down his guard a little. "I'm sure you are. But no one wants an unexpected expenditure, do they?"

Marvin had reappeared and he leaned over to give the pup a pat and a bit of an ear rub. "You've got a great dog. I never had one growing up."

"But you like them." Her voice was softer. "That's pretty obvious."

"I do. Very much." Marvin leaned into a scratch, which delighted Cole immensely. "You're such a good boy, aren't you, Marvin? Mmm…that feels good."

When he looked up, Brooklyn was smiling. Damn, she was so beautiful when she smiled. He was going to have to step carefully there.

"He likes you, too. You can stop by for a game of fetch when you need to," she offered.

It was unexpected and he frowned. "Really? You're inviting me to play with your dog?"

She shrugged. "Dogs are great healers, Cole. From what you said, you probably need him as much as he needs a good game of throw-the-tennis-ball."

"Thanks," he said quietly, standing again. "Maybe I'll do that."

But as he said his goodbyes and made his way down the path from her house, he wondered what kind of recovery she'd needed, and if Marvin had been there for her. He hoped so. The thought of Brooklyn, such a strong, beautiful, independent woman needing some sort of healing made his stomach tie up in knots. If she'd had to recover from something, he hoped she hadn't had to do it alone.

CHAPTER FOUR

BROOKLYN KNEW THE day the executives arrived because the helicopter made an appearance, swinging low over the house before disappearing over the trees to the landing pad. She stepped away from the window and went back to printing shipping labels. She'd spent too much time thinking about Cole and that moment when he'd touched her hand. Something had happened between them, like a bolt of lightning. The startled look on his face had told her he had felt it, too. It made everything more complicated.

She should just brush it off and regain her common sense. But the past few nights, when she'd gone to bed, she'd lain awake thinking of how he'd brought Marvin a present and the way he patted the dog and rubbed his ears. Marvin was the most important thing in her life, really. As much as it would be more convenient for her to still hate Cole, his actions suggested an unexpected kindness and gentleness.

Kindness didn't translate into trust, though. He was a long way from accomplishing that.

Better to focus on the present. She needed to go over to the mainland again today. She'd finished dyeing another batch of yarn and had packed up new orders to be shipped away. Fall was a busy time for her. As the weather cooled, people picked up their knitting needles again and started on a number of projects. Even though it was only early October, Christmas orders were already flooding in.

She should forget about Cole and think more about the holiday season and building up her stock.

The seas were calm and the day clear, and the trip seemed to take no time at all. The first stop for her was the post office, which took a fairly long time as she had a number of shipments. Then she drove down to Liverpool to visit Delilah. Even though Brooklyn had her own yarn business, there were many specialty yarns that she sourced elsewhere. Right now she was hoping Delilah had a new shipment of alpaca yarn. She loved working with it, and her customers liked it, as well, since it was lighter than wool and wasn't scratchy.

Delilah was at the store but more than happy to go to lunch. They headed to a local inn and dined on hearty chowder and fresh bread.

Delilah, who was in her midforties, took a look at Brooklyn and angled her head, as if assessing. "There's something different about you. A different kind of energy." She thought for a moment and shrugged. "You've perked up."

Heat slid up Brooklyn's neck. "I love the fall. It's my favorite time of year."

"I don't think so. What's going on in your life?" She leaned forward. "Have you put up that online dating profile like I suggested?"

Brooklyn laughed and spooned up more chowder. "No, I didn't. It's nothing, really. I mean, I met the new owner of the house. Otherwise I've just been busy." She raised an eyebrow. "After what I just spent at your store, you can tell I have orders piling up."

"What's he like? Is he old with a big paunch and stinking rich?"

She laughed, but the image of Cole standing at her door with cake and wine stuck in her head and her heart gave a little thump. "He's stinking rich, from what I gather. He's maybe thirty-five? And quite good-looking."

"Ooh. Some island romance in your future?" She waggled her eyebrows suggestively.

"Yeah, and wouldn't that be awkward. You don't… you-know-what where you eat, Del. Besides, he'll be here a bit and then have to go back to New York. That's where his businesses are. He'll only be on the island now and again."

To her surprise, the thought made her a little lonely. She was used to having someone else for company. The summer hadn't been that bad, because the weather had been great and she'd had the gardens to keep and her own vegetable plot. In the wintertime, though, she often got storm-stayed. During those times, she'd often gone up to the big house with Ernest and Marietta and they'd played cards and eaten great food and it had been more than pleasant. Her house was cozy as anything, but the thought of facing the winter without any company at all… Maybe she should consider finding an apartment or something in town. But how could she afford two places? Right now she was mortgage-free and the business was more than enough to keep her comfortable. But if she had to add a thousand a month or so to her bills, it would make things tight.

She sniffed a little. A thousand a month was probably Cole Abbot's wine budget. Or whiskey, or scotch, or whatever pricey alcohol he drank. She'd looked up the wine he'd brought. She was used to the ten-to-twenty-dollar bottles. The one he'd brought had been sixty. She was saving it for a special occasion.

"So, young, rich, not a troll," Delilah said, ticking each attribute off on her fingers. "Remind me again why you're not making a move to tap that?"

Brooklyn snorted. "Thanks, Del, for getting right to the point."

"Any time." Her face softened, and she patted Brooklyn's hand. "Look, I just want you to be happy. And I know you don't need a man for that. I just worry that you… Well, you've closed yourself off to possibilities because of what happened."

Del was one of the few people who really knew about Brooklyn's trauma. Being a victim of a violent crime had changed Brooklyn, made her more wary and less trusting. Sure, she'd done all sorts of therapy and she was doing well. But she'd also built the life she wanted and didn't like the disruption.

She'd had enough counseling to understand that she liked guarantees. She wasn't a risk-taker, and in her mind, love was the biggest risk of all.

"It's not that, Del." She took a sip of her tea and sighed. "I mean, I'm not physically afraid of a relationship." The assault hadn't been sexual. It had been a straight up robbery, and looking back, it seemed like something from a movie. It certainly felt like it had happened to someone else. The fear had been cold and debilitating. The hard press of the gun dug into her ribs and she could still feel the painful grip of his big hand on her arm. For a few terrified moments, she'd been his hostage. But when he got into the car, she'd managed to scramble out the passenger side and he'd sped off. She'd been safe, yet forever altered.

"No, sweetie," Delilah said gently. "You're afraid of

living. Everything happens in good time, but sometimes people come along that shake us up a bit." She smiled. "Maybe this guy is going to shake you up."

He already had. "He likes Marvin, and Marvin likes him back, the traitor," she confessed. "Then again, pats and treats go a long way with dogs."

Delilah grinned. "Not just with dogs. I'm partial to pats and treats myself."

"Delilah!" Brooklyn started to laugh and put down her teacup. Delilah had been married to the same guy for fifteen years and they were still adorable together. "This is why I love you."

"And here I thought it was because you get a bulk discount at the store."

"I'm nicer than that."

"I know that. I hope you do. Anyway, if this guy isn't going to be on the island that much, why not have a thing or see where it goes? God knows you deserve it."

Brooklyn had gone "home" to recover, really. The trauma from those five minutes in her life had resulted in crippling fear and panic. Life was much better now, but she didn't like change. Didn't want it.

Even one as sexy and intriguing as Cole Abbott.

When she returned home later that afternoon, she put her supplies in the house and took Marvin out for a walk on the beach so he could get a good romp in before the weather changed. The forecast called for rain later in the evening, and Brooklyn could feel the change in air pressure and humidity as she threw a stick of driftwood for Marvin. He was four now, and his energy level was still that of a puppy, though he definitely had more discipline. He came running back and dropped the stick at her feet, panting happily, eyes flashing as he waited for her to throw it again. She did, then walked on, the sharp wind buffeting her ponytail, pulling strands out to blow around her face, and puffing her jacket out behind her. The calm seas of earlier were now gray with little white caps. Tonight would be the perfect night to finish her shawl and then move on to holiday projects.

Delilah had given her food for thought. Not that she wanted to have a torrid affair or anything. It was more the reminder that she'd hidden herself away here.

She'd even withdrawn from her family. Her parents lived in Halifax, where her dad worked for a courier company and her mom was a nurse. Her brother and sister no longer lived in Nova Scotia; her sister was a geologist working in Alberta, and her brother an environmental engineer for a US company based out of Maryland. Brooklyn took the stick from Marvin and threw it again, watching him spin up sand as he chased after it. Brooklyn had been in her third year of her science degree when the assault happened. Then everything had changed.

She got to the end of the sandy stretch and climbed the path to the grassy expanse above. Darkening skies told her she should get home soon; she wasn't keen on getting caught in the rain, especially with Marvin and his wet dog smell. She called for him to come and was answered with a bark that sounded farther away than she anticipated. Frowning, she directed her gaze toward the sound of the bark and saw Marvin's golden coat running through the tall grass, headed toward Cole.

Not fair, considering Delilah's words still echoed in her head. Hopefully she could remain cool and detached and not blush.

Cole lifted a hand in greeting, and Marvin bounced and danced beside him.

"My dog is incredibly undisciplined," she said as he approached. "Sorry."

"Don't be. Marvin's great. I wish I'd had a dog as a kid. My folks said no because they are dirty and then pets aren't allowed in dormitories."

"Even for rich kids?"

He laughed. "Even for rich kids. Merrick was a great school. It's where I met Jeremy and Branson. But no dogs, sadly."

"Jeremy, as in your Realtor?"

He nodded. "Yes, that's right."

"And Branson is…"

"Branson Black."

She tried not to let her mouth drop open and failed. "The novelist."

"That's the one." Cole grinned. "We've been best friends since we were thirteen."

Brooklyn had been brought up in the city. All her classmates were God knows where. She'd made friends here, though. Good ones, like Delilah. Besides, in a small town, everyone pretty much knew everyone else.

Which meant most knew something about why she'd moved home while in university and holed up on the island. It was a hard place to keep secrets.

"Aren't your guests on the island?" she asked, waving the stick for Marvin. She tossed it and he ran off, while Cole chuckled.

"They don't need babysitters. Right now they're settling in. Getting downtime." He grinned. "I confiscated their phones when they arrived. Cue looks of panic."

"That's torture." But she grinned in response.

"You would think so. I let each person send an 'I've arrived' message and then that's it for four days. Either people are napping, or working out, or trying to figure out a way to work without being connected. Switching out of that mindset is hard, and it takes time. We'll get together tonight at dinner."

"Cool." They walked on, down the path toward the lane that ran the length of the island from her house to his. Marvin trotted around with the stick of driftwood in his mouth, proud of his new possession. A gust of wind buffeted them and there was a bit of mist in it. The rain wouldn't be far off now.

"Looks like we're in for some nasty weather."

"Just some rain." She put her hands in her jacket pocket. "By tomorrow night it'll be clear again. But it was choppy on the water today. I hit some big waves on the way back."

"You're not scared doing that?"

She laughed. "I've been piloting around this island since I was old enough to see over the wheel. And when the weather is really bad, I stay home." She let out a sigh. "Honestly? Sitting by my window with a glass of wine, watching the rain? It's cozy and pretty relaxing."

"Hmm. I kind of wish I could do that tonight. Instead I'm going to try to deal with five VPs who are going through tech withdrawal."

She bit down on her lip. Had he just said he wanted to spend the evening with her, or had he been speaking theoretically? She tried to imagine Cole in her small living room and couldn't make it fit. Then she thought of the great room at the house, with the windows facing the water, and could totally picture him sitting there, swirling a brandy or something, watching the rain. A very different world from hers.

Their steps had slowed as they reached the lane. To the right was his house, gray and imposing, absolutely stunning. She'd been inside lots of times when Ernest had owned it, and wondered what sort of changes Cole had made to the decor. Maybe someday she'd get to see inside again. But not today. Today he was…well, if not working, he was busy with his guests.

"I meant to ask you. Do you know if Ernest had someone taking care of the grounds? I have my caretakers, but they had a few questions about what's in the shed and about a couple of the plants in the garden. If you knew who they could contact…"

She smiled. "Send them down to the house, or have them call me. I can give them the details."

"You don't have to do that."

"Cole, I looked after the grounds for Ernest. I love gardening. He paid me a monthly wage and I mowed the grass, tended his flower beds and did his snow removal."

Cole stopped and stared at her. "You did?"

She started laughing. "Did you think I had someone here to do it for me? Granted, my little flower beds and lawn are tiny in comparison, but if I want off the island in the winter I have to clear the lane so I can get to the dock. There's a nice little tractor up there with a blower attachment. Works great."

"Oh. Well." He stared a moment more, apparently still recovering from his surprise. "This monthly wage thing…" An awkward silence followed.

"I can live without it. I knew when Ernest sold the house that gig would come to an end. To be honest, Ernest was too old to do it all, and he wouldn't hear of me doing it without being paid. It worked for both of us."

"I see. I just don't want to deprive you of any income."

She lifted her chin. It was the second time he'd made that sort of comment to her, insinuating she was down on her luck. She was actually doing pretty well for herself. She had a new holiday pattern going up on a popular site this month, and because she'd built a solid reputation for accurate and clear pattern instructions, every time she sold a new pattern, she saw increased downloads.

One of the things she really wanted to do was put together her own book of patterns and find a publisher.

"I'm doing fine, thanks. Of course you should have your own employees take this over." And to be honest, it would feel strange, working for Cole.

"Raelynn would also like your recipe for that soup you made the other day. I raved about it."

"Oh, well, that's easy enough. As I said, send her down. I'm not headed anywhere for a few days."

"Thanks, Brooklyn. I appreciate it."

She looked over at him. "I suppose this means we're being friendly now." She deliberately used the verb instead of the friend noun. Acting friendly didn't necessarily constitute friendship.

"I suppose it does."

And he smiled.

He was pretty gorgeous at any time, but when he smiled it was something different altogether. His eyes got tiny crinkles in the corners and his whole body seemed to relax with it. Right now, in the gloominess of the coming rain, his eyes seemed grayish blue, but she'd noticed the other day in the sun that they were a clear, bright blue that seemed to look right inside her. Kind of like the ocean, changing color depending on the weather and the storms going on inside.

"You should get back to your guests. They're probably trying to figure out how to get internet on your TV."

He grinned again. "I turned off the Wi-Fi."

"Sneaky." She couldn't help but smile back.

"I know we'll be outside some, but I'll make sure we don't invade your privacy."

"Thank you. I appreciate it."

They said their goodbyes, but as Cole walked away, Brooklyn sighed. She almost wished he'd invade her privacy. She couldn't imagine making a move herself, and knew without a doubt he was not for her. And yet a part of her wished he might be, just a little. Even though he was exactly the wrong kind of man, and not at all what she needed.

CHAPTER FIVE

By the third day of their visit, Cole's VPs were bright and energetic and far more relaxed than he'd expected. Some of it he credited to the scenery, fresh air, the wonderful food that Raelynn provided to the group, and full nights of sleep. They'd taken the boat to the mainland today and had gone to the Sandpiper Resort for a delicious lunch. They'd stayed for two hours, talking about their respective divisions, brainstorming ideas in the casual setting. The downtime had refreshed them and Cole could feel the renewed excitement and energy around the table. It was exactly what he'd hoped to achieve.

Once they were back on the island, Cole turned on the Wi-Fi and they had an online session with an expert on balancing an executive workload with wellness to avoid burnout.

Cole looked at the group when the facilitator left the session. "So what did you think? Tomorrow's our last day before you return to real life. What takeaways do you have?"

Duncan leaned forward and put his elbows on his knees. "I gotta tell you, Cole, when you took my phone I was pretty ticked off. But when I caught myself reaching for it over and over, I realized what an addiction it's become. I've become used to having it all the time, which means I'm always working. I think it's contributed a lot to my stress level. I still miss it." Everyone laughed a bit. "I'm trying not to go crazy wondering what's happened to the company in my absence. But I've slept better the last two nights than I have in months. Maybe years. I didn't realize how much I needed the break until I took it."

The other men nodded in agreement. "I found the first day and a half really hard," James added. "I don't know what it's like to have nothing to do…and then not have any tech to keep me from being bored. This was really like a work/tech detox for me, and one I can see I really needed."

Cole smiled, pleased at the feedback. "I know it's hard not to feel as if things are going to fall apart if you're unavailable, but they're not. If you have the right people in place, they all know their jobs. You can trust them. Nurture their talents. Have confidence in their abilities, which makes for better employees. And has the by-product of cutting you some slack. Look at me, for example." He looked at each man, right in the eye. "I'm the president and CEO. I took on responsibility for everything for a long time. But that's not sustainable and certainly not healthy. Instead I have great people in place who know their jobs.

"You guys, it starts with us. From the top down. I don't want to see any of you crash and burn out. It's not good for you, for your families, or for Abbott."

Everyone nodded thoughtfully.

"Tomorrow is our last day. I'd like for us to have a working breakfast midmorning where we can discuss your ideas for taking this back to not only your job but to your divisions. What changes you think would work with regards to your staff and their workload. Now that you've had a chance to unplug and get your creativity fired up again, let's see if we can leave with some action items. Sound good?"

They broke up and had a few hours until dinner, so two of the execs decided to take a walk on the beach, one was going to hit the gym, and the fourth had rediscovered a love of cooking and had agreed to help Raelynn with the dinner. Cole was left alone, pleased at how the day had gone, glad that he'd been able to give his own VPs a chance to decompress and recharge. If he'd done that now and again, he might have avoided the full-on breakdown.

It didn't really surprise him to find himself gravitating toward the rambling house in the trees. He hadn't spoken to Brooklyn since that day on the beach, though he'd seen her briefly this morning as they'd driven the golf cart from the house down to the dock. She'd been in her front yard raking leaves, her hair in a high ponytail and a pair of jeans hugging her backside.

Marvin was nowhere to be seen, but that was okay. He didn't need the dog to be chasing the cart or anything. Still, he'd wondered about her. What was she doing to fill her days?

He wandered toward her place, trying to think of an excuse for dropping in. He was nearly at her yard and still hadn't come up with anything plausible. Maybe he should turn around and go home again.

Instead he found himself on her front step.

He knocked. There was a flurry of barking, and then her footsteps as she came to the door and opened it.

Her hair was gathered up in a messy nest on the top of her head, and she wore a stained sweatshirt and sweatpants. "Oh. I'm sorry. I'm interrupting something, aren't I?" A strange, sharp odor permeated the air.

"I've been dyeing yarn the last few days," she answered. "That's the smell. Do you want to come in?"

He didn't want to intrude, but he was incredibly curious. How did someone hand-dye yarn? Marvin was standing just behind her, tail wagging, no longer barking in alarm but as if waiting to greet a friend. "Hey, Marv," he said, stepping inside. "I have to admit, I'm curious. I've never seen hand-dyed yarn before."

She led him through the house, to a back porch that had lots of natural light and counters. Several basins were lined up, and maybe four had dye inside and swirls of yarn soaking. On the other side of the room, drying racks were set up, with hanks of yarn lying across the wooden spindles. A small fan kept air circulating, and Cole spied one of the windows cracked open, even though the day was cool.

"This is it. My custom yarn business happens here," she said, tucking a stray piece of hair behind her ear. "I usually take three or four days and do a bunch at a time. Some are custom orders, and others are colors I've done before that are good sellers." She nodded at the drying racks. "Today I've done a lot of holiday ones."

Indeed. One looked like blocks of candy cane colors—red, white, green. "I didn't think of it being dyed in chunks of color," he said, wandering over toward the drying rack.

"When you ball it up, you'll see it's actually variegated. This one I call Peppermint Stick."

He grinned. "Cute."

"I do solid colors, too." She pointed at a deep, vibrant red. "That one is a big seller. This year I'm adding something new to my online shop, too. Kits. Comes with a pattern, the right amount of yarn, and any notions needed. I'm pretty excited about that."

"What sort of kit?" He was fascinated by the whole thing.

She picked up the red yarn. "A Christmas stocking, for example. This is a gorgeous color. I'll add some white with a pattern to knit a snowflake into the front and back. Then some white kind of trim for the top, and the pattern, and voilà. A home-crafted stocking for your mantel or as a keepsake for your kids or grandkids. I'll even include instructions for sewing in names with the white yarn."

"That's really, really neat." He was impressed. Even though her setup was low tech, clearly it worked fine. "Would it be easier if you had more space? You could do more at a time. How many can you dye in a day?"

"The rack holds five and I have two racks. Plus, the yarn has to sit in the dye for a good while, and then there's all the rinsing. I also only use eco-friendly dyes. It makes the cost go up a little, but my customers are willing to pay." She looked up at him, her eyes alight with enthusiasm. "Most people think of the fiber being sourced, but don't consider the dyes that are used in production."

She went over to the rack and picked up a circle of yarn. "When it's dry, like this is, I twist the hank into a skein." She deftly pulled the circle taut in her hands, started twisting it tightly and folded it in half so that it twisted around itself. Then she tucked one end inside the other and—poof!—it was done, just like that. "I put a tag on it and it's ready for shipping or knitting."

"You did that so quickly." He was still awed at the setup, and it wasn't just the fumes coming from the dye basins.

"I'll show you. Here."

She picked up another circle. "Okay, so put your hands inside the hank here."

"It's called a hank?"

"It is." She held his hands and spread them until the yarn was tight. "Now, make an L with this hand, and use one finger on this hand."

She maneuvered his fingers and he tried not to think about how she was touching him. But she was in her comfort zone now, wasn't she?

"Okay. Now take this finger and make a twist."

He did. The motion and the thickness of the yarn made it awkward, but he twisted again, and again, each time a little more difficult as the twist tightened.

"Now bend your elbow and use it to halve the twist." She took his arm and helped him. The moment he bent the yarn, it wrapped around itself. He laughed. "Well."

"Seriously." She was smiling at him. "Now look. You tuck that end under so it stays together." She touched his hands again, helped him secure the skein. When it was done she smoothed it out. "Congratulations. You did it."

He grinned back at her. "It's really neat that you do this. That you make a living at it."

"It's an okay living. I'm a staff of one and my facilities are my great-grandma's summer kitchen, but it works." She met his gaze evenly. "I live a pretty simple life. I don't need much."

He respected that. Even admired it. It wasn't his life, and he wasn't sure he'd be good at that much simplicity. But how would he know? He'd never had the choice.

He held the yarn in his hands, the soft weight of it foreign and pleasant. "Well, I admire you. And I'm kind of jealous. I graduated and went right into business with my dad. A few years later he died, leaving me everything. I was kind of thrust into the role."

She took the yarn away from him and put it down on a table. "That sounds like a lot."

He nodded. "I was younger than you, and a sudden billionaire with a dozen companies to oversee. And I'd lost my father, so I didn't have him for advice or as a mentor."

He wasn't sure why he'd told her all that. It wasn't as if it was a secret; his dad's death had made the business pages and the news of his stepping into the CEO position had followed. But that last part…it made him feel a little bit vulnerable. He wasn't sure anyone understood what an adjustment it had been. How scared he still was of failing.

And how his dad had shared his business acumen but hadn't really taught Cole what it was like to be a man. Numbers and figures had been his way of communicating, but never anything personally meaningful. Anything he'd learned in that regard, he'd learned from his best friends.

"But you did it. And are a tremendous success," she reminded him quietly.

"I had the support of the directors, which helped." At least with the numbers and figures. Not so much with the loneliness.

"Until you crashed."

"Until I crashed."

She was very close to him now, close enough he could touch her if he wanted. And he wanted. It wasn't the smart thing but he was kind of tired of always feeling pressure to do the smart thing. Or the most fiscally responsible thing. He wanted a chance to be human. Mess up. Get his hands dirty.

"Cole," she said softly, and he realized he'd been staring at her lips like a fool.

"You are definitely not what I expected," he murmured, shifting his gaze from her mouth to her eyes. "Not at all."

"Nor are you," she replied, and her words were a little breathless. "But this isn't a good idea."

"I know. I'm not sure how much I care, though."

They'd drifted closer together until they were nearly touching. Cole held his breath as his heart pounded. And then he decided to abandon all caution and just do what he wanted to do—kiss her.

He curled a hand around the nape of her neck and leaned in, touching his lips to hers. They were soft and warm and opened a little in surprise, and she let out a small breath as he fit his mouth over hers more securely. She lifted her hand and let it rest on his arm, holding on and yet still holding back, just a little. She tasted like tea and cinnamon and vanilla, an intoxicating blend that made him think of home—or at least the home he hadn't had but always imagined.

All too soon he shifted back, not wanting to press his case, or go too fast. There was something fragile about her he couldn't put his finger on. Oh, she wouldn't break. She was a strong, stubborn woman. But there was something else, a vulnerability, that he sensed in her sweetness and hesitation.

"Oh, my," she said softly and bit down on her lower lip. It was so sexy he nearly groaned.

"I should probably get back. Everyone is leaving tomorrow, and Raelynn is cooking a farewell dinner tonight. Lobster's on the menu."

"Sounds lovely." She took a step back, then frowned a bit. "Listen, Cole…this probably isn't a good idea. I mean, you want to buy my house. Something between us muddies those waters. And I don't plan to sell, which means we'll be neighbors. Also awkward. So as much as I'm flattered…"

"No more kissing?" He was profoundly disappointed. He'd enjoyed kissing her very much. She was a thorn in his side, but he was starting to like her a lot. She was, as Tori liked to say, "good people."

"No more kissing," she confirmed. She shoved her hands into her sweatshirt pockets, a telling bit of body language he was curious about. Withdrawing and also protective…she didn't have to be afraid of him, though. He would never hurt her.

"I won't lie. I'm disappointed. But if that's what you want…"

"It is, yes. But it might be nice if we stayed on friendly terms. It does make living on the island together easier."

"Because you're not going to sell." He nearly smiled, but tried not to.

But she did, a sweet little uptick of the corners of her mouth as her eyes sparkled at him. "Because I'm not going to sell."

He nodded, then felt compelled to add, "You know that what I am willing to pay would set you up in a house and leave capital left over to run your business properly."

"But it isn't home. And right now…this is home."

She was definitely attached, and he couldn't honestly say he blamed her. There was something warm and inviting about the old house, and he'd already found himself captivated by the island.

"So I don't get the real estate deal and I don't get kisses. It seems I'm getting the rotten end of this deal."

She nodded, a sober expression on her face. "It appears you are," she replied, and damned if they weren't flirting after all.

"I'll just have to come up with a better offer." He held out a hand and gestured toward the door. "Shall we? I really do need to get back."

She led him to the front door. Marvin looked up from his doggy bed and his tail gave a thump, but he didn't get up and rush over. It was almost as if he was used to seeing Cole there. Like Cole somehow…belonged.

That was ridiculous, wasn't it? This was just a dog, and a slightly tired old house, and not his life at all.

"Helicopter tomorrow," he warned Brooklyn. "Fastest way to get my people from here to the airport."

"Thanks for the warning," she said, smiling a little. "Have a good dinner with your guests."

He almost wanted to invite her to join them. Also ridiculous, but he was prolonging their goodbye and didn't know why.

So he said goodbye and went back to the graveled lane, toward the big house on the bluff.

Brooklyn kept her eye on the forecast as the week progressed. A midseason hurricane had formed to the southeast and was spinning its way north. The US eastern seaboard looked to be getting a miss, but Nova Scotia was another story, if the models were accurate. Right now it could go a little either way. A direct hit would be nasty. A bit to the right would bring lots of rain. To the left, crazy winds. Either way, it was a category three now, and they'd had a very warm autumn. Maybe it would only be a tropical storm when it hit, but right now forecasters were predicting a category one.

Which didn't sound that bad. Except she'd seen what even a category one could do. Widespread power outages. With her generator, that wasn't a huge deal. But the seas would be whipped up and rolling, which meant getting to the mainland would be out of the question. Her little boat wasn't up to it. She'd have to make a trip over and stock up on anything she might need.

Her needles clacked and she grinned. Wine, chocolate, dog food…all the necessities for being storm-stayed.

She spread the shawl out over her lap and admired the fine, even stitches and the soft yarn. This might be her favorite piece ever, and that was saying something. She imagined wrapping herself up in it this winter, with a cup of hot cocoa and a good book or DVD. She'd have Marvin for company, as always. And yet as she picked up the knitting again, a sense of unease slid through her. Cole would be gone, wouldn't he? And she'd be alone on the island. Not that she minded; she was used to it. But he wouldn't be here. With his smiley face and teasing voice and…well, just everything.

She'd gotten kind of used to him, after all. He made things interesting.

Her cell rang and she reached over to grab it, looked at the number, and frowned. It was a number that she didn't recognize at all. "Hello?"

"Hey, Brooklyn, it's Cole."

"You got my phone number." She wasn't sure if she was pleased or not.

"I got it from Jeremy, my Realtor, who had it because of…well. When I was trying to buy your house from under you."

She laughed out loud at his bluntness. "Fair enough. What's up?"

He was calling her. *Calling her.* It shouldn't make her giddy, but there were a whole list of *shouldn'ts* where

Cole was concerned and she had so far ignored every single one.

"I'm having a dinner at my house tonight with my friends. Jeremy and Tori are coming over, and Branson is back in town with Jessica. I hate being a fifth wheel, so I wondered if you'd like to join us."

Oh, my. She wasn't sure if he meant for this to be as his date or if she was a chair filler. And she had no idea how to ask, either. "Dinner? With your friends? But I don't know them. Won't it be awkward?"

"Naw. It's just casual. They haven't been over to the island since I moved in, and I thought it would be nice to do it now since it looks like we're in for some weather later in the week."

She hesitated.

"Of course, if you don't want to, that's fine. I know it's last-minute."

Which was a paltry excuse because living somewhere with a population of two pretty much guaranteed an open social calendar.

"I could probably come. I guess."

"Great! Come any time after six. We'll have pre-dinner drinks. Everyone's spending the night, so we can all indulge a little."

Oh, my. What had she agreed to? A cozy little dinner party with a bunch of billionaires, and her with a solid low five-figure income, no degree, no prestige… what would they have to talk about? When it was just her and Cole, she tended to forget he was so rich and accomplished. She was suddenly having second thoughts.

"Don't even think about backing out. I can hear your brain turning."

"Who said I was having second thoughts?" If she was good at anything, it was bluffing. Bluffing being

strong, bluffing being independent, bluffing being...
whole. But that was another story and one she was not
planning to share with Cole.

He just laughed lightly. "Raelynn is cooking up a
feast. Come hungry."

"Should I bring anything?"

"Just yourself. See you at six."

He was gone before she could say another word. It
was fine. She'd met Tori before, and she was lovely. And
it was just dinner. She could excuse herself if it was too
much and walk home. Besides, she was curious to see
what changes Cole had made. Ernest had had a decorator do the house, and she'd always thought the furniture a little heavy and dark. Had Cole kept the same
vibe or done something very different? She knew he'd
done some renos, but the work crews hadn't been there
a very long time.

She put the knitting away and decided to take a bath
and think about what to wear. She was having dinner
with not one but three billionaires, wasn't she? And Jeremy's wife and Branson's girlfriend. There was no question that she was Cole's date. Even though it was a casual
"round out the table" date, they were still paired up.

Second thoughts bubbled up again.

The bath and lavender salts helped to relax her, and
she dressed in black leggings and her favorite long
sweater that she'd knit herself, with drop sleeves and a
V-neck. It was knit out of cashmere in a pinky-red rhu-
barb shade, and she slid on her favorite boots, brown
leather ones that were well loved and classic, stopping
at just below her knee. There was a bit of a debate in
her head about wearing her hair up or down, but she
decided to put it up in a top knot because she liked how
it emphasized the V-neckline.

And because her clothing choices were still some-what casual, she took extra time with makeup, going a little heavier than usual with her eyes and then a neutral lip. When she was done she pressed a hand to her stomach to calm her nerves. Dinner. It was dinner, for Pete's sake. Not an actual date. Not really. They weren't going to be alone or anything.

There was an odd little beep outside her house and she peered out the window. One of the golf carts was parked out front, and the man behind the wheel had to be Raelynn's husband, who worked as the caretaker. She laughed out loud. Even on this tiny island, Cole had somehow managed to send a driver to get her.

She went outside and approached, smiling at the man sitting patiently. "Hi, I'm Brooklyn."

"Dan," he replied, grinning back.

"Dan, I just need to let my dog out before I go. Do you mind waiting?"

"Of course not. I've heard about your dog. Cole talks about him."

"He does?"

He nodded. "My dad says that Cole was never allowed to have a dog at the house, but he always liked them. The Abbott house wasn't one for…well, I don't know. It was a bit sterile."

She filed that tidbit away, but what he'd said prompted another question. "Your father knows Cole?"

"He was Cole's father's chauffeur for years. I spent most of my childhood near the Abbotts."

Interesting. Brooklyn wondered why Cole had then hired Dan. Keeping it all in the family?

There was no time to ask, nor did she want to pry. Instead she went to let Marvin out, and once he'd had a pee and said hello to Dan, she put him back inside and slid into the cart. "Shall we?" she asked.

The sun was fading and there was a distinct chill in the air, though it wasn't what Brooklyn would call cold. It took no time at all and they were at the house. Lights glowed from the windows, and Dan dropped her by the front door. "Let me know when you want to go home, Ms. Graves."

"Please, call me Brooklyn. It's a small island and we should all be friends."

He smiled at that, a big genuine smile. "All right. Anyway, just let me know. There's no need for you to walk home in the dark."

She appreciated it, though she fully planned to walk. She knew this island like the back of her hand, dark or light. And there was something magical about being on an island, surrounded by the Atlantic, and looking up at the stars. It was awesome and humbling.

He drove away and Brooklyn was left with her next dilemma. Knock? Or let herself in? With Ernest, she'd always just knocked and stuck her head in the door, calling out. They'd had that sort of relationship. It was different with Cole, so she lifted the door knocker and rapped it smartly against the huge solid wood door.

CHAPTER SIX

THE DOOR OPENED and Raelynn smiled out at her. "Brooklyn! I'm so glad you came."

An ally. Brooklyn smiled back. She'd met Raelynn days earlier, when she'd come up to the house to chat about the gardens and Raelynn's plans for winter upkeep. The New Yorker was quick to learn and really entertaining. Brooklyn had laughed more in her company than she had for ages.

"Me, too. Dan picked me up. He's a nice guy, your husband."

Raelynn blushed. "We've been together for about six years. When Cole hired us to work as a team, well, it was a dream come true."

The couple wouldn't stay on the island in Cole's absence but would travel back ahead of him when the house was open. Apparently they'd be the ones maintaining everything during the retreats when Cole wasn't present, too. When Raelynn had told her that, Brooklyn had realized how much Cole must like and trust them.

Raelynn stepped aside. "Come on in, and I'll get you a glass of wine."

"That sounds lovely."

Together they walked through the foyer. Brooklyn

expected to see Cole and his company seated in the vast living room, but instead laughter came from the kitchen. She entered and Cole's gaze found hers, his eyes lighting up with pleasure.

"You're here! Everyone, this is Brooklyn, my favorite neighbor. Brooklyn, this is Jeremy and Tori, their baby, Rose, and Branson and Jessica."

Jeremy reminded her a little of JFK Jr., only with shorter hair, and Branson…well. His nearly black hair tumbled over his collar and he looked a bit like a sexy pirate. She could see why Jessica stared at him with stars in her eyes. Tori and Jessica were both lovely in a way that made Brooklyn comfortable and not awkward. Maybe she'd expected them to be different—more coiffed and manicured, perhaps. Instead Tori snuggled Rose on her arm and smiled widely, her hair in slight disarray, and Jessica had the most adorable smile and freckles on her nose.

"I'm your only neighbor, so thanks for that dubious distinction. I'm very pleased to meet you all. Well, Tori and I have met before, briefly. It's good to see you again." She thanked Raelynn when she was handed a glass of wine. "Welcome to Bellwether Island."

"I hope Cole hasn't been a jerk," Jeremy offered. "When he sets his mind to something, he goes after it."

Her face heated but she hid behind taking a sip of wine before she answered. "Not at all. He knows my position on selling and so the subject is dropped. We've become friends." She smiled sweetly. Very sweetly.

Branson burst out laughing. "You were right, Cole. She's a firecracker."

Tori came over and touched her arm. "Good for you. Cole needs someone to put him in his place from time to time."

Jessica was grinning, leaning against Branson's arm. "I think you're pretty great," she said. "It takes a tough cookie to live out here full time."

The warm welcome was a pleasant surprise, so Brooklyn smiled and relaxed a little more. "You're a painter. I don't know if anything on the island inspires you, but you're welcome anytime."

Jessica nudged Branson. "See? That's what you should have said when I showed up at your lighthouse."

Branson rolled his eyes and everyone laughed.

Raelynn was working behind them and finally shooed them out. "Okay, you bunch. I have work to do in here and you're in the way. Starter course in ten minutes."

Starter courses. It reminded Brooklyn of the fact that in her life, a starter course meant maybe a platter of vegetables and dip before a meal. How many courses would there be?

They moved into the living room and Brooklyn paused at the threshold. Cole had definitely decorated differently than his predecessor. While the glow of the lamps threw a warm and welcoming light, the color scheme was vastly different from Ernest's. Instead of cream and gold and brown, the room was painted a light gray, with a darker gray sofa and chairs, a glass-topped coffee table and a massive rug that covered the floor in shades of gray, blue and white.

It reminded Brooklyn of the gray waves and white caps of the ocean on a blustery day, brought inside, and she loved it. It was an extension of the landscape, blending in rather than keeping it out.

"Do you like it?" Cole asked, once he saw her face.

"I do. It's very different from what was here before. But it suits the house and…you."

"Thank you." He smiled at her. "Did you want another quick tour? I've made some other changes. I nearly forgot that of course you would know what it was like before."

She was curious. "I'd like that. But we can do it another time. You have guests."

He waved a hand. "They'll be fine for five minutes. Come on."

He'd taken a den and made it into a boardroom, complete with a huge table and executive chairs, and some sort of smart board. "Some of our retreats will be team building or brainstorming getaways."

The common areas had all been repainted into that same restful gray, cool and relaxing. Artwork decorated the walls, though Brooklyn didn't recognize any particular artist. In the main areas, the artwork was black-and-white: driftwood and dunes and cliffs. Cole had moved in and brought the ocean with him, and she had to say she loved it a lot. It felt fresh and modern and yet peaceful, with an underlying energy she couldn't quite pinpoint but made her feel grounded and strong.

"Did you have a decorator?"

"Yes." He led her up the stairs. "I brought in someone from New York. I think he did a good job, don't you?"

"It fits. It fits this island, and you, too. I loved it when Ernest lived here, but this is even better, I think."

"I'm glad you approve."

She looked up at him. "Oh, get real. You don't really care if you have my approval or not."

He tilted his head and met her gaze. "You know, that should be true. But lately I find myself caring about what you think very much."

"Cole…"

"I know. I'm just saying. Somehow I don't want to disappoint you."

After a tour of the guest rooms, he took her down and showed her the gym. By that time, Raelynn was calling them to the dining room, and she let out a sigh at the beautiful table setting.

There were three bowls with fresh flowers on the table, lending their sweet scent but low enough that the blooms didn't impede anyone's view of each other. Rose had started to fall asleep and was now sitting in a carrier nearby, covered with a blanket and staring dazedly at a bar holding very colorful and interesting shapes.

The table had had the extension leaves taken out of it so that it sat six. Cole was at the head and Jeremy at the foot, with Jessica and Branson on one side, and then Tori on an angle to Jeremy and Brooklyn on an angle to Cole. They were definitely paired up, but Brooklyn couldn't bring herself to mind. They all seemed to get along so well that it didn't matter anyway.

The first course was a ginger-carrot soup, perfectly seasoned with ginger and a hint of cumin and cayenne. Brooklyn decided to ask Raelynn for the recipe, and then the cook returned with asparagus wrapped in Parma ham. It nearly looked too pretty to eat with the vibrant green and crisp pink of the ham, and went perfectly with the dry Riesling Raelynn had poured during the soup course. The starters had been simple but delicious, and Brooklyn savored each bite as conversation flowed easily around the table.

Brooklyn was already wondering how she was going to make it to the main course when a small plate was placed before her, containing a kale and apple salad with pumpkin seeds and pomegranate arils. She looked up at Cole and said, "Where did you ever find Raelynn? She's a fantastic chef."

He grinned. "I'll tell her you said so. She was working for a caterer and ran a party for my mother maybe six years ago. Incidentally, she also met Dan that night. She stayed with the caterer even after she and Dan married, and when I bought this place, I offered them the caretaker jobs."

Jessica put down her fork. "They don't mind being so isolated?" She looked at Brooklyn and smiled. "Not that it isn't lovely, but when someone is so used to the city, this can be a bit of a shock."

"None taken," Brooklyn replied. "It is isolated. Even for me, and I've pretty much been here my whole life." She thought about Raelynn and Dan living above the garage. She was sure Cole had it decorated nicely for them, but she understood now why he'd thought buying her out would provide them with a home of their own.

"They won't stay all year round," Cole said. "Only when it's required. And maybe through the summer." He leaned back in his chair, toying with his wineglass. "I'd like to be here in the summer months more. Enjoy the beach, maybe do some deep-sea fishing."

Jeremy laughed. "Look at you, slowing down."

Cole lifted an eyebrow. "And you, settling down. Whatever, bro."

Everyone laughed a little, and then Branson said, "That's not in the cards for you, Cole?"

Unease settled in Brooklyn's stomach. She was here as Cole's date, after all. She tried to keep a relaxed posture, even though the question seemed rather pointed, and did and didn't involve her at the same time. But Cole just shrugged easily. "Dude, you know me. I have too much going on, even if I have slowed down a bit. You and Jeremy can carry that flag. The single life works for me."

Jeremy gazed into Tori's eyes. "I'm definitely okay with that."

"Me, too," Bran said, leaning over and kissing Jessica's temple.

It was so obvious to Brooklyn that the other two couples were deeply in love. What in the world was she doing here? It had become horribly awkward. She suddenly felt like nothing more than a seat filler.

Thankfully, Raelynn returned with their main course, a maple-glazed salmon with tiny smashed potatoes and steamed vegetables. Brooklyn couldn't remember ever sitting down to such a feast. It was so different from her actual life, but everyone else was acting as if this happened every day. Did they always live like this?

There was a new wine for the salmon dish, a pinot noir that was delicate and lighter than she normally liked her reds, but matched the salmon beautifully. Dear heaven, actual wine pairings in addition to all this food. And this was a "casual" dinner! She couldn't imagine what fancy would entail.

It was Jessica who totally switched gears and eased the knot in Brooklyn's stomach. "Brooklyn, I love your sweater. Is that cashmere?"

She nodded and smiled. "Thank you, and yes, it is."

"Did you make it yourself? Tori tells us you run your own knitting business."

Brooklyn glanced at Tori, who was smiling at her. Sure they'd met, but she was surprised that she'd been a topic of conversation. "What?" Tori asked. "People in town know who you are. Anytime you put something in the store in Liverpool, it goes like hotcakes. My mom actually downloaded one of your patterns for a baby blanket last winter."

"Oh, I hope it turned out! Which one?"

"The lacy carriage blanket. She said it knit up like a dream."

Jessica jumped in again. "I think it's beautiful. You'd pay through the nose for something like that in Manhattan."

Brooklyn chuckled. "I can't imagine there being a market for hand knits in Manhattan."

Cole stepped in. "Actually, you might be surprised. A little market research would tell you for sure."

"Which sounds a lot like big business. I'm pretty happy running my little one as it is, and on my own time."

She took a bite of the salmon and wondered why her heart was beating so fast. Everyone was so friendly and lovely, so why was she feeling like a complete fish out of water?

Branson was the one who stepped in. "Actually, I think Jess and I get that. What you do is very creative. It's not always a great idea to commoditize our creativity."

"Exactly." Brooklyn smiled at him and let out a slow breath. "I don't mind living simply if it means keeping my joy."

"Amen," Jessica said.

The subject changed again and Brooklyn focused on enjoying the flavorful main course. By the time dessert arrived, she wasn't sure she could eat another bite, until her serving of crème brûlée was placed in front of her.

She looked up at Raelynn. "You are evil, Raelynn."

Raelynn laughed. "Thank you. I'll take that as a compliment."

"You should. This is my favorite dessert."

She knew she shouldn't indulge anymore. But she couldn't resist as she took her spoon and broke through the crust to the custard below.

It was nothing short of heaven.

After dinner, they all retired to the living room again. A fire had been laid in the fireplace and it crackled merrily. Tori went to their guest room and put a now sleeping Rose to bed. Brooklyn wasn't sure she should stay much longer. She was not a part of this group. It was clear that Cole would have been fine without a dinner partner, so why had he invited her? Why had he kissed her in her grandmother's porch? What did he even want? She knew what his purpose for the island was, but that was all. That was professional. And perhaps a little personal, but she had no idea what his motives were.

And yet she didn't believe he was playing games, either. He didn't seem the cavalier type.

Maybe she should just ask him. But not now. Not when his guests were curled up on his expensive furniture.

"I really should be going," she said with a smile. "But thank you for inviting me and for such a lovely dinner. I don't need to eat now for a week!"

Cole looked up, a frown appearing between his eyebrows. "So soon? It's only nine."

"I've got to be up early in the morning. This time of year I start getting a lot of orders. I don't want to fall behind."

"You must be getting a lot of holiday business starting," Tori said. "How do you keep up? Don't you worry about having carpal tunnel after knitting so much?"

"So far so good," Brooklyn replied. "But yes, this is a really busy time of year. It was so nice meeting you all and joining you for dinner, though." And she meant it. She'd felt awkward, but it wasn't because of anything anyone had said or done, not really. It was just an awareness that they lived in a world that was foreign to her.

"I'll call Dan to run you down," Cole said.

"No, please don't. It's a beautiful night and I'll walk."

"I'll walk you, then."

She was aware that the other two couples were hanging on their every word. "It's okay, Cole. You stay with your guests."

"Oh, we're fine," said Tori lightly. "We can spare him for half an hour."

"See?"

She wasn't going to win, and to protest further would only make it more awkward. "All right, then."

They headed out into the evening. With the sun now down and the moon rising, the air had taken on a distinct chill. She hadn't thought she'd need a jacket over her sweater, but it was colder than she'd expected. Probably because the sky was perfectly clear, with a blanket of brilliant stars above them.

"Wow," Cole said, pausing on the gravel in front of the house. "You can see forever when there's no light pollution."

"Right?" She hugged her arms around herself and tilted her head to stare into the darkness. "There are a million stars tonight."

He was closer to her than she realized, because when he spoke again she jumped, startled by his nearness and how his soft voice was so close to her ear. "Stars make me feel both incredibly small and also like I belong to something vast. That probably doesn't make sense."

But it did make sense to her. She'd often felt the same. "When my brother and sister and I were kids, we used to lie on the sand and stare up at the stars." She laughed as the memory came rushing back. "My mom hated it because we always ended up with sand in our hair and bites from sand fleas on our legs and arms. It was my grandma who washed out all the little grains of sand and put calamine lotion on so we wouldn't scratch."

She turned her head and looked up at him. There was a small smile on his face but his eyes seemed sad. "What?" she asked.

"Nothing. I just never did anything like that as a kid. Of course, I didn't have brothers or sisters, either."

Brooklyn thought it sounded unbearably lonely, and that those kinds of memories were something not even privilege could buy. "Then come on," she said impulsively, taking his hand and pulling him off the graveled path.

Cole let Brooklyn drag him along because he was simply enchanted by her. He had been, all through dinner. She'd shown up looking so incredibly beautiful, with her hair gathered up and the graceful curve of her neck exposed. He'd thought about what she might do if he kissed her right where her neck met her shoulder, if she'd sigh a little or break out in goose bumps. She'd enjoyed dinner, too. He'd stolen looks at her as she'd tasted each dish, sipped the wine that Raelynn had chosen for each course. It was a casual dinner with friends but to her it had been special, hadn't it?

Even the question about his single status hadn't fazed him…much. And that was surprising.

Now she was pulling him through tall, crackly grass

as they made their way to the beach, ignoring any path. No matter where he was on the island, he could hear the ocean, but the shush of the breakers now reached his ears, and something built in his chest, something unexpected that he wasn't sure what to do with.

In this moment, he didn't want to be anywhere else but here, with her. Especially with her. And that complicated things so much. He did dates. He didn't do... more.

"Come on," she said, jumping down over a small dune and into the sand. She took off her footwear and left it at the edge, and let go of his hand as she danced toward the water. She was maybe ten feet away from the waves when she stopped, opened her arms wide and lifted her face to the sky.

Oh, damn. This wasn't a little complication; it was a huge one that he wasn't sure what to do with.

She spun around and called to him. "Come on!"

He took off his shoes and socks, and the cool sand squidged between his toes. He'd gone business casual tonight, so he was wearing nice trousers and a tailored button-down. Not exactly beach attire. She trotted back and grabbed his hand. "Come on, slowpoke. We're going to look at the stars."

He laughed and followed her, and then to his surprise, she dropped down onto the sand and made to lie down.

"Wait!" He stopped her as he shrugged out of his jacket. "We can put this under our heads. So we don't get sand."

Her smile was wide as she took his jacket, then spread it on the sand. "Okay, come on down."

He wasn't sure if he'd get any fleabites...after all, this was Nova Scotia in early October. Wouldn't it be too cold or something? And right now he didn't actually care. He lay down on the sand beside her and put his head on his jacket. They had to lie close together to share the "pillow," and he liked the feeling of her body next to his.

"Look up," she said, her voice barely more than a breath, and he opened his eyes to the sky above.

It was so big. Inky blackness stretched endlessly, with thousands of stars blinking at them. The ocean swept in and out, lulling him into relaxing. And yet he was so very aware of the woman beside him that it was impossible to relax completely. He sensed her every breath and could smell her floral shampoo. And when she reached out and hooked a few of her fingers in his, his chest tightened.

Brooklyn Graves was a beautiful woman. Not just outside, but inside, too.

"Look," she whispered, pointing up with her free hand. "There's a satellite moving across the sky."

The silver light moved in a precise arc and he watched it for several seconds. "Do you know the constellations?"

"Not really," she replied. She slid her fingers away and he missed the contact. "I mean, I know the Big and Little Dippers. But the rest… I like making things up instead. Kind of like when you see shapes in the clouds? I like to find them in the stars."

God, she was so pure, wasn't she? How many women had he met in his lifetime who would indulge in a bit of whimsy to make up their own constellations? It struck him that maybe he'd spent a lot of his time with the wrong sort of woman.

And wondered if that was because of the example set at home. His mother had not been a nurturer. It was something that he and Jeremy had in common. Jeremy had had a stepdad. Cole had still had his father, but his father had barely been around. His first love was always Abbott Industries. And when his will had been read, his instruction to his son was "Please don't ruin my company." Nothing about being happy or finding love...and when Cole had looked at his mother's impassive face at the cemetery, he'd wondered if they'd ever loved each other at all.

He let out a long breath, wishing he knew how to let go of the past. But it popped up now and again, and more often lately. He couldn't imagine living in a loveless marriage—or worse, loving someone only to have them stop loving you.

Especially when you weren't really that lovable to begin with.

"That was a 'deep thought' kind of sigh. You okay?"

He felt her gaze on his profile and stared at the stars. "Yeah, I'm fine. Just thinking."

"What about?"

"My family." He debated whether or not he should say more. He didn't talk about his personal life. But there was something about Brooklyn that invited him to be open. "My mother would never have done this. Neither would my dad. To be honest, I'm not even sure why they had me. I spent my whole life trying to gain their approval, or rebelling at never getting it. Now it's too late anyway."

"Even for your mother? I know your dad is gone, but she's still living, right?"

"Yeah. We don't have much of a relationship. She wasn't very maternal."

"I see."

"I spent a lot of time looking for validation, and not

enough time actually living. Being here on the island has hammered that home, and sometimes I'm not sure what to do with it."

"It sounds like you made a lot of life changes after your health scare."

"Let's call it what it is. I had a breakdown. Of course it was all kept super quiet, because if it had gotten out, Abbott stock would have plummeted."

"That's a lot of pressure to put on a single person, Cole."

He didn't answer, because she was right.

"So what are you going to do? Walk away?"

"No." That he was able to answer definitively. "I do know I have to stop being self-destructive. Being a workaholic is not the answer. But I still need to have a purpose and a reason to be busy. I can't just hide away here. It's nice for a little while, but not forever."

"Balance."

"Yeah. It's one of those words that get thrown around a lot, but for me it means making sure I take time out, that I don't burn out, that I don't have to do everything myself. It sounds like it should be easy, but when you've lived that way your whole life, the habits are hard to break."

He'd been on the island a few weeks, and he was already getting antsy to get back. He did actually like his job. He liked building things and helping people and solving problems. And so far he had not ruined the company. On the contrary.

"You have wonderful friends who support you." She nudged a little closer and he wondered if she was cold.

"Here," he said, sitting up a bit and holding his arm out. "You're cold. Snuggle in."

She hesitated for a moment, then just when he

thought she was going to say no, she slid closer and let him pull her next to his body. She fit there so well. Made him want things he'd never wanted in his life.

They stargazed a few minutes more, silent but for the waves slipping over the sand. He wondered what he should do. He could send her home and say he needed to get back to his friends. He could walk her home and say good-night, and be a gentleman. He could turn toward her and kiss her soft, full lips, even though they'd agreed they would not be sharing kisses again.

He should send her home. Get back. Forget about this impulsive beach trip and make plans to head back to New York soon. She wasn't the kind of woman he could or should play games with.

He rolled to his side so he was facing her and rested his head on his hand, braced by his elbow.

Her lips twitched. "You're supposed to be looking at the stars."

"I'm looking at something more beautiful than stars."

"There's a line."

"It's not a line if it's true."

She turned her face toward him. "What do you want, Cole?"

He struggled with how to answer. He couldn't lie. He couldn't say nothing, and he couldn't say more than he felt. So he let his gaze lock with hers as he admitted, simply, "You."

Her chest rose and fell with a big breath, and her eyes widened. "But that's all, right? You're not looking for a relationship or a girlfriend or whatever."

"I won't lie to you, Brooklyn. I won't do that just to get what I want, okay? I don't use manipulation."

"But you want me."

"I do. Quite a bit, actually. But we agreed not to kiss

again, so I'm lying here, admitting what I want, knowing that it all hinges on one word from you. Because I never, ever want to treat you unfairly."

Her throat bobbed as she swallowed, and her eyes softened. "Even when you were trying to buy my house, you were always honest. I… I trust you, Cole."

The way she said it made him think that it was not something she admitted very often.

And then she surprised him by lifting up and shifting so that her mouth was against his.

He used gravity to his advantage, moving forward until she was back down on the sand, her head on his jacket, and he was braced above her, tasting her lips, which held the faint taste of vanilla and brown sugar from dessert. She was so sweet, so perfect. Her sweater was soft beneath his hand as he ran his hand up her arm and then behind her neck, cradling the soft skin and baby hairs there. She responded by nudging her left leg in between his, twining them together as he deepened the kiss. Her fingers gripped his arm as he slid his lips off hers and finally tasted the delectable hollow of her throat and she gasped, arching up. Without thinking, he ran his hand under her sweater to cup her breast in his palm, the pebbled tip pushing through her bra.

This was going far faster than he'd anticipated, and while his desire was yelling at him to take this as far as she'd let him, his caution—and conscience—told him to slow down. She wasn't his to ravish. She was his to protect.

And he had no freaking idea where that notion had come from, but it made him temper his advances, removing his hand from beneath her sweater and instead indulging in long, sweet kisses that drugged his mind.

At some point they slowed to gentle sips and nibbles,

and then he pressed his forehead to hers. "Brooklyn. Please don't ask me to be sorry we did that. I'm not. No matter what happens, I'm not sorry."

She pushed away a bit. "What do you mean, whatever happens? Is there something I should know?"

Cole looked her fully in the eyes. "I don't live here. This house, this island, is part of my life but not all of it, not like it is yours. It's here for me to retreat to, for me to help others, too. Men and women like me, who forget to take care of themselves in their high-pressure lives."

"It's a piece of the puzzle that is Cole Abbott," she murmured.

"Exactly. And I like you and I want you…but I don't want to build up expectations that aren't realistic."

"So this is a fling."

"No." He put his hand under her chin and lifted it. "Not a fling. You mean something to me, okay? Flings are…a couple of dates and some hot sex and not calling each other back. That's not us." It had been him, though. More times than he cared to admit.

And that alone scared him. The fact that he was saying all this out loud was terrifying. And yet he wanted to deal with her the way he ran his business—with integrity. She deserved it.

"But you'll be leaving."

"Yes, and soon."

She sighed, then sat up. Grains of sand clung to her sweater and he thought about the story she'd shared from her childhood. "Are you still close with your family, Brooklyn?"

She pulled up her knees and rested her arms on them, staring out at the dark ocean. "Not like I used to be. We're kind of spread out now."

But there was a hesitancy, a guardedness in her tone

that made him curious. She could run her business any-where. Why here, and why so isolated from everything? What was she running from?

He didn't have a chance to ask her as she jumped up from the sand and started brushing off her bottom. "You need to get back. You've left your guests a long time."

He gathered up his jacket, but then held out his hand. She paused, then took it, and they went back to where they'd abandoned their shoes. Once they'd brushed the sand off their feet and their footwear was back on, they took the narrow path toward Brooklyn's house.

The porch light was on, welcoming her back, and he fought against a sense of both wistfulness and home-coming. He was starting to realize how very much he'd wished to have someplace that felt like home and not just a dwelling…even if it was a dwelling he shared with other people. The closest he'd ever felt was Merrick, when he and Jeremy and Branson had been in board-ing school together.

Back then it had been the people who had made it his home. But that wasn't true now. He'd only known Brooklyn a few weeks. He was at a loss to explain why the house felt so comfortable.

"I guess this is good-night," he said softly.

"Thank you for dinner. And for introducing me to your friends. They seem very, very nice."

"They are."

"And tell Raelynn her food was exquisite."

"All right."

He kissed her lightly this time, not pulling her close, but a gentle, slightly lingering contact that left his lips aching for more. But he'd do the smart thing and go home, have a whiskey with his pals and put this whole thing in perspective. Stars and moonlight did strange things to a man, didn't they?

"Good night," he said and stepped away.

"Good night. I'll wait to let Marvin out until after you're out of sight. Otherwise you won't get away for another twenty minutes."

He chuckled lightly, but his chest was tight at the feelings he was developing for this woman and her dog.

So he turned away and walked out of the circle of her porch light and back toward the mansion on the hill, waiting for him.

CHAPTER SEVEN

BROOKLYN WATCHED THE forecast carefully over the days ahead. The hurricane had been a category three as it barreled its way north, and now, maybe thirty-six hours away, had been downgraded to a cat two.

She made a trip to the mainland for supplies before the surf started picking up. Batteries, lamp oil, dog food and easy-to-prepare foods were top of her list. It wasn't her first storm, and she was fully prepared to spend a few evenings knitting by lantern light with a glass of wine if it came to that. There was still water in her rain barrels she could use for plumbing, and she filled two ten-gallon jugs that she'd use for drinking and cooking.

All models pointed to a direct hit just south of here as it made landfall, and even if it ended up as a category one, Brooklyn was pretty sure she'd lose power for several days. She had a small generator that would run her fridge and a few other things if required, but she relied on low-tech solutions to weather any outages.

She also hadn't heard from Cole since the night of the dinner party. She missed him. Of course, that in itself was a bad idea, so she didn't bother to initiate contact, either.

Instead she figured she'd have one lovely evening to remember; the night she stargazed with a billionaire and they made out on the beach. She smiled a little. It was a damned good memory, to be honest. One of those "there was this one time" stories. Had she really said she trusted him, and meant it?

Starlight was a funny, funny thing. Because for the first time in forever, she'd forgotten to feel threatened. Forgotten to be cautious.

She grabbed her lamps and filled them with lamp oil to shake away the unsettling thoughts. When the power went out, the darkness was the kind where a person couldn't see their hand in front of their face. Her favorite lighting was from the oil lamps. It was so warm and cozy. If she got cold, she'd put a fire on in the fireplace. She'd already brought wood into the back porch for that very reason.

Marvin sat by her feet. He'd been keeping rather close today, a good indication that storm weather was on its way. Outside it was sunny, but the air was still. Brooklyn was glad she'd gone over to the mainland and was already back. The surf would pick up soon, ahead of the storm. The wind would slip in, full of restless, restrained energy that shushed through the leaves. It was mild, too, the tropical air humid and heavy.

She wondered if Cole was prepared. His boat was still at the dock, and unless the helicopter had come while she was in town, he hadn't left the island.

Lamps filled and fresh batteries in her flashlights, she called Dan and then took Marvin and headed to the main house and garage. Marvin trotted ahead, and she called to him when they neared the garage where Dan and Raelynn lived. Dan met her in the drive, wearing a pair of rubber boots and a windbreaker.

"You're sure the tractor will tow his boat?"

She nodded. "Pretty sure. We only have to get them

out of the water and to the boathouse. Then at least they won't smash up against the dock, and they'll be away from the trees."

Dan nodded and opened the garage door. "The key is in it. You're in charge, Brooklyn. I don't have a lot of experience with boats. Limos now…that's more my style."

"Don't worry. I know what to do. You just have to take orders." She grinned and winked at him, and he laughed. She liked Dan a lot. He and Raelynn made a really cute couple.

Brooklyn hopped up on the tractor and whistled for Marvin, who hopped up on the step beside her left foot. While Dan waited, she pressed in the clutch and brake and turned the key, the diesel engine rumbling to life. Marvin looked like she'd just given him the world's best present. He loved riding on the tractor. It was maybe bigger than required, but Ernest had always wanted the best. And she had to admit, in the winter, it did a heck of a job at snow removal once the blower attachment was installed.

They'd go to the boathouse and get the trailers, and then take the boats out of the water. Brooklyn wasn't taking any chances. Her boat was her only way on and off the island.

Cole went to his window when the strange rumbling sound touched his ears. To his amazement, he saw a big orange tractor heading down the lane, with Brooklyn in the driver's seat and Marvin's golden head beside her. Dan was walking behind, and Cole wondered what the heck they were up to.

More than that, he wondered why the sight of her driving a tractor made him so…curious. Her self-reliance never failed to impress him, but he hadn't imagined her using large machinery. She looked cute and incredibly capable.

That curiosity had his feet moving forward, stopping in the foyer for a light jacket. The storm was sending warm, moist air over the region, but he wasn't overly worried about any power outages. There was a huge generator wired in to his electrical panel, and he'd already told Raelynn and Dan to come to the main house if everything went dark.

Right now he wanted to know what Brooklyn was planning to do with that tractor.

When he started the downhill grade to her house, he saw exactly what she was doing. She and Dan had hooked a boat trailer to the tractor and right now Brooklyn was backing it to the water. The tide was in, so the ground held firm against the weight of the tires. Once the trailer was in the water, she locked the brake and hopped down, leaving the tractor running and giving Dan instructions.

Cole knew he should help, but he was fascinated watching her work.

She walked down the dock and unmoored her boat, guiding it expertly onto the trailer. When it was secured, she motioned to Dan to put the tractor in gear and pull them out. Dan released the brake and touched the throttle.

The tractor strained against the weight, but bit by bit pulled the trailer forward until they were on the firm lane leading to the boat shed. Once they got there, she got the boat into the shed and unhooked the first trailer. Brooklyn swung the tractor around, backing it up to get the second trailer.

This time Cole approached, seeing as the second trailer was for his boat, and not her responsibility. Besides, he wanted to help. All his life this sort of thing had been for the "help" to do, but he wasn't above a little hands-on labor.

"Hello," he called out, and when Dan and Brooklyn turned around, he lifted a hand in a wave.

"Oh, hey!" Brooklyn called back to him, while Marvin heard his voice and made dizzying circles around Cole's legs.

"Marvin, take it easy, dude," Cole said, but laughed and gave the dog a good rub. "I see he also likes the tractor."

"We don't use it much in the summer. Unless a tree goes down or something, or we have to move the boats." She shoved her hands in her jacket pocket. "Ernest had a boat, too. Hence the two trailers."

"Well, let me help this time, since it's my boat."

"Sure. Dan's got his boots on. I'll back up the tractor, you can pilot it in, and Dan can help secure it. Easy-peasy."

Marvin hopped back up in his spot of honor and they worked as a team. It took no time at all to get the boat on the trailer. The boat was heavier than hers, though, and took a little more work on the part of the tractor to get it up top to the shed. To Cole's surprise, she backed the trailer in expertly, so both boats were protected from the elements.

To say he was impressed was an understatement.

Together they shut the boathouse doors and she killed the tractor engine. "Would you two like a cup of coffee or something?"

Dan looked like he wanted to say yes, but reluctantly shook his head. "I told Raelynn I'd be back up to do some hurricane prep. We still have to move the patio furniture and stuff inside."

Cole appreciated it but didn't want to begrudge the guy a simple drink. "There's time, Dan. No need to rush back."

"Seriously," Brooklyn said, "a pot takes five minutes to brew. And because you both helped, the boat thing went pretty fast."

"All right then. If you do, Cole."

"Sure."

Cole watched as Dan chatted to Brooklyn and Marvin trotted behind them. Dan was a friendly guy and so easygoing. He and Brooklyn were relaxed, like old friends. He thought back to his dinner party and how sometimes Brooklyn looked a little awkward or uncomfortable. He wasn't usually so aware of their differences in lifestyle, but watching her drive the tractor and laughing with Dan, he realized that in many ways they were as different as the sun and moon.

"Cole, you coming?" she called back.

"Yep. Be right there."

Marvin stood before him, tennis ball in his mouth. The moment Cole made eye contact with the dog, the tennis ball was dropped at his feet. Cole chuckled and picked it up, then threw it into the grass. He did this twice before Brooklyn came back, a cup of coffee in her hands. "Here, stop playing with the dog and have a coffee."

He smiled up at her. "But he asked so nicely."

She snorted. "He always does."

He went to take the mug from her and their fingers touched. The contact sparked a memory of that night under the stars, and how they'd touched each other, gently and carefully, and he knew staying was the wrong move. But he couldn't leave now, not with Dan coming out onto the front porch with his own cup. Cole would have to remain polite and no more. Otherwise he was going to find himself in a place he couldn't get out of.

They all sat on the front porch and sipped their coffee, talking about the forecast and what they might expect. None of them were strangers to hurricanes; the storms often made their way up the East Coast. But this was the first time Cole would be on a tiny island in the ocean and not comfortable in the family mansion or an elite boarding school. Maybe they weren't far from the mainland, but once the storm came in, there would be no getting off the island until it passed. It was a different sort of feeling, being at the mercy of Mother Nature.

"The storm's still a cat two," Dan said. "That'll cause some serious damage."

"And depending on when it hits, the storm surge could really be devastating." Brooklyn frowned. "Cole, is your friend Branson ready? His place is lovely, but so close to the shore. The cliffs aren't very high, either."

"You know it?"

She smiled. "Everyone knows that property. The lighthouse was a legendary make-out spot in high school."

Dan laughed and Cole was left wondering if she'd ever gone to the lighthouse for that sort of activity. But he wasn't going to ask. He didn't need that picture in his brain if she confirmed it.

"I hope so. Jeremy, too. We're all right in the path."

Silence fell for a few moments, and he noticed the wind had an eerie sound to it. "It feels weird."

Brooklyn smiled a little. "The wind? Yeah. The waves are gonna pick up really soon. By tomorrow night we'll be in the thick of it. But you wait. Before it hits? There'll be tons of surfers out catching the swell." She shook her head. "That's not for me. Last time we had a storm this big, power was out on the mainland for five days. I guess I'm chill about it once I'm prepared, but I don't see it as something to play with."

Cole looked over at her and saw lines of worry near her eyes. "You know if it looks bad, you can come out to the house and wait it out with us. Marvin, too."

"Oh, we'll be fine. Not our first rodeo."

He knew she would be. She was one of the most independent, capable women he'd ever met. "Of course you will. But you're welcome just the same."

"Thank you."

He downed what was left in his cup and stood. "Well, thanks for the coffee, but I should probably be getting back. I've been working with the New York office today, and I have a call at four that I need to prep for."

"I'll head back with you, and take the tractor," Dan agreed. "But you can ride shotgun if you want to, boss."

Brooklyn laughed and snorted, and Cole couldn't stop the smile that spread over his face. She was so darned artless.

"I'll walk. And see you there." He met Brooklyn's gaze. "Thank you for moving my boat. Please be careful during the storm, okay?"

Her smile slipped and she nodded. "I will. You do the same. And we can check in when it's over."

"The invitation still stands. You and Marvin are welcome any time."

She nodded.

He tried not to think about her down here all alone if things got scary. She was a big girl and could take care of herself.

But damned if he didn't want to. Why did he keep having that impulse?

CHAPTER EIGHT

HURRICANE PAULA ROARED into Nova Scotia as a strong category one. Before it ever made official landfall, power was out all over the south shore. Brooklyn stared out the window at the wind and rain. It wasn't raining heavily yet; this was just one of the outer bands getting started. But this was gearing up to be a doozy, and for the first time ever she was nervous about being here at the house.

It was only four o'clock and still daylight, but soon darkness would fall as the worst of the storm wreaked havoc on her island. Marvin sat at her knee, never moving. He was a loyal companion, always at her side at any sign of trouble. She patted his head and rubbed his ears. And thought of Cole and Dan and Raelynn, up at the house, hopefully safe and cozy.

There was a large crack and a whoosh and she jumped up and ran to the window. One of the trees in her front yard had broken off, tilting awkwardly into the lane. She looked down at Marvin again. The sound had startled him and now he was panting. Good heavens, this was just the prelude. And as much as she loved the little house, she realized she really didn't want to be alone right now. Not when there was company to be had.

"Come on, Marvin." She went to grab his leash and

filled a zipped baggie with kibble. Then she took her waterproof pack and put the kibble and a change of clothes inside, along with her toothbrush. There were three people at the house and he had extended the offer, after all. Things would be fine until morning, and then she'd come down and run the generator as cleanup began.

She pulled on her raincoat and boots, fastening the hood of her jacket around her chin with the Velcro closing. With Marvin's leash tight in her hand, she locked the door with the other hand and tested it, then kept her eye on the handful of trees nearby, just in case they too succumbed to the wind. A gust buffeted her and she staggered, but then she gripped the leash and started toward the other end of the island. Marvin squinted against the driving rain but trotted along beside her.

To her right she could see the coastline, and the wild spray that filled the air as the big waves crashed onto the rocks.

Paula was far more dangerous than her name sounded.

By the time they got to Cole's, Marvin was soaking wet and she was breathless from fighting the wind. She knocked on the front door, suddenly wondering if this was an awful idea. Marvin was going to be wet and probably make a mess; she'd be dripping everywhere. A nasty gust of wind slammed into them both and she hunched forward. What if he hadn't heard her knock?

She just raised her hand to knock again when the door opened, and Cole stood there in the breach. His mouth was open in surprise as he took in what she was sure had to be a bedraggled sight—one woman in a canary yellow raincoat and a very wet dog with his tail not quite between his legs, but definitely in a displeased position. Another gust of wind sent a wash of rain over them and partly into Cole's foyer. "You'd better come in, before you blow away."

She stepped inside and let him close the door, but didn't move inside. "I'm soaking wet, I'm afraid. And going to drip over your foyer."

"That's what towels are for. Hang on."

He disappeared for a moment, then came back with two fluffy towels. He took Marvin's leash while she removed her raincoat and boots, and then used a towel to blot her face and arms. She was just about to reach for Marvin when he started an all-over body shudder and shook, spraying water all over the foyer and Cole's clean pants.

"Oh, Marvin!" Brooklyn let out a huge sigh. "I'm sorry, Cole. What a mess."

Again, he laughed. "It's water. It won't hurt anything." He took Marvin's.towel and started rubbing it over the dog's back and down his legs. "Yeah, you like that, don't you?" Marvin wore a blissful doggy expression and Brooklyn rolled her eyes. That creature loved anything to do with pats, scratches or rubs. He didn't even mind when Cole lifted his feet and dried off each pad.

"Is it okay that we're here? With the power out and all, and then a tree came down in front of the house, and I just thought…"

"You thought what?" He stood, holding the towel in his hands, watching her intently.

Heat rushed into her cheeks. "The worst of the storm is set to be after dark. It just felt…a little lonely. I mean, there are lots of times when I've weathered storms alone because there's no one here. But you are here, and Rae-lynn and Dan, and—"

"You don't have to explain. I told you that you were welcome to join us and I meant it. There's lots of room, we've got power thanks to the generator, and we'll be cozy as anything."

"I'll try to make sure Marvin behaves himself."

In response, Cole reached down and unclipped Marvin's leash. "Don't be silly. He's a great dog. Come on, Marvin. Let's get a treat."

At the word "treat," the dog's ears perked up and he followed closely on Cole's heels as Cole started down the hall toward the kitchen.

"He doesn't really eat people food," she cautioned. The last thing she needed was for Marvin to have some sort of gastro episode in the middle of the storm.

"How about some cheese? Or some carrots?"

Brooklyn followed the duo into the kitchen. "I suppose a little would be all right. I did bring kibble with me."

"Perfect. Let me find a bowl for water."

He dug around in the cupboards until he found a stainless steel mixing bowl, which he filled with water and put on the floor. Then he went into the fridge and grabbed a platter. It contained cubed cheese, meats and had a bunch of green grapes in the center. "Hungry?"

She'd eaten lunch but it had been a simple grilled cheese. "I wouldn't mind a few grapes."

"Great. Make yourself at home." He took three cubes of cheese and went over to Marvin. "Marvin, sit."

Marvin's butt hit the tile floor.

Cole turned to Brooklyn with a wide smile that made him look ridiculously boyish. "I didn't think he'd really do it."

"Ask him to shake a paw, and offer your non-cheese hand."

He turned back, leaned over. "Marvin, shake a paw." He held out his hand, and Marvin lifted his paw and placed it on Cole's palm.

"Good boy! Have a piece of cheese." Cole fed him the cube of cheddar. Marvin took it delicately, and once more Brooklyn marveled at the wide smile on Cole's face. He really did love dogs. It was a crying shame that he was in his thirties and had never had one. Marvin added so much to her life.

"There's a fire on in the fireplace. Why don't you bring your grapes and come in? Do you want a coffee? Brandy or cognac?"

She'd forgotten that she was moving into the lap of luxury by coming to Cole's. "I wouldn't say no to coffee, but show me where the stuff is. I can make it. You don't have to wait on me."

"Don't be silly. I know how to run a coffee maker."

He did, too. Before long there were two steaming mugs. He even steamed milk for hers and poured the froth in, making a rich, aromatic latte. "See?"

She wasn't used to fancy coffee. But she certainly wasn't going to say no. "Thanks. That smells great."

She followed him to the living room. Even though the storm raged outside, and she could see it through the windows, there was warm light from a tall lamp and the flicker of the gas fireplace. It threw some heat and Brooklyn picked a chair near the fire, settling into it with a sigh. It was so incredibly comfortable she nearly sighed again. Cole sat on the sofa opposite her and lifted his mug to taste his coffee.

Marvin went up to the fireplace, stared at the flames for a moment, and then turned around twice before flopping down in front of it.

Brooklyn laughed and looked over at Cole. "That's it. He's made himself at home for the duration."

"Good," Cole decreed. "And how about you?"

She smiled faintly. Cole looked delectable in his slightly damp trousers and thick-knit sweater. "I'm getting there. But I feel a little odd being here. It's a gorgeous house, Cole. I keep feeling I'll break something expensive."

"Don't worry about that. I'll buy another." He flashed her his grin and she smiled in return, but only for a moment.

"Yes, but you see, that just highlights how different our lives are."

He shrugged. "Does it matter? I mean, it's only money."

She stared down in her cup for a moment before looking up and meeting his gaze again. "The people who generally say that are the ones who have lots of it," she countered. "At one point, my family owned this whole island. They had to sell most of it for financial reasons. For a lot of people, money means freedom. Freedom to choose what sort of life they'll have. The less money, the more limited the choices."

"I realize that." His voice had softened. "I just meant that I want you to be comfortable and not worry about how much something here costs."

"I know that. It just…got my hackles up a bit." She gave a little laugh. "Pride. I still have some, apparently."

"You sure do." He drank more of his coffee. "Why don't you sit over here with me? The heat from the fire will still reach you, and it feels weird talking to you way over there."

The room was very large and it did seem as if there was a lot of space between them. She probably shouldn't, but she got up and moved over to the sofa, sitting at the other end and tucking her feet up beneath her. "Better?"

"Much." His soft eyes met hers. "I'm very glad you're here, Brooklyn."

A gust of wind rattled the window and they both looked over. The window was streaked with rain and the beach grasses were waving furiously.

"It seems so strange being inside with power while that's going on out there," she remarked.

"Ernest was smart and had the generator wired in. With only two houses on the island, I'm guessing it'd be the last on the list to have power restored. You could go days without it here."

She nodded. "One time when I was small, we got caught in a nor'easter in January. No generators on the island back then. We cooked on my grandmother's woodstove and used oil lamps for light." She smiled fondly at the memory. "We melted snow for water and we did puzzles and played cards. Good memories."

"It sounds perfect," Cole said, and she noticed his smile wasn't quite as immediate as before.

"Did I say something wrong?"

"Oh, no, of course not. I'm just finding that every time you share a memory, I envy you your childhood a little more."

"Yours was lonely. But then you met Branson and Jeremy."

He nodded. "Yes, I did. And they saved me. Anything I learned about affection and loyalty and friendship, I learned from them."

It sounded awfully sad just the same.

"I think we're opposites," she replied softly. "My

family gave lots of love and support. But it's the real world that's let me down."

"How so?"

She hesitated, and he must have sensed her discomfort, because he said, "Never mind. If you're not comfortable talking about it, we won't."

It was a moment in which she could choose to trust him or not. They'd become friends, but she wasn't yet sure what sort of friends. They'd made out on the beach and it had been glorious. But since then he'd been perfectly platonic, as she'd asked.

She liked that about him. Even as she thought about kissing him again, she liked that she'd set a boundary and he'd accepted it without question. She liked it a lot.

Marvin got up from the spot in front of the fire and came to her side. He sat and put his head on her knee, and her heart softened. "Marvin is not a trained therapy dog, but you'd think he was. He's my best friend in the world."

Cole's gaze was steady. "If you don't want to answer this, I'll respect it. Is there a reason why you'd need a therapy dog?"

Brooklyn swallowed around the large lump in her throat. It had been a few years now, and it wasn't exactly a secret. After all, it had been on the news and the communities in this part of the province were small. But choosing to tell someone was different.

Because it was telling, and not just having them know.

Cole slid over on the sofa and took her hand in his. His hand was warm, in contrast to her cold one. He chafed it a bit and said gently, "You don't have to tell me if you don't want to. The last thing I want is to upset you."

She looked up at him. "Are you even real?"

"What do you mean?"

"I mean you're rich and you look like…that, and it's crazy that you're this nice as well. I keep wondering where your flaws are."

"Oh," he said darkly, "I have them. Never fear."

She sighed as he twined his fingers with hers. Marvin still pressed close to her knees, and she felt very comforted and protected in that moment. Something that was in short supply most of the time, even though she faked bravery whenever she was out of her comfort zone.

"It happened a few years ago, in town, in the middle of the afternoon."

Cole held on to Brooklyn's hand firmly, waiting for her to go on. She'd paused, and he would be patient, because he sensed what she was going to say was important. And it was unusual and flattering that she trusted him with whatever her story was. Not many people did. Only two, really. Jeremy and Branson. The truth was that other than his best buddies, Cole didn't have close relationships. And fears? He hadn't lied. He was 100 percent a commitment-phobe and, despite seeing it in his best friends, wasn't sure he really believed in love, either.

But he liked Brooklyn, more than any woman he'd ever met. There was something so real about her. He never questioned her motives. She was unfailingly honest and authentic, with no hidden agenda.

And right now, a wild storm was raging outside and she was holding onto his hand for dear life. He knew he should be cautious. That he should not want to get involved in whatever personal things she had going on. But she was also letting him in, and there was something addictive about knowing someone trusted you enough to share a secret. It wasn't something that he was used to. It was also something he usually avoided, but with Brooklyn, it felt oddly safe.

He rubbed his thumb over her hand, encouraging her to go on.

"I was home for the weekend, and I went into the liquor store to buy a bottle of wine for my mom and me. We were going to have a wine and movie night, because I was heading into finals and needed some downtime to chill.

"So I'm waiting in line with my wine, and this guy comes in. I didn't think anything about it. I barely even noticed him. And then he walks up to the cashier in front of me and pulls a gun out of his jacket."

"My God," Cole exclaimed. "In a town that small? Does that sort of thing happen often? I mean, I kind of pictured a crime rate of about zero."

"Bad things happen everywhere," she whispered.

"I'm sorry. Go on."

She hesitated and he waited. Not that he wanted to pressure her, but he got the feeling she needed to say it. Marvin let out a whine and nudged her leg, and she reached down with her other hand and patted his head. "Thanks, Marv," she murmured. "Okay." Her voice strengthened. "We all did exactly what he said. We didn't move. The cashiers gave him the money. But they'd also hit the panic button, and once he had the money he started to freak out. So he grabbed me and dragged me outside with him."

Cole swore. She'd been part of an armed robbery. No wonder she was skittish.

"His car was outside. I'd dropped my bottle of wine and it broke everywhere, and I had a piece of glass in the top of my foot. He opened the driver's side and shoved me in, and then got in after me. There was a split second where I froze, but then I remembered watching a show and hearing that the one thing you should never do is go to a second location with someone, so I unlocked the door and jumped out, hoping he wouldn't use the gun. He didn't. He took off, and I was left there on the sidewalk."

She was trembling now, so he slid closer and enfolded her in his arms. "You're safe now," he said gently and kissed her hair. His heart hurt for her. What a terrifying ordeal. "You were smart and did everything right."

"That's what the cops said. I was able to give a good description and a partial plate. He was arrested shortly after."

"So you got Marvin."

"Not at first. I went through all the victim services stuff, and some counseling, but I really struggled. I left school, which I still regret sometimes. Eventually I got Marvin, and then I came over to the island for a few days to get away. It was the first time I'd felt peace in months, so I asked if I could move over here for a while. Two years and counting and I'm still here. My grandmother deeded me the property so it would be in the family but she wouldn't have to deal with it. Marvin's been with me through all of that."

Cole held her close but was gratified to see that she'd stopped shaking. "He's quite a dog," he said. "And you're quite a woman."

"I ran away. That's not so remarkable. Heck, I still fight a lot of panic when I go into town. Waiting in line anywhere is torture. And I have a handful of places I like to go and that's it. I'm still horribly afraid."

"You also live on this island by yourself, run your own business and are as competent a person as I've ever met. Maybe certain situations trigger you, but I promise you, they don't define who you are. The way you stood up to me when I arrived…"

She laughed, a sound thick with emotion. "Oh, Cole. I thought I was going to throw up the whole time. But this place means so much to me. There was no way I was going to give it up without a fight."

He thought for a moment, then turned a bit and made her face him. "You listen to me," he said. "You are brave. Being brave doesn't mean not being afraid. It means being afraid and doing it anyway. There is nothing I respect more, Brooklyn. And I'm honored that you shared it with me." Honored and a bit terrified, but he'd work through that.

She looked down and bit her lip. He didn't want to make her cry, but couldn't she see how remarkable she was? "What were you taking in school?"

"Chemistry. I was trying to get into the pharmacy program."

He grinned. "Smarty-pants."

She finally smiled. "Whatever."

The wind howled around the windows and Cole realized that at some point it had gotten dark outside. "Looks like we're stormed in for sure, now," he commented. "I'm glad you came. I'm glad that my house is a place you feel safe."

She turned her liquid eyes to his and said simply, "You love my dog. That's my first litmus test."

Did he? Did he love Marvin? He looked down at the yellow fur and big brown eyes and realized he did, in fact, love this dog. He was friendship and loyalty and love all wrapped up in one four-legged package. He was the friend that Cole had wanted his whole life, and Cole was even more glad that Brooklyn had him to keep her from being lonely. Maybe moving to the island had been an extreme reaction on her part, but she'd been through something rather extreme. Who was he to judge?

After all, he wasn't the king of perfect life choices, was he?

"Rae and Dan will be coming over soon for dinner. You don't mind, do you?"

Her face brightened. "No, not at all! I like them both, very much. It was one of the reasons I came up here today. I kind of liked the thought of, well, everyone together."

"Me, too," he said, and realized it was true. Raelynn and Dan were employees, but they were more than that to Cole.

"Hey, Cole?"

He looked into her face. Her tears had dried, but her eyes remained that steady, piercing blue that had reached in and grabbed him from day one, when he'd expected an old lady and was met with her instead.

"Thank you for listening. And for letting go of the idea of buying me out. It means a lot."

"You're welcome," he said, unsure of what else to say. He had never agreed to let go of his desire to purchase her property, but now that she'd said it, he knew he could not pressure her to sell and take away her safe place. Even if it was a place to hide.

Everyone had a right to hide if they wanted to. He looked around the huge living room. Even him.

CHAPTER NINE

THE RAIN SLASHED and the windows rattled, but Cole's kitchen was the port in the storm for the four occupants of the island. Brooklyn looked around and felt a warmth that had eluded her for a long, long time. These people felt like her friends. The class difference didn't seem to matter, even though Brooklyn was always aware of the opulence around her.

Cole had spared no expense in updating the house, and she'd caught a glimpse of his sweater tag before dinner. She was pretty sure that it cost as much as most of her wardrobe put together. The towel he'd given her earlier had been of the finest, plushiest cotton. Cole Abbott was a man used to the best.

But he was also a lot more fun than she'd imagined.

The four of them had eaten a delicious meal of carbonara and salad that Raelynn had prepared, eating in the kitchen rather than the formal dining room. Once the mess was cleaned up, Cole had opened up another bottle of wine and suggested they play cards. Brooklyn wondered if he'd done that because of what she'd said earlier, and making her want to feel at home. Either way, the result was that they were now sitting around the kitchen table. Rae, as she asked Brooklyn to call her, and Brooklyn had glasses of Shiraz at their elbows, while the men had switched to scotch.

The game they all agreed on was hearts, and so far Dan was trouncing everyone. He never seemed to end up with the queen of spades, and as the evening progressed, the storm howled and shook the house, and Raelynn topped up their glasses once more, Brooklyn couldn't remember a time when she'd had so much fun.

Cole's eyes were the color of cornflowers as they twinkled at her over his cards, and she grinned back. The smile playing on his lips was mesmerizing, and she found herself staring at his mouth for too long as she remembered kissing him on the beach.

"Your turn," Raelynn said, and Brooklyn dragged her gaze away and back to the cards in her hand.

This was the one hand where she couldn't pass three cards to anyone. She was stuck with what she had, and she was getting tired of always ending up with a mitt full of hearts counting against her. She also had the two of clubs, so she started the hand and placed each card carefully. One after the other she ended up with hearts, and the other three were teasing her about how badly she was playing. But in the end, she played the queen of spades and reveled in the shock on their faces when they all realized she'd taken every single heart and the queen, too.

Which meant she had no penalty and they all had to count the points against themselves.

"Oh, that was sneaky!" Dan exclaimed, pointing his finger at her. "Damn you, Brookie!"

She burst out laughing. "Brookie? No one has called me that since I was nine!"

Raelynn joined in, and Cole raised an eyebrow. "Brookie," he said, his smooth voice teasing.

"Don't even think about it," she warned, leveling him with a glare.

He grinned and sat back in his chair. "Deal again. I need to redeem myself."

At some point they switched to playing rummy and Raelynn got up to make popcorn. Finally, about midnight, Raelynn and Dan decided to call it a night.

"You're sure you don't want to stay here?" Cole asked, frowning. The apartment over the garage wasn't powered by the generator, so they'd be going to a dark home.

"We've got flashlights and blankets." Rae winked at him. "Don't you worry about us. We won't get cold."

Brooklyn snorted and that set everyone laughing again. The pair bundled up in raincoats and headed out into the storm to make the short trek to their apartment.

"I had fun," Brooklyn said. Her brain was a little fuzzy from the wine, but the evening had been long and there'd been more sipping than drinking. It was a pleasant, warm feeling brought on by the excellent shiraz and the company.

"Me, too," Cole said. "Way more than I usually do. Cutthroat hearts was so much better than gallery openings and charity benefits."

"Oh, that sounds dull as dirt," she remarked.

"It is, most of the time." He leaned against the kitchen counter and tilted his head as he studied her. "Is this what normal people do on a Saturday night?"

"Around here? As often as not. Maybe a movie. Or watching the hockey game on TV."

"That sounds heavenly."

"Oh, be serious."

He pushed away from the counter and came to her. She was in the midst of picking up dirty glasses from the table and he stayed her motions with a hand on her wrist. "No, I mean it, Brooklyn. I'm so glad you came here tonight. You have this talent for making people at home no matter where you are."

Heat rushed into her face, both from the praise and from the intimate touch on her arm. "Thank you," she said, working hard to accept the compliment and not brush it off. He was being earnest, and she respected that.

And his gaze dropped from her eyes to her lips and clung there, while her pulse leaped and her breath quickened. They shouldn't kiss again. It would muddy the waters. And yet…she wanted to. Tonight their relationship had changed. They were no longer casual acquaintances. She'd shared something personal with him, and he'd invited her into his home. They'd laughed together. Trash-talked over cards. They were real friends now.

Friends who apparently also had this buzz of attraction humming between them.

She was the one who made the first move. It only took a step for her to be a breath away from him. She held a wineglass in each hand and was glad of it, or else she might have put her arms around his neck and drawn him close. But she did lift her chin, a silent invitation, and met his gaze evenly. Cole Abbott surprised her, and in the nicest way. Maybe this would complicate things. But she'd had enough shiraz to lose a bit of caution where Cole was concerned.

"Brooklyn," he murmured. "Be sure."

And still she held his gaze, even though inside she was trembling.

He leaned forward. It didn't take much, and his lips touched hers. At the first contact her eyelids fluttered closed, and she focused on the feel of his lips. How could they be firm and yet so soft at the same time? He tasted slightly of the scotch from earlier, warm and mellow and expensive. His hand curled around the nape of her neck and his fingertips rubbed the tight tendons there, so perfectly that she nearly moaned with pleasure.

But she wouldn't. Because kissing was one thing, but losing control was another, and she was not going to lose control. Not tonight. This felt too fragile. Too... new. Different even from their interlude on the beach—deeper somehow.

"You taste good," he murmured, nipping at her lips.

"So do you."

They kissed a while longer, not rushing, until there was a whine at her feet.

Marvin sat there looking up at them, an anxious look in his eyes.

Brooklyn took the opportunity to step back and clear her head from the seductive haze that was Cole. "Well, hello, sleepyhead." Marvin had curled up in front of the fire and snoozed most of the evening. "I suppose you need to go outside."

Cole took the crystal glasses from her hands. "I'll deal with these. You take him outside. Or if you want, we can go out together. It's not as bad as it was, but it's still a storm and it's pitch-black outside."

"My things are by the front door," she said, patting her leg for Marvin to follow. "But I wouldn't say no to the company."

Brooklyn headed to the front door, but instead of his usual trot, Marvin plodded along behind her. "You can't still be sleepy," she chided him, reaching for her raincoat. "You've been a lazybones all night."

He looked up at her and whined again. Maybe it was the storm, she reasoned. Marvin wasn't himself, but they were in a strange house with the remnants of a hurricane blustering outside.

"What's wrong?" Cole joined her a moment later, shrugging on a jacket.

"Marvin's slow. And whining a bit. Hopefully he's not scared."

Cole handed her a flashlight. "Here. We should have a light."

Together they opened the door and went outside. Marvin hesitated in the doorway, but then went down the few steps to the path and found a nearby bush to pee on. He started to trot away, so Brooklyn and Cole followed, the flashlight beam illuminating the rain that seemed to be falling sideways in the brisk wind.

But it was definitely not as bad as earlier. The worst was probably over now.

Marvin hunched over and Brooklyn followed with a poop bag; she wasn't about to leave his mess on Cole's lawn. But when she went to him, she saw him straining with very little progress. And then when he did have success, there was blood.

Her heart froze a little. His uncharacteristic lethargy, the whining, the blood…something was wrong with Marvin. And they were stuck on this island with no power, and no way off. Even if the storm eased, the sea was too wild for either of their boats.

"Cole?" She called through the wind, and he ran over to her right away. Had her voice sounded as panicked as she felt? "There's something wrong with Marvin. There's blood, and…" Her throat closed over.

Cole took the flashlight. Marvin was whining, loud enough they could hear him over the wind, and tears of fear stung her eyes. "Marv, what is it, huh? You not feeling good, buddy?"

"Let's get him inside."

She nodded, and they urged the dog to follow them back to the house. She toweled him off carefully, trying to stay calm. "There you go, sweetie. All dry." She looked at Cole. "Let's see if he'll drink."

They went back into the kitchen, and then Brooklyn realized that Marvin hadn't eaten the kibble she'd put out at supper time. She'd had a fine time, eating and drinking and laughing and kissing Cole…and her best friend had been getting sick.

"He didn't eat," she whispered.

The dog sniffed the bowl of food, looked at the water and turned away.

"Okay," Cole said, taking her hands. "Who's your vet?"

"Dr. Thorpe in Liverpool. But he's unlikely to have power…"

"Does he have a cell number?"

She nodded. "He gave it to me once when Marvin was a puppy and we had an emergency. I think it's still in my phone…"

Cole squeezed her fingers. "Okay. I know it's late, but call him. See if he has power."

Tears slipped down her cheeks. "Even if he does, we can't get off the island. Not with the swell being what it is."

"First things first. You call. I'm going to check into some things." He paused and kissed her forehead. "Marvin's going to be okay, Brooklyn."

She sniffed and pulled her hands away. "Okay. I'm going to look for the number."

Cole slipped away and went to another room, and Brooklyn retrieved her phone. With shaking fingers, she scrolled through her contacts until she found Dr.

Thorpe's number. He didn't answer for the first four rings, but on the fifth he picked up, and she let out a breath, determined not to cry or panic.

As they were talking, Marvin started to throw up. There was only bile, which she relayed to the vet as calmly as she could, as well as Marvin's other symptoms. With a promise to call him back with any updates or an estimated time of arrival, she clicked off the call, started crying again and went searching for something to clean up after Marvin.

Cole came back and found her on the floor, a contrite and subdued Marvin beside her. "Did you reach him?"

She nodded and balled up the paper towel she'd found under the sink. "I'm to watch him for worsening symptoms and call him immediately if he gets worse or if we manage to get to the mainland." She looked up at Cole, her eyes wet. "There's no way. Even if we could handle the waves, the boats are locked away and we'd have to get them out of the boat shed and launch them..."

She got up and went to the garbage can, then washed her hands. "Oh, Cole, I'm so sorry this has happened when you've been so kind."

"Don't be silly. You haven't done anything wrong." Marvin was now lying on the kitchen floor and she saw the worry crease Cole's forehead. "I made a few calls. If we can hold out another few hours, I might have a way for us to get him to the vet."

She stared at him. "How?"

"My helicopter pilot. We have the pad here. He's monitoring the winds and will call me the moment he's cool with taking off." He came forward and cupped her face in his hands. "It won't be a fun flight, but it'll be short. You just have to hang on a little longer."

She nodded, incredibly touched amid all the worry tangling in her stomach.

Then watched as Cole, in his thousand-dollar sweater, knelt down gently, picked up all eighty pounds of her sick dog in his arms and went toward the living room. She followed him, swallowing sobs at the caring and loving way he was handling her beloved pet. And in the living room, instead of putting him on the rug in front of the fire, Cole put Marvin down on the sofa and sat down beside him. "There you are, dude," he said soothingly, and Brooklyn sat down on the other side of Marvin.

"Cole, your sofa…he might be sick again. Or… worse."

Cole met her gaze. "So what? It's just a sofa. He needs to be comfortable and loved. And you need to be beside him."

She had no idea how to answer, so she simply stroked Marvin's head and prayed he'd be okay, and that this was some weird thing and he wasn't very ill at all.

Cole and Brooklyn sat with Marvin into the night. Though Cole tried feeding him by hand and offering him water, the dog wouldn't eat or drink. He threw up again, but Cole had retrieved the towel from earlier and put it nearby. It saved the sofa and towels were easily replaced.

Dogs weren't. Even though Cole had never had such a companion, all he needed to do was see the look of anguish on Brooklyn's face to know that Marvin had to be okay. Cole would do anything in his power to ensure it. Even wake his pilot and have a chopper chartered in the tail end of a hurricane.

Besides, he was horribly fond of Marvin himself.

Other than his two best friends, he'd never received such an enthusiastic greeting as he did when he entered Brooklyn's yard and Marvin came running out to meet him, barking and with a wildly wagging tail.

His cell rang and he jumped, then answered it. The call was brief, and then he clicked off and met Brooklyn's hopeful gaze.

"He'll be here in about an hour. It'd be faster, but he's got to deal with the wind. Call the vet and give him the heads-up. You're sure he has power?"

"The clinic is also on a generator. I'll call him."

"I'm arranging for a car to meet us at the airstrip."

"Cole, I don't know what to say." Her eyes were luminous with tears and gratitude. "This is… I can't even tell you."

"Hush. Make your call and I'll make sure we're ready to go."

It took some doing to get a car service, and a promise of a very nice monetary incentive. He also called Dan, updating him on the situation and letting him know there'd be a helicopter landing shortly. He wasn't surprised when Dan and Raelynn showed up ten minutes later, concern etched on their faces. They weren't just employees, they were wonderful people and Brooklyn had won them over, too.

Too. There was no denying that he was more involved with her than he ever intended. That kiss in the kitchen tonight had been soft and sweet and so different from anything he'd ever experienced. For a guy who didn't do intimacy, he was up to his neck in it right now.

Raelynn had made tea and pushed a cup in Brooklyn's hands. "Here. Drink some of this and breathe."

It was good advice, but everyone was on edge. Marvin had gotten down from the sofa, but he was so devoid of his usual energy. He once again sniffed at the bowls but turned away. He whined pitifully and then lay down on the floor, resting on his side.

Cole saw Brooklyn's face start to crumple again, so he went to her and squeezed her shoulder.

Moments later they heard the rhythmic *whomp-whomp* of the helicopter approaching. Cole shrugged on his jacket, then held out Brooklyn's so she could slip her arms in. When Dan gave the go-ahead, he once again hefted Marvin into his arms—the dead weight made him stagger slightly—and headed toward the helipad.

Brooklyn jogged beside him, carrying a blanket that Raelynn had pressed into her hands.

"Hang on tight," the pilot shouted over the noise, but his face wore a grin. "Fasten your seat belts. It'll be bumpy but short."

Brooklyn's face was pale and he wondered if she was afraid of the helicopter or for Marvin. She'd mentioned going on a ride with Ernest once, but that wasn't in the dark in nasty weather, either. He patted her hand and gave her a headset. Then he put on his own.

"Don't worry," he said into the mic. "Dave's a former navy pilot. He's used to landing on a pitching deck. Dry land is a breeze, right Dave?"

"Yes, sir," Dave answered. "Ready?"

It was not an easy trip, even though it was, as Dave promised, a short one. Wind buffeted the aircraft and more than once Cole's stomach did a hollow flip. Brooklyn's fingers were tight in Marvin's fur, and Cole's brow wrinkled in concern as Marvin panted heavily. Was it the stress of the ride, or his illness? Thankfully, they weren't in the air very long, and were soon nearing the tiny Liverpool airport. Dave set the chopper down expertly and promised to stay nearby for the return trip whenever Cole required it.

For the third time, Cole lifted Marvin—still bundled in the blanket—out of the helicopter and to the waiting cab he'd convinced to pick them up.

The cabbie lifted an eyebrow at the sight of the dog but said nothing about it as he opened the back door for them. "Dr. Thorpe's vet clinic," Cole said as Brooklyn crawled in the other side. He realized that the dog had always been sandwiched between the two of them since he'd started getting sick.

"Have to take the long way. One of the roads is flooded. Heck of a storm," the cabbie said.

"Whatever gets us there fast and safe," Cole replied.

The sun wasn't yet up, and power was out, making everything eerily dark. The headlights illuminated a narrow swath, but enough that Cole could see downed branches and a few trees snapped off. Lights were on at a square building, though, with a parking lot out front. "Looks like the doc has a generator running," the driver said, pulling in. "Lucky for you, eh?"

"Very." Brooklyn leaned forward toward the front seat. "Thank you so much for coming out to get us. It means a lot."

"Oh, no problem."

Cole knew it was no problem because he'd paid handsomely for the service. But he admired Brooklyn's kindness and courtesy. She appreciated people, and he liked that about her.

Dr. Thorpe came out and met them at the door, and for the first time, Cole didn't have to lift Marvin. Cole was in good shape, but eighty pounds of deadweight dog was a challenge. He and Brooklyn followed the vet into the building and then into an exam room. Cole stood back while Brooklyn relayed Marvin's symptoms, and then the two of them went to the waiting room while Dr. Thorpe and his assistant, who Cole quickly learned was his wife, did the examination.

He looked over at Brooklyn, who was leaned back in the chair with her eyes closed. She looked exhausted, with circles under her eyes and swollen lids where she'd cried. "He's gonna be okay," Cole reassured her. "He's in good hands now."

She opened her eyes. "I know. Part of me is relieved and glad that we're here. The other part of me is now nervous for the diagnosis."

"Get some rest. You've been up all night, and it's nearly time for the sun to come up again."

"I will once Dr. Thorpe has come out to talk to us." But she turned her weary head in his direction. "But thank you, Cole. You moved heaven and earth to get us here. I can never repay you. You're a good man."

Cole flushed under her praise, but the words that rang in his ears were the ones calling him a good man.

He was a successful man. A relatively smart man. A very rich man. But he wasn't sure he'd ever been called "good," and the compliment went straight to his heart.

He wanted to be a good man. And more accurately, he wanted to be a good man for her.

Wasn't life just full of surprises?

CHAPTER TEN

BROOKLYN NEVER DID fall asleep. It seemed hours until Dr. Thorpe came out and told them that Marvin had a foreign object in his stomach, and that he needed to do more tests. He further explained that exploratory surgery was most certainly necessary and as quickly as possible, to remove the blockage and ensure the fastest recovery. Brooklyn agreed right away, and Dr. Thorpe had disappeared to carry on.

Now she couldn't sleep. Not while she was waiting. She was exhausted, and sometimes she sat with her eyes closed, but that was only because her lids were so heavy. Her brain was too busy to close down, as well.

Cole didn't sleep, either. He sat next to her and held her hand. Dr. Thorpe had told them to feel free to use the coffee machine, and Cole got up and made her a cup of coffee and handed her the paper cup before making one for himself. Minutes ticked by, lots of them. The sun came up, and at seven thirty one of the front office staff came in. "Oh," she said. "I didn't realize there was an emergency call. Do you need anything?"

"We're fine, thank you," Brooklyn said.

"Well, let me know. I came in to cancel today's appointments and to feed the animals we have kenneled in the back."

Finally, after what seemed an eternity, Dr. Thorpe returned with a smile on his face. "Good news. Turns out it was a bit of netting. We removed it and will watch him carefully for the next bit, run some fluids and make sure there are no complications. In a few days, he should be good as new."

Brooklyn let out a massive sigh of relief. This whole time she had been fighting against the thoughts about what she'd do without her beloved pet, but now that he was going to be okay the possibilities crowded her mind and she was both thankful and overwhelmed.

Cole stood and shook the vet's hand. "That's great news."

"Getting him here quickly helped. The sooner we can treat these issues, the better the prognosis. Marvin's in excellent health otherwise."

Brooklyn frowned, trying to think of what Marvin might have eaten and where. "Netting? I guess he might have picked it up on the beach. We do walk there every day. But I didn't notice him eating anything strange."

"It's hard to say. Dogs are like kids. The moment you have your back turned…" He grinned, and Brooklyn could see the tiredness behind his dark brown eyes.

"I can't thank you enough, Dr. Thorpe. Thank you for coming in and for having a generator." She smiled weakly.

"You're welcome. I'd like to keep Marvin here until tomorrow at least. Particularly where you're on the island, making sure he's good and stable is important. It's not like I live just around the corner."

"Of course. Whatever you think is best. Can I see him?"

"Certainly. He's still out, though."

Brooklyn went back and bit her lip when she saw

Marvin resting, still unconscious from the anesthesia. His tongue hung out of his mouth, but his breaths were nice and even. She patted his head and gave him a kiss, and said a little prayer of thanks that he was going to be okay.

When she went out to the waiting room, Cole was chatting with the woman at the desk. "Hey," he said, smiling at her. "Jen says that power's out almost everywhere, but she heard that the lights are on at the Sandpiper Resort. If they have a room, why don't we head there and get some sleep? That way you can be close to Marvin. If he can go home tomorrow, I'll have Dave fly us all home. If not, we can always fly back and bring a boat back to pick him up. But for today, you can get some sleep and not have to worry."

Right now she was so tired the thought of a comfortable bed nearly made her weep. "If they have a room, I'll say yes. I'm ready to drop."

"Same. Give me a few minutes to sort some arrangements."

He was looking after everything, and while she was thankful, it also felt a bit strange. She wasn't used to people taking charge and making sure her comforts were seen to. She wasn't quite sure how she felt about it really, or if her unsettled thoughts were all part of the emotion and fatigue of the past few hours. So she let it go, deciding they could talk about it later.

One cab ride later and he had them checked into the only room left at the Sandpiper. "We're lucky to have not lost power," the woman behind the desk said with a smile. "But that also means we're full up. You got our last room."

"Perfect." Cole sent her a winning smile and then held out his hand to Brooklyn. "Shall we?"

The only room left was of course the suite, complete with a patio overlooking the ocean and a massive king-size bed with six pillows and a silk duvet that looked like a fluffy cloud. "Big enough for the both of us," Cole said, his voice utterly practical. "What do you want first? Sleep or food?"

Brooklyn yawned. "Sleep."

"Then in you go." He pulled down the covers and she crawled inside, fully clothed. The mattress felt absolutely heavenly, the pillow cradled her head perfectly. Her whole body melted into the fine linens.

"You're going to sleep too, right?" she asked, closing her eyes.

"You bet I am."

"Okay. Good." She was starting to drift off when she said, "Cole?"

"Yes, Brooklyn?"

"Thank you. So very much. I couldn't bear to lose him."

"I know. Sleep now."

She thought she felt his fingers brush the hair off her face. And then she remembered nothing.

When she woke, it was to the sensation of something warm pressed up against her back. She blinked against the brightness of the room—they hadn't bothered to shut the curtains—and remembered that she was in a gorgeous hotel suite with Cole. And that it was Cole who was spooning her right now, his breaths deep and even against her ear.

Brooklyn didn't want to move, it felt so good.

A few short weeks ago he'd come to the island with all intentions of getting her to sell her house. Now he was snuggled up next to her, after they'd weathered a hurricane together and he'd singlehandedly saved her best friend.

Because if they hadn't gotten Marvin prompt attention, the outcome might have been very different.

She'd had him pegged as an entitled, spoiled, rich jerk, but he hadn't borne out that initial impression. Indeed, he was caring and funny and generous.

And, boy, did he know how to kiss.

He snuffled a bit behind her and shifted, and she let out a sigh. His hand moved over her arm, and she hummed a little at the soft, soothing touch. When was the last time someone had casually grazed her arm like that? Or held her? She hadn't let anyone this close in years. Especially physically. It had only taken a few brief minutes on a spring afternoon to instill an aversion to having her space invaded. The attack had made it impossible for her to be intimate with anyone. But now she felt no panic. She hadn't on the beach the other night, either. All she felt with Cole was safe and protected.

Well, perhaps more than that.

"Did you get some rest?"

His voice sent ripples of pleasure down her spine. "I did, thank you."

"Good. You needed it."

She rolled over to face him, and was suddenly aware of the room they occupied. She'd been too tired and overwrought earlier, but now she realized that the suite they were in was stunning. It was probably nothing next to Cole's regular accommodations, but to her the huge space, luxurious bed linens and sweeping views were nothing short of amazing. She could never afford a night in a place like this on her own.

She definitely didn't want him thinking she expected it or...worse, that she was taking advantage. "Cole, I want to pay my share of the room." She didn't mention the helicopter ride or the cabs, though. They were both aware of the differences in their lifestyles. She wished she could afford to split the cost straight down the middle, but her finances would never withstand it. Instead, she'd feel forever in his debt. She didn't like that. Didn't like feeling indebted to anyone.

He studied her for a long moment, then nodded. "If you feel you must, but it's not necessary, okay? I would have done the same for any friend."

She believed him. And not just because it assuaged her guilt, but because Cole was turning out to be the kind of man who told the truth. "Any friend?" she asked. She seriously doubted Cole's friends ever needed this sort of help.

He smiled at her, his eyes still a little soft from sleep. "To show you I mean it, I'll share a funny story. I was traveling for work but found out that Jeremy was back in New York, licking his wounds because Tori had left him. I dropped everything, hopped on a plane and then Branson and I showed up at Jeremy's office and staged a romantic intervention."

She snorted a little. The picture of the two men offering relationship advice to Jeremy seemed utterly unreal. And yet… Jeremy and Tori were very happy. "I'm trying to imagine that."

"It really happened. He was miserable and taking it out on everyone around him. Anyway, I told you so you can see that I mean it, Brooklyn. When people are important to me, it's a pleasure to be able to help them." His eyes darkened. "Sometimes I wonder what I can possibly do with all my money. Helping friends is a good start."

Still, one thing stuck with her. "We're friends?"

A slow smile crept up his cheek. She was beneath the covers and he was on top, but it felt intimate just the same. "Aren't we?"

"I suppose we are," she conceded. "It's just unexpected."

"For me, too. But I'm not sorry."

She waited a few moments, trying to put her thoughts into words that wouldn't offend him. Finally, she met his gaze. "You're much nicer than I expected."

"Thank you?" He phrased it as a question. "Glad you think I'm nice. Not sure I'm as glad you didn't think so in the beginning."

She laughed softly. How lovely was it that they were still facing each other, talking? Was this what her grandmother had used to call "sweet nothings?"

"I had this idea of who you were. Especially after some of the things you said at first, about working hard and playing hard, and offering to buy me out without batting an eye at the price. You're in your mid-thirties, and not married. No girlfriend you've mentioned. I had this image in my head of a playboy, but that isn't being borne out by your behavior."

His smile widened. "Oh, I'm glad." His hand was still on her arm and his thumb made little circles. She wasn't even sure he knew he was doing it. "Here's the thing, Brooklyn. I did work hard and play hard for a lot of years. But things changed after my heart scare. I'd been trying so hard to be like my dad in some ways and very unlike him in others. I wanted to follow in his footsteps at Abbott, but I was determined to stay away from marriage, since he and my mother barely spoke. In the end, he died a young man because he was a workaholic. That is not a path I'd like to follow."

"Do you feel you've let him down somehow by slowing down, or adjusting your priorities?"

His eyes widened in acknowledgment. "Man, you hit the nail on the head. I do. Abbott Industries was everything to him. He was so damned good at it. I made a different choice, and on one level I know it was the right one. But I still haven't quite moved past the idea that I've failed or something."

"There's nothing wrong with searching for some balance in life. Or…getting off the hamster wheel."

"Intellectually I know that. I guess…" He halted, looked down and then lifted his gaze again. "I've always been looking for approval. My parents didn't have a good marriage. Certainly not overtly loving, and I'm an only child. It always seemed Dad's hopes were pinned on me. There was never any question of me not taking over the business. It was just a matter of when."

"And you're okay with that? Didn't you ever want to do something else?"

He smiled a little. "I went through a stage where I wanted to be a football quarterback. And then one where I thought I should be in a rock band. But seriously…no. I love the company. I want to see it succeed. And yet…"

His voice trailed away, and Brooklyn reached out to touch his cheek. "What is it?"

"Dad was a workaholic in an unworkable marriage. I don't want that for myself. So… I've never been much for relationships. I mean, that's just setting myself up for failure, isn't it? And I'm desperately trying to find the right balance so I can keep Abbott strong enough to withstand this economy, without putting myself in the hospital."

"Good thing you don't have high expectations of

yourself, then," she quipped and smiled. "That's a lot of pressure on one person."

"I have a lot of responsibilities."

Brooklyn didn't quite get that, because she had deliberately set up her own life to be simple. Perhaps too simple, really. She loved the island, but was it enough to keep her through all her days?

When Cole had arrived on the island, she'd wanted nothing more than to keep everything exactly the same. But was that reasonable? Staying exactly the same meant she'd never be married, or have children of her own. She'd live alone in her grandparents' house and what, knit for the rest of her life?

"What is it?" Cole asked. "You suddenly looked very sad."

"Nothing, really. Just realizing how life carries us along with it no matter what we plan."

Before he could ask her what she meant, her phone buzzed. Grateful for the interruption, she rolled over and retrieved it from the table beside the bed. Dr. Thorpe had sent through a photo of Marvin, who was awake and apparently very groggy.

Power's on for real and Marvin's awake.

He'd punctuated it with a smiley face.

"Look," she said, rolling back and showing him the screen. "Marvin's loopy but conscious." She felt so much relief she was lightheaded with it. "Again, thank you so much."

"Turns out this has worked out okay for me," he said softly, brushing a piece of her hair behind her ear. "I'm here with you, aren't I?"

And yet his words about not wanting a relationship still echoed. Brooklyn struggled to define what was happening between them. They were neighbors. Friends. She wasn't exactly poor, but she had a very modest existence next to his lavish one. He had a high-powered career and she made a small living out of what had been a hobby. Their lives intersected in one small way—being on the island at the same time. But that was it.

So what did she want from this moment, right now, in a hotel room? It wasn't sex. Not that she didn't think it would be spectacular, because after what had happened on the beach she was sure there would be fireworks. But it would also make her incredibly vulnerable, and she wasn't ready for that. Not when there was no future in it.

"Cole..."

"Don't say it. I can see it on your face, and it's okay. Let's just get up, order some food and figure out what's next."

He wasn't going to push. She appreciated it and respected him for it. She was also a little disappointed in herself. Why was it so hard to reach out and take the opportunity before her?

Her throat tightened. The answer was simple, but certainly not easy to acknowledge. The truth was, one afternoon out of her lifetime had changed everything. It had made her seek guarantees, and in the absence of guarantees, she couldn't bring herself to take chances. And that was okay, wasn't it? Everyone made choices based on past experiences. After all, Cole had made several choices based on his upbringing and his father's death. He'd just said so.

Moreover, the only guarantee she wanted from him was that he'd leave her property alone, and he'd essentially done that already.

So she smiled as Cole rolled off the bed and reached for the in-room dining menu. In a matter of hours she'd be taking Marvin back home and life would get back to normal, wouldn't it? And despite her recent "is this all there is" thoughts, she was at least happy that she'd had the power to make those choices for herself.

Cole ordered up a feast of brunch foods: omelets, home fries, crisp bacon, a fruit platter with ripe berries, grapes and melon, pastries, and lots of coffee.

When their bellies were full, they ventured outside to the mile-long beach and listened to the pounding surf left over from the storm. The sun had come out, but there was a mess of driftwood and seaweed strewn behind on the normally pristine white sand. The crisp breeze was invigorating, and when they returned to the resort, they learned from the staff that power was slowly being restored across the province.

The island was sure to still be without, but she could manage with the generator—

The generator! In her haste last night, she'd forgotten to start it up at the house. Now it had been twenty-four hours and her fridge and freezer were sure to be thawed. Dammit! All her food would be wasted.

When she said as much to Cole, he frowned and fired off a text to Dan.

"It's too late," she lamented. "Dan can't do anything, Cole. It should have been done first thing this morning at the latest. I was planning on returning home this morning and starting it up if the power wasn't back on."

But Cole merely smiled and handed over his phone.

Thought of it and went to the house this morning. Damage is minimal and the generator's working fine. Will refuel it tonight.

She stared at the screen. "Dan did that?"

"Apparently. See? Nothing to worry about."

It had been so long since she'd relied on anyone, or even had someone look after her welfare, that she wasn't sure what to say.

"Have you checked your email or anything?"

She shook her head. "No. I've been trying to save battery." Indeed, her phone was now down to 32 percent. "And my data."

"I was going to check mine back in the room." He looked down at her and took her hand. The wind was cool in the aftermath of the storm, the tropical humidity gone from the air and leaving a distinctive fall feeling behind. "I'm sure they'll have charge cords at the desk. Unless you want to go home tonight. I can put Dave on standby."

She hadn't even thought of Dave. "Oh my gosh, is he still at the airstrip?"

Cole chuckled. "No. I sent him back to Halifax just after you went to sleep. Whenever we need him, he can be back here in a few hours. If you want to go home tonight…"

They could go back to the island. She could always return for Marvin with the boat tomorrow. It would be rough sailing, but the seas would be calmer than today. Or they could stay at the resort tonight and take Marvin home tomorrow if he was ready.

It would mean spending the night with Cole…

"I've got the room for the night anyway, Brooklyn, so it's entirely up to you."

There was only one bed. It was a giant one, but…

Cole sighed and looked out over the water. Brooklyn wasn't sure what to make of the dejected sound. Was he frustrated with her? With the situation?

"It's entirely up to you," she offered. "You've been so kind already. I will work around whatever it is you want."

He didn't look at her. "What I want is you. I told you that once before. So keep that in mind when you decide if you want to go home tonight or if you want to stay."

Then he turned his head to look at her. "I want you, Brooklyn. Even if it's for one night only."

That was it, then. He still wasn't looking for a relationship or anything more than a fling. The only thing left to decide was if she was willing to accept one night in his bed, or if she would protect her heart and her body and do the safe and sensible thing.

CHAPTER ELEVEN

COLE SAW THE struggle on Brooklyn's face and mentally prepared himself to call Dave and ask for a return flight to the island.

She liked him. He knew that for sure. But he also knew she was the kind of woman who played it safe. The walk on the dunes the other night had been an exception to the rule, but it had given him a taste of what she could be like when she dropped her guard and let her passion out to play.

He liked that woman a lot. He liked her anyway, but that night was branded on his memory with its sweetness and vulnerability and trust.

But when it was over, he'd sensed that it wasn't something to be repeated. And he might have promised her that nothing would happen tonight if they stayed. Nothing *would* happen if she didn't wish it. But he wasn't going to pretend that he didn't want it to. Because he did. He wanted to be with her, hear her say his name, feel her body against his. He wanted to be held in her arms, hear her throaty laughter in the dark. The choice was hers.

She met his gaze, her blue eyes troubled. "I don't know how to… I mean, I…" she stammered. "Cole, I don't know how to be casual, or…damn. I don't know how to say this without it sounding prudish or judgy or old-fashioned. It's not about that, really. It's more…"

She stopped again, and his heart softened. "Being vulnerable. Or…perhaps separating the physical from the emotional." Her cheeks reddened. "That's probably as good an explanation as any."

"And because we both avoid the word *love* like the plague."

She laughed a little, and he was glad. Facing this head-on was probably the right thing. Ignoring things unsaid would only lead to a mess.

"Well, that, too." She bit her lip for a moment before speaking again. "We have very different lives. They've intersected while you've been on the island, but let's not pretend that we actually exist in each other's spheres, both geographically and socially. What's between us… maybe it's real or maybe it's purely situational. But I… I'm not sure I can do sex in a situational way."

He nodded, disappointed but knowing he'd get over it. "I'm more than walking hormones," he replied. "I won't deny that I'm very attracted to you. But nothing will happen that you don't want to happen, if that's what you're worried about. You're very much in control, here, Brooklyn. Heck, there's a sofa. If you want, I'll sleep there. Or another room might free up for tonight." He put his hand along her cheek, the skin smooth and cool from the ocean breeze. "Whatever you want, that's what you'll have."

"What I want isn't fair." Her hair whipped around her cheek and she raised her hand to tuck it away. "I want to kiss you right now, right after saying that we can't be together. I'm a big mess of mixed signals, and I know it. But I think I'd like to stay, and we can take Marvin home tomorrow. If that's okay."

"Of course it's okay." His heart was pounding against his ribs, from wanting her, from her acknowledgment of wanting him, too. "And fair or not, I want to kiss you, too."

He put his other hand on her face so that she was cupped in his palms like a precious chalice. Then he leaned forward and kissed her. Her lips were cold but the inside of her mouth was soft and warm, and his body responded to the sweetness of the kiss.

Staying in the same room with her, in the same bed, would be torture. But one he was willing to undergo if it meant a few stolen kisses and the feel of her in his arms.

He ended the kiss and sat back on his heels, stunned by the sudden realization.

It wasn't just wanting her. It was about intimacy, and connection, and something far more substantial than a night in a hotel room.

It scared him half to death, and for a moment he considered calling the pilot and going back today anyway.

And then he looked at her shining eyes and left his phone in his pocket.

After their walk, they took a shower—separately. Neither had a change of clothes, but there were plush robes in the closet and they put those on instead. Cole tried to ignore the soft aloe scent of her damp hair, freshly washed with the hotel-supplied toiletries, but he wasn't having much luck. It seemed as if everything about her assaulted his senses. The fresh scent of her post-shower, her hair, darker when wet, and curling around her shoulders. If he touched her, it would be game over for him. The white robe, her skin, still pink from the hot water in the shower… If he touched her, would she make that little sound of pleasure like she had the night on the beach?

He busied himself with the menu again and they chose dinner items. He was pleased to see the inspired offerings on the dinner menu. Maple ginger salmon was paired with a sweet potato and bulgur dish as well as miso-roasted Brussels sprouts, and he ordered a bottle of Riesling to go with it. When dinner came, the wait staff set it up on the table in the seating area. Cole looked over at Brooklyn, who was watching the whole thing with wide eyes. He wondered if she'd ever had room service before today. If she had slipped into a hotel robe or enjoyed the finer things that she so obviously deserved.

He tipped the staff generously and then turned to Brooklyn. "Shall we?"

She giggled a little. "Oh, Cole! They saw us in our robes. Do you suppose they think that we…? Oh, my."

He chuckled. "So what if they did? I'm pretty sure it's not the first time. Come on, let's eat. This smells incredible. Tori was right. This inn is a hidden gem. What a gorgeous place."

She stepped forward then, and he lifted the dome off the plated meal. The colors, presentation, aroma…his stomach growled in response. Then he held her chair for her until she sat down. Just because they were in a hotel room didn't mean he'd lost his manners.

"Tori used to work here, right?"

Cole took his seat. "Yes, that's right. It's how she and Jeremy met."

Fork in hand, Brooklyn met his gaze. "I'd think your speed is more like…the Plaza. Or what's the other one in New York? The Waldorf Astoria."

She was so adorable. He wished he could take her there. Maybe he could. He had to go back to Manhattan soon; he couldn't avoid the Abbott offices forever. What if she went with him for a taste of the Big Apple?

"You've never been to New York, have you?"

She shook her head. "I've never been much of any-where." She popped half of a sprout into her mouth and closed her eyes. "Oh, wow. I don't even really like Brussels sprouts and this is delicious. Not bitter at all."

He tried one, as well, and flavor exploded on his tongue. "You know," he said, after he'd swallowed the bite, "I'm really no different in New York than I am here. Maybe more relaxed, I suppose, but the same person. I don't go through a personality change."

She nodded. "I'm glad to hear it. Still, this isn't the life you're used to."

"Maybe it's better."

Where had that thought come from?

She laughed. "Do you really think so? It's a different lifestyle here. Slower, yes, but don't you miss, I don't know, theater and restaurants and…whatever it is you usually do?"

"You mean work in my office until nine p.m.? Hate to break it to you, Brooklyn, but last night, playing cards and having a few drinks? I don't remember when I last had that much fun."

He lifted his glass. "So why don't we toast? To sim-pler lives and happier times."

She raised her glass and touched the rim to his, her eyes glowing in the mellow light from the nearby lamp. They each took a sip.

"And to Marvin," she added.

He grinned. "Of course." They drank again. "And to making the best of a bad situation," he finished. "Be-cause a private dinner for two is a heck of a nice way to spend the day after a hurricane."

"Cole…"

"Eat," he said softly. "Honestly, I don't care if we watch

a movie and raid the snacks in the minibar. I'm just happy to be spending the evening with you, Brooklyn."

That much, at least, was 100 percent true.

Brooklyn savored each bite of the amazing dinner and every last drop of the Riesling. Now she was warm and full and, if she were honest, seriously reconsidering her words of the afternoon.

Cole looked so approachable in the robe that all she wanted to do was untie the belt at his hips and see what happened. She wasn't brave enough, but it didn't stop her body from being hyperaware of his. He was across the room right now and she was already imagining what it would feel like to have his skin against hers.

She wasn't a virgin, but it had been a very long time, and truthfully she was starting to care for Cole—a lot. He would walk away one of these days and she knew the island would be lonely without him. If they were to indulge themselves—and it certainly would be nothing more than an indulgence—she wasn't sure she could untangle her emotions from the act, and that would leave her not just lonely but potentially desolate.

But oh, the temptation was very, very real.

The awareness only intensified as they found a movie on TV and got into the bed to watch it. It was a legal drama, and Brooklyn found herself caught up in the story line. At one point Cole paused it and got up to get refreshments. There was a small bottle of prosecco that Brooklyn thought sounded nice, so he did the honors and popped the cork for her, then fixed himself a drink from the small bottles and mix. There were snacks, too—nuts and chips and chocolate. He brought an assortment over and put it on the bed between them, shot her a boyish grin and plopped back into the bed.

The movie continued and Brooklyn stole glances at him, contentedly munching potato chips and sipping on whatever he'd mixed with his soda.

The prosecco fizzed lightly on her tongue, slightly sweet but not overpowering. The air in the room changed, however, when the main characters of the movie escaped danger and found themselves alone, full of adrenaline, and gratitude for being alive.

Cole shifted slightly on the bed, but Brooklyn couldn't look over. She refilled her glass with the rest of the prosecco and tried to ignore her intense awareness of Cole at the moment, instead focusing on the screen. But that only made things worse. That Cole remained equally silent ratcheted the tension up another notch. Was he feeling it, too? That undeniable pull, made tighter by what was happening on screen?

She stole a glance at him and found him watching her. But he didn't move, didn't speak. He had said today on the beach that she was in control. At the time she'd thought it was control to say no, to keep things platonic. But now that word, *control*, took on a whole other meaning.

If she wanted something to happen, it could. And it could happen how she wanted it to. Everything was within her reach. All she had to do was reach out and grasp it.

She might not have another chance. She'd set her life up as she wanted. Why couldn't she have this one night to remember?

The scene switched, but Brooklyn reached for the remote and hit the mute button, sending the room into silence. Cole's neck bobbed as he swallowed, but he didn't move, didn't shift his gaze. Her stomach was a tangle of anxiety and anticipation, but she took a breath and lifted her chin.

Control. Power. Maybe it was finally time to reclaim hers.

She shifted and knelt on the bed, then reached for the tie on Cole's robe and tugged it gently. The knot fell away easily, and she reached down and opened the robe. Glory, he was beautiful, all lean muscle and definitely ready for her. Still he remained silent, as if speaking would break the tenuous spell.

Then she reached for the belt on her robe and undid it. Fear spiked... Long time, new man, lights on, and even a little body insecurity all played into her nervousness. But her need and longing overrode the sensation, and she let the robe gape open. Neither of them wore anything beneath the soft fabric, so they were not quite naked but were undressed all the same.

"Brooklyn," he finally whispered. "I don't... I can't..."

She loved that he was struggling to put words together. He was normally so self-assured, knowing exactly what to say. The feminine power of the moment seeped into her, emboldening her. She moved forward until her knees were next to his thighs. Then she slid her right leg over his so that she was straddling him, their bodies close together but not joined. Everything in her was crying out for completion, but she'd be damned if she'd hurry.

Control.

"Touch me," she said quietly, her voice roughened by desire. "Please, Cole. I'm dying for you to touch me."

"Show me where," he said, and she thrilled at taking the lead.

Brooklyn reached for his hand and guided it to her

breast, loving the feel of his warm fingers against the sensitive skin. Her eyes closed for a moment as she absorbed the sensation, the tenderness of it, imprinting onto her memory the look of awe on his face as she'd opened her robe. She felt utterly beautiful and desirable, and free to take whatever she needed or wanted.

And what she wanted was what he wanted, wasn't it? She reached down and touched him, heard the harsh hiss of his breath as he inhaled. She opened her eyes only to find his closed, his head back against the pillow, strain tightening his face. All because she was touching him. His hips nudged against her and there was a fleeting feeling that this couldn't be real.

To prove she was wrong, she shifted and then settled, and they both stilled, struck by the magnitude of what she'd just done.

It was more than need. More than desire. It was… right. Like something clicked into place in that moment, key to lock. Her heart trembled as Cole's eyes opened and found hers. "Brook," he whispered, and tears stung the backs of her eyes.

She would not cry, even though this was the most beautiful moment she could ever remember.

Instead she started to move, dying to use this unexpected power to give him pleasure.

In the end the pleasure was mutual. Her robe slid off her shoulders and pooled at her hips. Skin grew slick and breaths quickened; he said her name and she called his in response. And yet they took their time and made it last, hovering on the edge of bliss as if they knew this was their one and only time. And when the final edges of their restraint frayed, any semblance of control was lost as they toppled into the unknown together.

CHAPTER TWELVE

THE ROOM WAS gray when Brooklyn woke the next morning. Last night they'd at least remembered to close the drapes to the room, and there was nothing but silence as her eyes adjusted to the dim light that entered through a sliver of window. Cole was asleep next to her, and neither of them was wearing a stitch of clothing. She'd slept naked with him…all night.

Now that day was dawning, reality poked its annoying head into the room. Today they would put on yesterday's clothes, and pick up Marvin, and fly back to the island and home.

She didn't want it to be over. Not yet. There was something so wildly wonderful about being in this bed with him, right now, away from both his world and hers, and in a world where it was just the two of them. She wanted to hang on to it a little longer, because that pesky reality kept wanting to have its say and she didn't want to listen. She'd have to, but not quite yet.

She shifted and the sheets brushed over her sensitive skin. Cole's lashes fluttered and she slipped her hand over his ribs, grazing the skin with her fingertips. "Mmm…" he murmured, eyes still closed. Her hand drifted lower and a smile teased the corner of his lips.

This time she let him have control, and she willingly

surrendered to his desires. He didn't speak and neither did she; they let their bodies do the talking. There wasn't an inch of her now that he didn't know, and the thought was both wonderful and overwhelming.

She wasn't sure they could stay just neighbors after this. And wasn't sure where that left them, either. Not together, but with this *thing* between them, always making it more.

Cole kissed her forehead and slid out of the bed to turn on the shower, and Brooklyn stared at the ceiling. This couldn't happen again. Somehow they'd have to go back to being neighbors, wouldn't they? And only through part of the year. Somehow she had to find a way to put them back on even terms where he could carry on with his life and she with hers...

Then again, maybe it wouldn't be that hard for him. After all, he did admit that he'd played hard in years past, which translated to no serious relationships. There was no reason to think this would be anything different. Heck, even yesterday he'd said he avoided relationships because of his parents' marriage. She was making a big something out of nothing. Or, as Gram would say, there was no need to borrow trouble until trouble borrowed you.

She waited for him to finish showering, then took her turn while he called Dave and set up a pick-up time for around noon. Instead of room service, they checked out and grabbed coffee and pastries at the inn coffee shop. Then it was off to the clinic in a taxi.

The clinic was back in business, which meant the waiting room was full of clients and dogs on leashes and cats in carriers. Brooklyn was suddenly nervous about Marvin, and taking him home. He'd had surgery, so was it really okay for him to be going home so early?

Dr. Thorpe popped out from the back of the clinic and beckoned for them to follow him through. There they found Marvin, moving slowly but with a steadily wagging tail and a happy-dog smile on his face.

"Hello, my boy." She knelt down and he came over, nudging her shoulder with his wide head, begging for pats. She couldn't stop the grin from spreading over her face, and she leaned back and caught his head in her hands. "Look, you crazy dog, don't go eating random stuff and scaring us again, huh?"

He licked her face.

Her cheeks flared as she realized she'd said "us" instead of "me," as if she and Cole were a couple.

Cole voiced the question that was on her mind. "Are you sure it's okay for him to go home?"

Dr. Thorpe nodded as Brooklyn got to her feet. "We could keep him another night, but he's doing well. I've got some medication for you to take with you, and a staff member will go over it with you, but he's young and healthy. I don't see any reason to expect complications. He needs to take it easy, though. For at least a week or two. No big runs on the beach. His stomach is bound to be touchy, too, so a bland diet is a good idea until he's healed. Mostly he just needs love and rest at this point."

"Love won't be an issue," Brooklyn assured him. She was fairly swamped with gratitude. "And I'll keep him on leash until he's good to go."

"If anything happens, we can be here fairly quickly." Cole spoke up, his voice quiet but with authority. "I've got to head back to New York in a few days, but my caretaker will be at the house and I'll keep the pilot on standby."

Dr. Thorpe grinned. "First patient I've ever had with his own air ambulance."

Brooklyn was still reeling from what Cole had just said. Not about the helicopter; at this point she was no longer surprised at his generosity. But he hadn't mentioned a word about going to New York. Of course, she'd known it would happen eventually, but he must have known before…

She swallowed tightly. Before last night.

She didn't feel duped, exactly, but there was no denying that if she'd known, she might have thought twice about sleeping with him. And there was definitely a niggle of doubt where he was concerned. Had he kept that little detail to himself because he suspected she would shut him down?

"Thank you so much, Dr. Thorpe."

"No problem at all. Call if you have any concerns or questions, okay?"

She walked Marvin out to the waiting room and then got all the paperwork and instructions from the assistant at the desk. She also pulled out her credit card to pay the bill, but the invoice showed a balance of zero.

She looked up at Cole. "You paid my vet bill?"

"If you're mad about it, we can talk. You can always pay me back."

"I will." She lifted her chin. He'd been a wonderful help, but he'd taken over a lot, too. She still had some pride. And that pride was stinging over his lack of disclosure. "Marvin's my dog, and I'm responsible for him."

"Okay, then." He said it easily, maybe too easily. They left the clinic and got into the waiting cab. Brooklyn's emotions were all over the place. She needed to pay her own way, but the vet bill and her half of the hotel bill would definitely take a chunk out of her small savings. But she didn't want his help, either. Didn't want their friendship to be predicated on whether or not he paid for things. Or…feeling constantly indebted.

This was the problem, wasn't it? Before, they were just friendly, getting along as neighbors. Now it was different. In the beginning, she'd let him pay for the dock because legally she could have made it difficult for him to make changes. That was business. This was…well, if not pleasure, it was personal. It changed the dynamic between them and she didn't like it.

Maybe it was better that he went back to New York now, so they could stop pretending they had something real.

"You're awfully quiet," he said, looking past Marvin's head to catch her gaze.

"Just thinking. There's a lot to do when I get back. I don't even know if I have power back. This morning the news was that some parts of the province might not get it back for three or four more days."

"As long as you have lots of gas for your generator, you'll be fine."

"I know."

She hadn't even been thinking about the practicalities, but she wasn't going to tell him that.

All too soon the drive to the airstrip was over and their helicopter was waiting. Cole lifted Marvin out of the car but the dog walked to the chopper under his own steam. Then Cole lifted him up again, careful of his incision.

When everyone was secured, Dave readied for take-off and Brooklyn let out a long breath. Once she was home she'd find the inflatable collar that she'd used the last time Marvin had had stitches, to keep him from licking. It was a little friendlier than a huge cone. Then she'd cook up some rice and chicken for him to eat until his stomach healed. She nuzzled his face with her nose. "I'm so glad you're okay, buddy. You scared me."

A happy lick was her reward.

Once they were airborne, Brooklyn got a good look at the devastation from the hurricane. Structures were mostly fine, but it was easy to see downed trees, and as they got to the coast, the mess left behind from the storm surge. She remembered that she had a huge tree in her lane that would need to be dealt with. In years past her dad would have made the trip with his chainsaw and they all would have hung out together. Maybe she'd give him a call and see if they wanted to make the trip from Halifax.

She let out a hefty sigh.

"What is it?" Cole reached over and touched her shoulder.

"Just a lot to do, that's all. But thank you so much, Cole. If not for you, Marvin could have died before I could get him to the mainland. I appreciate this more than you know."

"Maybe you can show your appreciation later." He smiled at her, his eyes twinkling. They had their headsets on, and she saw Dave smile a little in the cockpit.

She wasn't going to answer. If they were to have a conversation, it wouldn't be in the air with a pilot listening in.

Dan and Raelynn were waiting when they landed, and Brooklyn was surprised at the feeling of pleasure she got, to see them waving at her. Dan came forward and helped Cole get Marvin out of the helicopter, and Raelynn practically showered the pup with kisses. "Oh, here's a good boy." She kissed his head and ruffled his ears. "I'm so glad he's okay, Brooklyn."

"Me, too. I'm sure he'll be up to no good before I know it."

Dan came forward and gave her a small hug. "Your generator's still working fine. Latest update is that we'll have power back tomorrow."

"Thank you, Dan. I appreciate that more than you know."

"It was no problem at all."

There was an awkward silence while they all stood there, as if wondering what to do next. Brooklyn finally jolted into action when Marvin pulled on the leash. "I'd better get this guy home. Plus, I'm dying for a change of clothes."

Cole thankfully took the bait. "Yes, me too. We left in kind of a hurry. I'll check in later, though, okay?"

"Sure," she responded, unsure of what exactly that meant or what she wanted it to mean. It was like last night was a whole world away, divorced from reality.

Cole changed into jeans and a soft sweater, then sat down to a delicious meal prepared by Raelynn. Their breakfast had been small and on the run, so he appreciated the homemade soup and substantial sandwich she placed on the table. Their internet was still down, so he was using his phone and eating up his data to work. Arrangements were being made for next week and his return to Manhattan. The first retreat at the house had gone well; one of his business acquaintances was planning a week here with his senior staff later in November. Granted, it wasn't the best time of year as far as weather and scenery, but Dan and Raelynn would make sure everyone was warm and cozy, and there was a facilitator coming with the group to guide their activities.

It was exactly what he'd bought this place for. And it would be much busier next summer.

He imagined Brooklyn here over the winter and wondered how she managed it. A good nor'easter would blow nearly as hard as the hurricane that had passed through, only colder and with snow, not rain. How did she manage being on the island alone for that?

What if…

He shook his head and spooned up more soup. No, it was ridiculous, wasn't it? She wouldn't leave the island. Unless… He thought back to last night and this morning, and the way she'd been in his arms. How she'd laughed playing cards, and the way she'd held his hand while they were waiting for news of Marvin. He cared about her so much. He might even…love her. It was a foreign idea in his brain; he'd never let himself even consider the word before. But Brooklyn was different, and the way he felt about her was different, too.

What if she came to New York for a while? It was still East Coast weather in the winter, but without the isolation. The more he thought about it, the more the idea had merit. She said she hadn't traveled, hadn't she? They could stay in his penthouse. Maybe do Thanksgiving at the family home in Connecticut. If it went well, she could go back in January or something, stay for a while. They could…

He sat back in his chair. What he was considering was having a relationship. And for the first time in his life, he wasn't afraid of the word.

How had this even happened?

Maybe because, for the first time, he'd been with a woman who he knew wasn't after his money. She'd turned it down, for Pete's sake! And had insisted on paying him back for the hotel and vet bills. She had so much pride. With Brooklyn, he got the feeling that his status worked against him, rather than for him…but she liked him anyway. She'd shared things with him, about her painful past. Was it possible she could love him, too?

"Are you all right, Cole?" Raelynn's voice interrupted his thoughts and he picked up his spoon again.

"Oh, yes, thank you. This is delicious."

"Brooklyn gave it to me last week. It's her grandmother's corn chowder recipe. I think her grandmother was a good cook from the sounds of it. I was thinking of asking her for more regional recipes for when I'm cooking for guests here."

"That's a great idea." Cole smiled up at her. "Thank you, Raelynn, for everything."

Raelynn's smile slipped, and she sat down in the chair next to him. "Cole, there's something I want to talk to you about, just to think about, of course."

Her face was tight with anxiety, her eyes worried. Cole frowned and pushed his near-empty bowl away. "What is it? Did something happen while we were gone?"

"No, not at all. We managed fine." She sent him a weak smile. "It's just…well, Dan would be upset if he knew I was talking to you, but I think it's only fair to be open and honest. The truth is…we've been talking about trying for a baby. You hired us here together, and I can still do the job after a short maternity leave, but it…might be on the radar in the near future."

That was all? He smiled at her. "Of course you two want a family. Are you pregnant already? Should I not have asked that?" He was unsure of the protocol of these things, but Raelynn's face relaxed at his reaction.

"No, not yet. I certainly wouldn't have indulged on the night of the storm if I had been. It's just that we both

really like it here. And living above the garage is fine
for the two of us—"

"But not for a baby."

"We could manage, but it's not optimal, no."

"Of course it's not." He had known that when they'd
first arrived weeks ago, but there hadn't been a huge
rush to make adjustments. There was probably room
in the house, but he could also understand the couple
wanting to have their own space for their family.

As far as the island went, Brooklyn's house was still
the perfect solution. Except she wouldn't sell it…and
she'd thanked him for letting the idea go. Which meant
that idea was firmly off the table.

Unless it wasn't…

"Leave it with me," he said to Raelynn. "I'm sure we
can come up with something. You're coming to New
York for Thanksgiving, though, aren't you? I'm sure
your families would like to see you."

She nodded. "That's the plan, for now, anyway. Unless you need us here."

He already knew there were no events planned for
that weekend, and he would still be in New York. There
was no reason for Dan and Raelynn to stay.

Which put Brooklyn here on the island alone—unless he could convince her to come along.

"I'll be back at dinner time," he announced, getting
up from the table. "I'm going down to Brooklyn's to
see how Marvin is settling in."

It wasn't subtle at all, and by the look on Raelynn's
face, she wasn't buying it, either. He didn't really care.
They needed to talk after this morning.

CHAPTER THIRTEEN

BROOKLYN EXPECTED COLE to show up, and he did, right around three o'clock. She'd settled Marvin and put his inflatable collar on. He looked ridiculous, but it kept him from being able to reach his incision and that was all that mattered.

The dog was pouting on his doggy bed and she'd changed into jeans and a warm sweater. She'd put on a pot of coffee. When she saw Cole walking down the lane, she reached into the cupboard and took out her special bottle of Irish cream. The conversation ahead might require a little fortification.

Marvin popped his head up when Cole knocked, but that was it. She answered the door and when they went back into the kitchen, Marvin's tail was thumping against the fabric of the bed. There now. He might not be himself, but he was happy to see Cole.

As she was. And that wasn't a good thing, she was thinking.

"Hey, buddy," Cole crooned, squatting before the bed. "How're you feeling, huh?"

Thump-thump.

"He's pouting about the collar," she offered and started pouring coffee.

Cole took the cup she offered. "I see you've got the necessities running off the generator."

"Fridge, freezer, water pump. And one power bar in the kitchen, for the microwave, coffee maker, and a lamp."

She held up the bottle of liqueur. "Care for some?"

"I wouldn't say no."

She put a splash in each mug. Irish cream coffee was a special treat she didn't indulge in often, but considering the craziness of the last few days, it seemed appropriate. "This reminds me of my granddad," she said, putting the cap back on the bottle. "He liked a drop in his coffee. We used to come over to the island on the weekends in the fall sometimes. He'd make his 'special' coffee, and we'd sit out on the front porch and smell the fall air."

"That sounds lovely." He looked into her eyes. "Would you like to sit out there now?"

She did, rather. She was feeling nostalgic this afternoon. Perhaps it was getting swept away for a few days, both in the emergency and the opulence of Cole's way of life. The storm had barely caused a blip at the mansion, and he'd merely had to snap his fingers to have a helicopter on its way, the last hotel room in town, room service. Maybe money couldn't buy happiness, but it could sure buy convenience.

It all seemed rather surreal now.

Marvin had settled into a snooze on the bed, so they went to the front verandah and sank into the cushions on the wicker chairs there. The wood creaked beneath their weight, and Brooklyn let out a sigh before she took a first sip of coffee and let memories wash over her. This had always been her happy place.

"Brooklyn, I came to talk about us."

She hadn't expected him to be so blunt. "Us?"

"Yes. Things have changed, wouldn't you agree?" When she didn't answer, he pressed on. "We spent the night together. That's not nothing. And it would be really great if you could look at me."

She did, the moment he said it. She lifted her gaze to his and felt that awful and wonderful turning in her stomach. He was in jeans and a sweater but it didn't matter. There was something in the way he carried himself, the way he spoke, that put him in another league. She was hard-pressed to pinpoint it, but she figured it fell into the category of "I know it when I see it." He had this presence about him that was confident but not arrogant, expensive but not ostentatious, and so very, very capable.

She could hold her own, but looking at him now, after what they'd shared, she found him a bit intimidating. Because any "us" would be horribly misbalanced, wouldn't it?

"It was one night, Cole. I'm not harboring any big expectations."

Was that disappointment on his face? She couldn't quite tell, but she could see by the tension around his eyes that her answer wasn't the one he'd been anticipating.

"I see." He took a sip of his coffee and then turned back to her again. "No, actually, I don't see. You don't strike me as the type to indulge in one-night flings, Brooklyn. I appreciate maybe you think you're letting me off the hook, but…" He cleared his throat. "But what if I don't want to be off the hook?"

Her breath caught. What was he saying? That he wanted them to be a thing? Have a relationship? That was ludicrous. They'd already decided things couldn't go further, that day he'd kissed her in the back porch.

And yet they had. They'd made love, twice. They'd passed "further" the moment she'd untied her robe and decided to follow her heart.

And that was it, wasn't it? Her heart was involved now. She truly, truly cared for him. And that was exactly why she had to walk away now. She would never fit into his life, and she didn't really want to. It would mean leaving this behind. The life she'd built for herself, by herself. She was a woman with a high school diploma from a tiny town, making a simple living. She had no business consorting with a billionaire, for Pete's sake.

"What do you want from me, Cole?"

He reached over and took her hand. "I want you to come to New York with me. I have to leave in the next few days and I know Marvin can't travel so soon, but I'd like for you to come stay with me when he's better. I don't want to say goodbye, Brooklyn. Not after last night. Not after everything. You make me laugh. I want to be near you all the time. And last night…that was so amazing." He put his cup down and turned his chair so he was facing her, and then clasped her other hand, too. "Please say yes. I care about you too much to say goodbye."

"You want a relationship with me." Her voice was tight and she couldn't quite sort out why. Any woman would be jumping for joy right about now. Why wasn't she?

"I want us to have a chance to explore what's happening between us. And realistically, I can't stay on the island forever. I still have responsibilities. But you could come to my world, couldn't you?" His face was alight with enthusiasm. "Have you ever been to New York? I can take you so many places. The theater. Restaurants.

Museums. Walking through Central Park with Marvin. Whatever you want to do."

Brooklyn frowned. Sure, it would be easy to get swept away, wouldn't it? It was a Cinderella dream come true, with the prince sitting here saying all the right things. But in fairy tales the princess was always ready to live in the castle. Brooklyn was sure she'd be a square peg in a round hole.

"I have work here, Cole. It is one of my busiest times, leading up to the holidays. I can't just jet off on a moment's notice." She met his gaze. "That's not how the real world works."

He frowned and sat back a little, perhaps a bit surprised at her sharpish tone. "So you can't dye your stuff in my penthouse," he reasoned. "But you could do everything else. Your business is online, right?"

"That's not the point."

"What is the point?"

She pulled her hands away. "The point is you expected me to jump up and say yes, I'd do what you wanted on a total whim, and when I didn't you're pouting."

"I do not pout."

She knew he wasn't pouting; he was genuinely confused and perhaps he had a right to be, considering what had happened last night. But she was already in it and it was too late to turn back now. "Yes, you are. You're used to getting what you want, and you think that my life is so insignificant that I can just pick up and leave because you've crooked your finger."

His mouth fell open. "When have I ever given you that impression?"

He hadn't, but panic was tightening her chest. The moment he'd stepped on the island, he'd threatened her very safe existence. She cared for him, she did. But it was a long way from there to relationship. Because who would be making all the sacrifices? She would.

"It's how you live, Cole. You pick up the phone and have a helicopter ready to take you where you want to go. You have a home in New York but it was nothing for you to drop more money than I'll ever make in a lifetime on this island, so you can have some sort of high-class retreat." She lifted her chin. "You are so used to getting what you want that you expected me to sell my home for the right price." A sudden thought took hold. "Maybe what you like in me is the challenge, because I'm probably the first person to say no to you in a very long time, huh? But what happens when that challenge is gone? Will you be bored of me then? And what's to become of me at that point?"

Cole looked stricken, and she had to turn away. She'd been harsh just now, even if her words had come from a place of real fear. She hadn't expected this invitation. Hadn't expected him to want…more.

Her friends would tell her she was crazy to not take a chance. They still believed in the fairy tale. But there was no security in those sorts of crazy dreams. If nothing else, Brooklyn considered herself a realist.

"I didn't realize you thought so little of me," he said quietly, his elbows resting on his knees. "And I thought you knew me better. I shared stuff about myself that I don't generally share with people, and I thought you understood. So if you think me asking you is because you're a challenge, you don't know me at all."

Her heart hurt, hearing the disappointment in his voice. "I would never fit into your life," she added, less angry now and more sad and practical. "We're from two different worlds, Cole. I'd be unhappy, I just know it. This is where I belong."

"I never said I wanted you to leave the island. Just to give us a chance. Brooklyn, I've never felt this way about anyone. You make me laugh, and you're the most genuine person I've ever met. I don't love you because you're a challenge. It's because you challenge me, and I need that. When I'm not with you I think about being with you. I made a commitment to balance my life better, and I think you were meant to be a part of that. Please, give this a chance."

The cramp in her chest went cold when he used the word *love*. Was that even possible? They'd known each other a matter of weeks. Did he even realize what he'd said? This was all spiraling too fast. "Cole, that's a big thing to say after we've spent one night together."

Hurt flashed across his face. "You surprise me. Yesterday we were walking the beach together. We shared something amazing. I can only guess that you're running scared right now, and that's okay. Believe me, I'm scared, too. I think the thing is, Brooklyn, I trust you. I believe that you're not interested in me because of my money. In fact, I think that point is working against me right now."

She couldn't deny it.

"I won't fit in there," she said firmly. "And you'd come to resent me. I shouldn't have let this go so far." She twisted her fingers together, knowing what she had to say and hating it just the same. "I shouldn't have slept with you, knowing we didn't have any sort of a future. Do you know, I wondered if you hadn't told me you were leaving because you thought if you did, last night, I would say no?"

"Exactly the opposite," he said roughly. "I didn't tell

you because I was still sorting through my feelings, deciding what I wanted to do. Then I imagined you coming to visit me, see me in my world, and I thought…" He ran his hand through his hair. "Well. It doesn't matter what I thought. You don't want to have anything to do with my world. You only want island Cole, who stays in your safe and secure world, and doesn't make you take any risks, right?"

She sat back. "Hey."

"No, not hey. You basically just said that I used a lie of omission to get you into bed, and I resent that. A lot. We were friends, Brooklyn. At least I thought we were. We shared things with each other, things that we don't talk about often. Maybe you regret what happened last night, but I don't. My motives where you were concerned were pure. Can you say the same?"

Brooklyn bristled at that and pushed out of her chair, going to the verandah railing and clenching it in her fingers. "They weren't impure, if that's what you're getting at. I wasn't angling for something."

"Weren't you? What happened? Did you decide to go for it because it was low-risk? Because I was always going to be leaving? Or did you think I didn't care? Do you think I flew you and Marvin to the mainland so I could impress you with my money? I sincerely hope not. It was my way of helping a friend in need. Maybe I was wrong. I believed you thought better of me."

Tears threatened now. He was hurt and angry and she had never wanted any of those things. Except, she realized, the low-risk part. And that she'd never considered that he might be hurt by it. She hadn't considered his feelings, because she'd got so caught up in what he was and not who he was.

"You're right. Not about everything, but some things.

And it shows we aren't right for each other. I'm sorry, Cole. That's all I can say. I'm sorry."

He sat for a moment in the silence that followed, then let out a long, slow sigh. Finally, he stood and faced her, his hands shoved into his jeans pockets.

"You disappoint me, Brooklyn. I'm surprised and disappointed."

God, of all the things to say. Those words gutted her. She'd spent years trying to get over the feeling that she'd let people down. She'd dropped out of her degree. She'd stayed away from relationships. She'd hidden herself away on the island because it was her happy place but moreover, her safe place. And while there was nothing wrong with searching out safety and peace, she'd always felt as if by doing so she was somehow disappointing those who meant the most to her.

Cole stepped forward, close enough that she had to look up to meet his gaze, and her insides trembled as he fixed his eyes on hers.

"You are so much more than you think, but you hide away so no one sees it. It feels like building your life here is a solution, but it's really just a way of avoiding dealing with what happened to you. And I can say that because of some of the things I did when my dad died, and again during my own health scare." His voice gentled and he lifted one hand to touch her cheek. "It's the difference between avoiding life and embracing it. I decided to stop running a few days ago when I accepted my feelings for you. But I can't force you to make that same decision. You have to do it on your own time. Maybe you never will."

He dropped his hand and backed away. "I'll be going in a couple of days. Dan and Raelynn will be here until after the holiday. If you need anything, don't hesitate to ask them. Goodbye, Brooklyn."

She couldn't answer, not even to say goodbye. She was too dumbstruck, too floored by what he'd said. Every instinct within her wanted to shout out that he was wrong. That moving here was embracing life, the kind of life she wanted.

But deep down she knew that was a lie. He'd seen it and called her out on it.

Fine. Maybe hiding away here on the island wasn't the right thing, but that didn't mean jetting off to New York City was the answer, either.

Brooklyn watched him go until he was out of sight at the end of the lane, and then she went back inside. Marvin was still sleeping on his bed, and she looked around her little house. She loved it. She did feel safe here. But even with Marvin for company, it was lonely. Especially now, with Cole gone for good.

Tears stung her eyes but she rubbed them away. She wasn't going to cry over Cole Abbott and his hurtful words. And she definitely wasn't going to cry over the decisions she'd made.

She was a strong woman, despite what Cole said. And that meant she'd get over him, too.

Cole strode into the executive offices of Abbott Industries and smiled as he greeted the receptionist at the front desk. "Good morning, Jennifer," he said brightly, and she waved as the phone rang and she hit a button on her headset.

It was good to be back. At least in most ways it was. The break on the island had been wonderful—for the most part—and he'd recharged. Now, though, it was time to get back and get to work. He'd handled most things remotely during his absence, but there was a different energy in the office. One he'd missed, he realized.

But he wasn't going to lie to himself and say he had no regrets. And if they weren't exactly regrets, he had feelings about what had happened with Brooklyn that weighed on his mind. Because he'd meant every single thing he'd said to her that day on her porch. Including the fact that he loved her.

This was his third day in the office and he had meetings scheduled for half of his time. One meeting was with the executives who'd gone on the retreat, to follow up on both their personal and professional thoughts since coming back to the "real world." He was looking forward to that a lot.

But first, there was a personal meeting he had to get out of the way.

He greeted his executive assistant and then took a deep breath before turning the handle on the door to his expansive office with a splendid view of the Hudson.

His mother was sitting behind his desk.

"Hello, Cole," she said, her voice warm and yet very…polite. In her late fifties, she still looked young and vibrant, with artfully colored hair and perfect makeup. Allison Abbott was a woman who took care of herself, always.

At least, publicly. As Cole knew, her private life had always been quite a hot mess.

"Mother," he said, putting down his briefcase. "Thank you for coming."

"I assumed that was what one does when one is summoned."

That stung a little. Not because it wasn't true, but because that was the nature of their relationship. "I've been slammed since returning. I thought the office was the easiest way." He didn't mention that she never came here anymore since his father's death.

He went to the door again to ask for coffee to be brought in. Then he lifted an eyebrow and said, "Maybe we can sit over here. Instead of you being behind my desk."

She laughed then, a sound Cole was unused to hearing. "Oh, Cole, I wondered if that would irritate you. You can be so stern."

Him? Stern? He hadn't considered it that way, but he supposed he came by the trait honestly. Still, he hoped he wasn't that way in all his personal relationships. Jeremy and Bran had never said such a thing. If anything, he'd prided himself a little too much on his social charm. Even if it did feel forced a lot of the time. It was one of the things he liked about Brooklyn, actually. He'd never had to put on a show. He'd been genuine, like he was with Bran and Jeremy, and Jess and Tori.

"You're very like your father in a lot of ways," she continued, and moved to sit on the small sofa in the rather huge office.

Cole's assistant brought in coffee and once they had fixed their cups, his mother looked up and asked, "Why did you call me here, Cole?"

He hesitated, lifting the cup to his lips and taking a revivifying sip while he considered his words.

"I want to talk about you and Dad."

She frowned. "What about us? Good heavens."

"I've never understood your relationship." His heartbeat quickened with nerves; this was a heck of a thing to talk about with one's mother. "I never saw any affection between you. You never did things together. And I felt…"

He halted, pursed his lips.

"You felt what?"

He met her gaze. "In the way."

Her eyes softened with what looked to Cole like regret, and her lips turned down a little. "I'm sorry about that. Your father's and my relationship was…complicated." She put down her cup and rested her hands in her lap. "Why are you asking this now? Have you… met someone?"

"What does that have to do with anything?"

She gave a delicate scoff. "Oh, Cole, we both know that falling in love with someone makes us question everything."

There was something in her voice that gave him pause. She fiddled with her fingers once more and he noticed that they were ringless. She'd stopped wearing her wedding rings. While a tiny part of him wanted to be outraged on his father's behalf, he knew he couldn't be. They'd had a cold marriage. Why shouldn't she take off the rings?

Why hadn't they divorced? Lord knew enough of his friends had had divorced parents.

"That's an interesting comment, considering it never really seemed like you—" He paused, reconsidered his phrasing. "Like you and dad were in love."

Her gaze slid away for a moment. "We weren't. But it doesn't mean I don't know what love is, Cole. Don't be naive."

Of course. He was looking at all this through tunnel vision. He'd always considered his parents as, well, parents. Not exactly…people. Which was rather selfish of him, really. Brooklyn would tell him to keep an open mind, wouldn't she? That people hid all sorts of pain behind personal façades.

"I'm sorry, Mother. That was uncalled for."

"Not necessarily. I know we failed you. I wasn't happy, Cole, and it affected every part of my life. Including how I parented you. I was awful at it." She met his gaze again. "I was not a good mother. I don't think I really knew how desperately unhappy I was until I—" her cheeks pinkened "—well, until I was free to be happy."

"And now you are?"

She nodded. "Yes. Oh, Cole, if you hadn't called me to your office, I was going to come visit anyway. I have news for you."

She wore an expression he'd never seen before. It was warm and peaceful and happy, and took a good ten years off her face. "What is it?"

"I want to tell you I'm getting remarried," she said with an unexpected softness to her voice. "And I wanted you to know before anyone else."

He sat back. Of all the announcements, this was the last thing he expected. "Remarried? To whom?" His brain jumped back over the past few months. The rings were missing from her fingers. Had she been seeing anyone special? How had he missed it? Then again, he'd been on his own private island, hidden away from the world.

"It's Edward."

"Edward...?"

"Mowbry."

"Your lawyer?" Cole let out a huge breath. "Good God, when did this happen?"

She looked him in the eye and said, "Thirty years ago."

Cole put down his coffee before he could spill it. "Wait. I would have been—"

"Five." She held his gaze, never wavering. "So yes.

It means I had an affair. Though I hate calling it an affair. It sounds so tawdry. I fell in love."

"Did Dad know?"

"Oh, he knew." Now that she'd made her announcement, she'd relaxed. She took a calm sip of her coffee. "Truthfully, Cole, we probably should never have married. His family had money, my family had money, we were in the right social sphere. And we liked each other well enough, but that's not enough to build a marriage on. We learned that very quickly."

"I don't know what to say." Cole was still trying to process everything. He'd idolized his dad, even though he'd often felt as if nothing he did was good enough. But they'd had their share of happy times. And Cole had soaked up every small bit of praise from his father like he was a man dying of thirst and his father's praise was lifesaving water. To learn she'd had an affair...

"I wasn't a good mother, and I can't change that," she said softly. "I was unhappy, and your father was always talking about you being the future of the company and it was like you were all that mattered and I was...nothing. When he found out about Edward, it was awful. He didn't speak to me for weeks."

"Why didn't you divorce him? If you were that unhappy?"

"Edward broke it off. And I didn't know how to do it on my own. Your dad would have put me through a horrible court case if I wanted any alimony. And he would never have allowed me to take you with me. So I stayed."

Cole sat there, his coffee cooling, his head full of everything she was telling him, trying to sort through it all. Maybe she'd stayed, but she hadn't been a very good mother. Certainly not nurturing.

"Would you have wanted to take me?"

Tears filled her eyes. "Oh, yes. And maybe… I don't know. Maybe I would have been a better parent. Any time I suggested anything, your father told me I was wrong and that he knew what you needed. I suppose you'd say I should have kept trying…but the criticism and coldness got into my head. I told myself he was right. I didn't know how to parent you. Then he insisted you go away to school…"

Cole shook his head. "Don't regret that decision. Merrick was the most wonderful time of my life."

"I do regret it. You should have had a home to come to, rather than a boarding school being your home."

Silence fell as that truth settled.

"And now that you're free, you and Edward…"

"Yes. Me and Edward." She cleared her throat. "Cole, you had all sorts of material things and advantages, but you didn't have love and affection. I need to own that, and tell you I'm sorry I failed you. I was so desperately unhappy that I simply didn't have love to give. And I was afraid if I ever let go of the tight control I had over my life, I'd fall apart and never be able to be put back together again."

Cole looked up abruptly and stared into his mother's face. He wondered if he should feel angry in this moment; after all, she was right. He had felt unloved through most of his childhood. And yet he was seeing his mother as another human being, with her own problems and stressors. And he knew that feeling of falling apart. How could he possibly sit in judgment of her and keep a clean conscience?

"It's okay," he said quietly. "Listen, I know what it's like to fall apart. And the good news is you can put yourself back together again. But I understand the fear. I really do."

"You should hate me. Or at least…not care. I came here expecting that."

It made him sad, that his mother would think such a thing. What a mess of a relationship they had.

"Mom, after Dad died, and I had taken over the corporation, I did fall apart. I didn't really say anything, and I made it seem as if I'd taken a much-needed vacation. Truthfully, I thought I had a heart attack and that scared the hell out of me. And then I went into a depression. Dad had worked himself to death, and I didn't want that for myself. It took that big scare for me to decide to not try to be a mirror image of my dad. It's why I bought the property in Nova Scotia. You'd like it there, I think. Gorgeous house, lovely beach…"

Wonderful neighbor. Best dog in the world. And the place where he'd left his heart behind.

"Anyway, my point is, there are worse things than falling apart." He smiled a little. "And I'm glad you told me. Wish you'd told me sooner."

"Your father wasn't a bad man, Cole. He just wasn't the man for me. And my unhappiness made me a poor excuse for a parent. That's not on your father, either. That's on me, and I'm sorry."

He hadn't expected the apology or the endorsement of his father. He'd guessed long ago that their marriage was one of appearances only. It was different hearing it articulated.

"So you really love Edward, huh?"

If he'd had any doubts, they evaporated when she smiled. Her eyes lit up and the lines of strain on her face melted away. "Oh, I do. He did get married, you know. And divorced. We crossed paths at an event months ago and it just…clicked. Like it had from the beginning."

Cole thought back to that first morning when he'd seen Brooklyn, expecting some middle-aged woman with a set of knitting needles in her hands, and instead being greeted by a woman with gorgeous waves of hair and shining eyes the color of an October sky. Yes, he could understand that "click" all too well.

He let out a breath. "But don't you worry that it'll… I don't know, be like before? That maybe you're…" His voice trailed away. "I'm sorry. I think I'm projecting onto you."

"Have you met someone?"

"Yeah. And you know, I thought I'd got past the whole 'not wanting a relationship' thing because she's different."

"What happened?"

"She's convinced that we're too different. And she needs guarantees."

His mother nodded. "Except there are no guarantees. You just…take your chances and hope."

"I've been scared to hope," he admitted.

"Me, too," she replied, and in an odd move, she reached over and touched his hand. "But Cole, I fell in love with Edward all those years ago. It didn't end well, and my heart was quite broken, but we've got a second chance. And that's really quite lovely. Maybe you and this woman—"

"Brooklyn," he supplied.

"Brooklyn. Maybe you can work things out. Because I do want you to be happy, Cole. Don't wait to be my age to share your heart with someone."

His throat tightened and he swallowed. "Well. I think this is the deepest conversation we've ever had."

"And long overdue." She smiled again and reached for her coffee.

"I'm happy for you," he said, meaning it wholeheartedly. "And I know you probably are planning some elaborate trip for your honeymoon, but you and Edward are welcome to stay on the island if you want. I have a couple who are working as caretaker and housekeeper there, and all it'll take is me sending word and they can have things readied for you."

"Does this mean you'll come to the wedding?" she asked, leaning forward, her voice hopeful. "Because I thought you'd be angry with me for marrying again."

He shook his head. "Dad's gone. Why would I want you to be alone and lonely? If you're happy, then I'm happy for you. Simple as that."

Tears filled her eyes. "We were such cold parents. I don't know where you got your big heart."

"Not everyone sees it," he assured her, chuckling. "Just a select few."

"Like this Brooklyn woman?"

He shook his head again. "Maybe before, but not now. She kind of handed it back to me."

"Then she's a fool."

"Maybe. Maybe not. She was pretty clear that we're over."

"I'm sorry, Cole."

"Me, too." He clapped his hands together and stood. "Let's change the subject. Clearly, this is an event that calls for more than coffee. I think you should call Edward, and we can set up a lunch date and all go out together. Have some champagne. What do you say?"

She stood, as well, her face beaming with approval. "Oh, that would be lovely. I'll call your assistant so she can coordinate it with your calendar."

That one line told him everything he needed to know about his mother's relationship with his father, and with him, thus far. He shook his head. "No, Mom. You call me. You don't have to have a relationship with my assistant. You're my mother."

"You're a better son than I deserve, but I'm not going to say no. Thank you, darling. I'll call you in a few days."

She moved forward, as if to buss his cheek, but she hugged him, too, an awkward thing but welcome just the same. "Thank you," she whispered and stepped back. "And don't give up if you love her, Cole. It's a rare thing. At least try to talk to her again, and listen to what she has to say."

He walked her to the door and said goodbye. And then went back to the sofa and sat down. He put his head into his hands and sighed. He missed Brooklyn. He loved her. And he wasn't sure how to go about fighting for her. How could he leave Abbott behind forever? It was a huge responsibility, but one he wanted. It motivated him to get up in the morning, gave him a purpose. He'd be on the island for a month and then be bored out of his mind and miserable. His mother had just shown him what happened to a person who was miserable in their life.

And yet living without Brooklyn was a painful thought. And he could see no way to do both. Brooklyn had been very clear about her needs, and he also didn't want to be the reason she ventured into a life she didn't want and was unhappy.

Maybe she was right. Maybe they were from two different worlds that couldn't be reconciled.

But damn, it hurt.

CHAPTER FOURTEEN

BROOKLYN LET MARVIN off his leash and watched as he ran down the beach, spinning up sand, as if his whole ordeal had never happened. She'd been a diligent nurse-maid to him, checking his incision, keeping his activity low, cooking him fresh chicken and rice until his stomach had healed. It had almost kept her mind off Cole.

Almost, but not quite.

The words he'd said to her that day still echoed in her head and made her question everything. Was she avoiding life? Hiding away on the island because it was safe and secure? Was she afraid to take a chance on them because she couldn't control the situation or the outcome?

Control. That was what it all came down to. To her, control equaled safety. Because for a very few moments one spring day, she'd had absolutely no control and she'd been in horrible danger. She didn't have to be a rocket scientist to figure that out. Her mind skittered back to the night they'd spent at the Sandpiper. He'd known, even then, hadn't he? Because he'd told her that she was in control of what happened between them. And she'd been the one to take the lead.

She and Marvin were nearly at the end of the beach when she saw two people heading down over the bluff. Dan and Raelynn, holding hands, and her heart warmed at the sight of them. It was a little bittersweet, watching their happiness. One night not long ago, she and Cole had walked down the same dune, hand in hand in the moonlight.

Marvin ran up to the couple, begging for pats as was his usual style. Moments later Brooklyn caught up to everyone. She hadn't spoken to them since Cole left. Dan had taken Cole to the mainland in the boat, and Raelynn had gone along to do some grocery shopping. They'd stopped at the house to see if Brooklyn needed anything, a truly neighborly gesture. She'd awkwardly declined.

Raelynn gave her a hug. "Oh, it's good to see you. And Marvin. He looks fully recovered."

"He is," Brooklyn answered, trying not to think of how nice that hug had felt. "And it's good to see you, too."

"Maybe now we've broken the ice and you can stop avoiding us," Raelynn continued, while Dan added a shocked, "Rae!"

"No, she's right," Brooklyn said, shaking her head. "I have been. Things ended on a weird note with Cole, and I wasn't sure what to say."

"Cole wasn't himself, either. He stomped around for the few days before he left. Wasn't fit to be around, really."

"I'm sorry."

"Not your fault," Raelynn said.

"Except maybe it is." Brooklyn watched Marvin as he raced around the dune below. "I didn't give him the answer he wanted."

"Yeah, well, he's still responsible for his reaction. So there."

"Rae…" Dan's voice held a weary caution that

Brooklyn found funny. It was so very…couple-ish. Clearly they'd already had this conversation.

Marvin brought back a piece of driftwood and Dan said, "That's my cue." He took the stick and went down to the beach to play some fetch.

Raelynn watched him go. "He's mad at you for breaking Cole's heart."

Brooklyn gaped at her. "Breaking his heart? I don't think I'm capable of that."

"Oh, I think you are." Raelynn's eyebrows shot up as she spoke. "He'd really fallen for you." Brooklyn opened her mouth to protest but Raelynn held up a hand. "I'm not saying you're wrong. I'm just saying that was the result."

Brooklyn didn't know what to say. She finally sighed and said, "We're too different. It would never work."

"Really, too different? I can't see how."

Brooklyn made a sound that was half scoff, half disbelief. "Come on, Raelynn. Look at his life, look at mine. He's a freaking billionaire, and I'm…well, I'm a thousandaire. That's about the size of my savings account."

Raelynn laughed. "Oh, for Pete's sake. That's just money. That's all…window dressing. It's in here that counts." She pressed a hand to her chest. "I've known Cole a while now. I've never seen him light up like he did with you. Or laugh. Maybe he needs someone like you. You ground him in a way bank accounts and employees never can, Brooklyn. And you need him, too."

"I do?"

Raelynn met her gaze evenly. "You're hiding away here. He can pull you out of that fear and uncertainty. And why shouldn't you enjoy some of the finer things?"

She raised an eyebrow. "It won't change you, if that's what you're worried about. You're too stubborn."

Brooklyn choked on a laugh, but she kept thinking of what Raelynn had said about Cole lighting up. She'd lit up too, every time he'd walked into a room or into her front yard.

"Cole is not stuck up. If anything, he's crying out for love. He didn't have much as a kid, as far as I can tell. He's had a lot of advantages, but not that. And yet he's one of the most giving people I know, expecting nothing in return."

Brooklyn knew well enough. She'd tried to wire the money for the hotel and vet bill to him, but he'd refused the transfer. She'd thought it was because he was still angry with her. But now she wondered if it was more than that.

"I hurt him, but I didn't mean to."

"We know that. Despite Dan's attitude, we both know that. But we also think you've made a big mistake, turning him away when you could take a chance on him. On you as a couple."

Silence fell for a few minutes. They listened to the crash of the waves, and the wind, and the plaintive wail of the gulls soaring overhead. It was cold, and Brooklyn shoved her hands into her jacket pockets before her fingers turned numb.

"I'm afraid," she finally said.

"We're all afraid of something," Raelynn answered, her voice steady and sure. "Every damned one of us. We can either let our fear rule us, or we can reach out for what we want and deserve in spite of it. Something made you quit, Brooklyn. Something made you wrap yourself in what was comforting and familiar. And that's okay for a while, but don't you want more? Don't you want love and excitement of the best kind, and surprises and…and life?"

Tears pricked the back of Brooklyn's eyes. It was basically what Cole had said to her, but without the blaze of hurt and rejection behind it. That she was avoiding life and playing it safe, and giving up the opportunity for something wonderful.

Because in all her life, there'd never been anything as wonderful as being in Cole's arms.

Could she do it? Could she go to him and ask for another chance? Could she handle a place as big and chaotic as New York, when even now she found going into unfamiliar places difficult? She wanted to believe she could, but even now, panic threaded through her, cold and tight.

"I can't leave Marvin," she said.

"Oh, good heavens. You don't even sound convincing saying that." She pointed at Dan, who was tugging on the stick that was in Marvin's mouth. "We'll take care of him. We're staying for at least another month."

Brooklyn's heart started to pound as she actually considered going to New York, fighting her demons along the way. "I don't know if my passport is still valid."

"Well, that might be a barrier. You should probably check." Raelynn was smiling now, her eyes glowing. "And we'll watch the house for you, too. Whatever you need."

"Raelynn… I don't know what to say. I'm still terrified. But I think I need to at least try, you know?" She swallowed against a lump in her throat. "I've been miserable since he left."

"He's a good man. And he loves you. Nothing in life is guaranteed, but please don't miss out on what could be wonderful because you're afraid to take a chance." Raelynn nodded toward Dan. "Trust me, the rewards can be more than you ever dreamed."

Someday, Brooklyn wanted to hear the story of Raelynn and Dan, but right now, she had some arrangements to make. She reached out and put her hand on Raelynn's forearm. "Can you help me with the details? I don't even know where to find him."

Now Raelynn's grin was wide. "Oh, yes. You find your passport. Then come up to the house and we'll get everything arranged. I'll help."

Brooklyn called for Marvin and then looked at Raelynn as a fizz of excitement started to run through her veins. "Why are you so determined to set us up?"

"Oh, honey. Because Cole is a great boss, but the few days before he left? I don't want to be stuck with that guy as my employer. He needs some Brooklyn sunshine in his life, stat."

Brooklyn grinned, then hooked Marvin up to his leash once he knocked up against her knees, tongue out and happy. "Thank you, Raelynn. I'll come back to the house when I've found my passport."

Dan came up the dune behind Marvin. "All good?" he asked.

"Better than good." Raelynn went to him and tilted her head up for a kiss. "We're going to dog-sit."

It had been years since Brooklyn had been on an airplane, and she'd found her passport though there was only six months left on it. Now she was buckled into her seat, preparing for landing at Newark airport.

The flight had been full, and since being trapped with no way out was one of the things that ramped up her anxiety, she'd spent most of the flight listening to a calming meditation app. It had helped.

With a couple of light bumps, they were on the ground, and before she knew it she'd grabbed her carry-on bag and was following the signs for ground transportation. She could do this. She could not hide forever, and this was a normal thing for most people.

It was better in the cab. The crush of people was held at bay and once she gave the driver the address, she sat back and watched the scenery as they left New Jersey for Manhattan. By ten thirty, she was dropped off outside a massive skyscraper. Inside were the executive offices of Abbott Industries, and Cole was in there, too. He didn't know she was coming. She'd thought about calling him, but then didn't want to in case she couldn't go through with it. Or…for him to tell her not to. She shouldered her bag, straightened the thick wrap she wore, and made her way inside.

One step closer.

Up the elevator, ten, twenty, twenty-five floors…

The doors opened and she thought she might be sick. Instead, she took a deep inhale and stepped off the elevator. She'd tackled some big things. She'd got on a plane and come here, faced crowds and a bit of the unknown and all because Cole Abbott might just be in love with her…and it was time she started living her life instead of settling for half of one. It had taken Cole to shake her out of that, so why would she let him slip away without fighting for him?

"May I help you?" The receptionist's voice was warm and pleasant, and Brooklyn stepped forward.

"Oh, yes, I'm sorry. I'm here to see Cole Abbott."

"Do you have an appointment?"

"No, I'm afraid I don't." Oh, Lord, what if he wasn't in the office today? Or stuck in meetings?

"He's in a meeting at the moment, but I can let him know you're here. It might be a bit of a wait, I'm sorry."

"I don't mind."

"Your name, please?"

More misgivings. What if this woman said her name and he didn't come out? "Brooklyn Graves," she answered, that sick feeling overtaking her again. What was she even doing here?

Then she straightened her shoulders and lifted her chin. She was here because for the first time in the past several years, something was more important to her than protecting herself. It was time she listened to her heart. And her heart said that there was something between her and Cole that was special, and that she'd been a fool to send him away as she had.

She kept going back to what Raelynn had said—that deep down they were the same sort of person, and the rest was just trappings. God, she hoped so.

So she waited in the seating area, dressed in a hand-knit shawl and clutching her ancient carry-on bag, daring to hope.

She didn't have long to wait. Cole came rushing around the corner, his tie slightly askew, his hair ruffled. His gaze clashed with hers and he stopped abruptly and stared.

"It is you. I couldn't believe it when I got the message."

Brooklyn was light-headed and her knees shook as she stood. "She said you were in a meeting. I didn't want to interrupt. I can wait…"

He shook his head. "No, the meeting can wait. We'll break until this afternoon. Come with me so we can talk."

She followed him down the hall to an office that was as big as her living room and kitchen combined. There was a massive desk on one side of the space, so neat and tidy she wondered if it was just for show. There was also a credenza and a five-foot filing cabinet, all in the same rich wood. In front of the desk was a smaller table with four chairs around it, as if for a small working group.

The other side of the office was made for comfort. There was a sofa, a couple of chairs, a beautiful glass-topped table; a couple of tall plants added some warmth to the space, and there was artwork on the walls. Best of all was the view of the river. She went to the window and stared out. This was such a different world from her own, but she found herself intrigued nonetheless.

"Surprised?" he asked.

"No." She turned and offered a small smile. "But then, I have no frame of reference, really. Other than, I don't know, movies."

He chuckled, and his eyes softened. "God, it's good to see you." Her throat tightened, and she was about to respond when he added, "What are you doing here?"

This was the moment to be brave, wasn't it? She'd come all this way, stepped out of her comfort zone, to be able to say the words she'd rehearsed. And now they were all gone.

His smile faded. "Is there something wrong? Did something happen?"

"Oh, no! Nothing like that. I'm just…now that I'm here I'm not sure how…" She sighed, met his gaze. "You were right, Cole, and I was wrong."

Lines furrowed his brow. "Wrong about what?"

She took a step forward, her pulse hammering with nerves, her breath short but feeling like she was on a train picking up speed, and no choice but to just go where it led. "About us. About me. You offered me something that I didn't know how to accept. That I was afraid to accept, because it meant leaving my comfortable, safe life behind." She ran her fingers through her hair. "Oh, Lord. What was I gonna do? Stay on that island forever, so I never had to put myself out there? How ridiculous."

He took two strides and took her by the hands. "Not ridiculous. You went through something life-altering, and you sought out comfort. How can I judge you for that when I did the same thing?"

"You did?"

"Sure. What did I do after my dad died? I buried myself in work until I couldn't hide from things anymore. And I thought I'd come a long way, but then there was you. I've never met anyone like you, Brooklyn. And yeah, maybe you were playing it safe, but you also know how to find joy in small things, to appreciate the simple, to value what money can't buy. You were so good for me, how could I not fall for you?"

The anxiety fluttered away, but her pulse was still racing, this time with hope and anticipation. "Raelynn said that we are similar underneath the obvious differences. I still don't know how to exist in your world. Maybe I'll never fit in. But Cole, I want to try. You changed everything this fall. Ever since the robbery, I've merely existed. But with you, I felt so alive. So I'm here to say that if you still want to give us a chance, I'm in. You might have to be patient with me, is all."

His smile grew until he was practically beaming. "You mean that."

"I got on a plane and braved the big city to find you. Would I have done that if I didn't mean it?"

"I'm sorry that you're still afraid—"

She waved him off. "No, don't be. The truth is, I'm still afraid because I've never made myself face it. I couldn't face so many things. I alienated people. I don't speak to my siblings enough, or my parents. I hide out on the island saying it's all nostalgia but it's not. Don't get me wrong, I love what I do. But that's not the same thing, is it?"

He shook his head. "It's not. I love what I do, too. But it's a lonely thing going it alone. And any time I was with you, everything was brighter. I wasn't lying, Brooklyn. I fell in love with you."

"I fell in love with you, too. I was just doing what I always do—be scared. I think I'd like to try something different now."

He wrapped his arms around her and held her close. "That's such good news," he whispered, kissing her hair by her temple. "Oh, Brooklyn, I've really missed you these past few weeks."

"Me, too. I moped around all the time. Tried convincing myself that I'd been right, sending you away. I'm going to be honest. It didn't take much convincing on Raelynn's part. She played matchmaker, but I didn't make it very hard for her."

"Remind me to give her a raise," he said, hugging her tightly.

"She and Dan are keeping Marvin while I'm here," she replied. "You blew into my life with your big real estate offer, but I ended up with two new friends, too."

Cole leaned back a little and looked into her eyes, then kissed her. A "Welcome home" kiss, a "Thank God you're here" kiss, an "I love you" kiss. Nothing had ever felt so good, so beautiful, so very right.

And when he let her go, she put her hands on either side of his face and smiled at him, tears gathering at the corners of her eyes. "I want to stop being afraid. I want to make you proud and fit in, but I don't want to lose myself. You can understand that, right?"

"Of course I can." He put one of his hands over hers. "I'll tell you something Jeremy and Bran don't know. When I had my breakdown, I started seeing a therapist to help me navigate my way out of the darkness. If you're willing, we can get you some help, too. Your fears are real, sweetheart. But you don't have to figure it out alone."

She nodded, so very, very touched, particularly that he'd made himself vulnerable, too. "I did some counseling after the robbery, and it helped, but it wasn't enough. I've always known that, deep down."

"Then I'll support you with whatever you need." He squeezed her fingers. "And that is not contingent on us being together, okay?"

He was such a good person. To think she'd thought him an arrogant billionaire flaunting about in his helicopter. He was so, so much more.

Then he kissed her again. "To be honest, if you hadn't shown up here, I was going to head back to the island soon. I know I left in a huff. I wanted to try again, to talk, to see if we could find a way through it. But I'm not complaining that you beat me to it."

He smiled again, then led her to the sofa and they sat. "I think if you're up to it, you should have a nice visit here for a week or two, and then go back to the island. You'll be missing Marvin, I'm sure. And I'll be joining you a week or so after that."

"You will?" She was thrilled.

"My mother is getting married, and I've convinced her to spend a few days with Edward at the house. That is, if you don't mind me bunking in with you."

Of course she didn't mind.

"They're honeymooning in Nova Scotia in November?" She faked a chill and laughed. "How'd that happen?"

"Oh, don't be silly. They're spending a few nights there. Then they're off to Italy for three weeks."

"And you're okay with the new man?"

Cole nodded. "I've known him my whole life. It's a long story, but it explains so much of my childhood. She came to see me, and she really talked to me for the first time. I'm starting to let go of a lot of my resentment. And it made me miss you even more. My parents didn't have warmth in their marriage, but I feel it every time we're together. We have something special, Brooklyn."

"We do," she answered. "More than I ever dreamed possible."

CHAPTER FIFTEEN

FOR THE FIRST time since the island had been settled, there was a wedding on its shores. The May sun was shining, the gulls were calling, and the waves were sending little frothy fingers over the sand as Brooklyn walked barefoot toward Cole, holding a bouquet reminiscent of wildflowers—baby pink roses, marguerites, baby's breath, purple clover. It was as wild and simple as she was, perfectly suited for an island bride on her wedding day.

He was waiting, in a suit the color of the sand beneath her feet, his brilliant blue eyes crinkling at the corners as he smiled at her walking down the "aisle." Her dress flowed softly around her curves, the silk caressing her skin as the breeze off the ocean fluttered the fabric around her legs. She'd anticipated the wind, so she'd left her hair mostly down in tumbling waves, except for a little from each side pulled back to anchor the frothy veil now billowing behind her.

For a simple look it had cost a fortune, but Cole's mother had insisted on taking her shopping in New York. She'd invited Brooklyn's mother along, as well, and while Brooklyn had been apprehensive about it, the two had gotten along just fine.

It seemed that Brooklyn sometimes erected barriers when there were none.

Now she was nearly to Cole, her heart bursting, wondering how on earth she'd got this lucky. Raelynn had preceded her up the aisle in her own dress of blush pink that matched the pale tea roses in their bouquets. Branson was Cole's best man, while Jeremy had performed usher duties and Dan was in charge of Marvin, who wore a white bow tie for the occasion.

Nearly there now, where the officiant waited. Past Jen and Delilah from the yarn store, past Branson's new wife, Jessica, who was expecting their first child, past Tori and Jeremy and her family and Cole's mother and her new husband.

And then she was there, standing beside him, reaching for his hand.

She'd moved her engagement ring to her right hand, and he toyed with it now, turning the stone in his fingers—a whopping two-carat cushion cut with a diamond-encrusted band that had nearly blinded her when he'd opened the box.

And then she met his gaze and was lost. Everything disappeared—the guests, the wind and the gulls and the ocean and there was just him, loving her, and her loving him, and the person in front of them, joining them to each other forever. Her lower lip wobbled as she said her vows; his voice was strong and clear as he made his promises. He slid a wedding band over her finger, and she did the same, pushing the platinum circle over his knuckle until it nested perfectly where it would remain. And then they kissed, and her veil whipped around her head, enveloping them in a curtain of tulle as a cheer went up from the small assembly.

Marvin barked at the commotion, and Brooklyn hadn't believed until this moment that it was possible to be this happy.

Back at the house, tents were set up and tables were covered with fine white linens and bouquets of flowers matching the one in her hand. A photographer took photos in the gardens and on the staircase in the house, and then they joined the guests who were mingling with cocktails. A delicious aroma rose from a line of chafing dishes; Cole had insisted on bringing his favorite caterer from New York to prepare the feast for the gathering, and even the cocktail hour was nothing short of amazing, with magnificent crab cakes, smoked salmon, asparagus tips wrapped in prosciutto, and a wine list that would grace the finest Michelin-starred establishment.

The dinner to follow was no less perfect, with lobster bisque, filet, and a crème wedding cake with fresh strawberry filling.

And through it all, Cole held his wife's hand as often as possible. Brooklyn had never felt so adored.

And when the evening descended, Brooklyn changed into a going-away dress. The guests would all remain on the island for the night, comfortably ensconced in the beautiful rooms of the mansion. Meanwhile, Dave and his helicopter flew in to escort them away for their wedding night. He took them back to the site of their last helicopter trip, the tiny Liverpool airport, where a chartered plane waited to take them to Martha's Vineyard. They'd spend a week there, hidden away from the world.

Brooklyn fell asleep, her head against Cole's shoulder as they made their way over the dark ocean to their honeymoon site. She woke when they landed and smiled bashfully as he kissed her hair. "Glad you had a refresher," he whispered. "Our night is just beginning."

Heat crept up her cheeks, the delicious sort. He was right, of course. But while they'd planned their day to the last detail, she still had one surprise left. A wedding present he was not expecting.

She waited until they were in the suite. Despite the coolness of the evening, Cole had opened the door to the private balcony just a little so that the light curtains ruffled and the scent of the ocean came inside. The room was lovely, all white and china blue, an oasis of calm and relaxation where they could settle into their first married days together. Cole stripped off his tie and his suit jacket, hanging them over a chair. He looked delicious in wrinkled trousers and his white shirt open at the throat. And they'd make the most of the king-size bed, she was sure of it.

As if reading her thoughts, he crossed the room and gathered her in his arms, then kissed her, holding nothing back. When he let her go, she was rather dizzy from it all, and looking forward to the rest of the night. But she put a palm on his chest and willed herself to calm.

"Wait," she said softly. "I have a wedding gift for you, and I've been waiting all day to give it to you when we were alone."

"Oh?" He waggled his eyebrows. "Tell me it's some skimpy lingerie under that dress."

She laughed. "That, too. But this is something else. Something special." She reached into the pocket of her new carry-on bag and took out a thick envelope.

"What's this?"

"Open it and find out."

He sat down on the edge of the bed and slid open the seal. Brooklyn watched as what the papers represented registered, and his gaze darted up to hers. "This is the deed to the house and your land."

"Now it's our house and our land. All you have to do is sign."

He stared at the sheaf of papers again, as if he couldn't quite believe it. "But Brooklyn, that's yours. It's been in your family for generations."

Oh, the dear man. She went to him and sat beside him on the mattress, and put her hand on his knee. "You silly fool. After today, you're my family. Now the whole island is back where it belongs. With one owner, one who loves and cherishes it."

For the past six months she'd discovered the true depths of her love for Cole. There had been moments where she wasn't sure she could handle city life and the demands that went along with his status, but she'd adjusted. She'd started going to therapy again, too, rather than hiding away and denying her fears. But the island was still their place, where they'd met and fallen in love and the place they loved most of all. It would be a summer home for them, a vacation house and a refuge when they needed time away. And someday, their children would run along the beach and collect driftwood and they'd go out and fish for pollock and mackerel.

"Sweetheart. This is just…thank you. Thank you for trusting me with it, for sharing this with me."

"I thought we could stay in the big house and Dan and Rae could have the house if they wanted it. Like you originally planned."

"Are you sure? You have so many memories there. I remember you saying you wouldn't take two million dollars for the house and land. But here you are just… giving it to me."

"That's because I got something much more valuable than two million dollars," she whispered, snuggling close. "I got your heart. And my love, I can't put a price on that. It's worth everything."

"I love you, Mrs. Abbott." The letter dropped to the floor as he pulled her into his arms.

"And I love you, Mr. Abbott. Happy wedding day."

* * * * *

COMING TO A
CROSSROADS

MARIE FERRARELLA

To
Charlie
Whose Kisses Still
Make the World
Fade Away

Prologue

The waitress carefully placed the two steaming cups of coffee on the table, setting one in front of each woman, then took a step back.

"Sure I can't interest either one of you ladies in a sweet roll or a doughnut?" she asked, looking from one woman to the other. "They were just baked this morning, and I can personally testify that they're absolutely heavenly."

Cecilia Parnell knew her friend Ruth was eager to be alone with her so that she could tell her what was on her mind. Instinct told Cilia that this had nothing to do with the house-cleaning business she'd built from the ground up and now ran with the help of a small squadron of exceptionally competent workers.

"Perhaps later," she told the waitress with a warm smile.

The waitress nodded. "I'll check with you then," she said and withdrew.

The moment she did, Ruth Bellamy sighed and leaned in over the small table. She had picked up a napkin even before the coffee had been brought to their table and she had begun working at it. She had quickly reduced the napkin into something resembling confetti.

When she spoke, Ruth's voice quivered with emotion. "I've never thought of myself as one of those mothers."

"One of those mothers?" Cilia questioned, waiting for her friend to elaborate, although she had a sneaking suspicion she knew what Ruth was trying to say and where this was all headed.

Ruth nodded, her fashionably styled silver-gray hair moving ever so slightly first against one cheek and then the other.

"The ones who interfere with their children's lives. Not that Liz has been a child for a long time." A bittersweet smile curved her lips as she recalled earlier times. "She wasn't even one when she *was* a child." Pride entered her voice. "She was the responsible one, always so serious, always so willing to shoulder responsibility—*more* than her share of responsibility," Ruth qualified, looking both proud and embarrassed at the same time.

Ruth blinked back tears, the shredded napkin in her hands now utterly useless.

Without a word, Cilia took a silk handkerchief—a recent gift from her daughter—out of her purse and handed it to Ruth. The latter took it and dried her eyes, then pressed the handkerchief back into Cilia's hand.

"I don't know what I would have done without her these last few years. She put her plans for college on hold without even telling me so that she could get a job and help me handle all those hospital and medical bills from Howard's treatment."

A sad smile curved the corners of the attractive widow's lips. "You'd think there'd be some sort of an unspoken understanding that said that if the patient didn't make it, the grieving family left behind was absolved from having to pay off the rest of the outstanding bills." Ruth was doing her best not to cry again. "It's only fair. I mean, they didn't live up to their part of the bargain. They didn't save him, so why should we…?"

She stopped abruptly, as if suddenly realizing

what she was saying. Ruth flushed. "I'm sorry. I didn't mean to carry on like this. I guess I'm still dealing with my own emotional fallout." She took a deep breath and then let it out slowly. "I'm afraid I'm not ready to deal with Howard's passing yet."

Leaning over the table, Cilia put her hand over her friend's, infinite comfort in the small gesture. "I understand, Ruth. Believe me, I understand. When I lost my husband, it felt as if I was the only one in the world who had gone through this kind of tragedy. I promise it'll get easier. Not immediately, but slowly, bit by bit, it will. You won't stop missing him, but it will get easier," she told the other woman.

Ruth took in another long breath. "I didn't ask you to meet me for coffee to come apart in front of you like this."

Cilia smiled understandingly and did her best to sound encouraging. "I know. Take all the time you need, dear."

Ruth framed her coffee cup with her hands, drawing in the warmth. She carefully took a long sip, hoping that would somehow help steady her nerves. To an extent, it did.

"Anyway, what I was trying to say is that Lizzie put her whole life on hold to help me deal with the bills and, eventually, with Howard's loss.

He was her stepfather," she said even though most of her friends had known that. "But he adored her, and the feeling was mutual. He was better than her own father had been." For a moment, she allowed herself to reflect on the past.

"I know," Cilia told her quietly.

"Howard was always able to talk to Lizzie even when I couldn't—not that she was ever a problem," Ruth said quickly, "but she was kind of headstrong and, well—" she shrugged haplessly "—you know what it's like between mothers and daughters."

Cilia smiled and nodded, her own set of memories slipping in. "Oh, I know, Ruth. Believe me, I know."

"Anyway, she worked really hard to make sure all of the bills were paid off before they got out of control. Because of that, she didn't have any kind of a life. She certainly didn't have anything that could have remotely passed for a social life. By now, she should have had her degree and gotten not just her MRS but her MOM as well," Ruth said, a fond expression on her face.

"Does she want those?" Cilia asked, thinking that perhaps her friend was putting her own hopes and dreams on her daughter. It had been known to happen. These days, not every woman wanted to sacrifice a career for raising a family.

"More than you could possibly guess," Ruth told her with feeling as she thought of her daughter. "But when Howard got sicker, she just pushed all that to the side. She took any job she could, holding down two and at times three part-time jobs so I could be at Howard's side. Well, those bills are finally all paid off now, but my debt certainly isn't."

"You're referring to your debt to your daughter," Cilia guessed knowingly.

Ruth nodded. "I most certainly am. I feel that because of her huge heart, which had her doing—as she put it—the right thing, I owe Lizzie as much as I can provide toward helping her get that college degree. But most of all, I owe her that home and family she couldn't even let herself think about because of what she felt was her obligation."

Ruth looked at her friend. "But in order to do that, I need help. Professional help. *Your* help."

Cilia knew the woman was referring to what she and her two best friends did as a sideline. Matchmaking. She nodded.

"Let me see what I can do," she promised Ruth. "And I'll get back to you."

"I have suggestions," Ruth added, an eagerness entering her voice.

This time it was Cilia who took a deep breath,

bracing herself. "I'm sure you do." Cilia turned and looked around for the waitress. Spotting the woman, she waved for her to come to their table.

As soon as she was close enough, Cilia said, "I think I'll have that sweet roll now."

The waitress beamed.

Chapter One

"I think I have a perfect match for the right lady!" Maizie Sommers declared before Cilia and Theresa were halfway across the threshold into Maizie's cozy, sun-drenched home.

Cilia had called her friends less than an hour ago, asking if the three of them could get together for a game of poker. Maizie had been thrilled, because she was just about to call *them*, inviting them over for the very same reason. Not that they actually played. The cards were just something for their hands to do while they talked over possibilities.

She could barely contain herself until her friends had arrived. The promise of matchmaking, of bringing two kindred souls together, had that kind of an effect on her.

Hearing Maizie's greeting, Cilia's mouth dropped open. "I haven't even told you why I asked you to call Theresa and make arrangements so we could hold our poker game here this evening," she complained.

Maizie led the way to the small gaming table. Along with a deck of cards and chips, there were three tall glasses of lemonade, one at each place setting.

"You don't have to, dear," Maizie told her friend. "We all know where this is heading." Sitting down, she smiled at Cilia as the latter and Theresa each pulled out a chair and followed suit. "You run a house-cleaning service. If Ruth wanted to talk to you about availing herself of your services for a thorough spring cleaning, you wouldn't have called me to find out if I was free to host a poker game at my place today."

"Maizie's right," Theresa said as she automatically picked up the deck from the center of the table and began dealing out the cards. "The only time we play this game is when we're brainstorming about possible matches because one of us has been approached by a concerned parent—usually a mother," she added with a knowing smile. Her blue eyes met Cilia's. "You can't deny that."

"I'm not *trying* to deny that," Cilia insisted. "I just wanted to be able to give you the full impact of Ruth Bellamy's request." She looked toward the woman who was responsible for initially forming their little extracurricular club. "Usually it's Maizie who brings us someone to match. Occasionally, it's you, Theresa. I guess I just wanted to savor my moment so I could balance out the tears."

Theresa put down the remaining deck of cards. "Tears?" she questioned, concerned. Of the three of them, Theresa was the most empathetic.

As usual, Maizie was more precise with her questions. "Whose tears?" she asked. The cards were forgotten for the time being. "Cilia, did someone make you cry?"

"No," Cilia replied, agitated that she wasn't making herself clear. "Ruth Bellamy was the one who was in tears."

"So I take it that she's still adjusting to having lost Howard?" Maizie asked sympathetically. She assumed that the answer to that was yes and went on from there. "She's had a long time to prepare herself for that inevitability—Howard's been gone for almost a year—but we all know it's never easy no matter how prepared you think you are," she said, putting into words what she knew in her heart the other two women were thinking.

"Granted," Cilia agreed, inclining her head. "But her tears were actually because of Lizzie."

"Lizzie? Really? I thought that her daughter was finally going to college at this point," Maizie said, slightly puzzled.

Cilia looked at her friend, astonished. When they had gotten together today, Ruth had made it sound as if this was the first time she'd talked about this situation to anyone. She should have known, Cilia thought. "You know everything, don't you, Maizie?"

Maizie neither confirmed nor denied her friend's supposition. She merely said, "I'm in the real estate business, Cilia. I hear things."

"Obviously," Cilia said with a sigh. "Well, anyway, Ruth feels extremely guilty because Lizzie, to put it in Ruth's own words, 'put her whole life on hold' in order to help her pay off all of Howard's remaining medical bills—which I gathered were substantial."

"I wish she had said something to one of us at the time," Theresa commented. "We could have held some sort of a fund-raiser for her, helped her defray at least some of the cost."

Although she agreed with Theresa, Maizie waved her hand at her friend's wishful thinking. "She's an extremely proud woman. And besides, that's all water under the bridge right now," Maizie told her friends. "What we *can* do now is find that sweet, selfless young woman someone who's worthy of her. Which brings me back to what I said when you first walked in. I think I know just the right young man for Lizzie, as it turns out."

Cilia laughed as she shook her head. "Of course you do."

"Because I'm in such an incredible mood, I'll overlook that slight sarcastic note in your voice," Maizie told her friend good-naturedly.

"Okay, I'll bite. *Why* are you in such an incredible mood?" Cilia asked, playing along.

Maizie was fairly beaming. "As it happens, my daughter paid a visit to my office this afternoon."

Theresa brightened at the mention of Maizie's daughter. "How are Nikki and that handsome husband of hers? Are they looking for a new house again?" she guessed, thinking that perhaps their family was expanding again and they would be needing more bedrooms soon.

"No," Maizie said, her eyes sparkling. "As it happens, Nikki asked if I—if *we*," she corrected herself pointedly, "could possibly use our 'collective magic' to find a match for this doctor friend of hers, who I gather she has recently taken under her wing."

"Collective magic of ours," Cilia repeated, rolling the phrase over on her tongue and smiling.

"I like the sound of that," Theresa said with an approving nod.

But Cilia was nothing if not all business, and she asked, "Why can't this doctor friend of Nikki's find someone on his own? What's wrong with him?"

"Nothing's wrong with him," Maizie said, coming to the stranger's defense as was her habit. "As a matter of fact, listening to Nikki, he sounds practically perfect. Once he was finished with medical school, his internship and his residency, becoming a general surgeon, he decided to offer his considerable services to a free clinic—which was when his fiancée of four years decided to dump him."

"Dump him?" Theresa cried, the game they were supposedly playing completely abandoned now. "Why in heaven's name would she do that?"

"She didn't want to have to help him pay off his student loans?" Cilia guessed.

But Maizie shook her head. "According to Nikki, it seems that the fiancée was counting on the young doctor to be able to support her in the lifestyle she has become very accustomed to." She could see that her friends weren't seeing the connection. "Apparently her father runs a prestigious medical practice in Beverly Hills. Everything was in place for Ethan to join the practice once he was finished with his studies."

"And he decided not to," Theresa concluded.

"I like this boy already," Cilia declared, nodding her head in approval.

Maizie's smile was bright enough to rival the sun. "I knew you would," she said. "Now," she continued, clapping her hands together as she turned toward Cilia for confirmation, "if memory serves, didn't Lizzie drive an independent cab service part-time? Chariot, right? Please tell me she still does," she implored.

Cilia nodded. "As a matter of fact, she still does. According to Ruth, Howard's bills are all paid off now, but Lizzie is still driving because now she's using that to help pay for her college tuition while she's taking her courses. Ruth said that Lizzie feels the Chariot job gives her flexibility."

"Why do you care if she's still a Chariot driver? He's a doctor—surely he has his own car," Theresa pointed out, not able to see how their friend's daughter's job made a difference in this scenario.

"Oh, he does," Maizie assured the other woman. "Although it's not exactly the latest word in automobiles. It's secondhand. His pride prevented him from letting his fiancée buy him a car she told him she wanted to be seen in."

"Better and better," Cilia murmured, underscoring her approval.

"And we know how unreliable these used cars can be," Maizie continued with a broad smile. "Anyway, long story short, Ethan and a couple of his friends are throwing a bachelor party for another friend who's getting married very soon, according to Nikki."

When Maizie paused to allow her words to sink in, Cilia urged, "Go on."

"Well, we all know how especially strict the 'don't drink and drive' laws are here, especially in Bedford. Landing in jail wouldn't be an auspicious way to end a party or a notable way to begin anything else, either." She smiled, seeing that her two friends looked as if they understood perfectly. "When she sees Ethan, Nikki is going to tell him to make sure that he calls a Chariot driver if he and his friends wind up inebriated and need a ride from the club."

"Club?" Theresa questioned, the single word all but throbbing with interest.

Maizie nodded. "Yes, dear, it's one of *those* places. Very popular with bachelors in search for a last hurrah before pledging their troth and undying love to their bride-to-be."

Theresa laughed. "You don't have to dress it up in fancy words, Maizie. I *do* know what bachelor parties are like these days," she told the unofficial leader of their group.

"No disrespect was intended, dear," Maizie replied, patting her fellow conspirator's hand. "So, let's get down to the particulars and make sure that we have a winning couple before we set these wheels in motion, shall we, ladies?" She glanced at her two best friends, waiting for a go-ahead signal, although she already sensed that they were both on board.

It was safe to say that while Maizie did have a remarkable ability to read the people she dealt with in her chosen line of work, the two people she knew best of all in the world were the two women who were sitting right here at her gaming table.

Their friendship dated back to the third grade, when she and Cilia came to a seven-year-old Theresa's rescue in the schoolyard. At the time she was being bullied by a small circle of so-called popular girls who felt they had the right to make themselves feel superior by making the diminutive Theresa feel inferior.

Maizie, with Cilia backing her up, put them all in their place.

And so their lasting friendship was born. Over the years, they had seen one another through a few bumpy, nonproductive romances before they each found lasting love that led to marriages, the latter giving every indication of lasting forever. And they did to the very end.

Maizie, Theresa and Cilia were there for each other for the births of their children and all the joys and heroic acts of patience all that involved. They were also there to hold trembling hands when each of them went through what felt like the ultimate, unimaginable heartbreak when first Maizie, then Cilia and finally Theresa lost the men they had thought would be with them forever.

They were also there to bolster and support one another when each nervously started their very own businesses in order to provide monetary support for their individual families after their husbands had died.

Maizie could truly say that no one knew her better than Theresa and Cilia, and she felt that they could honestly say the same about her.

While they weren't actual sisters by virtue of blood, they were even closer than sisters because of everything they had gone through and weathered together.

"You know what's necessary," Maizie said rhetorically to Cilia. "We'll need a list of interests, photos and assorted information to pull this off."

Theresa nodded, the corners of her mouth curving. "In other words, the usual."

Maizie's smile was even wider. It was almost as if she didn't really need to put things into words anymore. "The usual," she echoed.

Their individual businesses reflected their personalities and their strong points. Maizie had gravitated to real estate, turning a one-woman office into a thriving business, while Theresa took her love of baking and expanded it, discovering to her delight that the public was more than willing to pay to sample her delicious baked goods. They were even more willing to pay to have her cater their parties and gatherings.

Cilia's talent was a love of neatness and organization, which she perfected and brought to other people. Those businesses, in turn, provided food and shelter for their families. It also created a feeling of satisfaction for each of them.

But what provided food for all three of their souls—completely without any monetary compensation whatsoever—was what they had initially done for each of their children: finding a match for them when they were far too busy to do any sort of looking on their own.

Because each of these four matches had turned out so well and so incredibly satisfyingly, Maizie and company haltingly decided to expand their base of operation just a little—strictly as a hobby. A sideline to nurture their souls and make them feel good about themselves.

Little by little, word spread about the dedicated career women who also had some sort of special insight when it came to making lasting matches. It wasn't long before concerned and worried mothers sought them out, as did the occasional father.

And the most amazing thing about this whole sideline hobby of theirs was that out of all the matches they had instigated, all the couples they had "magically" brought together while pulling strings from behind a curtain, not a single one of these matches had faded away or fallen apart.

Each and every one of them had lasted.

And as Maizie talked with her friends, comparing details, making mental notes, maybe it

was the euphoria of past victories that was in-
fusing her now, but she had a good feeling about
this match that was even now in the making. She
just hoped that she wasn't getting carried away
by the moment and by the fact that her near-to-
perfect daughter had actually come to her and
asked for help with a match, of all things.

History, she thought, looking around at her
friends, was repeating itself.

Dr. Ethan O'Neill fingered the small, lami-
nated business card in the pocket of his sports
jacket. He'd done it two, possibly three times
already, just to assure himself that he still had
the card with Chariot's general number on it. He
worried that it might have fallen out when he
took out his wallet to pay for a round of drinks.
Looking at his friends, he had a growing suspicion that they were going to need the number by
the time the evening was finally over.

He wasn't all that much of a drinker. Back in
his undergraduate days, he'd learned how to *really* nurse a glass of beer, or the occasional glass
of whiskey, for a good part of the evening.

However, Jimmy, Wayne and Pete each had
their own brand of poison, and they were really
knocking back those glasses. As for Joel, the al-

most bridegroom, it had turned out that he had a real fondness for tequila.

Ethan got the feeling that Joel was working up his nerve to walk down the aisle, even though the wedding was nearly three weeks away.

When it came time for yet another round, because he was the most sober one in his small group, he found that he wound up paying more often than the others did. But then, what did he have left to spend money on now that Catherine had terminated their engagement?

At least his friends were still with him. And, drunk or not, their values were a lot less shallow than Catherine's had turned out to be.

He sighed as his hands tightened around his glass. Four years gone, just like that. He wondered if she even missed him.

"Sure I can't talk you into having something with more of a kick to it, buddy?"

Ethan blinked and realized that the bartender, a bald, barrel-chested man in his forties or maybe fifties, was talking to him.

"On the house," the man added with a smile that seemed oddly sunny.

"No, that's okay," Ethan answered. "I'm fine. But I think my friends could probably stand to get refills," he said, nodding in the general direction of the rest of the bachelor party.

"I take it that you're the designated driver?" the bartender asked as he began to refill the other four glasses. "I hate to tell you this, but if you get pulled over for some reason, I'm pretty sure that your blood alcohol level's probably just a little over the legal limit if you get a particularly zealous police officer."

"Not to worry, I've got it covered." Ethan glanced at his friends, who were sounding progressively rowdier and louder. "I've got all of us covered."

The bartender nodded. "You're a good friend."

"Not really. I'm just not in the mood to celebrate," he confessed.

"Then, out of sheer curiosity—if you don't mind my asking—what are you doing here tonight, raising a glass?" the bartender asked.

Ethan shrugged. The breakup was still very fresh in his mind. He knew that Catherine wasn't exactly a selfless soul, but he hadn't thought of her as being heartless. At least, not until recently.

"I gave my word I'd come," he told the bartender. "Didn't seem right not to. The bridegroom needs all the help being propped up as he can get."

The bartender, Harry, nodded. "Like I said, you're a good friend," he declared as he went to fill another patron's empty glass.

"Yeah, that's me, all right," Ethan murmured to himself under his breath as he raised his glass to his lips again. "Mr. Nice Guy."

Chapter Two

If she didn't know better, Liz Bellamy would have said she was sleepwalking, or rather, sleep driving—never a good idea, she mused philosophically.

It was either that or her body was somehow moving in slow motion through a tall vat of molasses. If it wouldn't have created a problem, she would have been tempted to pull over to the side of the road and just grab at least a short catnap before she finally clocked out, turned her car north and headed back to her place for the night.

"Face it, Elizabeth Bellamy, you're not as

young and energetic as you used to be," Liz muttered under her breath.

At almost thirty, she felt that was an exceedingly sad thing to admit to herself. She could remember a time when she used to have enough energy for at least two and a half people. These days there were times when she only had enough energy to sustain half a person—or at least it certainly felt that way to her.

Of course, on the other side of the coin, Liz consoled herself, most of the time she was adhering to a less than sedate pace, which involved going to school and holding down one job, and sometimes two, in order to make those proverbial ends meet.

And one of those so-called ends involved her college tuition, not exactly a small sum by anyone's standards.

Looking back over her day, it had consisted of four classes, the last one of which had run almost twice as long as it was supposed to. Actually, all of the professors who taught classes she was required to take in order to earn her degree seemed to drone on and on endlessly today. After she had numbly stumbled out of her last class, her late afternoon and evening had been no better. This was one of the evenings that she drove for Chariot.

Most of the time she found driving people to their destinations at least passably interesting. Sometimes, depending on the personality of the fare she was driving, she even thought of it as fun. This evening's passengers, however— if she was allowed to rate her fares—wouldn't have even gotten three stars. Not a single one of them. For that matter, a couple of rather boisterous, highly critical fares wouldn't have even received one star.

Especially not the one who had gotten sick in her car. Usually she considered herself to be a very sympathetic person, but this particular fare's unceremonious parting with his meal wasn't the result of the sudden onset of some sort of a flu or bug but the very real result of having just too much to drink, obviously too fast.

The man had been loud and possessed a cutting, viper-sharp tongue, which he only paused using long enough to clear out some apparently much-needed space in his stomach. She could only assume that he was making room for more alcohol. When she got the man to his destination, he grumbled over the charge, threw the money at her and finally piled out of her vehicle, mumbling something about her "doing something about that awful smell." He wound up staggering into some waiting woman's arms.

His wife, Liz guessed by the pained expression on the woman's face. As she drove away, heading for a car wash to clean the mess out of her car, she felt nothing but pity for the poor woman in her rearview mirror.

Yes, Liz thought now with a sigh, she was definitely ready to call it a night and go home. Besides, she reminded herself, she had a test to study for. She needed to get home and to bed so she could get up early—and hopefully bright— in order to study the complex information so it was still fresh in her mind when she took the test.

With all this working and studying she was doing, Liz knew that by a lot of people's standards she was trapped in a rat race. But this was a rat race of her own choosing, and in the end, it would all be worth it. Because she would have finally completed all her courses to get that precious degree she was after—and then she would be growing bleary-eyed putting in long hours in a science lab.

A science lab where she hoped one day, if she was good enough and diligent enough, she would finally be doing something beneficial for humanity. That, to her, meant that good people wouldn't have to die from diseases like the one that had claimed her stepfather years before his time.

"See? You've got your priorities straight." She paused as she came to a light and frowned slightly. "Okay, Lizzie, you're talking to yourself again. Definitely time for you to go home."

As if some unseen force had heard her, her cell phone, the one she kept exclusively for her Chariot job, began vibrating in her pocket. Because the last bunch of fares had been almost noisy enough to wake the dead, she had turned her ringer up to loud so she wouldn't wind up missing a call from her next fare.

However, at this point, there wasn't supposed to be a next fare.

"She's not here," Liz said to the ringing noise, aiming her words toward her pocket. "She went home. Better yet, she died. Let someone else pick up this fare."

The cell phone continued ringing.

A feeling of guilt, possibly thanks to her strict parochial schooling, came out of nowhere and wrapped its tentacles around her so tightly, it began to interfere with her breathing.

"C'mon, give me a break," she all but begged the ringing phone. "Finally!" she declared the second that the phone had stopped ringing.

But the next moment, as if to defy her, the cell began ringing again. Liz rolled her eyes.

"Okay, okay, you win," she cried, pulling out

the phone and putting it on speaker so she didn't have to hold on to it. "Hello, this is Liz, your Chariot driver. Do you need a ride somewhere?" she asked, hoping against hope that this was a wrong number and not someone who needed a ride.

The person would probably ask her to drive them to somewhere in north LA County. With the exception of her last fare—a man who finally rated five stars—all the other fares had been a trial to her patience.

"Yes!" Ethan cried with enthusiasm, happy that the line had finally been picked up.

He had just about been ready to give up and try to call for a cab when the person on the other end had finally answered her phone. Dr. Connors had recommended taking Chariot, and he had found that it was always best to go with someone who had been recommended rather than to just approach this cold turkey. He had never had to use the services of a Chariot driver before.

"My buddies and I need rides home," Ethan told the lyrical-sounding voice on the other end of his cell phone.

Maybe he had had more to drink than he'd thought, because the voice that had answered his call sounded as if it belonged to an angel.

C'mon, Ethan, get a grip. It's a safe bet to

assume that angels don't drive around in Char-
iots. At least not the kind that have an engine
and four tires.

Buddies. Uh-uh, back away now, a little voice
in Liz's head warned. The word *buddies* meant
that there was more than one passenger involved.
Still, she couldn't very well just hang up. She
needed something tangible to go on before she
turned the man down and referred him to someone else.

"Buddies?" Liz repeated. "How many people
is that exactly?"

"Three. Plus me," Ethan answered. "It would
have been four plus me, but the guy we threw
this bash for got a ride from a friend of his."

Ethan didn't add that this friend was a new
friend, nor did he think it prudent to say that the
friend was one of the rather exotic waitresses
at the club they'd gone to. He didn't think that
Joel, once he finally came to his senses, would
really want word of this particular little adven-
ture to get around.

Ethan had already tried to talk Joel out of
letting Cinnamon drive him home, but Joel had
been rather adamant about it, saying that he
knew what he was doing. So, against his better
judgment, Ethan had decided to back off.

"Four?" Liz repeated doubtfully. "I'm afraid

my back seat can only hold three adults." She hoped that the man would take the hint and let her turn him down gracefully. These days it was all too easy to get labeled as being an uncooperative driver, and she didn't need that. But the idea of having to drive to four different destinations wasn't exactly overly thrilling either at this hour.

Ethan laughed. "They're not all that adult," he told her, then realized the woman might get the wrong impression. He definitely didn't want to scare her off. "Don't worry, they're harmless. So am I," he added quickly in case she might have thought he was attempting to put moves on her. "I—"

"Good to know," Liz said, cutting in and still trying to wrap this up, "but that still makes you four adults in the back seat, and you just won't all fit there."

"How about if one of us—if I," he specified, "sit in the front passenger seat? You can fit us all in then, can't you?" he asked. "Full disclosure, the others aren't feeling any pain, but I still can." *That didn't come out right*, he thought, searching for a way to gracefully redeem himself while untangling his tongue. "That is, I mean—"

Maybe she should just pretend to lose the connection, Liz thought. "Well, I…"

Ethan could hear the hesitation in her voice

and the beginnings of a refusal. Suddenly he thought of a way to sweeten the deal and get the driver to say yes.

"How about if we'd each pay separately for the ride? I mean the full fare," he clarified. "Seeing as how you would be dropping each of us off one by one, that would only seem fair, right?"

"Right," she agreed, but money really wasn't the point. "But—" she began to explain again, except she didn't get the chance because the potential fare spoke up again.

"Okay, then it's settled. We're at the corner of Culver and Alton, just past the shopping center," he told her. "We'll be the group of four guys standing in front of Bar None," he added for extra clarity.

"The nightclub," Liz said. She was well aware of the location as well as the kind of nightclub it was.

Ethan was afraid that might be a deal breaker for her. He suddenly wanted to meet this Chariot driver who didn't seem all that interested in making money. After Catherine had run over his heart with a backhoe that left dollar signs in her wake, the thought of someone who *wasn't* shallow or fixated on the accumulation of money intrigued him.

"It's more like a restaurant with poor lighting," he corrected. "So, when can we expect you to get here?"

Jimmy, he thought, glancing over at his friend, was sinking rather fast, and the sooner they got him home, the better.

The word *never* rose to Liz's lips, urged on by self-preservation. She didn't want to be driving around heaven only knew where, dropping off four men who had doubtlessly been partying too hard. Especially not when her body was begging her to call it a night so she could crawl into bed and drop off into unconsciousness in less than sixty seconds.

But although he didn't know it, ultimately this Ethan person had said the right thing. He had appealed to her business sense by offering what amounted to almost four times the fare for what was in essence one long drive.

It was too good to pass up, and she knew it.

Liz did a quick calculation, taking the lack of traffic into account. "I can be there in about fifteen minutes," she told him.

"We'll be right here, waiting. And Liz, thank you," Ethan said just before he hung up.

She couldn't remember a fare ever having thanked her *before* she had arrived.

"Well, at least he's polite," Liz murmured as

she closed her phone and put it on the passenger seat next to her. "That's something."

She reminded herself of all the long hours she had put in, keeping her stepfather company while her mother had taken the time to run a few quick errands. There were times, especially toward the end, when she had stayed up into the wee hours of the night, holding her stepfather's hand and talking to him even after she was certain that the man couldn't hear her anymore and had drifted off to sleep.

"You can do this, Lizzie. Driving four slightly inebriated men home—how long can it take, right?" she asked herself.

Liz didn't bother answering, because deep down, she knew what the answer to that question was. The answer was "long," not to mention that some people would say that she was being uncharacteristically naive.

But she wasn't. If anything went wrong, she could always call the number of the man who ran the local branch of the company. Protective of all the drivers in his branch, Alan Parker had given the emergency number to her as well as to all the other drivers. He referred to it as a 9-1-1 for Chariot drivers in case something went wrong and a fare decided to either pull a fast one by skipping out on paying the driver or, worse, tried to take advantage of one of the female drivers.

Although to her knowledge, since Alan had instituted the 9-1-1 call number, the only driver who had used it was Herb Abernathy when the fare he was driving, a huge, overbearing bull of a man, had attempted—unsuccessfully, as it turned out—to shake him down and steal *his* money.

Liz pulled over at the next light and double-checked her glove compartment to make sure she had the number handy. She did, and looking at it, she committed the number to memory so if these partying bachelors—or whatever they actually were—got too rowdy for her to handle, she could call for help immediately.

She was about to start up her car, then stopped again. *The hell with memory*, she thought. Liz proceeded to program the number into her business phone *just in case*. She had always been a firm believer in better safe than sorry.

Taking in a deep a breath, Liz put the phone within easy reach up on her dashboard. Now she was ready, she thought, starting up her car.

Within minutes, she was less than half a block away from her fare, or rather, her fares. Almost unconsciously, her attention was drawn toward her pocket and the container of pepper spray her mother had insisted she carry with her.

Apparently, her mother had read numerous articles about every single potential warning sign a female Chariot driver should take to heart. By going over a long list of every single thing that could potentially happen to her, her well-meaning mother had managed to rob her of her feeling of confidence, not to mention the feeling that she would be able to protect herself in practically any given situation.

Liz didn't think of herself as a superheroine, but neither did she think of herself as a walking victim with a neon sign flashing on her forehead saying, *Please come save me.*

Rounding the corner, Liz felt that she had spotted her fares: four well-dressed, if slightly disheveled, young men who looked as if they had been partying a bit too hard.

All except one, she amended as she drew closer. One of the men looked to be in better condition than his friends. It was the one with darker hair and really chiseled features. He looked to be slightly taller than the other men around him—although that could have been because he wasn't slouching like the other three, she decided. She had a feeling that he was probably the one who had called her—only because he looked as if he could still make out the numbers on his keypad.

Pulling her vehicle up to the foursome, Liz slowed it down and then came to a full stop. "Did one of you call for a Chariot?"

At the sound of her voice, all four men turned in her direction.

"I didn't, but you are a sight for sore eyes!" one of the slightly fuzzy, bleary-eyed men cried in relief. "Hey, fellas, this means we don't have to walk home," Jimmy announced happily.

"Hey, maybe you were going to walk, but I was going to hitch a ride if push came to shove," Pete told his friends.

"Not me," Wayne announced. "I've got to save up my strength for the wedding."

Jimmy scrunched his eyebrows together as if he was trying to understand what Wayne had just said. "What's that supposed to mean? Why would you need strength?" he asked.

Wayne's grin all but split his face. "In case Stephanie changes her mind about marrying Joel, of course. She's going to need someone to console her," he told the others, his grin turning into an almost moronic smile on his face. "Am I right, Ethan?" He looked over his shoulder at the only silent one in the group.

"You, Wayne, are never right," the man he had

just addressed said good-naturedly. He moved his way to the front of the group. "As you can see," he told Liz, "you came just in time." He glanced at the inebriated group. "A few more minutes and I'm not sure if my friends could pour themselves into your Chariot."

She looked at the group uncertainly. Part of her was entertaining a bad feeling about this venture. "About that…"

Anticipating her taking a pass on driving his friends and him home, Ethan quickly said, "Don't worry, if one of them has an accident in your car, I'll pay to have it cleaned."

She supposed that she couldn't ask for more than that. After all, she didn't want to seem unreasonable, and she had to admit that the guy who'd called her number, asking for a ride, *was* cute.

Liz got out of her car and rounded the hood, then opened up the rear passenger door. "Then by all means, please get in," Liz told the group.

Her eyes met Mr. Tall, Dark and Handsome's vivid blue eyes just as he smiled at her. His dimples shot straight into her heart. "Thank you."

That was the second time he had thanked her tonight, and she still hadn't done anything.

Chapter Three

The next moment, one of the would-be fares, Pete Jones, suddenly sank down and wound up sitting on the sidewalk. He looked as mystified as any of them to find himself in that position. He glared at his friends almost accusingly.

"Hey, how come all you guys suddenly got so much taller than me?" he asked, slurring his words.

The only sober-looking man in the group—the one Liz assumed had called her—leaned over his friend and pointed out, "We're not taller, Pete. You're sitting on the sidewalk."

"Oh." Pete blinked, as if that helped him process the information. "Why am I doing that?" he asked. His bewildered question was punctuated with a hiccup.

Oh dear Lord, what have I gotten myself into? Liz wondered, watching the group to see what would happen next.

"My guess, Pete," Ethan said as he took hold of his friend's arm in order to help him up, "is that your legs couldn't hold you up. Hey, Wayne, Jimmy—" he turned toward the other two men, who, in Liz's estimation, looked just as inebriated as the man communing with the sidewalk "—a little help here?"

"Sure," the thinner of the duo answered, his tongue as thick as Pete's. "What do you…do you want us…to do?" Hiccups broke up his phrasing.

"Help me load Pete into the back of the Chariot," Ethan told the two men.

This man was being incredibly patient, Liz thought. More patient than she was feeling, but he was apparently doing the best he could to manage the situation, so she kept silent.

For now.

Rather than comply, Wayne and Jimmy turned to look at the vehicle with its wide-open rear passenger doors. Jimmy blinked again, as if he was trying to focus his eyes—or maybe his brain.

"You mean you called this for us?" he asked.

"Yes, it's a Chariot, and this lady is going to be driving us home," he said as Pete's knees buckled and he did something resembling a grand plié.

"Her name—name's Chariot?" Wayne questioned, displaying his first glimmer of interest in the driver.

"No, that's the car service," Ethan answered. Struggling to hold Pete upright, Ethan looked apologetically at the driver. "They're not usually like this," he told her. "You wouldn't know it, but they normally hold down very responsible positions in their fields."

"You're right," Liz answered. "I wouldn't know it. Luckily, having a normal IQ is not a requirement in order to ride in a Chariot." She looked uneasily at the man who Ethan had managed to get into an upright position. "He's not going to throw up, is he?" Twice in one day was more than she should have to put up with.

"Lord, I hope not." Ethan looked at his inert friends. "Wayne, Jimmy, c'mon," he urged, a sliver of impatience evident in his voice.

Well, at least he's human, Liz thought, continuing to watch the little floor show before her unfold.

When Wayne and Jimmy looked blankly at

the man who was struggling to hold their friend upright, Liz decided that this wasn't going to go anywhere for at least another few minutes. His friends might well be intelligent, the way he claimed, but right now they were acting dumber than a bag of doorknobs.

With a sigh, Liz circled around her vehicle and crossed toward Ethan and his uncooperative drunken friend. To Ethan's apparent surprise, she leveraged her shoulder under Pete's arm.

"C'mon," she told Ethan.

The relief on Ethan's face was indescribable. "This is definitely service above and beyond the call of duty. Thank you!" Ethan said, genuinely grateful.

"No need to keep thanking me," Liz told him. "I'm doing it so we can get going. I don't want to be out here all night." Her words were punctuated by muffled grunts as she helped Ethan maneuver his friend into the car.

Pete seemed to suddenly come to life. "Oh wow…you smell…good!" He turned his head toward Liz. "Who are…are you?" he asked.

Liz deliberately turned his face away from hers. Pete's breath was practically suffocating her. "I'm your driver."

"She's driving us home, Pete, so behave yourself," Ethan said sternly, hoping that would be the end of it.

Pete hiccuped, and for a second, it looked as if whatever he had just tasted was going to come back up. But then he swallowed. Elaborately.

"You think we...we can...we can go the slow way home?" he asked, attempting what amounted to flirting with the driver.

"Not a chance," Liz answered, glancing at the two men who were still outside the car. They were obviously trying to prop one another up. "Are they going to need a special invitation?" she asked Ethan.

Having gotten his friend into the vehicle, Ethan peered over his shoulder and realized who she was talking about. "Jimmy, Wayne, get into the car. Now!"

"You don't hafta sound like...like a drill sergeant. We're comin'," one of the men mumbled, although it was impossible to say which of them it was.

Liz watched dubiously as the other two men piled almost comically into the back seat, each ineffectively trying to carve out a space for himself. The moment they were finally in, she closed the door and got in behind the wheel. Eager to leave and get this over with, Liz waited until

Ethan was in the front passenger seat and had buckled up his seat belt.

As she started up her car, Liz asked her only lucid fare, "You know their addresses, right? Because I don't think any of these guys could find their way home on a bet right now."

Ethan laughed, grateful she hadn't thrown up her hands and just left them in front of the bar. Given the way his friends were behaving, he really wouldn't have blamed her if she had.

"You're probably right," he agreed. "I'm sorry about them. If there's any damage done to the vehicle, I'll take care of it," he assured her again.

The beautiful driver who had come to their rescue looked at him somewhat apprehensively. "Exactly what do you mean by *damage to the vehicle*?"

The question was no sooner asked than Pete began to make heaving noises.

Liz frowned and looked back at Ethan. She had already had to clean out her car once today, and once was more than enough. "That better not be what I think it is."

"Pete… Pete…gets carsick when…when he's not…sitting in the front," Jimmy managed to get out, gulping in snatches of air.

The idea of having the inebriated man sitting up front with her was definitely not what she had signed on for. But when she looked at the man who was sitting there now, he nodded his head, looking extremely sincere as well as apologetic.

That meant that the guy who had spoken up in the back was probably right, Liz thought and sighed. "I suppose it's worth a try. Put him in the front—but we're driving him home first," she specified.

"Absolutely," Ethan promised. Only then did Liz pull over her car, albeit reluctantly.

Getting out of his seat, Ethan opened the back passenger door. The second he did, Pete all but fell into his arms.

"Are we there yet?" Pete asked, breathing the question against Ethan's chest.

Liz could see that Ethan was trying not to breathe as he answered. "Not yet, pal. Just keep everything down a few more minutes, okay?"

"I'm trying, buddy. I'm…trying," Pete slurred, the very picture of misery. He tilted his head back. "But I dunno if I can."

Ethan managed to get his friend into the front seat. Even before he closed the door, Liz asked, "Address?"

He rattled off a local address and closed the front door, then got into the back himself.

Liz started up her car again. "I know a short-cut," she announced. With that, she took a slight detour, driving away from the local street she was on.

Mentally, she crossed her fingers, hoping the man in the front seat would keep everything down in the time it took her to bring him home. To that end, she zipped through a number of lights just as they were about to turn red.

She wound up making it to her destination in what amounted to record time.

Miraculously enough, Pete didn't throw up, although he had made noises to that effect twice.

"I'm impressed," Ethan told her sincerely as he got out of the car.

He quickly hauled Pete out of the front seat. In his estimation, it seemed to be getting easier. Or maybe it was just his adrenaline at work.

"Don't be," Liz told him. "I was inspired."

"Understood. So, what's the fare for getting him from the bar to his apartment?" Ethan asked.

She appreciated that he didn't try to double-talk his way out of their agreement: paying full fare for each trip rather than taking the sum of the distance traveled and dividing it up. She told him what she felt was a fair charge for the distance she'd traveled.

Ethan nodded. "More than reasonable," he

told her. As he fished Pete's wallet out of the man's pant pocket, his friend giggled.

"Hey, I'm…tick…ticklish, man." The next moment Pete was back sitting on the sidewalk, but this time at least it was in front of his garden apartment.

Ethan opened the wallet and found only a dollar. "Hey, Pete, when did you go through all your money?" he asked.

Pete raised his shoulders and then let them drop. "I dunno. At the…the club?" It was a question, not an answer.

Uh-uh. Liz had a bad feeling about this. Part of her wanted to tell the other two men to get out and just drive away from the entire group, chalking it up to a lesson learned. But having watched Ethan looking after his friends—who certainly didn't seem appreciative—softened her. So, against her better judgment, she didn't start up her vehicle and pull away but went on waiting.

Ethan had Pete back on his feet—sort of. "I'll just get him inside and be right back," he promised, indicating the door to his far right.

Liz had no choice but to nod. "Go ahead."

The moment that Ethan managed to reach the apartment door and unlock it, then disappear inside with Pete, Wayne leaned over from the back seat, wrapping his arms around the headrest.

"So, what are you doing later tonight?" he asked Liz. He wasn't slurring badly anymore, but his breath was still very pungent.

Without thinking, Liz answered what she'd been thinking of since before she had picked up the four men. "Getting into bed."

Wayne's arms tightened around the headrest as he tried to lean in closer. "Hey, that sounds good!" He flashed a toothy grin.

"Alone," Liz emphasized sternly.

Wayne looked crestfallen. "You sure you don't want company?"

"Hey, leave the lady alone, Wayne," Jimmy said, speaking up. Just when she thought there was hope for the man, he ruined it by saying, "Can't you see that I'm more her type?"

"I think it's only fair to tell you two that I have a Taser in my purse," Liz informed them in a totally serious voice.

"No, you don't." Wayne laughed. Then, because he wasn't a hundred percent sure that she didn't, he hesitantly asked, "Do you?"

She turned in her seat to look at the two men. "If I take it out, I warn you that I'll be forced to use it."

Jimmy actually looked panicked and almost

sober now. "No, that's okay, that's okay. We don't need to see it. We really don't!"

"You don't need to see what?" Ethan asked, getting into the car again. "By the way, here's Pete's fare," he said, handing Liz the amount she had quoted when she arrived at Pete's address.

The sight of Ethan almost made Liz sigh with relief. She had been bluffing about having a Taser. If the drunken duo had wanted her to show the weapon to them, she wasn't sure what she could whip out of her purse. She had nothing in there that could have looked like a Taser, even to these two intoxicated men.

"Ethan, don't sit too close to her," Wayne hissed as if Liz wouldn't be able to hear him warning his friend. "She's got a Taser." As he told Ethan about the alleged weapon, he was cowering in the farthest part of the back seat.

Ethan raised one eyebrow as he looked at the driver. "Is that so?"

She was not about to lie or deny, not while his two friends were still in the car. So instead Liz said, "I find it keeps people from doing something that neither of us really bargained for."

He was guessing that the Taser didn't exist; however, he wasn't about to bank on that. But he had a pretty good guess why she had threatened them with it. Ethan sighed. "Guys, what did I tell you?"

"We *were* being nice," Jimmy protested.

"Yeah, we were going to have her come partying with us. We're really good at partying," Wayne told her, holding up his right hand as if he was taking an oath.

"Again, I apologize for anything they might have said," Ethan told her.

"You might think about having that put on the front of your T-shirt the next time you go out with these guys," Liz told him. She saw that he was searching for something to say in response and took pity on him. "Just give me their addresses so I can call it a night."

"The driver sleeps alone, Ethan, so there's no use in making any plans," Wayne told him just before he surprised everyone by suddenly passing out in the back seat.

Despite her comment, Ethan said, "Again, I apologize. They're *really* not like this. It's just that they've had too much to drink."

"You think?" Liz quipped. "Never mind, just give me his address so we can drop him off next."

"Are you familiar with the new apartment homes they just finished building last year?

They're located on Oak Street and Lindstrom?" Ethan asked her.

When it came to Bedford, she was familiar with every street, every development and shopping center in the city as well as the immediate surrounding areas. The way she saw it, it was her job, but she didn't bother saying as much to Ethan.

Instead, she said, "Oak Street and Lindstrom it is," and made a right at the next light.

When Liz pulled up in front of the apartment complex, she was on the lookout for the closest entrance. Finding it, she glanced at Ethan, waiting for directions. "Now what?"

"Now I see if Wayne's got any money in *his* wallet and pay you before I get him into his apartment," Ethan told her, getting out of the vehicle. "And you," he warned, leaning in over Jimmy. "I want you to behave yourself—or I'll let her use her Taser on you. Have I made myself clear?"

"Absolutely. You got it, Ethan. Scout's honor." Jimmy all but saluted.

Meanwhile, Ethan had located Wayne's wallet, pulled it out and looked inside. "Looks like we're in luck. Wayne didn't spend everything on entertainment." Counting out a number of bills, he folded them and handed the amount to Liz.

She didn't bother counting the amount—she had watched Ethan do it. "This is too much."

"No, it's not," he told her. "Seeing what you're putting up with, you've earned that and more." He slid the wallet back into Wayne's pocket. The latter didn't seem to even notice. "Be right back," Ethan promised.

"Hey, we going somewhere?" Wayne asked, coming to as Ethan drew him out of the vehicle.

"You are going home and to bed," Ethan told his friend, guiding the stumbling man toward his ground-floor apartment door.

"I am? With who?" Wayne asked, his eyes almost shining.

"Don't start," Ethan warned.

Suddenly, the man was almost weeping. "I miss Cindy," Wayne lamented, referring to the woman he had recently broken up with.

Ethan looked at the man sympathetically. "I'm sure you do. I know how you feel. We'll talk about that next time," he promised as his voice faded behind the apartment door.

Liz caught the tail end of the conversation, and it had her wondering about Ethan.

"Okay, two down, two to go," Ethan announced when he returned to the Chariot less than five minutes later. He began to open the front passenger door, then stopped before he started getting in. "If you'd rather, I can sit in the back again now that there's actually room."

She really didn't mind having him up front. "You might as well continue sitting up front. It can't be that much farther, can it?"

"As a matter of fact, the next stop is only five blocks from here," he told her, then gave her the exact address.

When they got there, Jimmy got out and was wobbly on his feet. As he tried to pay for his ride, he dropped the money and nearly fell over picking the bills up. He bunched them up, quickly paid Liz and then rushed to his door. He looked over his shoulder in her direction twice before getting into his apartment and locking the door.

"I think he's afraid of me," Liz commented.

"Yes, I think so, too," Ethan agreed with a laugh.

She debated with herself for a moment, then decided to go ahead. "If you don't mind me asking—"

"You're entitled to ask anything you want after what you had to put up with tonight," he assured her.

"How did you wind up being friends with those guys?" Liz asked.

"We grew up in the same neighborhood." A

fond smile curved his mouth. "I wasn't always as tall as I am now. Wayne, Jimmy and Pete kept the other guys from beating up on me. I returned the favor by coaching them for their college entrance exams." He looked at her, the infectious smile going right under her skin. "I guess you could say we have history."

She smiled at him. "I guess you could. Okay," she told him, starting up her car again, "let's get you home before it's tomorrow."

Chapter Four

"So," Liz asked as she started up her car to begin the last leg of her trip for the night, "what was the occasion for the celebration? Or was this just a typical guys' night out?"

"No, it definitely wasn't a typical guys' night out," Ethan assured her. "It was a bachelor party."

Liz spared a glance in her lone passenger's direction. "For you?" she asked after a beat. *It figures, all the good ones are always taken.* She saw the guarded expression on Ethan's face and felt that maybe she needed to explain why she had asked the question. "The reason I asked is because you seem oddly sober, especially compared to the rest of your friends. I thought maybe it was because you had to show up lucid and clear-eyed to the rehearsal dinner with your fiancée and her family."

She shouldn't have asked anything. It was late, and she was getting really tired.

"The bachelor party wasn't for me," he told her. "But I did think one of us had to be able to make sense if we got pulled over on the way home. And then I had a couple of shots over the course of the evening and decided that maybe I shouldn't risk it." He laughed softly under his breath. "A DUI wouldn't look good on my record."

"News flash, it wouldn't look good on anyone's record," Liz told him. "At the risk of sounding curious again, just what record are you referring—"

Liz didn't get to finish what she was about to ask, because the word was suddenly replaced by a sudden, loud shriek brought on by surprise. She had always thought of herself as an exceptionally careful driver, but the only explanation for what happened was that she must have driven over particularly sharp broken glass or something of that nature, because out of the blue, she heard the unnerving sound of one of her tires blowing out. Simultaneously, the car lurched to one side.

Gripping the steering wheel, her heart pounding, Liz steered into the swerve. Several nerve-racking moments later—moments that felt as if they lasted forever—she finally managed to prevent skidding, but also prevented what could have been a fatal accident.

She was able to get her car out of the path of an oncoming truck.

Yanking the wheel as hard and as far to the right as she could, she drove them to a safe stretch of land.

Adrenaline pumping wildly through her veins, Liz guided the car toward the far right lane before she finally felt it was safe enough to stop. Her heart pounding in her chest, she pulled up the emergency brake.

For a moment, they both just sat in her car, listening to their hearts pound, neither one saying anything. They were just glad to be alive.

Finally, blowing out a long, relieved breath, Ethan said, "That was probably the most impressive driving I've ever witnessed."

Liz's smile was etched with relief. "You can thank my stepfather for that." The words came out of her mouth before she could think better of them.

"I will," Ethan said with such sincerity, she knew he meant it. "Just tell me where I can find him and I'll thank him in person."

Liz stared straight ahead into the darkness. "You can't."

Ethan could tell from her tone that she wasn't giving him a flippant answer. "Oh."

Wanting to get past the awkward moment, Liz moved on. "*His* father had a farm up north, and we visited there for a month every summer. Howard taught me how to drive on an old car that he proudly told me he rebuilt when he was a teenager. He kept it stored in his father's old barn, and it was his pride and joy. Even so, he taught me how to drive defensively on it because he loved me."

"Sounds like a really great guy," Ethan told her with feeling.

For a second, her smile was far away as Liz recalled those summers they had spent together, before her stepfather had begun to succumb to the disease that finally stole him away from her mother and from her.

"Yes, he was. All right," she said, turning on the hazard lights and taking a deep breath, "I'm going to go assess the damage."

She got out and shut the driver's-side door. When she heard the other door being shut, she realized that Ethan had come out as well.

"I didn't mean for you to come with me," she protested.

He wasn't the type to remain on the sidelines. "I thought maybe I could help," Ethan told her.

By now Liz could see what the damage was. The right front tire had totally blown out.

Right behind her, Ethan let out a low whistle. "Really impressive driving," he repeated, thinking what could have happened to them if she hadn't been as in command of the situation as she was.

"Thanks." Belatedly, Liz looked at her passenger. It was dark, except for the hazard lights, and she really couldn't make out details all that well. "Are you all right? I mean you didn't smack your head or feel as if you got whiplash or anything like that, did you?" He seemed all right, but that could just have been due to the poor lighting. "Maybe you should just sit in the car until I'm finished."

"Finished?" Ethan repeated, confused. "Finished with what?"

"Well, we're not going anywhere until I change that tire," she said, jerking her thumb in its general direction. She paused to peer at him more closely. "Are you sure you didn't get hurt?"

"I'm sure," Ethan told her, more interested in something else she'd just said. "You're planning on changing the tire?" he questioned. "Why don't you just call a towing service? Chariot has to have some sort of contingency for that. They'll come out and change your tire for you."

"They do, but waiting for them to come could take a while," she told him as she popped her trunk. "Besides, I've got everything I need to change a tire right in my trunk."

"I take it your stepfather showed you how to change a tire," Ethan guessed.

"No, he talked me through it, and I changed the tire," she corrected. "Said it would stay with me longer that way.

"Ordinarily, if I had a leaking tire, I would just fill it with that can of compressed air and sealant I have. That's supposed to be good for fifty miles, which is always enough to get me home from wherever I am. But this baby," she said, looking at the shards that were once part of her tire, "it just blew to smithereens, so I'm going to have to take the whole thing off." She walked to the rear of her vehicle and popped the trunk. "Luckily, I have a full-size tire in my trunk, not one of those teeny, cute little pseudo-tires."

The more she talked, the more fascinating Ethan found her. His Chariot driver was unlike any other woman he had ever known.

"You're probably the most resourceful woman I've ever met." As he said that, he took off his jacket and then carelessly tossed it in the car.

"What are you doing?" Liz asked, wondering if she had given him the wrong impression.

Did he think this was an opportunity to do whatever he wanted with her? Other than the truck that had come barreling toward them before she got them out of the way, the road had been fairly deserted in both directions. Liz really wished now that she had signed up for that course in self-defense her mother was always trying to convince her to take. She wouldn't be feeling quite as vulnerable right now.

Grabbing the lug wrench, her fingers tightened around it.

His back to Liz as he assessed the tire again, Ethan said, "Well I'm not about to watch you wrestle with the tire. I *am* bigger than you are."

The man was trying to be helpful. Liz relaxed. But as far as she was concerned, size didn't matter in this case. "Have you ever changed a tire before?" Liz asked.

"No," he admitted. "But I am a fast learner."
He flashed her a smile. "I figure you can talk
me through it, like your stepfather talked you
through it."

Liz sighed. "Look, Ethan, I appreciate the
offer, but—"

"Good. Then let's get to it, shall we?" Ethan
suggested.

She was still very dubious. Maybe the man
was trying to impress her and could wind up
getting hurt in the process. She didn't want that
on her conscience.

"You don't earn your living with your hands,
do you?" she asked.

"No more than anyone else," he said evasively.

Liz noticed that he had avoided her eyes when
he said that, which just raised her suspicions.
"What *do* you do for a living?"

Ethan paused—he could tell she wasn't about
to drop this unless he gave her an answer, and he
wasn't about to lie. For one thing, he had no gift
for lying. He usually stumbled over anything that
took him more than a couple of words to explain
if it wasn't truthful. It was rooted in the fact that
he didn't expect anyone to lie to him, so he felt
that it would be a breach of good conscience to
lie to someone else.

Though he knew he was probably leaving

himself open to a lecture, Ethan told her the truth. "I'm a general surgeon."

Liz's blue-gray eyes widened as his words sank in. "A general— Go sit in the car," she instructed, pointing toward the front seat.

"I'm not a *clumsy* surgeon, I'm a *general* surgeon," Ethan emphasized.

"That may be, but I really doubt that you have to hoist any of your patients up on the table with a jack before you operate on them. A jack could slip if you don't know how to do it right."

She made it sound ominous, Ethan thought. He began to protest that he could handle a jack, but she waved away anything he was going to say.

"Don't worry, I won't think any less of you if you can't change the tire," she assured him.

"*That* wasn't my concern," Ethan informed her. Although, if he was being truthful, that *did* enter into the general framework of the situation.

"Oh, then what was?" Liz asked skeptically.

"I didn't want you to have to struggle getting the blown tire off and the new one on. It doesn't take an Einstein to know those things are heavy," he said. "Now will you *please* just accept my help so we can get the tire on the car and get off this road before some drunk or sleepy driver plows into us?"

Liz sighed. "You do make a compelling argu-ment," she told him, which was her way of apol-ogizing. A half smile curved the corners of her mouth. "You sure you're not a lawyer?"

He shivered as if the very idea left him cold. "Wouldn't be caught dead being one."

"Going counterclockwise, loosen the lug nuts with the wrench," she instructed, then com-mented, "That's a pretty strong opinion. Any particular reason that you feel that way?"

He frowned at her last instruction. "Shouldn't I jack up the car first?"

"Not yet. You have to get the lug nuts loos-ened about one-quarter to one-half a turn," she told him.

"Which is it, one-quarter or one-half?" he asked.

"It varies. Trust me," she said when he looked at her dubiously. "We'll play it by ear. Or, I could just take over—" she offered.

"One-quarter to one-half," he murmured.

"You didn't answer me. Why did you say that you wouldn't be caught dead being a lawyer?" Liz asked.

Busy trying to loosen the lug nuts, the mus-cles in his arms straining so hard he could have sworn he felt each one individually, it took Ethan a minute to answer. He wanted to use words rather than just grunts, and right now all he was capable of was grunting as he worked to get each one of the incredibly tight nuts loose. It was not an easy proposition, getting each of the lug nuts loose.

When he could finally speak, Ethan found himself gasping just a little. "That sounds like something a bartender might say," he commented, sparing her a glance, "not a Chariot driver."

Liz laughed. *Lucky guess*, she thought. "Actually, I'm both—but not at the same time."

At this point, she was crouching beside him in case he needed help or suddenly decided to stop pitting himself against the lug nuts and handed over the wrench to her. But he didn't. He went on fighting the good fight.

Sweat was creasing his brow and looked as if it was going to be sliding into his eyes next. Shifting her weight, Liz pulled out her handkerchief and, very carefully, aware of every stroke, she wiped his brow.

She also managed to startle him a little.

Ethan pulled back his head as if he was getting out of the way of a mosquito, then realized it was the driver, trying to be kind. Because his hands were filthy by now, he didn't try to take the handkerchief from her. Instead, he kept very still for a moment, letting her finish wiping away the perspiration before it could get into his eyes. All the while telling himself that he wasn't reacting to this sweet-faced blonde's touch as he felt her fingers grazing his skin.

"Thanks," he told her when, finished, she bunched up her handkerchief and slid it back into her pocket.

Her smile was quick and fleeting. "Just doing my part," Liz answered. Rising to her feet, she told him, "*Now* you're ready to jack up the car." When he laughed as he got up, she had to ask, "What's so funny?"

"I don't know. It's like I heard a little voice saying, 'Put me in, Coach. Put me in now.'"

"All right, if you say so," she replied, thinking that maybe working with his hands made the man punchy.

Jacking up the car took no real effort at all, especially not after what he'd gone through loosening the lug nuts.

"So, a bartending Chariot driver. How does that happen?" he asked. One by one he worked loose the lug nuts until he had them all the way off.

"It happens when there are college bills to pay," she told him, her voice sounding as if she was distancing herself a little from the conversation.

"Student loans, eh? Those can be brutal," he agreed.

With all four of the lug nuts finally off, Ethan gripped the tire by its treads and slowly pulled the shredded tire off its mount. He set the old tire on its side, then picked up the new tire. He lined up the rim with the lug bolts and pushed the tire into place.

"I think I can see the light at the end of the tunnel," Ethan declared, feeling exhilarated.

"Me, too," she agreed, but her mind was elsewhere. His comment had caught her attention. "How do you get to be a general surgeon without having a staggering amount of student debts to pay off yourself?" she asked. "It's not that I don't believe you." The man was changing her tire. She would have believed that he could walk on water if it meant that he'd get the job done faster. "It's just that I'm curious."

"Scholarships," he answered her, beginning to tighten the lug nuts one by one, first by hand, then using the lug wrench, but only so far. "Lots and lots of scholarships. You'd be surprised how many organizations out there are ready—make that anxious," he amended, "to give away sizable checks to perfect strangers. Not enough to pay for an entire education, mind you," he qualified, "but stitched together, those generous checks can make an impressive dent in those staggering monthly payments. As for the amount that was left over, I picked up a job here and there to fill in the gaps, although," he said, not wanting to give her the wrong impression—the wolf had never been at his door, huffing and puffing, "there weren't too many of those."

"Jobs or gaps?" she asked.

"Gaps," he answered.

She nodded. "So where do you hang your shingle?" she asked. "*Do* people still hang shingles?"

"Probably," he said, working on the last lug nut. "But I don't."

Since he didn't add anything, she took a guess. "Are you part of a group?"

Ethan shrugged, dismissing the small storefront clinic he showed up at religiously. "It's no place you would have heard of."

She took that as his way of closing the subject, so she dropped it, although she was still curious. Noticing that he was finally finished and that the tire was officially changed, she quietly began picking up the tools and deposited them, one by one, back into the trunk of her car.

Securing the jack in its place, she then

reached into the trunk and took out a thermos and a towel. Armed with both, she turned back around to face Ethan.

"Here," Liz announced, holding both items out toward him.

Ethan looked at the offerings, then at her, quizzically. "What am I supposed to do with this?"

"There's water in the thermos," she told him, then prompted, "I'd suggest pouring it on your hands and then using the towel to get some of that grease and dirt off," she said, nodding at his hands. "I've seen my dog looking cleaner after rolling around in the mud. Here, put your hands out, and I'll pour. As a surgeon, scrubbing up must be second nature to you."

Ethan laughed as she splashed water over his outstretched hands. "More so than changing tires. A *lot* more," he said with feeling.

"Well, I really appreciate the sacrifice," she told him.

He let her pour the water on his hands, turning them after a beat until both sides of both hands were wet.

"Well, I got something out of it, too," he said, taking the towel from her.

"Oh, what?"

He smiled at her. "Now I get to put 'changed tire' on my résumé."

She grinned. "Never know when that might come in handy."

Ethan was finished with the towel and handed it back to her. Liz noticed that he had a smudge on his cheek. Dipping the towel into what was left of the water, she proceeded to gently remove the black streak from Ethan's cheek. She wasn't prepared for the simple action to generate a bolt of excitement through her—but it did.

"Now you're clean," she proclaimed, then amended, "Or as clean as you can get without taking a shower."

Ethan nodded. "First thing when I get home. I wouldn't want to scare anyone."

"I really doubt that would *ever* happen, even if you came walking out of the ooze," she murmured under her breath.

"Did you say something?" Ethan asked her as he got back into her car.

"Just that it's getting really late," she answered, saying the first thing that came to her mind.

Sometimes, Liz thought, starting up her car, a girl just had to lie.

Chapter Five

Early Thursday morning, Nikki Connors breezed into the Well Being Clinic's tiny back room, which served as an office for Ethan and whatever doctor had volunteered their services for at least part of that day. Thursdays were Nikki's day.

The tiny room also doubled as a medical storage area, leaving very little room for movement.

"Well, you look none the worse for wear, Dr. O'Neill," Nikki observed, putting down her medical bag on top of what was supposedly a desk. In fact, she thought with a pleased feeling, her friend looked as if he was positively thriving. "I thought you told me that you and some of your friends were throwing that bachelor party for… Joe, was it?" Nikki was doing her best to sound as if she wasn't as invested in Ethan's answer as she actually was. "Did you wind up calling it off?" she asked innocently.

"Oh no, it was definitely on," Ethan told her. "And his name was Joel."

"Joel," she echoed, nodding her head. She pulled up one of the two rickety chairs and sat down. "So, tell me *all* about it," she coaxed. "We've got about ten minutes before Dame Edna throws open the doors and patients start pouring in," she said, referring to the nurse who had come out of retirement to work at the storefront clinic. Lowering her voice, Nikki added, "Don't leave anything out."

There wasn't all that much to leave in, Ethan thought, sitting down opposite Nikki, but he humored the woman he thought of as an older sister.

"Well, Wayne, Jimmy and Pete got *really* soused. And as for Joel, last I saw, he got a ride from the entertainment and went home with her. To be perfectly honest, I'm not sure about the wedding going off as planned."

"How about you?" Nikki asked nonchalantly.

"Did you get soused or were you the designated driver?"

While he answered, Nikki was casting about for a way that her mother and those matchmaking friends of hers could bring Ethan and the Chariot driver together again, so she didn't hear Ethan's response immediately.

"That's no to both," he told Nikki.

Bringing herself back to the present, Nikki blinked. "Come again?"

Ethan smiled. "Well, I didn't get drunk, but I didn't drive the guys home, either."

"Oh?" she asked with what she hoped was just the proper amount of surprise. "Why not?"

"Because I had had a couple of shots," Ethan explained, "and although I didn't feel like I was intoxicated, I really didn't want to take a chance with our safety."

"So what did you do?" Nikki prodded innocently. "Call a friend?"

He laughed. "Anyone I called at that hour of the evening, asking them to pick up three very sloshed guys and me, would not have remained a friend for long. No, I used the Chariot number you gave me," he said, giving credit where it was due. "I'd never used it before, but I have to admit it's pretty efficient. I specified my location and where I want to wind up, and within

minutes, a driver in the area connects with me."
Ethan grinned. "Kind of like a fairy godmother."

Nikki laughed at the image. "Except she comes with a meter instead of a wand."

"Yeah, there is that, too," he agreed, thinking back to the way Liz had just seemed to appear out of the gathering evening mist.

"What did she say when she saw that there were four of you who had to be dropped off in four different locations?" Nikki asked. She was attempting to urge him on with his story before Edna came in to interrupt them.

"I put that in with my request. Wait." He looked at her uncertainly. "How did you know the Chariot driver was a she? I didn't say anything about gender."

He had caught her up short for a moment, and she searched for something plausible to use as an excuse. And then she remembered. "You said the driver appeared like a fairy godmother. I doubt you would have described the driver that way if it was a guy. I mean, a genie maybe, but definitely not a fairy godmother."

There, that should do it, Nikki thought.

She watched her friend's face to see if he had bought her explanation. To her great relief, he did. That had been a close one.

Neither Ethan nor the Chariot-driving young

college student would ever know just what machinations had to be orchestrated in order to have Liz and her Chariot available and in the vicinity of the nightclub where the bachelor party had taken place. But then, Nikki thought with a smile, Lucas, her husband, was a good sport. He had even told her that he could see how much this meant to her. So he had agreed to become an accessory to the setup so that Ethan could meet the woman who was so much better suited for him than that "cold-blooded, self-centered snob"—Nikki's words, Lucas had specified— he had been engaged to.

Because Catherine Van Houghton's father ran a very successful practice, Nikki had found that their worlds did sometimes converge. It usually involved fund-raisers. Catherine had no interest in any sort of charitable donation or work, but she did enjoy parading around in gowns that were obviously in a price range over and above anything else found at the party. Making others envious was apparently her sole source of enjoyment.

The woman, Nikki had long ago decided, was shallower than a puddle. She'd never understood how someone who had such a generous soul as Ethan could have ever gotten ensnared in her web.

Ethan nodded. "I guess that makes sense."

"Was she nice?"

Nikki's question came out of the blue and threw Ethan for a moment before he realized what she was asking and about whom.

"Actually, yes, she was. She even tolerated Jimmy hitting on her."

Amusement touched her eyes. "What happened?" Nikki asked.

"She put him in his place," he answered simply.

"By hitting him?" Nikki guessed. She hoped that hadn't thrown a wrench into the works. She could see Ethan getting in the way of flying fists. But a quick survey of his face told her she was worrying for nothing.

So far.

Ethan laughed, remembering what had happened that evening. "By telling him about the Taser she had in her purse."

"Did she? Have one?" Nikki added when she realized her sentence was incomplete.

"She might have, but I don't think so," Ethan admitted. "She told Jimmy if she took it out to show him, she intended to use it. He got pretty quiet after that."

I like her already, Mom, Nikki thought.

"So," Nikki concluded out loud, "the evening was uneventful."

"After the blowout, yes," Ethan agreed in an offhand manner as he shifted in his chair, getting ready to get up.

"Hold it, back up a minute," Nikki ordered, clamping her hand over his wrist. "What blowout?"

"The front tire blew right after she dropped off Wayne." In Nikki's opinion, Ethan fairly glowed as he said with a touch of pride, "I changed my first tire, although she had to talk me through it."

She was doing her best to get clear about things. "So there was no one in the Chariot except for the two of you?" Nikki asked.

"No, there wasn't," he confirmed. "Liz— that's the driver—was going to change it herself, but I told her I didn't want her struggling with the tire after what she'd already done. Good thing, too," he reflected. "Those lug nuts were a real bear to get off. My biceps ached the next day. But it was one of those good kind of aches, you know?"

Nikki felt as if she was getting this story in torn bits and pieces that she had to reconstruct in order to make sense out of it.

"What was it that Liz had 'already done'?" she asked him.

Just then, they heard a very sharp clearing of

their only nurse's throat. Edna Vincent, looking like a nurse who had served in at least the Korean War if not WWII, was standing in the doorway, a reproving expression on her very long, very thin face. Edna had a face that looked as if it hadn't smiled in at least a decade, possibly more.

"Doctors," Edna said when her cough hadn't gotten the response she was looking for, "the patients are getting restless."

Without sparing Edna a look, Nikki held up her hand to indicate to the formerly retired nurse that she needed a moment longer.

"We'll be right out as soon as Dr. Ethan finishes what he was telling me." Looking at Ethan, she said, "Go on."

"When that tire blew out, she drove like a pro. She held on to the steering wheel and kept that car from crashing *and* from colliding with an oncoming truck. You should have seen her, Nikki. She was absolutely magnificent."

Perfect!

Nikki smiled in satisfaction. "I'll bet." She heard the sharp intake of breath to her right. "Yes, Edna, we're coming," she told the severe-looking woman, who was shifting from foot to foot.

"So," Nikki said, addressing Ethan, "are you planning on seeing this race car driver again?"

"She was our Chariot driver," Ethan protested. "She'd probably think it was creepy having me call her out of the blue. Besides, I *can't* call her out of the blue. I don't have her actual cell number." The number he had used was one that had connected him to the drivers in the general area.

"Oh, that can be gotten," Nikki assured him with the wave of her hand. When he raised an eyebrow, she realized that could be taken as a slip and quickly covered it up by saying, "I'm sure that Chariot headquarters or whatever they call themselves has her number on file." She slanted a glance in Ethan's direction. "Unless you don't want to see her again."

"Oh, I do," he said with feeling he didn't bother hiding. "But I don't want her to think that I'm stalking her. I can't just show up on her doorstep—even if I knew where that doorstep was."

Meanwhile, Nikki was busy working the problem before her. "This Liz person knows she picked you guys up from a bachelor party. Did any of you happen to tell her about Joel's wedding?" she asked.

He didn't even have to think about that before answering. "Well, yes, but—"

"Great!" Nikki declared. "Then you can ask her if she would mind being your plus-one. Tell her it's your way of repaying her for being such a good sport—or such a good driver. Take your pick—or use both," she added cheerfully, saying whatever it took to get him to agree.

Ethan nodded, thinking the suggestion over. "I suppose that could work," he told Nikki. But because he had an aversion to doing something that could be seen as offensive to another party, he qualified, "Let me think about it," just as they walked out of the tiny back office.

"About time," Edna told the duo. She was standing right outside in the hall, her arms folded in front of her sunken-in chest. "I don't need to put up with this aggravation. I don't know why I just don't retire."

"You can't retire, Edna. You know you're what keeps everything running around here. Without you, everything would just fall apart," Ethan told her with sincerity. "And we're sorry about keeping you waiting all this time. I just got caught up in what I was telling Dr. Connors."

Edna raised her chin and sniffed through her distinctly Roman nose. "*I'm* not the one who's been waiting," she informed Ethan. "The patients are getting extremely *im*patient."

"You could try smiling at them and maybe sweet-talking," Nikki suggested with a straight face. "It might be a whole new concept for you."

Ethan steered Nikki to the side and said to her in a lowered voice, "Nikki, leave the woman alone. You know Edna can't help being the way she is. She's been that way longer than either one of us has been alive."

"Your problem, Dr. Ethan O'Neill, is that your heart is just too big and too kind," Nikki said as she picked up the first chart on the scarred extended table that served as the clinic's reception desk. "I'll take Mrs. Klein," she told Ethan, opening the folder and glancing down the page. "Unless you'd rather because she's your patient."

He appreciated Nikki's thoughtfulness. "Yes, I've seen her before, but I think she'd probably prefer to talk to you. Sometimes a woman relates better to another woman, especially when it comes to certain problems. That was why I was glad when you signed on to volunteer at the clinic."

"My pleasure, Ethan," Nikki said, flashing a wide smile at the younger doctor.

Edna moved in closer, looming over them and scowling like a dark rain cloud. "I hate to break up this mutual admiration fest, but the patients—" she said, pointing toward the waiting room.

"Nose to the grindstone, Edna. Nose to the grindstone," Nikki replied, walking by the woman and out into the waiting room. Raising her voice, Nikki called out, "Mrs. Klein?" as she scanned the sea of faces looking back at her.

Out of the corner of his eye, Ethan saw the dour-looking nurse nodding slightly to herself in what seemed like approval.

Why, you old fraud, Ethan thought. *You actually like Nikki, don't you? You just probably like giving her a hard time even more.*

He had been concerned for no reason, he thought.

The next moment, he wondered if maybe he got in his own way a lot like that. Like creating reasons not to do something that he actually *wanted* to do.

Brightening, he picked up the next file on the reception desk and read off the name across the top as he walked out into the waiting room.

Ethan had to admit that the more established doctor had given him something to think about.

Something that he knew he really *shouldn't* be considering, but something that nonetheless kept sneaking into his mind time and again over the course of an extremely long day.

And even after he and Nikki had seen the last patient—almost two hours after the clinic's official closing time—Ethan kept going back to and thinking about what she had suggested.

So much so that it prompted him to suddenly ask, as he locked the front door and pulled down the shades, "You really think I could get that driver's phone number from Chariot?" He turned to look at Nikki, hoping she could talk him into it. "Isn't that a little, you know, unethical of them?"

"Tell you what, let me handle it. I could call in, tell the dispatcher or whatever that one of my friends used their service the other night and was very impressed with both the service and the driver's driving skills and professionalism." She congratulated herself for throwing in that last part, confident that it would cinch the argument. "I'd then go on to give them the date and destinations she drove all of you to so the company can track down the name of the driver who was behind the wheel. How's that?"

He wasn't quite sold on her plan. "Why would they give it to you?"

She wished he didn't have such a detail-oriented mind. She was just making this up as she went along, because she already *knew* Liz's name, her number and where she lived, thanks to her mother. She was just looking for a way to get him to think she was ferreting it out.

"Leave that to me. What I need you to do is go home and make sure you give that woman a five-star rating for the drive. Since it involves her livelihood, I'm sure she keeps up on her ratings. A five-star rating will make her more amenable to you," she told him.

"I don't have to do that," Ethan answered as he picked up his medical bag and his jacket.

"Oh yes, you do," Nikki insisted. "These days almost everyone is dependent on getting good ratings. Grocery cashier, people behind the post office desks, Chariot drivers."

"I know," Ethan cut in, "that's why the first thing I did when I got home that night was go online and rate her. I gave her a five plus."

"Five plus?" she echoed. "You can do that?"

Ethan walked her out the back door and into the tiny parking area behind the clinic, then he accompanied her to her car. "I augmented the rating with an explanation why I thought the driver was outstanding, and in case you're wondering, when I cited the driver, I used her driver number, not her name, so it sounded as if I was being neutral."

Nikki smiled as she got into her car. Ethan really was such a cuddly, adorable human being.

Liz Bellamy, brace yourself. Dr. Wonderful is

about to enter your life and make you happy to be alive, Nikki thought.

And then, as she started her engine and pulled out of the lot, she mentally tipped her cap to her mother.

Looks like you and your friends have done it again, Mom.

Chapter Six

Liz didn't discover the small, well-worn notebook until almost two days after her blown-tire thrill ride. The truth of it was, when she had returned from her last Chariot run that night, she had been too exhausted and too shaken by the thought of what could have happened to her as well as to her passenger when that tire blew. She was just grateful for the training that her stepfather had drilled into her until it was like second nature. But she definitely didn't have the strength or wherewithal to clean her vehicle the way she always did when she came home after spending all that time driving strangers around.

And the next morning, after being unable to fall asleep, Liz had wound up *oversleeping* and almost missed her class—and her test. She managed to get to the classroom by the proverbial skin of her teeth.

The moment classes were over for that day, she had raced to her *other* part-time job that she had mentioned to her handsome fare. She was a bartender at a small local Chinese restaurant.

Liz had gotten that position through a form of nepotism. Young Lee, the stately older woman who owned and ran the restaurant, had known her ever since she had been a little girl. She and Young's youngest daughter, Sandra, had gone to school together. But more important than that, Young had always been partial to her because she was so studious and hardworking.

Fortunately for her, Liz thought, Mrs. Lee thought those qualities, and thus she, were up there, right at the head of the line. Plus, the sacrifices she had made in order to help pay her stepfather's medical bills were not lost on the honorable woman, either.

Liz might not have even found the pocket-size notebook at that point, either, but she refused to go to bed that second evening until she checked over her car. She was on call the next evening. That meant washing her car and vacuuming the interior.

She was relieved to discover, after having given her vehicle a second once-over in as many days, her car was none the worse for its unexpected, harrowing ordeal. Miraculously, there wasn't a dent or so much as a ding to commemorate the event.

Liz felt that she owed one of the charitable organizations she occasionally gave to a generous donation. Or at least generous in *her* terms, which at times, depending on her bills, was not all that much. But thanks of some sort were definitely owed to the angel she firmly believed she had watching over her. Liz was not about to let that go until she could pay that debt forward.

Liz had already made up her mind to double up on her driving until she earned an extra amount that she could put toward the donation. To her that meant that her vehicle had to be in top condition.

After washing and drying the outside of her car—because a car wash would have subtracted from her profit—she proceeded to vacuum its interior. A quick survey first of the front and back areas assured her that there were no discarded wrappers or snack containers to clog up her machine. Turning the vacuum cleaner on, Liz went over the upholstery slowly.

When she stuck her hand in between the front passenger seat and the cushion comprising its backrest, at best she expected to find a few crumbs that had worked their way into the seat's crease. She did *not* expect to find a small, worn notebook.

Without doing any actual reading, she saw that there was a lot of writing on those small, cramped pages. This had to be a commemoration of someone's past. She immediately couldn't help wondering who it belonged to and if it was important.

But Alan from Chariot's local office hadn't contacted her to say that someone had called in, asking if a notebook had been turned in. That probably meant that it *wasn't* important, she decided. Besides, in this day and age, if anyone wanted to remember anything of importance— or even something in general—they dictated it into their cell phone. It was just handier and easier that way, Liz thought.

But, as she flipped open the notebook and looked at it a little more closely, she realized that there was *extensive* writing on three-quarters of the pages. This had to be important to someone.

Liz's mouth dropped open. Apparently, someone had been using this—and might still be in the process of using it—as a journal.

She tried to remember if she had picked up an older man or woman during the last day she had driven for Chariot.

There had been one passenger who definitely fell into the senior citizen category, an elderly woman. But the passenger had held on to her purse with both hands, keeping it close to her chest as if she expected to be mugged at any second right there inside the car.

Thinking, Liz remembered carrying on a steady stream of conversation—which in actuality amounted to a monologue on her part—during the whole ride. She had done so in order to try to put the woman at ease. It had to have worked, Liz congratulated herself at the time, because the elderly woman had given her five stars and had mentioned something in her review about her having a "nice, soothing voice."

Still, Liz supposed, the notebook could belong to the woman, even though she hadn't seen the woman take it out at any time—*and* she had looked in her rearview mirror several times to check on her fare's condition.

Maybe there was a name written in somewhere either in the front or back of the notebook that could help her identify who the thing belonged to. Or at the very least, there might be something tangible for her to work with.

Liz flipped through the pages with her thumb, taking in the preponderance of writing on them. In her estimation, all this writing represented an awful lot of thoughts. She could not, in good conscience, just toss this notebook away or even put it aside for the time being and allow it to collect dust until she got around to reuniting the owner with the notebook.

Thinking of the task ahead, Liz sighed, trying not to get overwhelmed.

She didn't exactly have an abundance of extra time, but this came under the heading of karma or balancing out the universe. Moreover, if she *didn't* try to find the owner of this journal, something bad was bound to happen to her.

In general, Liz wasn't a superstitious person, but there were certain things that she refused to risk by ignoring.

Liz was disciplined enough to finish cleaning up her vehicle and then store her cleaning tools before she went on to her next task. She managed to curb her considerable curiosity until she went back upstairs to her third-floor studio apartment.

But once she had closed her door behind her, Liz immediately opened the notebook and scanned both the inside cover and the page facing it.

The owner's name was entered in such tiny, neat letters that she almost missed it. Especially since the rest of the writing appeared to be far more illegible, written in script that seemed far more suited to a doctor than...

The thought stopped her cold.

A doctor? The man she had come close to touching death with had been a doctor.

Ethan.

Admittedly, part of her had thought that Ethan was kidding when he told her that he was a doctor, because, well, how would she have known if that was the truth or not? A lot of people partying for the evening liked to pretend to be something they weren't just to build themselves up for that small island of time, especially if they weren't ever going to see that person again, she reasoned.

Liz pressed her lips together, reassessing her analysis.

No, Ethan hadn't been like that. He certainly hadn't instantly pounded his chest, telling her about being a doctor—a surgeon, at that, she reminded herself. As a matter of fact, she had had to drag that information out of him, as if his chosen vocation was just a fact of life and definitely nothing that needed to be held up to the light and revered.

Besides, whether he was or wasn't a doctor was ultimately easy enough to ascertain. She could just google the man—provided, of course, that he had given her his actual name.

The thought had her immediately drawing in her breath. Not over the fact that Ethan might have lied to her, but over the fact that her mind was actually entertaining those kinds of dark thoughts.

When had she gotten so cynical?

She used to believe everything anyone told her, falling back on her old rule of thumb: She didn't lie to anyone, so then why would anyone want to go out of their way to lie to her?

But somewhere along the line, that iconic and innocent belief of hers that had sustained her through so much had become a casualty. And with its passing, it had left her at the mercy of a darker, far more disturbing reality.

"Okay, time to get a grip on your brooding thoughts, Lizzie, and reunite Dr. Ethan with the thoughts he felt were worthy of commemorating and putting down on paper. But first," she said out loud, as if she was an old-time announcer on the radio, "it's time to check those latest reviews of yours and see where you can improve your services to the world at large."

She was thinking about her latest Chariot ratings, fully aware that she would not be the only one who was looking at them. The people who ran the local office checked everyone's ratings religiously—as did her mother, although Ruth Bellamy only checked hers, and for a different reason than the local office did.

Her overly concerned mother checked her ratings because she was worried that one of the passengers she had driven somewhere might have made a derogatory comment or shared a dark thought that he'd had about his "beautiful" driver.

Liz knew that if she could have gotten away with it, her mother would have wrapped her up in bubble wrap and kept her stored somewhere in the house. And while, in a very odd way, Liz could understand where her mother was coming from—she'd lost her husband, which in turn had taught her that *nobody* could control their destiny—living life isolated like that wasn't living at all. And she knew that her mother knew that.

It was just easier on her mother to wish that it wasn't so.

After turning on her computer, Liz went directly to the Chariot website. Once there, she accessed the ratings page for the local drivers. She didn't have any time to read any of the evaluations sent in about the other drivers in her area—she never did. Instead, she went straight to her own ratings.

Taking a deep breath, she braced herself and raised her eyes.

Liz was a firm believer that it was always best to be prepared for the worst, just in case—because one time—*just* one time—she had been slammed between the eyes by some vengeful idiot who was completely disgruntled that he couldn't get her to agree to earn a higher tip by taking him up on what he felt was a perfectly logical proposition.

The key word there had been *proposition.*

As prepared as she felt she was going to be, Liz pulled up her page and started reading.

And then she smiled.

While the other two ratings that had been input from that day were good in their own right, the one that obviously had to be written by her very last passenger of that fateful day was nothing short of fantastic—as well as heartwarming.

She read the review with its accompanying five-plus stars again and again for a total of three times. She was smiling a little more broadly each time she came to the end.

When she finished reading the review for a third time, Liz leaned back in her chair and sighed happily. "How about that?" she murmured. "You really *are* a good guy, Dr. Ethan," she said, addressing the page on the computer as if it was the man she had dealt with the other night. "If nothing else, I'm going to get this notebook back into your hands as fast as humanly possible."

Glancing over the rating with its glowing words, she searched for any indication of an email address or some other avenue of communication she could use in order to get in contact with this man who was not just a feast for the eyes but, in her opinion, had a beautiful soul to match.

But there was nothing.

None of the multiple ways of conveying messages via social media were evident.

For a few minutes, Liz felt exceedingly frustrated. But then she recalled that she did have another way available to her. The same one she had initially thought of before she had gotten distracted. It was an old-fashioned online device that she had used before when she had tried to track someone down. At the time all she had had was a general location, an approximate age and the person's name.

"Luckily, you're not John Smith," Liz said, addressing the notebook he had left in his wake. And she now believed that Ethan O'Neill was her passenger's actual name.

Wait, Liz thought suddenly. Maybe there was something in these pages that would give her a clue—or better yet, an actual address.

She got as far as opening the book and flipping to the second page. In order to do what she wanted to, she realized that she was going to have to start reading what was on these pages. Of course she would be doing that reading for the most innocent of reasons, but when push came to shove, she knew that it was actually another excuse for an invasion of privacy.

What if Ethan had shared his innermost thoughts about the path he was taking? Or maybe a woman he was dating? Or something even more serious.

Did she have the right to do that? To invade his private thoughts like that?

She wouldn't allow her mind to go that route or come up with some fabricated reasoning allowing her to go ahead and start reading.

She had no business reading his thoughts. They were his own, she silently argued.

Still, when he had lost the notebook, it and the thoughts in it could be considered public property, right?

Oh Lord, now she sounded like one of those lawyers—lawyers that Ethan had said he wouldn't be caught dead being.

Okay, back to the first method she had come up with, she thought. If that failed to produce the results she needed, then she supposed that she would be within her rights to see if there was some sort of an address or general location for Ethan in the notebook.

Her conscience assuaged, Liz pulled up the website that she knew could at least get her some sort of information about Dr. Ethan O'Neill. She knew that for an extra fee, she could find out if he had ever been married, if he had ever been divorced and for another fee over that, she could also learn if Ethan had some sort of an arrest record on file.

None of that interested her.

All she wanted was to be able to find an address for the man so that she could return his notebook to him.

A thought suddenly occurred to her. What if Ethan had only just now realized that it was missing? That would certainly explain why he hadn't already called the local office asking about it, because they would have in turn called her.

Poor man—if he *did* realize that his journal was missing, he was probably worried that he'd never see it again.

Well, if nothing else, at least she could put that fear to rest for him.

With a smile, she began typing.

Quickly.

Chapter Seven

There were days when his work at the clinic really felt rewarding. It didn't even have to be anything overwhelming or of major proportions. Sometimes the reward was the smile of a relieved mother whom he had reassured that her little boy or girl would recover from a high fever without any ill effects.

Sometimes the reward was the gratitude he saw in a patient's eyes when they were told that they didn't have some sort of mystery ailment that would eventually eat away at their stomach lining—that what they had was just a case of really bad indigestion.

Ethan had come to discover over the course of the months he had spent at the clinic that there were hundreds of tiny victories to be celebrated. Victories that were spread out over the days and weeks he worked here at the clinic, sometimes being the only physician there the entire twelve-plus-hour day.

Most of the time, though, he wasn't fighting the good fight alone. He could usually count on at least one of the volunteers coming in for part if not for the whole of the day.

However, as it turned out, today had all the makings of what could be whimsically called— by someone with a sadistic streak—a perfect storm. At the last minute, the volunteer physician who was scheduled for that day couldn't make it, and even Edna, always so dependable, was nearly an hour late getting to the clinic. Scowling like an ominous thundercloud, the nurse offered no excuse for her late arrival, but as a result, she was surly all day—or even surlier than usual.

On top of that, the patients, usually at least happy about the medical attention they received if not downright grateful for it, were angry and annoyed at having to wait so long. And they seemed to have no qualms about voicing their displeasure in very vocal, sometimes graphic terms.

Ethan didn't have unreasonable expectations. He was used to the occasional vocal outbursts. What he wasn't used to was a patient like Fred Hadley suddenly becoming physical and taking a swing at the patient sitting next to him when that patient insisted that *he* was supposed to be the next one to be seen and not Hadley. Out in the waiting room at the time, Ethan had to jump in between the two swinging, belligerent and cursing men.

It was times like these that he *really* wished he had access to a security guard, at least somewhere in the area, maybe one who was charged with keeping the peace in general at the strip mall.

But there was no such person, and he had to handle it all himself, much to the horror of some of his other patients.

He had just managed to push the two men apart when Edna descended on all three of them, her eyes shooting daggers. The nurse sternly informed the two combatants that "Mr. Hadley signed in first, and since your complaints are both of the non-serious variety, protocol will be followed. There will be no extra points for whining."

Her words seemed to carry weight, but it proved to be too late for Ethan's eye, which had been on the receiving end of the brutish Hadley's fist.

Ethan's eye stung now as he drove home, hours after the incident, but he was relatively sure that his eye wasn't going to swell shut. However, he did have one killer headache. That hadn't abated over the course of the day, but as always, he still managed to push on through it.

The amazing thing was that Edna had stopped by twice during the course of the afternoon to ask him how he was feeling. The first time he had believed he was hallucinating. Realizing that he wasn't, he was rather gratified at the show of concern.

There was a heart in that old crone after all, Ethan had thought with a small smile.

Pulling up to his apartment complex now, he drove into his designated space, grateful that his apartment was located on the ground floor. He really didn't feel up to having to climb up any stairs right now. As it was, he could have sworn that every step he did take reverberated in his temples.

Getting out of his car, Ethan totally focused on putting one foot in front of the other until such time as he reached his apartment, when he intended to fall facedown in his bed.

That was why he almost didn't see it.

As a matter of fact, he wound up stepping on the notebook before his subconscious alerted him that something was off. The welcome mat in front of his door wasn't level.

Taking a step back, Ethan looked down and was completely surprised to see what appeared to be a notebook partially tucked under his doormat.

His notebook.

Recognition instantly flooded over him, in part blocking out the dull throbbing in his temples. He had been so busy the last few days, he hadn't even noticed his journal was missing. In his defense, he only wrote in it sporadically, so he wouldn't have noticed it was missing until he reached for it and discovered that it wasn't in any of his pockets.

"Where have you been?" he murmured to the journal, flipping open the front cover.

There was a small, neatly printed note tucked inside the journal.

Unlocking his front door and opening it, Ethan held on to the journal and its note until he was inside. Once he was, he locked the door and turned on the light.

And then he started reading.

"'I found this stuck under the front seat cushion. Hope losing it didn't create too much trouble for you. Best, your Chariot driver, Liz.'"

Ethan had thought he was far too weary to smile.

He wasn't.

Especially when he saw what was written right beneath her name. The woman had included a phone number. Whether it was a number that would connect him directly to her, or the number at Chariot's local office, where he assumed he could leave a message, he didn't know. But he intended to find out.

Funny how things turned out, Ethan thought, crossing to his sofa. He had been debating whether or not to act on Nikki's suggestion about inviting the woman to be his plus-one to Joel's wedding—a wedding he had learned was apparently still on despite Joel's lone drunken transgression.

This, he thought looking at the journal in his hand, was the omen he'd been waiting for.

His dating skills were nothing if not dusty. He had never considered himself one of those charming rogues who were capable of approaching a woman and putting the moves on her as long as she had some sort of a pulse. If Ethan had to describe himself, he thought he was more of a wingman. *Anyone's* wingman.

But there was something about this woman who had gone out of her way to locate him because he'd lost something she thought he needed that really spoke to him and made him want to move outside his comfort zone.

At the very least, he could take her out for coffee to express his gratitude, although he was still nursing high hopes about asking her to accompany him to Joel's wedding.

He glanced at his wristwatch. It was almost ten. That wasn't late, but it wasn't exactly early, either, he argued.

Ethan told himself that logically he should wait until morning. He'd be fresher then, and with luck, this blasted headache burrowing holes into his skull would be a thing of the past.

But then he recalled that tomorrow was his even *earlier* day at the clinic—he opened the doors at seven thirty, and the first volunteer wasn't due in until nine thirty. That meant he wouldn't be able to call Liz until who knew when.

He rolled the thought over in his head, looking at it from all angles.

Liz had said she had a crazy schedule as well, so after all this agonizing, he might *still* wind up connecting to her voice mail.

Well, there was just one way to find out, he

told himself. Placing the note she'd written on the coffee table in front of him, Ethan took out his cell phone and carefully input the neatly written numbers on the last line of the note.

His cell phone connected to the number, and after a second, he heard it ring on the other end. Mentally, he began to count off the number of times it rang. He could feel his disappointment growing larger and larger with each ring.

In his experience, most people had the number of rings on their phone set to four before voice mail kicked in. But the phone on the other end of his call kept ringing.

"Five…six…seven…eight…" He made up his mind to give the phone on the other end ten rings, then give up.

When he suddenly heard the other end being picked up, despite the hour, his exhaustion and his throbbing temples, Ethan instantly came to attention.

"Hello?" he heard a woman's melodious voice ask uncertainly.

It had to be her!

"Is this Liz—um—" It suddenly occurred to Ethan that he hadn't gotten her last name the other night.

Nice going, he upbraided himself.

"Yes," the melodious voice on the other end

answered and then suddenly asked, "Ethan? Is that you, Dr. O'Neill?"

Relief washed over him. He didn't have to continue fumbling and possibly coming off like a socially challenged, tongue-tied fool. He and Liz had experienced a life-or-death situation in the short amount of time they had spent together. He could *talk* to her without being uncomfortably aware of the fact that she could shoot him down at any moment.

He instinctively felt that Liz was, at bottom, a decent, kind person. And he could certainly work with that.

"Yes, it's me," he answered. "I hope I'm not calling too late."

He heard her laugh, and the sound instantly seemed to warm him. "There is no 'too late' in my world, Ethan. There're just endless hours feeding into one another. I take it you found the journal I left for you—*your* journal," she corrected herself.

"Yes, yes, I found it," he answered. "That was really awfully nice of you to go out of your way like that to return it to me."

He could actually *hear* the smile in her voice when she answered. "Again, I'm a Chariot driver. There is no 'out of my way.' Besides, I wouldn't have felt right about not returning the journal to you once I found it and realized it was yours. It looked as if it was important," she confided. "You had an awful lot of writing in it. Oh, and don't worry. If you're wondering, I did *not* read any of it.

"Don't get me wrong," she explained, lowering her voice as if she was sharing a secret with him. "I *was* sorely tempted to read it, but reading it would have been a violation of your privacy."

"A violation of my privacy," he repeated in total amazement. "You're serious."

It was half a question, half a statement and a completely new experience for him.

"Yes. Why do you sound so surprised?" she asked.

Delighted by the woman he was talking to, Ethan couldn't help laughing. "You, Liz, are definitely in a class all by yourself. I don't know anyone else who would worry about invading someone else's privacy, especially if they were in the least bit curious about what sort of thoughts a person might think needed to be written down."

Specifically, he was thinking of the way Catherine would have handled this situation. Catherine, who felt that everything fell within her purview to look into and investigate if she was so inclined. Catherine did whatever she damn well pleased.

The only boundaries he knew of in his former fiancée's world were the ones she kept around herself and her own personal information. That was somehow off-limits. But that certainly didn't extend to him or, for that matter, anyone else who Catherine had dealt with.

Catherine.

There was a bullet he had dodged. Ethan congratulated himself, not for the first time. Admittedly, it had gotten too easy to just let things slide and go along with whatever she wanted rather than put up a fight or even raise an objection to something she wanted him to do or agree to.

In the beginning, he had been rather dazzled by her beauty, which was considerable. But just like the old adage went, beauty was only skin deep, and, he had come to the conclusion, what Catherine had just beneath the surface was pretty damn ugly. Just before the end came, he had given up waiting for her to change, because after all, Catherine didn't think there was anything wrong with her. In her eyes he was the deficient one. She had called him an unimaginative boor and a hopeless stick-in-the-mud more than once.

When she called him that the day he had told her that he was going to work at the free clinic, that had been the last straw. Horrified and incensed, Catherine told him that he had to choose—it was either working at the clinic, like a fool, or remaining engaged to her. When he told her he chose the clinic, Catherine stared at him as if he had lost his mind. And then she had, presumably, gone through all the stages of mourning at lightning speed: shock, disbelief, horror and then fury. A great deal of fury.

Ethan felt as if he nearly got whiplash watching her go through all of them.

"Well, then, forgive me for saying it," he heard Liz telling him, bringing him back to the present, "but you need to upgrade the class of people you interact with. You don't seem to know any very nice ones."

"No forgiveness necessary," Ethan assured her with a laugh. "You are right on-target, at least about someone I know. Listen, to get back to the reason I called. I was wondering if I could thank you some way for being so nice and dropping off my journal. I mean, you could have had some disembodied voice from your local office call me over the phone to tell me where I could go in order to pick up my journal."

"I just eliminated a step," Liz said, making it sound as if it had been no big deal on her part and that she hadn't had to find the time to squeeze in the errand between jobs. "This just seemed easier than asking someone at the local office to notify you. And you don't need to thank me. Just think of it as a good deed that you can pass on if you should ever have the opportunity to do so."

So, she was one of those, he thought. Someone who thought in terms of good deeds. Something else that set her apart from Catherine, he couldn't help thinking.

"I'll be sure to do that," he replied. "But in the meantime, how about I buy you a cup of coffee at this little restaurant I know? It serves great coffee, and the word hasn't been invented yet to describe the pastries they serve there. They're baked on the premises—"

"By a little old lady who gets up every morning before dawn to fill the order," Liz guessed, tongue-in-cheek. It was in keeping with the rest of his description, she thought.

"You peeked," he accused, doing his best not to laugh.

"Well, I figured that you only wanted the best," she answered, playing along.

His smile deepened as he thought of the woman on the other end of the call. "Actually," Ethan told her, "that's true."

Why such a very common, playful answer should generate a warm shiver and send it shimmying up and down her spine like that left Liz totally mystified. But that didn't change the fact that it did. Liz pressed her lips together, determined not to overanalyze her reaction.

"All right," Liz agreed. "Where and when— and keep in mind that between my schedule and the one you told me you had, this just might take some elaborate coordination on both our parts."

Elaborate or not, he was determined to make this happen. "Well, fortunately, I've got one of my friends volunteering at the clinic tomorrow, so I can probably manage any time after nine thirty. How about you?" he asked.

There was a pause on the other end, and he heard the sound of papers being shuffled. She hadn't been kidding about her schedule, he thought. He found himself crossing his fingers.

"Ethan?" he finally heard her say after a long beat.

"Yes?"

"My last class is over at eleven, and I don't have to be anywhere for about ninety minutes after that. Give me the restaurant's address, and I'll meet you there," she told him.

Yes!

Trying not to sound as if there was a small, cheering chorus in his head, Ethan gave her the address of the Sunny Day Café.

Chapter Eight

The café was steadily growing more crowded.

Liz looked at her watch and wondered for the second time in the space of ten minutes whether she had somehow gotten her destination wrong. But she sincerely doubted that there were *two* restaurants called Sunny Day Café within the city of Bedford. It wasn't as if the place was part of a chain.

That left time as the only variable in this little equation.

She could have sworn she and Ethan had agreed to meet here at eleven thirty. It was past eleven thirty. It was now twenty minutes after twelve. With more people entering the café every few minutes, it was only a matter of time before some couple would ask if she would mind moving to the counter so that they could use her table. That was one of the reasons she was currently on her second cup of coffee, which she was now diligently nursing as well as daintily nibbling on her second piece of pastry. The first one had disappeared into her mouth in a flash because it had turned out to be even more wonderful than she had been led to expect from Ethan's initial description of the baked goods.

Resisting the temptation to look at her watch again, Liz decided to give Ethan another ten, no, nine more minutes, she amended. Nine more minutes would make it a full hour that she had been nesting here.

As far as she was concerned, giving a man an extra hour to show up for a coffee date that *he* had been the one to schedule in the first place was being more than reasonable on her part.

Besides, today was supposed to be the day that she would grab more shifts driving for Chariot. That would start in half an hour from now.

Or at least it was supposed to, she thought, looking at the door again. Waiting for Ethan to show up was going to make her late—if she let it.

He now had eight more minutes, Liz thought.

Her countdown was down to four minutes when the café door opened and Ethan finally came in, looking, she had to admit, as if he had just run the last few miles from the clinic on foot.

Right. She was imagining things, Liz told herself. But he *did* look as if he had already put in a full eight-hour day.

Seeing Ethan looking around the small café like a misguided puppy desperately trying to find his way instantly tugged at Liz's heart. All the semi-angry thoughts that had been forming in her mind for that last forty-five minutes just evaporated.

Liz held her hand up in the air, waving her fingers to catch his attention.

The look of relief she saw on his face the second he spotted her waving at him was gratifying to witness, Liz thought. She forgave him for being late without even having to hear his excuse. She instinctively knew that whatever had kept him away hadn't been of Ethan's own choosing.

"I am *so* sorry," Ethan apologized in a semi-whisper the second he was close enough to her to speak. He slid into the chair opposite Liz's at the small table for two. "There was an emergency at the exact same time I was about to walk out the door to meet you." He knew that had to sound lame, but it was the truth.

She was just happy that he had finally shown up and that she wasn't being stood up.

"That's how emergencies like to do it," she said, nodding her head. "At the most inopportune times. I think that's what they based that old saying on—the one about the best-laid plans of mice and men. It goes for doctors, too," she told him, doing her best to keep a straight face.

He was relieved and drained at the same time. While he hadn't actually run the distance, he felt as if he had, all the while upbraiding himself that he had left her number on the desk in his tiny office. He'd had no way to reach her, and he was afraid that she wouldn't still be waiting here once he finally made it to the café.

Trying to sound as if he wasn't breathless, he asked, "Have you been waiting long?"

"Not anymore," she told him, her eyes sparkling. She didn't want to go over that ground. As far as she was concerned, that was in the past and she was all about moving forward. "So, was it a big emergency or a little emergency?" Liz asked, genuinely curious.

"A man's heart stopped, but I got it going again." The man had actually fallen at his feet just as he was about to leave. But in his estimation, that sounded far too melodramatic. He hadn't told her about the man's heart attack so that he could be seen in any sort of favorable light—he just wanted Liz to understand he hadn't been late because he had just arbitrarily lost track of time. He had been detained by unfortunate circumstances beyond his control.

"So, definitely a big emergency," Liz concluded, clearly impressed by the matter-of-fact way Ethan had answered her question. Were these kinds of emergencies just everyday occurrences for him so that he made it sound as if this was the norm? She hoped not, because then it would mean that his soul had gotten numb. "And then what?" she asked.

"And then the paramedics took him to the hospital," he told her. He looked over toward the counter, noting that there was what appeared to be a cross section of humanity, tall, short, well-groomed and motley looking as well queuing up in front of it. The only thing this collection of people had in common was that they all wanted to place their orders. "Don't worry, the man is in good hands."

"If you ask me, he was in good hands when he came to the clinic to see you," Liz said, her eyes on his. She pushed her still half-filled cup toward him. She could tell he was getting ready to get in line. "Look, in the interest of time, would you like to share my coffee and pastry with me?" she offered.

Ethan was sincerely tempted for a number of reasons, but ultimately, in his mind, sharing her coffee and pastry somehow seemed excessively cheap. "No, I'll just go up and get my own," he told her, beginning to push his chair back and get up.

"If you do," she pointed out, "you're going to spend most of the time I have left standing in line, waiting to be served." Liz nodded down at her coffee and pastry. "It would be a lot easier just to share mine. I promise that except for an occasional allergy attack if I'm within close proximity to strawberries, I'm in the pink of health."

"Strawberries?" he questioned as he sat down in his chair again. She was right, he thought. He didn't want to waste what little time they had left together by standing in a line.

"So I'm told," Liz answered. "My mother maintains that I broke out in hives from strawberries when I was a little girl. Of course, it wasn't because I actually *ate* the strawberries, but because my cousin Alex decided I was too pale. In what his mother, my late Aunt Betsy, called an 'inspired' moment, he smeared strawberry jam all over my arms and legs." She rolled her eyes. "Talk about sticky…"

"How old were you at the time?" Ethan asked, stunned by the vivid image that description created in his mind's eye.

"I was three. Alex was four." Ethan found her smile incredibly infectious as she went on to confide, "Our mothers never left us alone after that."

"I wouldn't have, either," Ethan agreed, then went on to honestly add, "I don't know if your cousin was being exceptionally creative or was just really troubled." Shaking his head, Ethan broke off what amounted to the tiniest sliver of the pastry that was sitting on the plate between them and then popped it into his mouth.

"Take more," Liz urged. "That's what my mother said about Alex years later when she referred to the incident. Personally, I think Alex was just a frustrated artist who used whatever he had available to him." She paused to take a small sip of what was now their joint cup of coffee. "He's off somewhere in Europe these days, 'expressing' himself, to use my mother's terminology."

"Hopefully he's not still using some woman's limbs as his extended canvas," Ethan said, watching Liz's face to see if he had perhaps overstepped some unseen boundary. It was all right for her to say that about her cousin, but she might feel protective about that same cousin.

"No, as far as I know, he's using canvas now to immortalize his vision."

Ethan nodded. "Good to hear." His attention shifted to the coffee he had just sipped. "You take your coffee the way I do. Black, no cream, no sugar."

"No nonsense," she added with a smile. "I don't drink coffee for taste, I use it for fuel to keep going."

"So do I," he commented. It seemed that the more he learned about her, the more he found that they had in common. He supposed it was silly to find that oddly comforting, but he did. When she laughed softly, he found himself captivated by the sound. "What's so funny?" he asked.

"I was just thinking that if everyone felt the way we did, all those trendy coffee shops that are sprouting all over the country would probably wind up going out of business."

Ethan shook his head. "Something else would take its place. A new type of snack food or some mind-blowing new fad would catch on instead." She had a way of appearing to listen intently to whatever he had to say, as if she was hanging on every word. It made a person feel as if they were the center of the universe, he thought. "People like having a variety of choices," he concluded, finding he was having difficulty hanging on to his thought. He kept getting lost in Liz's smile.

She was nodding at what he had just said. "Like all those cable channels."

He grinned. "Yes, like that." He found that she was so incredibly easy to talk to—and he was really unwilling to have this small time they were sharing together end. He searched for a way to continue it. "My grandmother once told me that when she was a little girl, there were only three main channels to watch. Not only that, but they would all sign off just after midnight."

Liz tried to understand what he was telling her. "You mean that there was nothing to watch on the TV monitor at that time?"

"Literally," he told her. "Except I think they called it a TV set at the time, not a monitor."

"Three stations, you said?" she repeated, rolling that concept over in her mind. "That would make a remote control almost useless."

His mouth curved. "There weren't any."

Her eyebrows drew together as she tried to understand what he was telling her. "There wasn't any what?" she asked.

"Remote controls," he repeated, clarifying what he meant.

That seemed really hard for her to believe. "Then how did they change the channels?" she asked.

"They got up and did it manually," he answered seriously.

Liz blinked and cocked her head, trying to envision doing that. "I don't—"

He didn't want Liz feeling dumb, so he quickly explained, "From what my grandmother told me, there was a dial on the television set. You got up and turned it each time you wanted to switch channels. It clicked when you turned it—although sometimes there was snow in between the channels."

"Snow?" she asked, confused.

"That's an explanation for another time," he told her, waving the word away.

She paused for a moment, trying to envision doing what he had just told her. "I guess that was how they got their exercise."

Ethan inclined his head. "Well, I don't know about the adults, but according to what my grandmother used to tell me, mothers would make their kids go outside and play games. Physical games," he emphasized. "According to Nana, kids didn't sit around in front of the TV, eating snacks and getting fat. They ran around playing games like tag, or handball, or they ran races. She said she and her friends came up with all sorts of active games to play in their heads to entertain themselves."

Listening to him, Liz smiled. "Sounds like fun, actually."

"Actually," he said, picking up the word she had just ended on, "according to Nana, they were a *lot* of fun. She was quite proud of the fact that she was as thin as she was all her life." He smiled fondly as he recalled something else. "Nana also went out of her way to make sure I stayed active and not attached to my computer games."

"She sounds like a really terrific lady," Liz told him.

"She was." Ethan thought of the older woman who, although loving, always spoke her mind. She had died before he had gotten engaged to Catherine, and for the first time, he was glad she had. He looked at Liz. "I think she would have liked you."

"That's a really lovely thing to say," she told him, touched. "And on that note," she began say, taking a deep breath as she began to gather up her things.

"You have to go," Ethan guessed. It wasn't

exactly a stretch, given that she was picking up her things.

Liz flashed an apologetic smile. "I'm afraid I have to get to my job at Chariot."

To her surprise, Ethan took out his wallet. Opening it, he grabbed a ten and placed the bill on the table.

A little confused, Liz raised her eyes to his. "Um, what's that?"

"It's a ten," he answered simply.

"I *know* what it is, but why did you just put it on the table?" she asked. "I already paid for the coffee and pastry, which would make that—" she nodded at the ten-dollar bill "—an exceedingly large tip."

"I said I wanted to take you out for coffee and a pastry in order to say thank you for returning my journal," he reminded her. "That implies paying for said coffee and pastry. Since you already paid the tab, I'm paying you," he concluded.

She shook her head. "I'm not a stickler for details," she told him. "Why don't we just say that you paid me back with your company and we'll call it even?"

He left the bill on the table between them. "Give it to your favorite charity, then," he told her.

"Right now, my favorite charity is me," she

answered glibly, thinking of the tuition she was currently juggling.

"Perfect," he said. "Problem solved."

She didn't exactly see it that way, although she sighed. "Well, in the interest of not causing a scene and in my getting out of here before it gets too much later, I'll accept this—temporarily," she specified, picking up the ten and putting it into her pocket.

"Good," he said. He thought about her using the word *temporarily.*

"I guess that means I'll get to see you again."

Caught by surprise by his reasoning, Liz was forced to nod. "Yes, I suppose you will." Holding her things, she began to weave her way out of the café.

Ethan was right behind her. "Great. How about the Saturday after this coming one?" he asked cheerfully.

She stopped dead as she was about to push open the café door and looked at him over her shoulder. "Wait, what?"

"How about next Saturday?" he repeated. Reaching over her, he pushed open the door for Liz and held it until she walked out of the café.

"Saturday?" Liz questioned, looking at him as she tried to wrap her head around the invitation.

"Yes." He gently ushered her out until she was

several steps past the café entrance. People were still going in. "You know, the day after Friday and before Sunday, except a week after this one."

"*That* Saturday?" she asked him, feeling a little off center.

He was getting closer to his subject at this point. "As a matter of fact, yes, that Saturday. And I think I should tell you that it also happens to be the day Joel's getting married." He talked faster now. "As it turned out, his fiancée decided to forgive him and go ahead with the wedding. I don't know if it's because she really loves the guy or because the deposit on the hall isn't refundable, but either way, the wedding apparently seems to be on."

"Hold it," Liz cried, putting her hands physically on Ethan's shoulders to anchor him in place. She caught herself thinking that he had awfully broad shoulders. "You're asking me to come to your friend's wedding with you?" she asked, trying to get it straight.

"Yes, I am." He looked at her, wondering if she was going to turn him down after all this. "Don't you like weddings?"

"They're a great institution," she answered. "But that's not the point."

"What is the point?" he asked innocently,

hoping she wasn't going to say anything to completely shoot him down or hand his head to him.

"The point is…" For a second, she was at a loss for words. Liz stumbled her way through her answer. "Don't you have someone else you'd rather ask?"

The man was a doctor and a good-looking one at that. He *had* to have a woman in his life—most likely several women. Why would he go out of his way to ask her? While it gave her a warm feeling, it really didn't make any sense to her. They were strangers.

Ethan's eyes met hers, and for a long moment, he didn't answer her.

Just when she was about to give up and tell him she needed to leave or she *was* going to be late—Ethan finally answered.

"No, I don't have anyone else I'd rather ask. I want to ask you."

Chapter Nine

Liz had doubts about accepting the invitation to attend the wedding next Saturday almost immediately. Not because she didn't want to attend it with Ethan—she really did. The man didn't have a single thing going against him. He was tall, handsome, warm and funny. And he was a doctor, for heaven's sake—which she knew would be the very first words out of her mother's mouth if she told Ruth about this pending invitation. Her mother wasn't easily impressed, but Liz knew the woman would see that as a definite plus in his favor.

No, Ethan wasn't the problem. The sad truth of it was she was hampered from being joyous about the prospect by several things. First of all, Saturday was her busiest day and an even busier night. Not just as a driver for Chariot, but also as a bartender at Young's Chinese Cuisine Restaurant.

People out on a Saturday night had more of a tendency to get tipsy. It had come to her attention that people also tended to tip more liberally the more inebriated they were. By going out with Ethan, she knew she would be giving up a nice piece of change.

And there was the other problem.

She didn't have anything to wear to a wedding. To a funeral, yes. She had that one nice black suit that she had bought to wear to her stepfather's funeral. But as for having *anything* that was more suitable to wear to an actual festive occasion, she had nothing.

Nor was she in any sort of a position to buy anything right now. Every last dime was accounted for, *especially* if there was nothing coming in for a day.

It was a catch-22 situation.

Liz was tempted to say as much to her mother when the latter called her unexpectedly the Thursday before the wedding. But she settled for asking her mother if there was anything wrong. Ruth didn't usually just call her out of the blue in the middle of the day. For one thing, her mother usually knew she wouldn't be able to reach her because of her crazy schedule.

"No, nothing's wrong, sweetie," Ruth replied, grateful that her daughter couldn't see her crossed fingers. "I'm just checking to see how you are and how everything's going these days for my extremely busy daughter."

The truth was Ruth had been doing her very best to contain herself ever since she had gone to Cilia for help and her friend had promised to see what she could do about finding someone for Liz. To Ruth, given Cilia's track record, that was as good as telling her to start looking for a venue where Liz and her prospective groom could hold the wedding reception.

Since that day, she had managed to force herself not to call Liz, but willpower only went so far.

Besides, it wasn't unusual for her to call her daughter out of the blue, Ruth stubbornly reasoned. They were close—they always had been. Consequently, she had waited as long as she could without exploding, then finally called.

"So?" Ruth asked cheerfully. "How is everything? Work still keeping you busy?" She thought that was a safe enough question to ask.

"Oh Lord, yes," Liz answered. "I can hardly catch my breath."

"And school?" Ruth asked, trying to get her daughter to talk about what was *really* important. "How's that going?"

"The same," Liz replied. "Everything feels like I'm caught in a total whirlwind. With everything that's going on, sometimes I'm not even sure what day it is," she confessed to her mother.

Sympathy instantly flowed out of every pore. "Oh darling, you're only one person. You can't push yourself like this or you'll just burn out. Or burn up," Ruth added with a warning note. "You have to realize that you need to pause once in a while, have a little fun. Enjoy a little me time," Ruth urged, trying desperately to provide an opening for Liz to tell her about the young man Maizie had arranged for her to meet.

"Yeah, well, that's probably not going to happen," Liz answered, her voice trailing off as she thought about her barren closet and her thin wallet. It was unrealistic of her to even have considered going out to this wedding with Ethan.

It was like pulling teeth, Ruth thought. "Wait, back up, dear. *What's* not going to happen? Was something supposed to happen?" Ruth asked.

She was so desperately eager to move this along she was almost bursting.

"I got invited to a wedding," Liz began and got no further.

"A wedding? That's wonderful!" Ruth cried. "You are going, right?" she asked as if there could only be one answer to that question.

"Mom," Liz said with a soul-scraping sigh, "I have *nothing* to wear. Really," Liz emphasized, keenly aware that was the standard excuse that most women said even when they were facing an entire wardrobe stuffed full of choices. Her closet, however, was the exception to that rule.

Undaunted, Ruth pressed, "But if you had something suitable to wear, would you go to this wedding?"

Liz sighed. She was usually exceedingly practical—however, this really was a different situation in her view. "Saturday's my best day when it comes to earning money, but yes," she admitted, "if I had something to wear to this thing besides jeans, I would go."

Strands of the "Hallelujah" chorus swelled and resounded in Ruth's head. She was going to hug Cilia the first opportunity she had. "Then let me buy you a dress you can go in, dear," Ruth proposed.

She didn't want her mother thinking she was

hinting for a handout. That wasn't how their relationship worked. "Mom, I wasn't telling you about the state of my closet so that you'd wind up spending money on me. I didn't mean for you to—"

"Oh my Lord, Lizzie, you have been there for me throughout Howard's terrible illness. Helping me, putting your own life on hold to help pay off the bills. Let me do this one little thing for you. *Please*," Ruth pleaded.

Liz could feel herself wavering, even though she knew she shouldn't. "Well…"

"It's settled, then," Ruth concluded. "Go, buy whatever catches your eye. If you ask me, you'd be the belle of the ball even if you were wearing burlap, but then, I'm prejudiced."

Liz laughed. The sound was a mixture of relief, amusement and gratitude. She really *did* want to go to this wedding with Ethan. If she turned the invitation down, who knew if she'd ever see him again?

Still, she had to ask, "Mom, are you sure about this?"

"Never more sure of anything in my life, my love. Trust me when I tell you, you'll be making me very happy if you go to this wedding with—" Ruth caught herself just in time. She had almost slipped and said Ethan's name. The jig would have been up at that point.

So instead, she cleared her throat and asked, "Who did you say you were going with, dear?"

"I didn't," Liz answered. "His name is Ethan."

"Ethan," Ruth repeated as if this was the first time she had heard the man's name. "Like John Wayne in that movie I always liked to watch. Remember, honey?"

Liz had to laugh. "Yes, Mother, like John Wayne in that movie you liked."

"How did you meet him?" Ruth asked innocently, knowing that logically would be her next question—if she hadn't already had all the details, thanks to grilling Cilia. "Is he someone from one of your classes?"

Liz was already busy mentally reshaping her schedule and framing her excuse to Young as to why she was going to need to take Saturday evening off. If she hadn't been preoccupied, she might have picked up on the fact that her mother sounded a little *too* innocent.

"No, Mom, Ethan was one of my fares." She decided to leave out the part that she had driven Ethan and his friends home from a bachelor party and that his friends had been pretty drunk at the time. She also decided that her mother didn't need to hear about the near accident that night that had consequently managed to bring her and Ethan closer together.

"Well, you'll have to tell me all about it some-time," Ruth declared in an upbeat voice, "but right now you, my love, need to go shopping."

Which she wouldn't be able to do if it weren't for her mother's generosity. Impulsively—something she rarely allowed to govern her—Liz made a decision. "Would you like to come shopping with me?" she asked.

For a second, there was silence on the other end of the line. And then Ruth all but cried, "Would I— I can be there in fifteen minutes. Ten if the local police aren't out patrolling the area."

The last thing she wanted was for her mother to get a speeding ticket because of her. "Make it fifteen, Mom. I'll wait."

She heard her mother sigh happily on the other end of the call. "Shopping with my daughter. Whoever this Ethan person is, Lizzie, he has my blessings," Ruth declared just before she hung up.

Liz stared at her reflection in her bedroom mirror. It was almost like looking at a stranger, she thought. It had been so long since she had had a reason to get this dressed up, she couldn't actually remember the last time that she had.

Since Ethan had told her this was an early evening wedding, she had opted to get a long dress. Initially, because she was so practical, she was going to buy a street-length dress. That way she could wear it whenever she needed to dress up for an event. But the moment her mother had talked her into slipping on this formfitting light blue gown with its mesmerizing side slit, it had been love at first sight.

Looking at herself now, it still felt as if she was moving through some sort of a misty dream. It certainly didn't feel real.

She half expected Ethan to cancel at the last minute, saying that another emergency had come up or, worse, he had changed his mind about going to something so important as a friend's wedding with a woman he hardly knew.

Lost in thought, Liz jumped when she heard the doorbell.

Terrific, she upbraided herself. A tire blowout and a careening car didn't make her flinch, but a chiming doorbell made her jump.

Very smooth, Lizzie. Answer it, for heaven's sake, before he goes away.

Taking a deep breath, Liz gathered her dress up and made her way over to the door. Once she reached it, she dropped her skirt and opened the front door.

Ethan was standing on the other side. Seeing her, he looked somewhat stunned.

When he didn't say anything, Liz asked him uneasily, "Is something wrong?" Had she left something unzipped or open?

"No, everything's perfect," Ethan answered in almost a hallowed whisper. He was standing there wearing a tailored tuxedo. "So perfect," he confided, "it almost doesn't seem real."

He looked exceedingly striking in his tux, she thought. He looked as if he had stepped out of the pages of a magazine, so handsome she nearly ached. She had an uncontrollable desire to run her fingers through his dark brown hair. A man like Ethan had to have encountered a great many beautiful women in his life. There was no reason for him to look so taken with her.

"You're making fun of me," she accused.

"Making fun of you?" he repeated in disbelief. "Are you kidding? I wouldn't dream of it." Then, in case she needed more convincing, he added, "May lightning come shooting out of the sky and strike me where I stand if it even so much as crossed my mind. I'm sorry. I didn't mean to stare, but—" He shook his head, still very stunned. "Wow."

"I'll take that as a compliment," Liz said. She had to admit, the way that Ethan was looking at her made her feel exceedingly attractive—and ready to take on the world.

"It was meant as a compliment," Ethan confirmed. "I mean, I already knew you were beautiful—inside and out," he quickly added in case Liz thought he was one of those shallow people who just evaluated what was on the surface and nothing more, "but even so—wow," he cried again, falling back on the three-letter word, because it did seem to sum up everything for him.

Relaxing, Liz could feel her smile going up to her eyes as she looked at Ethan. "I believe you already said that," she teased.

Her smile widened as she picked up the small clutch purse her mother had insisted on getting for her. She'd said it matched the high heels that she had also insisted on buying.

"But I didn't mind hearing it again," Liz told him truthfully, her mouth curving.

"That's good, because I seem to find myself kind of tongue-tied at the moment," he confided. "You really are a sight to behold."

Her eyes crinkled as her smile widened. "You look very nice, too," Liz told him as she locked her door and then followed him out.

"Nobody's going to look at me," Ethan assured her. He was having trouble drawing his eyes away from Liz. The gown was adhering to her body like a breathtaking second skin. He'd had no idea when he'd first met her that she was *this* gorgeous. "They probably won't even look at the bride once they see you walk in."

Liz laughed, slipping her arm through his as they walked to his car. "Now you're just exaggerating."

"I'll have you know that I'm known for my honesty," he informed her with a straight face. "Exaggeration doesn't enter into the picture."

He really did seem serious. She slowed down a little before they could reach his car. "If you really think I'll upstage the bride, maybe I shouldn't go," she said seriously. "The bride should always have center stage on her big day."

"I agree," he replied, then added, "We'll hide you behind one of the tall plants." And then he grinned. "But you are definitely going to this wedding with me. Now that I've seen you in that dress, there is no way I'm going to go and endure this thing on my own." He looked at her again, an appreciative look in his eyes. "You are absolutely coming with me," he informed her again, hoping she wasn't being serious about not going.

"You sure it'll be all right?" she asked.

Because although she enjoyed having Ethan compliment her, if he was even the slightest bit serious about her taking attention away from the bride, there was no way she wanted to be guilty of that. Her sole intent on wearing this clingy light blue dress was to look pretty for Ethan, not to detract in any way from the bride. She had never been one of those women who thrived on being the center of attention.

To be honest, quite the opposite was true.

"If it were any more all right," he told her, "it would probably be illegal."

She cocked her head, confusion marking her brow. "Come again?"

"That's my awkward way of telling you that you look gorgeous, and if you don't attend this wedding with me, I'll be traumatized for the rest of my life."

Liz laughed. He certainly did have a way of delivering a compliment.

"I sincerely doubt if you would even be traumatized for the rest of the day," she countered, unable to keep her mouth from curving in a wide, deep smile.

Ethan arched a single perfectly formed dark eyebrow. "Yes, but are you really willing to risk finding that out for sure?"

She pretended to think his question over before finally getting into his rather small sports car. "I guess not."

Given her dress, getting into the passenger seat was not an easy feat. It took her a minute or so to situate herself and then buckle up.

"Nice car," she observed.

"You like it?" he asked.

His eyes swept over the interior as if he hadn't seen the car before, and then he put his key into the ignition, but he didn't immediately start up the car.

"I am the proud third owner. It belonged to a cousin of mine, and he sold it to his friend. When the friend got married, he sold it back to my cousin, because he didn't think it was a proper car for a married man. My cousin then sold the car to me. He said he figured it would be good for my image—until it turned out that I didn't need an image."

"Oh, why's that?" she asked, curious.

Maybe he shouldn't have said anything. No woman wanted to hear about a man's ex right off the bat.

Ethan shrugged. "Long story," he told her, hoping that put it off, at least for now.

Liz smiled, nodding.

"Okay. Then I guess you'd better talk fast if you want to finish before we get to the wedding."

Chapter Ten

Ethan weighed his options. Ordinarily, he was an open person, but discretion did play a considerable part. And discretion told him that although he liked this woman—more than he'd thought possible, given how little time had gone by since they had met each other—he still didn't know her well enough to share this personal part of his life.

At least not yet.

"If you don't mind," Ethan said after a long moment, "this isn't the kind of story to just rattle off while traveling to a wedding."

Something in his voice caught her attention. "So it's a serious story," Liz concluded.

It certainly wasn't a happy one, he thought. And the more he reflected on it, the more disappointing it grew. "You might call it that."

"What would *you* call it?" Liz asked, genuinely interested.

He spared her a glance. "Truthfully?" he asked.

Her mouth curved. "Well, if I had a choice, I'd rather you didn't lie to me, so yes, I'd opt for truthfully," she told him.

Ethan thought back over the course of the entire almost five-year relationship. Now that it was behind him and the shock of the breakup was in perspective, he could be honest with himself.

"What I'd call it," he answered, "was an unfortunate waste of four years."

"Hmm." Liz mulled over his choice of words. "I take it you're referring to a relationship and not to the time you spent in medical school."

Ethan laughed softly. She had hit the nail right on the head. "Beautiful, an extremely good driver and really sharp to boot," he said, assessing the woman sitting in the passenger seat. "From where I'm standing, you're a triple threat."

She definitely didn't see herself as anything remotely like that. "Trust me, I'm not a threat to anyone, triple, double or single."

"And she has a sense of humor as well," Ethan added with a smile. Not to mention that the woman was apparently modest, he thought. She was *so* different from Catherine. "I might have to beat my friends off with a stick just to keep you to myself today."

That caused Liz to think. "Are they the same friends who had such incredibly liquid limbs when I picked all four of you up in front of Bar None?"

He nodded. "The very same ones," he answered. "They're all going to be at the wedding." A thought suddenly occurred to him. "That won't be a problem for you, will it?" Although he couldn't for the life of him see why.

"No. To be honest, considering their conditions, I really doubt they're going to even remember me." She smiled at him. "You were the only one who was sober that night."

About to make a right at the corner, Ethan glanced in her direction just before he made the turn. "Luckily for me."

Liz made no comment; she merely smiled at him. It was the kind of smile that was enough to light up every fiber of his being.

After having gone through and survived almost five years with Catherine before she had walked out on him, he had seriously doubted that he would even so much as notice another woman, much less find himself actually attracted to one. In light of the evening that promised to be ahead of him, he was very glad that he had turned out to be wrong.

"Listen," Ethan began just as they were approaching the Evergreen Country Club, where Joel and Stephanie's wedding and reception were being held, "if you find you want to leave at any time during the reception, all you have to do is let me know and we'll go."

That caught her off guard. "Just like that?" Liz asked.

She had assumed that he had to be there for the duration, since he had thrown the bachelor party. In her opinion that meant he and the groom were close friends. Maybe she was wrong.

"Yes," Ethan told her. "I don't want you feeling uncomfortable. The whole point of attending the reception is to have fun."

Given his relationship to the groom, she didn't quite see it that way. "I thought the whole point of this was to watch your friend and his wife start a brand-new life."

Parking his car fortuitously close to the reception hall, Ethan got out and circled around to Liz's side. Given what she was wearing, he thought she just might need help getting out of his car.

"Trust me, they started enjoying that new life almost a year ago," he told Liz with a smile. "This is just the symbolic celebration and fanfare that goes with it."

"Interesting way to put it," she commented.

"Well, you'll find that I'm an interesting kind of guy." Ethan offered her his arm. "Ready to blow off a little steam?"

She slipped her arm through his just as she sighed contentedly. "Ethan, if you want to know the truth—"

"Always," he assured her, beginning to escort her toward the entrance.

"—I have been ready to blow off some steam for months, possibly even years," she amended.

"Then I'd say we'd better get to it," Ethan said as he ushered her to the massive doors.

Although Ethan wound up telling her at least twice during the first couple of hours that they could just pick up and go the second she wanted to, they wound up staying at the reception for the entire four hours.

Although she didn't know the couple, Liz

found the wedding ceremony to be sweetly touching.

In contrast, the partying that followed was nothing short of frantic. When she scanned the large reception hall, it seemed to Liz as if everyone there was throwing themselves into having the very best time they possibly could.

Even the older guests got really caught up in the partying.

And right from the start, Ethan apparently was not about to let her hang back.

"Would you like to dance?" he asked Liz after the bride and groom had had their first dance together and the band had started to play another song.

"Maybe you should ask someone else," Liz suggested modestly. "I'm really not much of a dancer."

He shrugged as if that was no big deal. "Funny, neither am I. Maybe between the two of us, we can come up with one good dancer," he told her, taking her hand and leading Liz to the dance floor.

She didn't resist, but she felt it only fair to tell him, "You're going to be sorry."

"The only way I'm going to be sorry is if I wind up dancing alone." Saying that, he wove

the fingers of one hand through hers while holding Liz close to him with his other.

Ever so gently, he began to sway to the beat
of the slow song that was playing. It took only a
second for them to be in sync with one another.

"I thought you said you couldn't dance," he
said softly.

"I can't," she answered without any false bra-
vado.

"Well, then, someone should tell your feet
and your hips, because they clearly are doing
just that." He smiled into her eyes, thinking that
if he wasn't careful, he could very easily get
lost in those same mesmerizing blue-gray eyes.
"You dance even better than you drive," Ethan
whispered against her ear as he drew her even
closer to him.

A hot shiver wiggled all through her, created
in the wake of his warm breath caressing her
cheek. Liz drew back her head to look at him.
"Now you're just making fun of me."

"At this close proximity?" he questioned,
amused. "I wouldn't dare."

She didn't understand. "What does proximity
have to do with it?"

"Well," he said pointedly, "from that position,
you could easily make me pay for any remark
I uttered that wasn't to your liking." His eyes

lowered for a moment to illustrate the point he was making.

She caught on instantly and frowned. "I am *not* a street fighter," she insisted.

"But you *are* street-smart," he told her. "I would have thought that being one would automatically make you the other."

Caught up in the music—and the realization that despite what he had initially said, Ethan was a really good dancer—Liz let him whirl her around for a couple of moments before she answered.

"Not necessarily, no." She smiled up into his face as she told him, "Never take anything for granted or you might wind up being very unpleasantly surprised."

Almost against his will, he thought of Catherine. In the beginning, he had just taken it for granted that she wanted the same things out of life that he did. But he'd quickly found out differently. She didn't want or value any of the same things. She valued material things, while he had a tendency to lean toward moral and spiritual victories.

In the end Catherine had called him a naive fool, among other things, for clinging to his values. That was just before she had haughtily informed him that he didn't deserve her.

Lord, she didn't know how right she had been about that, Ethan now thought. He felt like an idiot, but only because he should have realized that fact way before he actually did.

All the clues had been right there in front of him. He had just needed to piece them together.

"Why are you smiling like that?" she asked him.

"I'm just enjoying your company," he answered. "And you also just said something that I completely agree with."

"Oh. That's good, I guess," Liz responded. Although she was slightly at a loss as to what it was that she had said that he found to be so agreeable to his own philosophy.

The song they were dancing to ended, but another one was beginning, this one with a faster tempo.

Ethan was still holding her in his arms. "Up for another dance, or would you rather sit this one out?"

He knew what he was hoping she would answer, but he wasn't about to pressure her if she had had enough for now. Although, he had to admit, he did like having an excuse to hold her like this.

"Oh, I think I can manage another dance," she answered whimsically.

"All right then," Ethan said, throwing himself into the dance in earnest.

"That was fun," Liz cried, trying to catch her breath as the fifth dance in a row ended. She leaned against Ethan, trying to brace herself. "But I think we could use a break."

"Oh, are we tired?" Ethan asked her, amused. He kept his arm around her waist, enjoying the contact while he could.

Liz drew in a deep breath. She wasn't in as good condition as she had believed, even with all the constant running around she did.

"Definitely," she managed to get out.

"Say no more," Ethan told her.

Taking her hand, he led Liz back to their table. As it turned out, Jimmy and Pete were now seated at their table. They were each there with their own plus-ones.

Jimmy glanced in their direction as Liz and Ethan approached the table. He grinned broadly at Ethan, and a look of mild recognition passed over his face. He squinted slightly as if he was trying to focus not just his eyes but his mind as well.

Rising, Jimmy nodded at Ethan. "Glad you could pull yourself away from that clinic of yours to come to Joel's wedding," he told Ethan with a good-natured laugh. Then, turning his attention toward the woman with Ethan, he put out his hand. "Hi, I'm Ethan's best friend." He cocked his head, studying her more closely. "Have we met?"

The woman who was sitting beside him and was apparently his date for the wedding groaned. "Now that's original," she murmured dismissively under her breath.

"No, I'm serious. You look kind of familiar— but I can't place you," he admitted. "And I really think I would have remembered someone like you," he added with an appreciative chuckle.

His date groaned again, more loudly this time.

Rather than make him jump through mental hoops, trying to recall the exact details, Liz told him, "We've met."

Jimmy looked as if he'd just caught the brass ring. "I *thought* so," he declared, looking pleased with himself for having been right. The problem was, he was still drawing a blank as to her identity and exactly where and when they had met.

"Refresh my memory," he requested.

Ethan picked that moment to come to Liz's rescue. "I don't think so, Jimmy," he told his friend. "If you can't remember, then that's your problem."

"Ah, c'mon, give me a hint." He looked from

Ethan to the woman with him, much to the annoyance of the woman he had brought to the wedding. It was obvious she didn't like taking a back seat to another woman, and until just now, she hadn't had to. "Please, Ethan?" Jimmy asked. "Trying to remember who your date is will drive me crazy all night."

"Well, can't have that, can we?" Liz said, deciding to put the man out of his misery. "I drove you home."

Liz watched the other man's face to see if the proverbial lightbulb went off.

It didn't.

"You did?" Jimmy questioned, clearly still at a loss about the details of the incident—or even the incident itself. "Did I, um, ask you to come in?" He was obviously trying to recreate the event in his mind and getting nowhere.

"Jimm*mmy!*" his companion admonished angrily.

Jimmy hardly spared her a glance as he waved at his date to be quiet. "I'm just trying to pin this down, sweetie." So saying, he did look at the other woman now, and he wasn't happy about what he saw. "Don't get that look on your face."

As much as she was enjoying this little drama and drawing it out for as long as she could, Liz had an uneasy feeling that, because of Jimmy's date, this was going to escalate. It could easily turn uncomfortable rather quickly unless she told Ethan's friend what he wanted to know.

She could see that Ethan wasn't about to butt in. Maybe he thought she liked putting his friend on the spot, but she really didn't.

"She was the Chariot driver the night we came back from Joel's bachelor party," Pete recalled, leaning in to put his two cents into the discussion. "Right?"

Instead of answering him one way or another, Ethan asked, "Is that what you think?"

Frustrated, Pete looked toward Liz for confirmation. "I'm right, aren't I?" he asked her.

Liz smiled and nodded. "Yes, you're right. I didn't think either one of you remembered," she told them honestly. "Neither one of you was feeling any pain that night."

Pete leered at her, then covered his heart as if her answer was physically causing him pain. It was obvious that he was intrigued by her. Far more so than he was with the companion he had brought with him to the reception. The latter, a rather lackluster brunette, seemed to be growing progressively more annoyed. She was shooting daggers at Pete and at her.

Okay, enough was enough. Ethan decided to come to Liz's rescue and whisk her away from his two friends. Taking her hand, Ethan drew her back toward the dance floor.

"Listen," he told her.

She did but didn't know what she was supposed to be hearing. "To what?"

Ethan smiled at her. "I think they're playing our song."

"Oh? And just what song would that be?" she asked, amused.

"Does it really matter?" he whispered against her ear as he slipped his arm around her again. They were dancing now.

Liz laughed. Somehow, this all felt so right, she thought as she allowed the music to seep into her veins and take her away.

"No, not really," Liz answered, falling into step with him. All that counted was sharing this with him.

Chapter Eleven

Liz really didn't think that she had any business gathering with the other single women when they all clustered together, each hoping to be the one who caught the bride's bouquet. After all, she wasn't a friend of the bride—or the groom, for that matter. Technically, as Ethan's plus-one, she was an outsider. Outsiders weren't supposed to be involved in anything so personal.

But when the host in charge of running the festivities called for all the single women at the reception to get into a group, Ethan had urged her to join the others.

Since there were so many other young women involved, Liz felt that the odds of her actually *catching* the bouquet were just a little better than zero.

Liz had just turned around to face the bride. At that moment, Stephanie, standing with her back to the group, tossed her bouquet into the group with an over-the-head, backward pitch that would have made any major league baseball player proud.

And just like that, all hell seemed to break loose. The women within the group scrambled to catch the bouquet. Liz just wanted to get out of their way. How she wound up being the one who actually *caught* the bouquet was an absolute mystery to her.

But suddenly, there she was, holding the stunning arrangement of pink and white roses, and guests all around her were cheering—except for the few who had viewed her as an interloper. They were less than gracious and appeared rather crestfallen.

Meanwhile, Liz could only stare, dumbfounded, at the flowers she had somehow wound up clutching against her chest.

"You know what this means, don't you?" a disembodied male voice somewhere in the crowd asked with a wicked chuckle.

Before Liz could even pretend to hazard a guess in response, someone else gleefully answered the question for her. "It means that Ethan gets to put the bride's garter on your leg!"

Loud whistles and clapping melded together, drowning out the rest of whatever the disembodied voices were saying.

When this part of the reception had initially gotten underway, Liz hadn't been paying much attention to whatever games were being engineered. However, she was aware that Ethan had been the one to catch Stephanie's lacy garter after Joel had slipped it seductively off his bride's leg and tossed it to the gaggle of waiting friends and groomsmen.

That was just after Ethan had coaxed her to take part in the group vying for the bridal bouquet.

Once she heard what was about to happen next, her heart began to beat twice as hard and fast. She decided that it was all part of the mystery surrounding her completely unexpected, unplanned catch of the bridal bouquet and not her very personal reaction to Ethan.

Liz looked around for a means of escape.

Instead, from out of nowhere, a chair was pushed forward and Liz found herself being seated on it. She was still holding the bride's bouquet.

The seductive slit on her gown played right into the scenario, leaving her leg exposed and ready for the garter. It was almost as if her gown had been created with just this event in mind.

Ethan came closer to her and their eyes met.

"You okay with this?" he asked her so quietly that she doubted anyone else could hear. She almost hadn't heard him herself.

Rather than answer verbally, she merely nodded her head, her mouth curving ever so slightly, indicating that it was all right.

Ethan knelt down beside her. His eyes holding hers, he moved aside her gown. And then, very slowly, he slipped the garter over her high-heeled shoe and then up along her leg.

Liz caught her breath. She could have sworn that she felt a tingling sensation sliding up and down her spine, rendering her hot and then cold all at the very same time. Her breath remained almost lodged in her throat as she never took her eyes off Ethan while he painstakingly secured the garter up on her thigh.

Because he wasn't playing to the crowd, which was urging him to go "Higher! Higher!" Ethan removed his hands from the garter when he had only gotten it halfway up her thigh.

Holding his hands up in the air like a rodeo competitor who had finished tying the calf he had roped, Ethan rose to his feet. He stood beside her chair and offered one hand to Liz, his unspoken meaning clear.

She offered Ethan a grateful smile as she wrapped her fingers around his hand and stood up beside him.

"Okay, c'mon now, kiss her!" someone within the crowd shouted.

"Yeah, kiss her!" Another voice from within the group seconded the motion.

The request was immediately caught up by others until "C'mon, kiss her!" became a full-fledged chant repeated over and over again.

Ethan turned toward Liz. "They're not going to stop, you know."

She took a breath as she nodded. "Yes, I know."

Still, his eyes held hers as if he was searching for something there to tell him whether she wanted him to back away or to move ahead.

After a beat, when she hadn't taken the opportunity to pull away, he took that as Liz's way of saying he had her permission to proceed.

So he did.

Leaning in, he brushed his lips over hers. Initially he thought that would be enough to satisfy the wedding guests.

Maybe it might have satisfied the guests, but it didn't do that for the participants.

The simple contact had unearthed something between them, a pull that he swore all but sucker punched him, robbing him of his very breath. It almost sealed him to the spot where he was standing, while his very soul seemed to be begging for more, for a second take.

A second take to show him that what had been created by the first kiss couldn't have been real. It had to have been a mistake.

To test his theory, Ethan brushed his lips against hers again, this time more forcefully and definitely with more feeling than the first time.

The results nearly blew him away.

He hadn't been wrong about the kiss. If anything, this time around it packed even more of a punch than it had the first time.

Just for a split second, Ethan found himself forgetting everyone else, even where he was. The only thing he *was* aware of was that something *really* special was happening.

As if to underscore that, his pulse began to hammer almost uncontrollably, setting what felt like a brand-new record for speed.

Liz had absolutely no experience when it came to kissing someone in front of an audience. She'd never been in a school play. She had never even been caught by a friend or relative while kissing her date. The main reason for the latter was because for the last number of years, there *had* been no dates. There'd only been work and more work, whether it took the form of school or the kind of work that yielded a paycheck. Work had completely dominated her life. There had been no time for socializing, no occasions of being set up by friends on blind dates. Nothing like that had even come close to happening.

Consequently, she had no idea how to handle what was going on now, how to respond to the people around her who were laughing and applauding, entertained by the kiss that she and Ethan were sharing.

At a loss as to how to react, Liz looked up at Ethan, waiting for him to take the lead.

What he saw when she looked up at him was vulnerability. That seemed to shoot straight into his gut. It dictated what he did next. Even though he wanted nothing more than to kiss her at least one more time, to give in to the chant that his friends had taken up, crying over and over, "Do it again!" Ethan deliberately put an end to it.

"Okay, you voyeurs, back off," Ethan announced loudly, albeit good-naturedly. "You've had your show. Now go back to your corners and behave."

Not waiting for a response, Ethan took Liz's hand and brought her over to where the seven-tiered wedding cake had been set up.

She had no idea why, since he had practically undone her just now with his lethal mouth, but she felt safe with Ethan. She smiled at him now, her manner conveying as much.

"You're a good sport," Ethan told her quietly. His eyes swept over her face slowly, as if to assure himself that she was all right. "Would you like to step outside for a breath of fresh air?"

Oh God, yes! she thought. It took effort not to blurt the words out.

She was relieved that Ethan was being this understanding about her feelings. And because he was, that put an entirely different perspective on the situation in her eyes. Had he been tempted to push his advantage—which part of her had a feeling that he must have somehow felt—she would have probably wound up walking out on him and the reception itself.

But Ethan had been exceedingly decent about the whole thing, even telling her again that they could leave at any time. That very fact made her feel as if Ethan was totally on her side.

And because she believed him when he made the offer to leave, that meant the world to her.

Smiling at Ethan, no longer the slightest bit wary, she answered, "I'd like that very much."

Taking her hand again, Ethan led her to the double doors that opened up to a private garden.

There were lanterns set up along the perimeter, giving the area a warm, golden glow. Part of the garden had been set aside for dancing after the meal had been consumed and the cake had been cut.

Right now the entire area was all but deserted except for a couple of hummingbirds that were swooping around, their wings going so fast they sounded like bumblebees getting ready to attack.

Surprised at first, Liz realized what was making the noise and smiled at the birds. "Hard to believe they can sound so ominous," she said.

"Just nature's way of protecting itself."

Liz laughed softly to herself. "I know how that is," she commented.

Ethan wasn't sure what he was going to say to her by way of a reply. He was aware of turning toward her—aware, too, of having her turn her face up to his.

The rest of it seemed to happen so naturally; it felt as if he had no choice but to react the way he did. Like it had all been written down somewhere in a sacred book and he was just following the steps.

Cupping Liz's cheek ever so gently with his hand, he tilted her head back just slightly and brought his mouth down to hers.

This kiss was strictly private, something to be shared and enjoyed just by the two of them, without an audience, without a single person there to so much as comment on it.

Liz felt her blood surging through every part of her body, responding to the man who had simultaneously created chaos and ecstasy within the very same space.

Her heart hammering wildly, Liz wove her arms around his neck and leaned her body into his, absorbing the warmth that Ethan was generating within her.

Trite as the sentiment might have sounded, time seemed to stand still as he went on kissing her.

As she continued kissing him.

She realized that, if she wasn't careful, she could very easily get lost in both the man and the kiss they were sharing, never to be heard from again.

It was only through exercising supreme effort that she managed to draw her head back, separating her lips from his. It was particularly difficult for her especially when every fiber of her being wanted nothing more than to continue kissing Ethan, continue getting lost in his arms, in his kiss.

In him.

Her churning adrenaline racing madly through every part of her body, Liz focused on separating herself from Ethan. Separating herself from the delicious moment and from the very real, very strong desire to see this through to the very end.

She couldn't very well make love with him here in the country club garden—if for no other reason than the fact other people at the reception would be coming out here soon. Being caught out here making love with this man—which was what she now knew she desperately wanted to do—was not in anyone's best interest. Not hers, not even his and certainly not in the best interest of the bride and groom. With that one simple act, the spotlight would be irrevocably stolen from them.

So, moving like someone caught up in a dream, she stepped back even as she pressed her lips together, both to end the kiss and to seal it in.

"I think I might have had enough fresh air for now," she managed to get out.

Her cheeks were an intriguing shade of pink, he observed. Ethan smiled at Liz as he nodded. "Then I guess that means we should go back inside."

"Yes," she agreed. "We should." Because if they remained out here much longer, she knew she couldn't be held responsible for her behavior.

Even as Liz agreed with Ethan, her feet felt like lead, wanting nothing more than to remain exactly where they were, out here with him. She had no idea if this was a fluke, a onetime occurrence that would never be repeated again, or a preview of what was to come. All she knew was that they needed to go back inside—before she wasn't able to comply.

"They're probably getting ready to serve the meal now," she said, grasping at straws for something logical to say.

He nodded. "That would be my guess." He looked at her just before they began to go back inside. "You're sure you're all right?" he asked quietly.

From somewhere, Liz managed to summon what she hoped was a carefree smile and flashed it at Ethan. "Oh, I'm just terrific," she assured him.

"Yes," he agreed, nodding his head, his voice rumbling along her bare skin, "you are."

The sound of his voice, with its unspoken promise of what was to be, all but undid her. With all her heart, she prayed that what was going on here wasn't just something that would pass, that this all-but-palpitating moment would be revisited in the not-too-distant future.

She truly wanted to see if they were as in sync as she felt they were. If they weren't, her imagination had just gotten carried away because this was the first time in forever that she didn't have to be rushing from one point to another, didn't have to juggle more than one thing at a time.

This was the first time that she could actually think of herself, not as a driver or a bartender or a student, not even as someone's daughter, but as a woman with needs and desires that had to be addressed. More than that, she had needs and desires that begged to be met.

She truly hoped that this was a sign of things to come and that when these things *did* come, they wouldn't wind up being wrapped in a tissue comprised of disappointment.

She felt Ethan's hand gently pressing on hers as they walked back through the double doors, as if to silently reassure her everything was going to be all right.

Somehow, she had a feeling that when the time finally came, she was *not* going to be disappointed.

Chapter Twelve

All in all, Liz had to admit that she had had a wonderful time. Up until the very end of the reception, just before she and Ethan finally left. Until that point, Ethan never left her side, making her have to fend for herself.

Whether they were at the table, or dancing, or mingling with the other guests, he was always with her, and he was the reason why she had enjoyed herself so immensely.

It was Liz's trip to the ladies' room before they left the reception that provided the only trouble spot to what had otherwise been a really fantastic day and evening.

Because it was while she was in the ladies'
room, using the facilities, that she wound up
overhearing a conversation. It was between two
of the more aggressive bridesmaids who had
tried to catch the bouquet. The women had gotten in each other's way, one all but body slam-
ming the other.

Liz recognized their voices. Neither one of
the women had looked very happy that she had
accidentally caught the bouquet.

"Why didn't he bring Catherine?" the taller
of the two bridesmaids asked. "If you ask me,
Catherine is a much better match for Ethan than
that aggressive flower catcher."

"Who knows? Maybe Catherine came to her
senses and decided that she could do better," the
second woman answered.

"Better than Ethan?" the first woman scoffed.
"C'mon, are you kidding me? Anyone with eyes
can see the man's a hunk."

"Yes, well, the word is that he's always going
to be a poor hunk." The second bridesmaid lowered her voice as if she was imparting a secret.
"He's working at that *free* clinic." She said the
term as if she was uttering curse words.

This seemed to be news to the first woman,
who drew in her breath, surprised. "What happened?"

"Beats me," her friend answered as they made their way out of the ladies' room. "But Catherine was smart to cut her losses," the woman said, her voice fading away.

It was only when Liz was certain that the two women had left the ladies' room that she finally ventured out of the bathroom stall. Washing her hands, then drying them quickly with a paper towel, she made her way out of the ladies' room.

This was *not* the way she would have wanted to end a perfect evening, Liz thought as she made her way back to Ethan. She had never been the type to let cattiness get to her. She certainly never took vain, petty words to heart.

But the short exchange she'd overheard between the two shallow women did raise a few questions in her mind. Questions that she knew wouldn't give her any peace until she had answers.

"You ready to go?" Ethan asked the moment he saw her crossing to him.

"You have no idea how ready," Liz answered with undue emphasis.

Ethan caught the inflection in her voice, and it made him wonder if something had happened. "Anything wrong?"

She offered him a small smile even as she

took herself to task for being too transparent. "I'm just tired."

Ethan had a feeling there was more to it than that, but she was entitled to her privacy and he wasn't going to press.

"Small wonder," he agreed. "I shouldn't have made you dance to so many of the songs, but you turned out to be such a great partner, I just didn't want to stop." He offered her what he hoped would pass as a contrite look. "I'm sorry."

Liz couldn't help laughing. "You have the nicest way of apologizing. Even if I was upset, I certainly can't find it in my heart to hold it against you after you put it so nicely."

Ethan shrugged as he helped her with her shawl. "What can I say? You bring out the best in me," he told her.

Right back at you, Liz thought.

As they worked their way to the door, she and Ethan said their goodbyes, pausing to exchange a few pleasantries with the groom and the bride's parents, all of whom seemed to be properly anesthetized, thanks to the champagne that had been downed that evening. Liz had a strong feeling that none of the words exchanged would be remembered by the parties involved by the time they reached the parking lot.

"I should have gotten you home earlier,"

Ethan apologized now as they made their way to his car. He had happened to glance at his watch as they left the country club. "I guess I lost track of time, but in my defense, you did look as if you were having a good time."

"That's because I was," she told him honestly. "It has been *months* since I had that much time to just enjoy myself, and I really can't remember the last time I actually got all dressed up."

Ethan pretended to give her a once-over. "Well, I'm happy to say that you certainly haven't lost the knack for that. And on behalf of all the men attending the reception today, I'd like to say that you really brightened up the room."

She laughed softly at his compliment. "The room was already bright, but thank you."

"Trust me, you turned heads," Ethan assured her, unlocking his car. He circled around to the passenger side and held the door open for her.

She could get used to this, Liz thought as she slid into her seat. "As long as I didn't embarrass you, that's good enough for me."

Closing her door, Ethan retraced his steps and went around to the driver's side, then got in. But rather than starting up the engine, he looked at her. "Why would you even think something like that?"

Liz shrugged. "No reason," she replied, thinking she needed to just drop the matter. This wasn't any of her business.

But she had always been a person who valued honesty more than anything else, and that meant that she needed to be honest herself before she could expect anyone else to reciprocate.

She debated silently while Ethan buckled up and even waited until he had started up his car and pulled out onto the road before she finally made her decision. Gathering her courage to her, she went ahead with presenting her question to him.

"Ethan?"

The way she uttered his name, it felt as if it was pregnant with all sorts of unspoken questions. Ethan did his best not to let paranoia get the better of him and tried to sound laid-back as he asked, "Yes?"

She took a deep, fortifying breath, then asked him the million-dollar question. "Who's Catherine?"

Whatever he might have been expecting her to ask, it was definitely *not* that. Ethan congratulated himself for not suddenly swerving to one side or coming to a sudden, skidding halt. Instead, he continued to keep his eyes on the road.

Only his hands tightened ever so slightly on his steering wheel.

"Who told you about Catherine?" he finally asked, doing his best to sound nonchalant.

Liz turned her head in his direction. If this woman had meant nothing to him, he wouldn't have that slightly guilty lilt in his voice.

"I'm hoping you will," she answered simply.

He hadn't stated that correctly, he upbraided himself. "I mean, how did you happen to even hear that name?"

As far as he knew, no one had brought up Catherine's name the entire time they were at the reception. How would Liz have even known to ask about his ex-fiancée? He must have missed something.

It really bothered her that she had to question him like this, but then, Liz reminded herself, it wasn't as if they had pledged their troth or any-thing even close to that sort of thing. He'd brought her to his friend's wedding. Beyond that, Ethan really didn't owe her any kind of an explanation.

But it still stung. She had just assumed that they were on a different footing than the one they seemed to be on.

Her mistake, Liz thought.

But part of her was still hoping that he would somehow redeem himself, even though he owed her nothing—certainly no explanations.

And yet…

She saw that Ethan was still waiting for her to give him some sort of an answer. She had to be honest with him.

"When I went to the ladies' room just before we left, I overheard two of the bridesmaids talking. One of them wondered why you had brought me to the wedding instead of Catherine. They were the aggressive ones who managed to knock each other out of the way at the bridal bouquet toss," she quickly added by way of edification. She didn't want him thinking that she was demanding an explanation—she just wanted to know why he had asked her to come with him when someone else obviously had a claim to his affections.

Ethan nodded, knowing exactly who she was talking about. "That would be Mia and Jackie."

"Friends of yours?" she asked.

"Oh Lord, no," he answered emphatically, rolling his eyes.

"Friends of Catherine?" she guessed.

"I think they wanted to be, but Catherine wasn't exactly the warm, welcoming type," he told her. "She would have looked down on them. She *did* look down on them."

Didn't sound as if he really liked this Catherine person, she thought. "Was she your girlfriend?" Liz finally asked him.

Ethan paused a moment, then told her, "She was my fiancée."

"Oh." *Fiancée.* The word seemed to burn itself right into her skin.

Well, she had certainly walked right into that one, Liz thought. But if he had a fiancée, why had Ethan brought her to this wedding? It didn't make sense. He didn't strike her as the two-timing type, but then, she certainly wasn't infallible when it came to judging people.

"Are you two on a little break?" she finally asked, trying to couch her question as best she could. She didn't want Ethan to see that she was hurt, disappointed and experiencing a host of other emotions.

Most of all, she wanted to be out of this car and in her home. Alone.

"On a little break?" he repeated. "No, we're not."

This was even worse than she'd thought. "Well, then—"

"We're on a permanent break," he told her with finality. "As of several months ago."

Liz wanted to ask him what happened. Most of all, she wanted to ask why he hadn't told her about this ex-fiancée, but she knew the man owed her no explanations. So she refrained from asking him any more questions, although *not* asking him was just furiously eating away at her insides.

"Don't you want to know why?" he finally asked.

"Only if you want to tell me," Liz answered, feeling that was the safest way for her to proceed.

"I didn't want to tell you," Ethan admitted, "but only because I am not proud of that period of my life."

Liz couldn't even begin to guess why he felt that way, but rather than speculate, she wanted Ethan to give her the details. That way there wouldn't be any misunderstandings.

"Why?" she asked.

"Because I didn't see what was happening right in front of me. And when I finally did, I kept hoping I was wrong, that somehow, it would all work itself out. But I finally had to face the fact that it wasn't going to do that—and that," he added with a sigh, "I had made a huge mistake."

"By getting engaged to Catherine?" Liz guessed, watching his profile closely.

"Yes," he admitted.

She still wasn't sure she was following him. "Why was it a mistake?" Liz pressed.

"Let me back up here," he told her, gathering his thoughts together. "Catherine's father ran a very successful medical firm located in Beverly Hills. Because I was marrying into the family, he was willing to have me join it once I completed my residency." There was no humor in the smile that curved his mouth. "My future was all laid out in front of me. My patients would be women who wanted to have someone help them realize the imagery goals they had for themselves. Fulfilling the fantasies of vain, shallow women, so to speak."

Liz could hear the emptiness he had to have felt. She made no comment; she just let him continue talking.

"I finally told Catherine that I was very grateful for her father's consideration, but I wanted to go where I could do the most good, where I felt I was needed." The smile on his lips deepened. "She didn't see it my way. We fought— she called me a blind fool and told me I had to pick. My choices were her and her father's practice, or the, quote, 'stupid clinic,' and if I picked that, it would be without her. I chose the latter. She flew into a rage. That was the last time I ever saw her."

Liz was quiet for a moment, then finally asked, "Do you regret your choice?"

Ethan didn't even hesitate. "Not for so much as even a second," he told her honestly. "What

I regret was that I spent over four years of my life being so unbelievably and completely blind."

As always, Liz focused on the positive aspect and tried to make him do the same. "The main thing is that you're not blind anymore." But still, she had to ask. "Do you miss her?"

He didn't understand how she could ask that. Wasn't she listening? "I just said I regretted losing over four years to that entanglement."

"But deep down, in your heart," Liz pressed, "do you miss Catherine?"

He thought about her question for a moment. "To be very honest, I miss the idea of having someone," he admitted. "But do I specifically miss Catherine?" He shook his head. "Not at all. I regret having to say that she wasn't really a very nice person. Drop-dead gorgeous on the outside," he said very honestly. "But she was a lot like that really tempting-looking meal you bite into, only to discover that, much to your horror, the inside tasted just rotten.

"Catherine's inside wasn't rotten, exactly, it was just incredibly shallow and empty."

They had reached her apartment complex, and he drove his car to the guest parking area.

"I'm sorry I didn't tell you about Catherine before, but to be totally honest, I was waiting for the right time to bring that up. That wasn't exactly the most stellar time in my life," he admitted, "and I didn't want you to think any less of me."

"I wouldn't have," she replied in all honesty.

He smiled as he pulled up the hand brake on his car and turned the engine off. "Well, Cinderella, we're here, and I managed to get you in just before midnight," he announced teasingly.

Opening her door, Liz slid out of the passenger side of the car. Ethan got out as well and circled to join her.

"Don't look so surprised," he told her when he saw the expression on her face. "I intend to do this right and walk you to your door."

Liz inclined her head. She should have known he would. "Very chivalrous," she replied. "Would you like to come in for some coffee or strong tea?"

"Why, am I drooping?" he asked with a laugh.

"No, but I thought you might want to have something to keep you awake for your drive home. I remember it's not far from here, but even half a mile could prove dangerous if you're sleepy."

"Well, I'm definitely not sleepy," he told her. "I think the conversation about Catherine took care of that for me."

"I'm sorry, I didn't mean to stir up any bad

memories," Liz told him. "I was just curious. Listening to those women made me feel as if I was some kind of a poacher."

"No," he assured her as they reached her door and he waited for her to take out her keys, "you definitely are not a poacher. Besides, I asked you out—you didn't ask me."

"Oh, right," she replied in a deadpan voice. "I forgot."

He straightened up as she opened her door. Suddenly, he didn't want the evening to end just yet. "Is that offer for coffee still good?"

Her eyes crinkled as she smiled at him. "It doesn't expire until just after the stroke of midnight."

"Then I will definitely take you up on it," he told her.

Liz pushed open her door. "By all means," she told him, "come on in."

Chapter Thirteen

Liz shrugged off her shawl as she walked into her kitchen and draped it over the back of one of the two chairs buffering the table.

"So," she asked, "have you decided whether to have coffee or tea yet?"

"I'll have coffee," Ethan replied. "Definitely coffee. Tea is only for when you're sick—and then only if someone is forcibly making you drink it," he concluded, making a face to show just how little he cared for drinking tea.

Liz nodded obligingly as she crossed to her refrigerator. She took out the can of coffee she had already opened earlier in the week.

"Mental note," she said aloud as if she was writing a memo to herself. "Do not offer Ethan tea again under penalty of death."

Amused at the supposed exchange she was having with herself, Ethan laughed.

"Well, maybe not death," he amended. "But as a last resort if there's absolutely nothing else to drink and the weather is below freezing outside."

Liz placed the coffee container on the counter beside her coffee machine. "Given that this is Southern California, I sincerely doubt the weather is going to drop down to freezing within our lifetime," she responded with a wide smile.

Measuring out enough coffee to make two extremely strong cups, she deposited the amount into the coffee filter and then poured in just enough water to mix with the crystals. The coffee maker began making percolating noises almost instantly.

"Now then," Liz continued, "I have milk, vanilla creamer, sugar—"

Ethan cut her short before she could go on reciting the contents of her refrigerator. "Just black."

She watched as the inky black liquid began to make its way into the glass coffeepot. Maybe she'd made it too strong.

Liz caught her bottom lip between her teeth.

"I should put in more water," she suggested, nodding toward the coffee maker.

"Black is fine," he reassured her.

She still had her doubts. "Black is one thing," she allowed. "But right now, once the coffee is finished percolating, if you want to consume it, you might have to cut it with a knife."

Ethan laughed at the image. "Now you're exaggerating."

"No, not really," she told him. "In its present state, if it fell on you, the coffee could probably flatten you, cartoon style," Liz added to help him visualize the ultimate results. "Still want it to be that strong?"

He grinned. "More than ever," he told her. And then he grew serious. "That talk about Catherine before, it didn't ruin the wedding for you, did it?" he asked. "Because you did seem to be having a really good time up until you came out of the ladies' room."

"That's because I was," she told him honestly.

Pouring Ethan a really black cup of coffee, she proceeded to pour a second one for herself, except that she only half filled her cup. She left the rest of the space for her creamer.

Taking his cup from Liz, Ethan looked at the one she was preparing for herself and raised a critical eyebrow. "But you said you drink it black," he told her. "That's creamer with a drop of coffee *in* it."

Liz shrugged good-naturedly. "Sometimes I like it with creamer," she told Ethan.

He laughed to himself. "You must save a lot of money on coffee."

Her mouth curved, and he found it infinitely appealing, not to mention extremely sexy. "Let's just say I don't run out of coffee very often."

Taking the cups into the living room with them, Liz and Ethan sat down on the sofa.

He took a long, appreciative sip and then looked at Liz. "You didn't answer my question," he reminded her. "Those women talking about Catherine didn't ruin the reception for you, did they?"

"When I overheard them talking, I wasn't thinking about the reception," she told Ethan.

He wasn't sure if he followed her. "What were you thinking about?"

Her eyes met his. "You," she admitted. "And whether or not you were just putting up a front, while inside, you were really missing Catherine."

He took another long sip of coffee, then set down his cup. "I'll let you in on a little secret," he told her. "Even when I was right there with Catherine, I was missing Catherine."

It was her turn to look at him in confusion. "I don't understand…"

He broke it down for her. "The woman I thought I was in love with didn't exist, except in the recesses of my mind. The real Catherine turned out to be extremely self-centered, to the point that there was room for only one person in her world—and that was her," he concluded. "Once I finally realized that, the relationship was over." He placed his cup on the small coffee table in front of the sofa. "I'd rather not talk about her. Catherine was just an unfortunate part of my past."

But there was more to it than that, Liz thought. "You indicated that her father was going to make you part of his medical firm. That would have been helpful to your career," she pointed out. "You must have regrets about missing out on that opportunity, don't you?"

She was getting the wrong picture, he thought. He was doing his best not to allow her perfume to distract him. "I didn't stay up all those nights, studying for medical exams just to wind up playing golf and belonging to a country club while squeezing in an occasional patient who is obsessed with whether or not the skin beneath her eyes is taut enough or needs another tuck. I *did* stay up all those nights studying so I could help people with *real* problems get better."

Replaying his words in his head, Ethan laughed at himself. "I guess that sounds a little hokey out loud," he observed.

She put her hand over his, as if that negated what he'd just said. "I think it sounds very noble."

Although he appreciated what Liz had just said, he laughed and shook his head. "That's not the way Catherine saw it."

Liz's brow furrowed ever so slightly. "Well, if you don't mind my saying so, Catherine sounds like she was an idiot."

"This probably sounds awful," Ethan confided, "but I don't mind at all." Because he wanted to have something to do with his hands, he reached for his coffee. But at the same time, he couldn't seem to tear his eyes away from her.

On automatic pilot, Liz reached for her own cup, also without looking. Except that she miscalculated where the cup was and wound up hitting his cup instead. Or maybe he wound up hitting hers.

Either way, the result was the same: hot coffee spilled everywhere. Quickly.

Black liquid pooled and spread over the coffee

table and then threatened to spill on the small runner that ran beneath it.

A mad scramble for something to wipe up the coffee before it could reach anything else somehow led to a great deal more sudden, unexpected contact. That in turn led to forgetting all about potential coffee stains on cushions, runners and tabletops.

But she looked at his suit jacket and suit and was simply horrified. He was soaked. "I am *so sorry*," she apologized, feeling awful. "I got coffee on your suit," she said, in case the dampness he was feeling wasn't enough of a clue.

Ethan waved away her apology. "Nothing a dry cleaner hasn't seen before, I'm sure," he told her. "Don't worry about it."

"I'll pay for it," she quickly volunteered.

But he shook his head, turning down her offer. "I can still afford to pay for my own dry cleaning."

"I didn't say you couldn't," she protested. "But it is my fault that the coffee spilled on your suit."

He could tell that she was about to rush off to get who knew what from the kitchen in order to try to erase some of the damage that had been perpetrated on his suit. Wanting to reassure her that everything was all right and that she hadn't accidentally ruined anything of importance, Ethan put his hands on her shoulders just to anchor her in place.

When she looked up at him, another apology hovering on her lips, the expression on her face seemed to burrow directly into his chest, taking his heart hostage.

Time suddenly stood still, making him keenly aware of absolutely everything. The way she was breathing, the way he could see her pulse throbbing in her throat. Most of all, it made him extremely aware of how much he wanted to kiss her at this very moment.

But if he did kiss her, Ethan thought, would she think he was just trying to take advantage of her, of the moment that had been accidentally created?

The debate was an extremely short one, because before he even realized it, Ethan was kissing her.

Instead of that simple act being the end of the matter, one kiss seemed to naturally lead into another—which in turn led to a third.

And then, suddenly, it felt as if someone had lit a match, not just under him, but under her as well. Passion just exploded between them.

Each kiss aroused a deep-seated hunger that he hadn't even been aware of existing until this very moment.

Working all those long hours at the clinic for the last nine months had drained him to the point that the only thing he had enough strength for was the drive home and then getting to his bed once he had unlocked his door.

Because his schedule was so hectic and full, Ethan found that he didn't even have any time to miss being with Catherine—not that there was all that much to miss after a while.

And if, as a man, he had missed the spirit-rejuvenating intimacy of lovemaking, he had never been the type who just availed himself of any willing woman to satisfy his mounting needs and urges. Instead, he had always needed to feel something for the woman he was with in order for the experience to be satisfying.

He felt something for Liz. So much so that he grew more and more aroused with every kiss that they shared. He became so aroused by her that he was beginning to have serious doubts he could put on the skids if he had to.

Which was why, even as he was sliding the zipper of her dress down her back, he forced himself to pull his head back. He looked at her, his eyes searching her face for an answer.

"Are you all right with this?" Ethan asked her, his voice thick with desire.

"Any more all right and I'd be on fire right now," she answered.

Then, to prevent any more conversation between them, which she saw only as delay, she stood up on her toes and surprised Ethan by sealing her mouth to his.

Anything else he might have wanted to say or ask dissolved in the heat of the moment and vanished.

Liz could feel her dress sinking down, then pooling around her ankles, resting there like a discarded blue cloud. Her body on fire, she began to tug away his coffee-dampened shirt—his jacket had already become a casualty along the way, on the floor now beside her newly removed gown.

Once she managed to get his shirt off his shoulders and down along his body, that left only his slacks as a barrier.

Her fingers felt like they had all turned into thumbs as she struggled to undo his belt.

In the end, he was the one who unnotched the belt, sending both his belt and his slacks down along his sinewy body and legs until they, too, became part of the discarded, forgotten heap on the floor.

They hardly took any notice. They were far too busy tangling their limbs together in an effort to feel the reassuring, overpowering warmth of bodies that were in search of one another, desperate to be completed. Wanting to complete the promise of what was being created in the wake of strong waves of desire.

Ethan wanted to rush the process, to get to the ultimate moment, but instead, he forced himself to take his time, savoring every part of her that was available to him.

His hands as well as his lips slid along Liz's warm, willing skin, feasting as if he had never been confronted with anything like this before. There had been a few women in his life before he had gotten engaged, but there hadn't been any since he and Catherine had gone their separate ways. He was reveling in this very heated moment, enjoying making love to every part of her as if he had never experienced lovemaking before.

Because, in a way, he hadn't. Certainly not with this sort of intensity, this fervor. It felt all brand-new to him. And, in a way, it was.

Liz could hardly catch her breath.

Ethan was doing things to her that she had only fantasized about. Granted, she wasn't a total novice to all this, but right now it almost felt as if she was. What was happening to her now was the difference between a chaste kiss and plunging, headfirst, into a swirling kaleidoscope of wild, unending heated emotion.

Liz drew in a long breath. She desperately wanted this to be an equal experience for both of them, but each time she felt she could reciprocate, he would begin doing something else, something even more wondrous, to her body, to all of her, practically sending her over the edge. Liz completely lost herself in the magic of his mouth, his igniting touch.

When he moved his mouth down lower, teasing her very core until she almost screamed as first one climax, then another rocked her body, she fell back, spent and thinking that would be the end of it.

But it wasn't.

It was just the prelude to what was to follow. Ultimately, he rocked her entire world two more times. And then he finally slid up along her heaving torso until their eyes were level. And then, as he captured her mouth again, she could feel him moving her legs apart, feel him becoming one with her. And once he had, he began to move, at first slowly, then more and more intently.

And faster.

With every move that Ethan made, Liz echoed.

Each move caused them to run madly together, striving to reach the very pinnacle of the mountain at the same time.

And when they finally did, that one moment seemed to freeze in time briefly. And then it finally exploded, sending them tumbling back to earth at breathtaking speed, clinging to one another in hopes of somehow preserving this one moment in time and making it last for all eternity.

But it didn't, although the euphoria did manage to linger for a while, enveloping them both in a soft, warm tissue of ecstasy, whispering seductively to them in words they couldn't really hear or make out. They could only feel the unspoken words silently undulating along their skin, a whispered memory to store away.

And that was enough for now.

Chapter Fourteen

Making love with Liz had been far more spectacular than he could have ever anticipated. Even so, Ethan had only intended to remain in bed with Liz for a little while longer. After that, he was going to get dressed and go home. He had *not* planned on lying with Liz in her bed after they had made love for a second time—at least, not for long.

And he certainly had not intended to fall asleep while lying there with her.

But he had.

Whether it was exhaustion that enveloped

him or a feeling of euphoric contentment that did it, he really didn't know. The only thing he did know was that one minute he was awake, and the next minute he had just drifted off to sleep, his arm still tightly wrapped around Liz's waist.

To make matters worse, he only realized that he had fallen asleep when he woke up the following morning. He woke up suddenly, roused out of a deep sleep by the strong, tempting scent of breakfast.

Ethan took a deep breath. Scrambled eggs, bacon and cheese if he didn't miss his guess, all of which was being prepared just a very short distance away.

His stomach rumbled in response, reminding him that it was empty.

Ethan pulled himself up into a sitting position. Even so, it took several seconds for his mind to catch up to his body. When it did, it began to orient him as to where he was as well as what day it was—minor facts that seemed to have gone missing from his brain when his eyes first opened.

The next glaring fact that burst on his brain like a water balloon that had found its target was that he was alone in this queen-size bed. It was something that hadn't been true when he'd drifted off to sleep—or he wouldn't have fallen asleep in the first place. He would have just gone home at that point.

It also occurred to Ethan that, other than the sheet that was now wrapped around his body like an ill-fashioned cocoon, he was naked. Not the best way to greet a new day in a strange bedroom, he thought as he tried to remember just where he and his clothes had parted company.

And then, just like that, it came back to him. He needn't have worried. His clothes—his suit, shirt and the rest of it—were sitting about two feet from him, all neatly folded on a chair that looked rather out of place in the functional bedroom. His best guess was that Liz must have brought the folding chair in to have some place to put his clothes so that they were the first thing he saw when he woke up.

Ethan hurried into them now, noticing that Liz had somehow managed to get the coffee stains out of his shirt and that she had dried it.

Fully dressed now, Ethan went into the kitchen in search of the woman who had managed to upend his world so intensely just a few short hours ago.

His brain still a little foggy, he found Liz in the kitchen just putting breakfast on the table. Another first for him, he thought, a warm feeling seeping into him. Breakfast usually came in a paper bag with a fast-food logo on its side, as did most of his lunches and dinners.

He indulged himself for a moment, watching her move about the kitchen, getting things ready.

"Hi."

Busy hurrying to get everything ready and on the table before she had to leave, the single-word greeting coming out of nowhere like that really startled her, and Liz jumped.

"You're up," she said needlessly, swinging around to look at him.

Ethan's easygoing smile was just a little endearingly crooked. "So are you," he observed.

A wave of awkwardness washed over Liz. This was an entirely new experience for her, having someone she had made love with the night before waking up in her apartment the next morning. Liz found herself at a complete loss as to what to say.

Banter with a fare was one thing—banter with a lover was entirely another matter.

So she fell back on the obvious.

"I made you breakfast," she said, nodding at the table.

"It certainly looks that way," Ethan acknowledged. "And it smells really great."

The compliment seemed to relax her, and she

smiled at her guest now. "And it doesn't taste bad, either."

Ethan glanced around the small kitchen. Everything had been washed and neatly put away. On those really rare instances when he did a little cooking, his kitchen looked as if a traveling circus had come through it, leaving chaos and a huge mess in its wake.

"Anything I can do to help?" he asked.

"Yes," Liz answered. "You can sit down and eat." Taking the chair opposite him, she sat, her shoulders looking slightly tense. And then he found out why. "I don't mean to rush you, but I'm going to have to leave very soon."

Six days a week, he worked like a demon from dawn to long after dark in some instances. But Sunday was his day off, and unless he got called in for an emergency—which had been known to happen—Ethan made a point of kicking back and catching up with the rest of his life.

Or just relaxing.

Although he hadn't given today any specific thought as to its structure, he was disappointed now to find out that Liz was going to be leaving shortly.

"You can't take a little more time off?" As he asked the question, Ethan absently cut into his omelet and put a forkful of it into his mouth. The flavor that greeted him exploded on his tongue like an unexpected surprise. He looked at her, pleased. "Hey," he cried, "this is really good."

Her smile moved from her lips up to her eyes. "Thank you."

"I mean, it's *really* good," Ethan emphasized, aware that compliments in Catherine's world fell like rain during the rainy season and left about as much of an impression.

But he couldn't remember the last time he'd had anything that resembled home cooking. So-called home-cooked meals that he made emerged out of his own kitchen and were, for the most part, things he threw together that initially came in a box that had microwave heating instructions printed on the side.

"Thank you," she said, then added, "I don't usually try to poison anyone with my cooking on a first date. Glad that you like it."

"Like it?" he echoed incredulously. "I'm tempted to propose to it."

Amused, Liz laughed as she shook her head. "Didn't anyone ever cook for you?"

Ethan knew she meant his fiancée, but he didn't go there. Instead, he answered, "My mother tried when I was a kid. She was a warm, loving person, but my mother and the stove had an ongoing feud that went on for years. She finally gave up and surrendered, allowing the stove to win. Takeout became a way of life in my house."

"Sorry to hear that," Liz said with genuine empathy. "My mother wasn't much of a cook, either," she confided. "But my stepfather was. He was always in the kitchen on Sundays, creating all these wonderful meals. He taught me everything he knew," she said, a fond look descending over her face for a moment as she thought of those years.

The next moment, she was back in the present—and the present required that she get moving. Finishing her breakfast, she quickly rose and went to wash off her dish and fork.

"I take it by the way you just consumed your breakfast that it's a no on you taking any more time off today," Ethan surmised. He paused to savor another bite of the breakfast she had so expertly prepared.

She looked really contrite as she told him, "I'm afraid not today. I promised the person who took over my shift yesterday that I'd double up and take over theirs today."

"All right," he said. "How about when you're done?"

Liz did a quick calculation. She'd be cutting it close, but it was doable. "Barring any massive traffic jams, I've got an hour between when that ends and my makeup bartending shift begins—"

"I'll take it," Ethan told her quickly. And then he took her hectic lifestyle into account. "Unless you have something else you'd rather do for that hour."

"To be honest," she told him, "I was planning to study for a test I've got coming up later this week—"

He couldn't very well put himself above her plans to earn a college degree. "Oh, well, then—"

"But I've got that pretty much down pat," she went on. "Why?" she asked, her mouth curving. "Just what did you have in mind?"

Doing anything with you, he silently answered. Out loud he said, "I thought it might be a nice day to take a walk on the beach or have a picnic in the park. What I do isn't really important." His eyes swept over her, drinking in every tiny nuance that was Liz Bellamy. "It's the company that matters."

She had to admit what he was saying sounded wonderful. But Liz was very aware that from everything she had gathered, the handsome young doctor who had also turned out to be a fantastic lover could very well be on the rebound right now. If he was, then the feelings he thought he was having might not actually be real.

"Are you sure about this?" Liz asked. "Wouldn't you rather be doing something else on your one day off? With someone else?"

"The answer to both those questions is no," he told her in all seriousness.

Finished with his breakfast, Ethan rose from the table to bring his plate over to the sink the way that she had.

But Liz got in his way and took the plate from him. She brought it over to the sink herself, quickly washing it. She placed it on the rack to dry next to her own plate.

"Well, if you're sure about that—" she began.

"I am," Ethan answered her without a second's hesitation.

Liz knew she shouldn't be getting carried away like this, but she couldn't help it. Smiling at Ethan's response, she told him, "Then I'll meet you when my shift is over. Just tell me where you'll be."

Ethan didn't bother to pretend as if he took her answer in stride. It was obvious that he was very pleased. "Tell you what, I'll make it easy for you," he told Liz. "How about right outside your apartment?"

She looked at him, uncertainly. "You're going to stay here?"

"What? No," he assured her. "I'm going to go back to my place so I can shower and change into something a little less formal than a tux," he quipped. "But I'll come back here later," he promised. He realized that he was making plans for them without consulting her. "Unless you have something else in mind."

"No," she assured him, a wide smile spreading over her lips. "Here is fine."

The smile was back in his eyes. "Then it's settled," he concluded. "I'll meet you here."

Since Liz was obviously ready to go, he followed her to the door and went out with her. As she locked her front door, Ethan couldn't ignore the longing that was building up inside him.

Even as he had warned himself to go slowly, he felt as if he had gotten his foot caught in the door of a race car just as it was about to pull away.

"Would it upset your schedule if I kissed you goodbye?" he asked Liz.

"Actually," she told him, pausing in front of her door for a moment, humor curving her mouth, "my guess is that it might even enhance it."

"Okay," he said, his eyes all but making love to her mouth, "let's put that to the test."

Slipping his hands around her waist, Ethan brought her closer to him. When there wasn't even room for a thin piece of paper between them, he leaned into Liz.

And then he kissed her.

The second his lips touched hers, he knew.

Yesterday hadn't been a fluke.

He could feel the effect of her lips against his, feel their kiss unfurling, drumming wildly within his chest.

If anything, yesterday had been just a preview of things to come. Her mouth definitely tasted sweeter this morning than it had last night, and in his opinion, last night had been wondrous.

Even when he forced himself to draw his lips away from hers, Ethan allowed himself to continue holding Liz for just a moment longer. It felt as if he had to step back from her in stages in order to be able to survive the ordeal.

"How long did you say this shift was going to be?" he asked her, his voice low and husky.

Too long, Liz thought.

Out loud, she told him, "It'll be over by six tonight."

"In other words, an eternity," Ethan assessed with a groan.

Liz laughed at his response. "Not quite that long," she told him.

"That all depends on which side of the clock you're standing on," Ethan answered.

He almost sounded serious, Liz thought. But then, the man was a born charmer, and charmers always knew what to say in order to turn a woman's head. It was a given.

Even so, she liked what he had said.

Liz was very tempted to kiss Ethan one more time, but she knew that if she gave in, if she did kiss him one more time, then she wasn't going to be going anywhere. The man had an utterly lethal mouth, and she would have liked nothing better than to lose herself in it, reveling in its effect, but she'd already done that last night. If this thing between them ended right now, she didn't want Ethan to think of her as a needy woman he'd had a one-night stand with.

It was far better to walk away with the memory of one beautiful night shining in her soul than to leave herself open to being considered as an object of pity.

C'mon, you have got to stop anticipating bad things, Liz upbraided herself.

"All right," she said brightly, "I'll be back here at six."

She was doing her very best not to sound overly excited or hopeful. She didn't add, "I'll see you, then" or even anything vaguely close to that. Instead, she told Ethan "Goodbye" and hurried to where her car stood waiting in her carport.

Liz didn't look back over her shoulder but just got into her vehicle.

She also deliberately refused to look in her rearview mirror as she pulled out of her space. She knew if she did, she would have been more than just tempted to pull back into her carport and go back to her apartment to spend the day with Ethan.

At the very least, she would have lingered for a while, and every minute she delayed getting to work was a minute she needed to make up—if not more than a minute, she amended.

Maintaining strict control over herself, she kept her eyes on the road as she drove away.

Maybe it was her, Liz thought, but it felt as if every single hour of her day dragged by with agonizing slowness.

Not that she wasn't busy. The entire day, she was ferrying a steady stream of new passengers. There was no break in the customers needing to be taken from one place to another. She found herself driving all over the city of Bedford, as well as a few of its neighboring cities.

Over the course of her day, she had crisscrossed not just Bedford, but practically the whole of Southern California.

Ordinarily, one tank of gas was more than enough to see her through a workday. Today, however, she had to stop and fill up not once, but twice. And while all of her passengers were exceptionally nice people—not a single surly one in the lot—she still found herself watching the clock and wishing time away.

That was something she had *promised* herself she was never going to do, because she, more than so many other people, was aware of how very fleeting time could be.

Although today seemed to have twice as many minutes in it as it normally had, eventually, those minutes did finally slip into the past. And, practically an eternity later, Liz was finally able to clock out after delivering her last Chariot passenger to a concert hall where the passenger was meeting her friends.

Finally free for an hour, Liz resisted the temptation to call Ethan. Instead, she glanced at her watch. It was a few minutes after six. Liz told herself that she would call Ethan once she got home because that way she could get in a wee bit more studying while she waited for him to arrive.

Even as she tried to convince herself that she

needed to take this slow, her heart refused to go along with that or accept it.

The simple truth of the matter was she couldn't *wait* to see Ethan.

Chapter Fifteen

Liz told herself that she was going to call Ethan only when she finally walked into her apartment. She managed to hold out until she parked her vehicle in its designated carport.

The second she pulled up her parking brake and turned off her ignition, she started to dial Ethan's number.

He picked up before the first ring was over.

"Hello?"

The sound of Ethan's voice slid up and down along her entire body. "Hi. I just got in," she told him.

"Good. I'll be right over."

Before she could say anything else to him, he had terminated the call.

Liz tucked her cell phone away. By "right over," she assumed that Ethan meant he would be driving over from his apartment. The thought of seeing him again had her stomach tightening in anticipation even as she told herself to keep calm.

No sooner had she managed to get out of her vehicle and into her apartment than she heard her doorbell ring.

Oh, please don't let it be my mother, she prayed. Ruth was the only one who would just pop up, unannounced, on her doorstep on a Sunday. And although she dearly loved her mother, now was not a good time for an impromptu visit.

Unless the person ringing her doorbell was an aggressive college student trying to get her to buy magazine subscriptions in order to help them win a trip to Cancún. That happened more often than she was happy about.

Braced and prepared to send the student on their way, Liz opened her door. "I'm sorry, but I'm not interested in—" she began dismissively, only to stop dead in the middle of her sentence when she found herself looking up into Ethan's handsome face.

Ethan gamely asked, "Not interested in what? I haven't said anything yet."

"Oh, I'm sorry. I thought you were selling subscriptions."

"No," he assured her with a laugh, "things aren't that bad yet." Ethan looked over her shoulder into her apartment. "Can I still come in?"

Coming to, Liz threw open her door. "Yes, please. I'm sorry, it's just that I wasn't expecting you to get here so quickly—how did you get here so quickly?"

"The usual way," he answered. "I drove."

Liz knew exactly how long it took to get from his apartment to hers. Since driving for Chariot, she had become familiar with practically every route and how long driving from one point to another took under normal conditions as well.

Ethan had gotten here inordinately fast.

"Faster than the speed of light?" she questioned.

"If that light had to drive here from the local coffee shop, then yes," Ethan answered. "And before you ask, I wasn't at the coffee shop all day. I estimated your approximate arrival time, and half an hour before your ETA, I drove over to the coffee shop."

"To buy a cup of black coffee?" Liz marveled. "That seems almost like a waste."

"It wasn't the coffee I was interested in," he replied with a grin. "But never mind that. Tell me all about your day."

She thought of the bartending job she had to get to in less than an hour. "Other than the fact that it's not over?"

"Yes, other than that," Ethan said, encouraging her to talk.

She thought for a moment before she began to answer. "Well, I drove twice the number of passengers I normally do. And, for a change," she added brightly, "they were all rather nice. Nobody got sick or belligerent."

"Does that happen a lot?" he asked her. "The last part, not the first."

"More than I'd like," she admitted. "I have to admit that I'd be happy if that *never* happened." Realizing that somehow she had wound up talking about herself, Liz quickly switched topics. "Are you hungry? Can I make you something?" she asked. Then, assuming that his answer would be a positive one, she went on to ask Ethan, "What would you like?" as she got up to her feet.

Ethan caught her hand, tugging her back down to the sofa. "What I would like is for you to sit down and relax a little. In less than an hour you're going to be on your feet again, taking orders and serving drinks. That means that right now, you should be sitting down and recharging your batteries."

"But if you're hungry—" she protested, under the impression that he probably had to be.

"I'll live," Ethan stressed. "Right now, the only thing I'm hungry for is finding out things about you."

"Me?" she questioned, caught completely off guard. "Why would you want to find out about me?"

"It's called getting to know each other," he answered with an amused smile. "I mean, I already know you're a fantastic driver and that you're putting yourself through college. What else?"

She shrugged. "That's it."

"That is *not* it," Ethan contradicted with feeling. "You're working two jobs, going to school when you can manage it, and you probably leap over tall buildings in a single bound when no one's watching."

She made an elaborate show of snapping her fingers. "Oh damn, you found out my secret identity. Now I'll have to kill you."

"Well, as long as it's for a good cause," he said whimsically.

Liz shook her head. "You do have a strange sense of humor," she told him.

"Said the woman who talked about her secret identity and killing me because I found it out."

She inclined her head. "Touché." And then she laughed, pleased. "You're just as weird as I am."

"I'll take that as a compliment," Ethan told her. "Besides, I have it on good authority that humor is a good way to unwind, especially when you repeatedly find yourself in stressful situations."

That, he thought, actually went a long way to describing both their lives.

"Lucky for me, my life is totally stress free," Liz quipped.

Not even a hint of a smile gave her away—for a whole ten seconds. And then she burst out laughing. Her laugh was infectious, and both she and Ethan laughed until there were tears in their eyes.

Finally able to catch her breath, Liz said, "Thanks, I needed that."

"Anytime," Ethan told her. "And that goes two ways, you know." When she raised a quizzical eyebrow, he said, "I haven't had occasion to laugh like that for a long time."

That didn't quite jibe with what she knew about him. "Not even at the bachelor party?" she asked.

The bachelor party had turned out to be more

stressful than he had anticipated. "That was more of a case of me trying to make sure my friends didn't do anything stupid and trying to get them all home with the same amount of body parts that they started out with." He thought back to that night. What in heaven's name had possessed him to think he knew how to throw a bachelor party? "At bottom, it was like trying to herd a bunch of wayward cats. Lucky for me this really great driver came on the scene and took the matter in hand for me." His eyes all but caressed her as he added, "She turned out to be a real lifesaver."

Although she liked the fact that he was grateful to her, getting compliments had always made her feel somewhat uncomfortable. Liz shifted a little in her seat.

"Don't you think you're exaggerating just a little?" she asked.

Not in his book, Ethan thought.

He wanted to hold her, to breathe in her scent. More than that, he wanted to make love with her again.

He cautioned himself not to act too aggressive. He didn't want to come on too strong or scare her off. But he couldn't help being honest. "If anything, I'm not saying enough."

She shrugged away his compliment. "Anyone could have done what I did."

"I'm not so sure about that," Ethan contradicted. "Compassion is not as common as you think. It kind of falls under the same heading as common sense—which isn't."

She didn't quite follow him. "Isn't what?" she questioned.

"Common," he answered. "As a matter of fact, common sense is pretty *far* from being a common thing. It's more like a unicorn. Very rare and hardly ever seen."

Liz looked at him, fascinated by his reasoning. "Do you really believe that?"

"I don't want to," he told her honestly. "But yes, I do."

"Not me," she told him. "I'd rather believe that if given a choice, people will come through in the end," she maintained. "In other words, they will live up to your expectations."

He decided to test her beliefs and see just how strong they actually were by voicing a really dark philosophy on life. "If you have no expectations of people, then you'll never be disappointed."

"But you will be," she argued. "Each and every time they live down to your expectations, you'll still be disappointed. I'd rather live with the possibility of hope than with no hope at all, because that way, there's always a chance of something positive happening."

Ethan caught himself laughing just then. He couldn't help thinking that Catherine would have eaten this woman alive if their paths had ever crossed.

Even so, he found Liz's philosophy not just delightful, but extremely heartening. He wished there were more people who thought the way she did.

Hearing Ethan laughing, Liz furrowed her brow. "Did I say something funny?"

"No, not at all," he told her quickly, doing his best to look more somber. But she just delighted him too much, so he gave up. "I was just thinking that the world should have more people like you. If it did, we would all be better off."

She didn't buy that for one minute. "Now you're just pulling my leg."

"I wouldn't dream of pulling any part of you," he told her, trying to maintain a straight face.

But the look in his eyes gave him away.

He was feeling that irresistible pull toward her again, the same one he had experienced last night. The one he had struggled earlier to bank down. Apparently, he had failed.

Before he could talk himself out of it, Ethan

leaned toward her, his eyes on her mouth. And then he was kissing her.

The kiss brought out all his needs, and he clamored for more.

"How much time do we have?" Ethan murmured against her lips in between deep, soul-wrenching kisses.

Liz could feel herself responding. She really wanted to give in to him, to herself. But her sense of responsibility was overpowering, and in the end, it won out.

"Not enough time for that," she answered, albeit not happily. "You do make me want things," she confided honestly, her voice thick with longing. "But I just can't let Young down. She did me a huge favor last night. She's the owner of the restaurant, and she wound up covering for me when she couldn't get anyone else to fill in. I can't pay her back for her unselfish act by not showing up today."

He could understand that and admired her loyalty.

"Okay," he said, reluctantly releasing her and drawing away. He took a deep breath, steadying himself. "Can I get a rain check?"

"Sure." And then her mouth curved. "But you know it never rains in California."

Ethan lifted his shoulders in a quick shrug.

"Who knows? I might get lucky and there'll be a sudden cloudburst."

Liz played along and nodded. "Well, we can always hope."

She was getting ready to leave, he thought. He could tell by her body language.

"Say," Ethan said as a thought suddenly hit him. "You mentioned you work in a Chinese restaurant, right?"

"Yes," she answered, waiting for him to explain why he was asking.

"Is it any good?" he asked.

"Best Chinese food in the county," she told him with enthusiasm. "Their shrimp in lobster sauce makes you think you've died and gone to heaven."

Ethan nodded, making his decision. "You've talked me into it."

"Into what?" she asked, confused. "I wasn't aware that I was talking you into anything."

He told Liz what was on his mind. "When you leave for your other job, I'll just tag along."

Liz frowned. "Ethan, as much as I like your company, I don't think that's a good idea."

He thought he knew why she might be hesitant about the arrangement, and he was quick to reassure her. "Don't worry, I don't intend to monopolize you. As a matter of fact, I'm not even planning on having a drink while I'm there. What I'm interested in—besides the bartender," he couldn't help qualifying with a wink, "is sampling the food. It's been forever since I had any really good Chinese food."

"Too busy?" she guessed.

That would have been the simpler answer to go with, but he didn't want even a hint of a lie marring their budding relationship.

"No," he admitted, "the truth of the matter was that Catherine didn't like Chinese food, or any kind of Asian food, for that matter. She had very specific tastes and required that I have the same ones."

Saying that out loud had him wondering why he had gone along with all her idiosyncrasies for as long as he had.

"Catherine sounds like a dictator," Liz told him honestly.

"Actually, now that I think about it, she was," he admitted. "All she needed to complete the picture was her own country to rule over. I think her father was planning on buying her one for her thirtieth birthday," he relayed with a straight face. "No danger of that."

"Why's that?" she asked.

"Because Catherine would have never admitted to turning thirty," he told her simply. "She was far too vain for that."

Liz couldn't contain her curiosity any longer. "If you don't mind my asking, how did you manage to put up with her?"

"That was relatively easy," Ethan told her. "As long as we interacted for only short intervals at a time, I could handle it. The important thing is that I've come to realize that that part of my life was a huge mistake and I've moved on from it."

And on to something far, far better, he thought.

"Now, speaking of moving, shouldn't we be getting a move on if you want to be able to get to work on time?" he asked Liz.

He was right, Liz thought, glancing at her watch. "Are you sure you want to get something to eat there?" she asked him.

"Why? Have you decided to rescind your endorsement?"

"No, definitely not," she said with feeling. "But Chinese food isn't for everyone."

"Well, rest easy," he said. "Because I happen to really love Chinese food. And I plan to make up for lost time now that the opportunity has come up."

"Well, then, I can tell you that you've really got a treat ahead of you," she promised Ethan.

His eyes swept over her and lingered just for a moment, drinking in the very sight of her.

They were going to the Chinese restaurant in a few minutes, but there would be other times, he promised himself. Other times when neither one of them had to be anywhere—except with each other.

"Yes," Ethan responded. "I know."

Chapter Sixteen

Although it had begun to feel as if the day would never end, eventually it did. Eleven o'clock came, and Young Lee's staff slowly began to close the restaurant up. By 11:20, Liz was walking into the parking lot with Ethan at her side.

"I don't think I have ever seen anyone eat as slowly as you did this evening," Liz confessed to Ethan in amusement as they approached her car.

"I had to eat slowly," he insisted. "Otherwise, the server would have been within his rights to ask me to leave in order to free up my table.

People were beginning to line up at the reservations desk."

She laughed. "You were at the restaurant for so long, I thought Mrs. Lee was going to make you part of the staff. Why *did* you stay so long?"

"Well," he answered, "I wanted to be able to walk you to your car. And then make sure you got home."

Liz wasn't quite sure she understood what he was telling her. "You're going to follow me home?"

"I'd like to," Ethan answered honestly. But he didn't want her to get the wrong impression or feel as if he was trying to crowd her. "But I won't if you don't want me to."

She liked the fact that Ethan was leaving the decision up to her. She also liked the fact that he wanted to make sure she got home safely, even though this was Bedford—considered to be one of the safest cities of its size in the country. There was something comforting about having someone care about her well-being who *didn't* respond to the name Mom.

This was all brand-new territory for her.

"I have no objections," she told him, doing her best not to sound as pleased as she felt. Her grandmother had once told her that men liked a woman who was hard to get. Although, Liz reminded herself, the only man her grandmother had ever had in her life was Grandpa, so her range of experience wasn't exactly extensive.

"Good, then I'll follow you home," Ethan told her. And once he got there, he told himself, he'd play it by ear.

Because it was after eleven o'clock on a Sunday, traffic was practically nonexistent once they had traveled a short distance on the freeway. For all intents and purposes, the weekend was over, and people were preparing themselves to face Monday morning. Consequently, Ethan and Liz had arrived at her apartment complex in what felt like record time.

Entering the complex right behind her, Ethan parked in the first available space in guest parking. Once there, he got out and made his way over to her carport. He managed to reach the carport just as she was getting out of her vehicle.

He closed her door for her. "You look tired," he observed.

Liz wanted to tell him that he was mistaken. That she had gotten her second wind and could keep going indefinitely. But that would have been lying.

The truth was always her first choice. "That's probably because I am," she confessed. Taking a deep breath, she added, "To tell the truth, I feel like I'm operating on fumes."

"Then we need to get you to bed as soon as possible." The second the words were out of his mouth, Ethan realized how that must have sounded. "I mean by yourself. Not that I wouldn't like to join you," he added in case she thought he was rejecting her. Nothing could have been further from the truth. However, he was putting her needs above his own.

"I'm trying to be thoughtful here. But the words just seem to be coming out all wrong," he confessed as he walked Liz to her door.

She smiled, placing her hand on Ethan's arm. "I appreciate it. The thoughtfulness, not the part about it coming out all wrong," she qualified with a grin. Liz paused as she unlocked her door, then turned toward Ethan. "Would you like to come in for a few minutes?"

"I would," he told her honestly. "But I won't. Like I said, you need your rest."

The fact that he wasn't thinking about himself, but about her, really touched Liz. So much so that from somewhere deep within the recesses of her soul, she felt a surge of untapped energy rising up and coming to the foreground.

Before she could stop herself, Liz wove her

arms around his neck, rose up on her toes and kissed Ethan. Hard.

Caught off guard, he kissed her back before he was able to put the skids on his response. Consequently, he came perilously close to losing himself in that kiss. Just as he had the night before.

But somehow, he managed to pull back, putting enough space between them to be able to tell her in all sincerity, "You're making it very hard for me to walk away."

Her eyes held him prisoner as she whispered, "Then don't."

And that was that.

All of Ethan's good intentions seemed to go up in smoke, a casualty of the heat generated between them. Ethan held himself in check only long enough to be able to move farther inside her apartment. Once he did, he pushed her door closed behind him.

After that, passion, fueled equally by desire and the memory of last night, consumed them both, taking them from the door into her bedroom.

Giving in, they continued enjoying one another until they were spent—but very, very content.

Yet even while she was in the throes of lovemaking, adoring every single delicious moment, a little voice in Liz's head warned her that this was all just a wonderful, fleeting occurrence. It cautioned her that she couldn't allow herself to get used to it—used to *him*—because all she could logically count on was right now, this minute.

Tomorrow was an unknown entity with its own set of ramifications that had nothing to do with what was happening now.

It was an eternity away.

Keeping that in mind, Liz was determined to enjoy what was happening *now*. Because what was happening between them was totally unexpected and absolutely wonderful. And that was all she could count on.

Some time later, Ethan cradled her in his arms. "You know, for an exhausted woman, you displayed an amazing amount of energy," he told Liz with an amused laugh as they lay in her bed.

She smiled, pleased at his compliment. Pleased, too, to be here like this with him. Feeling like this was all so wondrously new to her. Liz knew better than to take anything for granted.

Her eyes crinkled as she said, "I guess you never know what you're capable of until that moment comes."

Charmed, Ethan pressed a kiss to her fore-head. "I guess not," he agreed.

He couldn't get over how completely different she was from Catherine. It amazed him that he had been willing to settle for so much less for so long. It was as if he hadn't even been think-ing back then, just going through the motions of living.

Ethan drew in a deep breath, trying to for-tify himself. "I'm going to have to go home," he told her.

"I know." There was a note of resigned sad-ness in her voice.

"I've got to be at the clinic by seven thirty," he added, then said by way of an explanation, "I never know what I'll find when I get there after my day off."

Her mouth curved just a little. "You make it sound ominous."

"Sometimes it is," he said honestly. "But it's not all bad," Ethan added quickly. "And I do like making a difference."

"I'm sure you do make a difference," she said with conviction. "In a lot of people's lives." It went without saying that in the short time they had known each other, Ethan had made a dif-ference in hers. "I understand perfectly," she as-sured him. "As a matter of fact, that's why I want to go into medical research once I get my degree. To make a difference."

He hadn't known that about her, and it surprised him. If she hadn't already had his complete attention before, she had it now.

"Any particular focus?" he asked.

Liz didn't even have to think about her answer. She had known it ever since she had made up her mind to go back to college.

"ALS," Liz answered. "It's the disease that killed my stepfather. He managed to last longer than most people, but it wasn't nearly long enough. I want to help find a way to eliminate it altogether."

"You do know that's a very tall, very frustrating order," Ethan felt obligated to point out.

"I know," she answered. "But if no one undertakes the battle, then the disease will be around forever."

Her reasoning blew him away. It amazed Ethan just how alike they were, how much he agreed with the way she thought. And he really liked the fact that she gave voice to things he had been feeling himself for a long time.

It was like he had found his soul mate. But even so, he knew he couldn't let himself get carried away. This sort of journey was one that was best undertaken slowly.

Even so, his arms tightened around her.

She raised her head in order to get a better look at his face. "I thought you said you had to go."

"I did, but I can spare a few more minutes," he told her.

She shifted around so that her body now faced his. The gesture was an unspoken invitation.

"Then let's not waste those minutes," she said.

The sound of her voice, sexy and low, suddenly rejuvenated him. And just like that, his body was ready to go again.

"Let's not," he agreed.

That evening was the beginning, laying the groundwork that in turn led to sporadic stolen minutes—sometimes even a stolen hour or two. It was time that was wedged in between her already overburdened, hectic schedule and his equally frantic one. Liz's schedule took her all over the city as well as to the local college and the Chinese restaurant, while his was completely stationary, taking place within the confines of the Well Being Clinic.

Because it turned out to be a lot easier for her to come by to see Ethan if she had several minutes to rub together, Liz did just that. And whenever she did stop by to visit him for a few minutes, she always brought food with her, something she had prepared in her kitchen so that he had a lunch to eat.

The first time she did stop by, Ethan's militant nurse, Edna, insisted that she had to sign in on the ledger first before she could see the doctor.

Thinking that the woman had mistaken her for a patient, Liz tried to explain to the nurse. "You don't understand. I just want to see him for a couple of minutes."

Edna's face transformed into a formidable scowl. "I understand, all right. That's what they all say, and I'm telling you that you need to wait your turn. The doctor will see you when he's ready to see you. Now sign your name," she ordered.

Liz glanced at her watch. She didn't have time for this. She'd only had a few minutes to spare, and they were presently ticking away. She could tell that the dour-faced nurse standing before her like the guardian of the gates of Hades was not about to move.

"Tell you what," Liz proposed. "Why don't you give this to the doctor?" She placed the brown bag on the reception desk.

Edna's brows narrowed even further into her perpetual frown. "The doctor doesn't accept bribes."

"It's not a bribe," Liz told the nurse. "It's lunch."

"Lunch?" Edna echoed. It wasn't obvious whether she believed her or not. "You brought him food?"

Rather than say something flippant, Liz explained the matter simply. "I had a feeling he wouldn't bring any himself, and given how pressed for time he usually is, I was afraid that he wouldn't just go out to get any on his own."

Edna studied the young woman before her at length before she finally concluded, "You're not a patient, are you?"

"No, I'm not," Liz answered. "I'm a friend of his."

"Huh" was the nurse's only response, delivered after another couple of seconds of close scrutiny.

Liz really began to feel for Ethan. If this was his help, he certainly had an uphill battle. "Anyway, I have to go. So if you'll just see that he gets this—" she nodded at the paper bag "—I'd appreciate it."

The nurse pursed her lips, looking at the paper bag, then at the young woman before her. "Sure, I can do that."

Liz inclined her head. "Thank you." Turning

on her heel, she was about to leave the clinic when the nurse called after her.

"What did you say your name was?"

"I didn't," Liz answered politely, then told her, "It's Liz Bellamy."

"And he'll know who Liz Bellamy is?" Edna asked, not looking all that convinced.

"I certainly hope so," Liz replied.

She turned to leave as another patient approached the reception desk, looking lost.

"Okay, I'll tell him," Edna responded, raising her voice just a tad, before she turned toward the patient. Edna had a new person to browbeat. "So, what's your problem?" she asked the woman point-blank.

A barrage of words, only some of which were intelligible, quickly came out of the small woman in response to the nurse's question.

It wasn't until ten minutes later that Edna was finally able to find the time to confront Ethan as he came out of one of the two exam rooms.

"Here," she declared, shoving the paper bag at him. "This is for you."

Stunned, Ethan looked at the bag. Since it came from Edna, he thought it safer if he just asked instead of looking into the bag. "What is it?"

Edna lifted her thin shoulders in a disinterested shrug. "I was told it was lunch," she said. "So it's probably lunch."

He didn't understand. This wasn't like the grumpy woman. "You brought me lunch?"

"Well, it wasn't going to come to you by itself," she informed him.

Maybe she was softening, he thought. "Edna, I don't know what to say."

"Well, that's a first," the nurse commented. "But before you get all mushy on me, I'm not the one responsible for this," she told him, waving a hand at the paper bag in his hands.

Okay, he was officially confused. "I don't understand."

"Neither do I," Edna said dismissively. "But this woman came in and asked me to give this to you."

Ethan was instantly alert. "A woman? What woman? When?"

"Some blonde woman," Edna said, annoyed by the questions. "Said her name was Liz Bellamy."

"Liz? Liz was here?" he questioned, immediately looking out into the small reception area. "Why didn't you call me?"

"Don't hand my head to me, young man," Edna snapped. "You were with a patient. You said never to interrupt you when you were with a patient unless it was an emergency."

As she walked away, she paused to look over her extremely thin shoulder. "You ask me, your taste is finally improving," she declared, and with that, she went back out into the reception area to terrorize the new patients who had just walked in.

Chapter Seventeen

"You managed to do the impossible," Ethan told her late that night when he swung by Liz's apartment.

He had called ahead to see if she would be home. The very sound of her voice invigorated him to the point that he suddenly had a second wind. He'd lost no time in getting to her apartment.

"Which impossible is that?" Liz asked, curious as she led Ethan over to the table.

The moment he had called her, Liz had quickly prepared a late-night dinner for both of them.

He smiled as he sat down. "You impressed Edna."

"Ah, the stern keeper of your gates," she recalled, visualizing the scowling woman. "She said that? That I impressed her?" The woman she had met hadn't seemed like the type to give voice to any praise.

"Not in so many words," he admitted. "But the inference was definitely there. If I read between the lines."

Liz laughed, spooning out a serving of beef stew for him and a smaller portion for herself. "I think you might have been blinded by those very same lines."

Ethan shook his head as he waited for her to sit down opposite him. "No, you have to understand the way that Edna thinks—she definitely likes you. Edna even said something about my taste in women definitely improving."

Liz took her seat at the table. "If you say so. Now eat." She gestured at his plate. "You need to keep up your strength. Nobody is going to have faith in a doctor who passes out at their feet."

He liked the way she looked out for him. This was definitely something new for him. "No danger of that happening, not with you bringing me lunches and feeding me dinner like this."

"Occasionally," Liz specified. "You make it sound like I do that on an everyday basis. It's only once in a while."

That wasn't to say that she wouldn't have been willing to do it every day, but she didn't want him to feel as if she was coming on strong. Besides, she couldn't really do it every day. The days when she had classes, she was far too busy to go out of her way all the way to the storefront clinic.

About to tell her that he saw right through her protest, the first spoonful of stew burst through, all but vibrating along his tongue. His eyes widened to the point that they looked as if they were going to fall out.

"Hey, this is *really* good," he exclaimed in abject wonder.

"You sound surprised," she noted.

He knew enough to backtrack if he didn't want to wind up hurting her feelings. "Not surprised, just really pleased. Have you ever considered owning your own restaurant?"

"My own restaurant?" she echoed. "Oh Lord, no!" Liz laughed, shaking her head as she dismissed the very idea. "My life is busy enough as it is."

Ethan paused as he allowed another spoonful of stew to wind its way through his system.

"Still," he told her, "it might be something to consider falling back on if you decide *not* to go into research."

She had had her heart set on going into medical research for a long time, but she smiled at how enthusiastic he sounded about her cooking.

"As long as you enjoy my efforts, that's good enough for me," she told him.

He considered her choice of words. "Oh, I think I'd use a stronger word than just *enjoy*," Ethan said as he made short work of the rest of the serving before him. "Damn, but this is good."

The sound of her pleased laugh lodged itself in his system, warming him as he surrendered his plate to her for seconds.

Ethan was a realist. He kept waiting for the sunshine throbbing within his system to grow a little dimmer and for disappointment to begin wiggling its way in, pushing aside the feeling of euphoria that was currently residing in his chest.

At the very least, he kept waiting for the perpetual smile on his face to fade away, or to fade just a touch. But even though he expected it, braced for it and mentally tried to prepare himself for what he felt was its inevitable advent, nothing changed. There was no dimness, no disappointment, and moreover, he couldn't get himself to stop smiling, not even a little.

He had initially thought that he felt the way he

did about Liz because, very simply put, he was on the rebound after his years with Catherine had come to such an abrupt end. But gradually, he was starting to realize that he felt the way he did about Liz not because she was a placeholder and not because he was using her to fill the void in his life. He was beginning to realize that he felt the way he did about Liz because of Liz. Because he had strong feelings about her.

That fact alone astonished him, because he had already made his peace with the fact that he just wasn't going to have strong feelings about any woman ever again.

And yet, here he was, looking forward to seeing Liz. Finding ways to see her despite each of them having schedules that would have easily exhausted any four other people. This was too perfect—which meant it was going to explode on him. Something always went wrong…and yet, he found himself wishing with all his heart, that this one time, it wouldn't.

Edna, of all people, noticed the difference in him and saw no reason not to mention it in her own winning way.

"You light up like a Christmas tree when that girl comes in," she told him, making the observation loud enough for Liz, who had just stopped by the clinic, to overhear her.

Ethan flushed somewhat. "Edna is not known for her subtlety," he told Liz.

"Oh? Did she say something?" Liz asked innocently as she came around the reception desk, then followed Ethan back into the tiny back office. "I didn't hear anything."

He laughed. They both knew she was lying, but he let it go. This wasn't the time or place to go into Edna's observation. That was best explored in the privacy of one of their bedrooms.

"Is this one of your quick visits sandwiched in between two different fares?" he asked her.

There was humor in her eyes as she asked, "How'd you guess?" She produced a paper bag out of the depths of her shoulder bag. "I brought you a chicken salad sandwich. It doesn't have to be refrigerated if you eat it in the next hour."

"I'll do my best," he promised.

He was about to tell Liz how much he really appreciated her stopping by like this and how he really did look forward to seeing her, but he didn't get a chance. A gut-wrenching, guttural scream coming from the waiting room managed to slice through anything he had to say.

Ethan was immediately hurrying out to discover the source of the scream, with Liz right on his heels, when they heard Edna cry out, "You'd better get in here, Doctor."

A second later, Ethan saw a young woman—little more than a girl, really, in Liz's estimation—sitting in a heap on the floor. Edna was hovering over her. The former was extremely pregnant. Her pretty young face was distorted with pain, and she appeared to be sitting in what looked like a small pool of water.

Edna looked at Ethan. "Her water broke," she informed him needlessly.

"I can see that," Ethan replied. Taking the pregnant teenager's hand in his, he squatted down to her level. "We need to get you to the hospital, Shirley."

"No, don't move me!" the teenager shrieked, her eyes wide and terrified. "It's coming! I can feel it coming! The baby's coming!"

"Shirley, this is your first baby," Ethan told the girl calmly in a soothing voice. "First babies notoriously take their time."

Her eyes looking as if they were about to pop out of her head, Shirley yanked Ethan in closer to her and told him between clenched teeth, "I said the baby is coming!" Her assertion was immediately followed by another mind-blowing scream.

"It's her body. She should know," Edna told Ethan in her typical flat, no-nonsense voice. And then the nurse looked around the waiting area.

For once, it was only half-filled. "You people need to get out of here," she announced.

"Hey," a large, burly man in a striped T-shirt protested. "I was next."

"You'll be next when you come back," Edna told him, leaving no room for argument. "Now go!" The nurse glared at the other patients. "That goes for the rest of you. Come back in a couple of hours," she ordered, pointing toward the front door.

"What if she's not done in a couple of hours?" another patient asked.

"Then you'll come back in a couple more," Edna told the patient. "Now go!"

To reinforce her order, Edna crossed to the door and held it open. The dark expression on her dour face left no room for any argument. Everyone had to leave.

Some grumbling, some compliant, all the other patients filed out of the clinic. The moment the last patient had left, Edna locked the door and then pulled down the blinds. It created a semblance of privacy against a background of cries and guttural screams.

Edna turned toward Liz who had dropped down on her knees beside Shirley, doing her best to comfort the semi-hysterical mother-to-be while Ethan had gone to change into scrubs and wash up.

The nurse crossed over to Liz. "You ever deliver a baby before?" Edna asked, although her tone seemed to indicate that she already knew the answer to her question.

"No," Liz answered honestly, "but you're here," she said, pointing out the obvious.

"Yeah," Edna agreed flatly. "Just one problem. My knees only bend far enough to let me sit down on a chair. Considering the position this mama-to-be is in, I won't be any help assisting young Dr. Kildare," she said, nodding her head toward Ethan just as he walked back into the waiting room.

Confused, Liz asked, "Who?"

"Somebody from a better era," Edna answered. She raised her voice just as Ethan came over to join them. "Your lady friend here is going to have to assist you," she informed him.

The declaration surprised him. Ethan looked at Liz. "How long was I gone?" he quipped, then asked seriously, "Liz, you okay with this?"

Liz certainly hadn't planned on any of this when she'd stopped by. She had only intended to be here for five minutes at most. But then, she had a feeling that the pregnant, screaming teenager on the floor hadn't planned on any of this, either.

"Just tell me what you need me to do," Liz told him gamely.

Shirley answered her instead of the doctor. "Get…this…baby…out of me!" the teenager screamed in agony.

"You heard the lady," Ethan told the two women. "Edna, I need clean towels, a blanket to put under Shirley and a basin filled with warm water. And if you can find a bottle of alcohol, bring that, too. We need to sterilize as much as we can."

"Yeah, yeah, I'll get them," Edna answered, beginning to shuffle off to the back room.

Liz rose to her feet. "I can get all that if you tell me where to find it," she said, wanting to spare the nurse the hassle of going back and forth.

"No, I need you right here," Ethan told her. "You're going to have to prop Shirley up when it comes time for her to push—which, all things considered, is going to be a lot sooner than I first thought."

He turned his attention to the moaning, twisting teenager. "Don't worry, Shirley, you're going to get through this." He smiled comfortingly at her. "It's the most natural process in the world."

Shirley shrieked again as another contraction seized her in its grip. When it finally passed, she all but collapsed back on the floor.

"Then why...do I...feel...like I'm...being yanked...*apart*!" she demanded.

"It might be natural, but nobody said it didn't hurt," Ethan told his patient. "Edna?"

"I'm here," Edna snapped as she shuffled back into the front room. "Hold your horses." She produced the towels and the blanket, placing the small pile on a chair. "I couldn't carry everything," she complained before Ethan could ask her where the basin of water and alcohol were. "I'll get the rest of it now."

Ethan merely nodded. "Help me with the blanket, Liz," he requested. "When I lift Shirley up, slip as much of the blanket under her as you can."

Liz did as he asked, moving as quickly as possible to get as much of the material under the teenager as she could. Although he tried to be as gentle as he could with her, Shirley still shrieked, sounding as if she was being pulled in two directions.

When he lay the screaming teen down again, Ethan focused on what needed to be done. He pushed her soggy, dripping maternity dress up.

A quick exam told him it was time.

"You were right," he told the unhappy teenager. "You really are ready to deliver this baby. It looks like you're fully dilated and ready to go."

His eyes shifted toward Liz. He really hoped she wouldn't freak out on him at the last minute, but she didn't seem like the type.

"Okay. I need you to prop our mama up by her shoulders until she's almost in a sitting position. Can you do that?" he asked Liz.

"No problem." She would have said that even if there was a problem. This was no time to think about herself, only the screaming teen who needed them.

"Shirley—" Ethan raised his voice as the teen screamed. "Shirley! When I tell you to push, I want you to push as hard as you can, do you understand?"

Shirley couldn't answer. She just nodded her head.

"Okay, now push!" Ethan ordered.

Amid ear-piercing screams, Shirley did as she was told until Ethan finally ordered her to stop.

The exhausted teenager looked at him as if he had betrayed her. "It's…not…here!" she cried.

"It will be," he told her. "Okay, again. Push!" Ethan ordered.

Liz could feel the pregnant teen's whole body

shaking against her hands as she propped the girl up.

"Okay, stop!" Ethan ordered less than a minute later.

Collapsing against the floor, Shirley alternated between screaming and crying. "It's… not…*working*!" she accused.

"It will," Ethan promised. "It will. Okay, again!" he ordered.

"I…can't…" she cried, shaking her head from side to side.

Liz leaned her face against the young woman's ear as she propped Shirley up against her chest. "Yes, you can," she coaxed. "You're almost there, Shirley. Don't give up now. You can do this. You know you can."

She raised her eyes to Ethan, who nodded. Liz pushed her hands up against Shirley's back, propping her up higher again.

"All right, push!" Ethan ordered. "Again!"

This time, just as it appeared that absolutely everything had been wrenched out of the exhausted mother-to-be, she squeezed her eyes shut, bore down and pushed as hard as she could with her very last ounce of strength. She pushed so hard, she was gasping and shrieking at the exact same time.

"It's coming," Ethan cried, encouraging the

teenager. "Your baby's coming…" He had his hands in position, waiting to make the monumental catch. When the baby finally emerged, Ethan immediately announced, "It's a girl." He looked up at the young mother. "You have a girl, Shirley. A lovely baby girl with…" He did a quick survey. "Ten fingers and ten toes."

Edna stepped in and took the baby from him. She quickly cleaned off the amniotic fluid from the little body as well as made sure the baby's nose and mouth were cleared of anything that might block the intake of air.

"I did it," Shirley cried, tears rolling down her cheeks as her daughter was placed in her arms. "I gave birth to a baby," she declared happily. Tears were shining in her eyes as she looked at Liz.

"I told you you could do it," Liz said, pleased beyond words that everything had turned out so well.

But it was obvious that the new mother barely heard her. She was far too enthralled with the new life she was holding in her arms.

Chapter Eighteen

Ethan slipped his arm around Liz's shoulders as he watched the EMTs wheel mother and baby out on a gurney and then load them into the back of their ambulance. He had already called ahead to the hospital and made arrangements with one of the obstetricians he knew to look after the new family unit.

He smiled now at Liz. "I'm glad you were here. You were a huge help calming Shirley down," he told her, closing the door again.

If anyone deserved any credit, it was Ethan, not her, Liz thought as she shrugged away his compliment. "Keeping people calm was just my Chariot driver training," she quipped. "Speaking of which," she continued, looking around for her purse. "I've got to clock back in. This was only supposed to be a five-minute break." Liz picked up her things where she had dropped them on the floor the moment Ethan had told her that he needed her help.

Ethan put his hand into his back pocket, ready to take out his wallet. "Let me make it up to you."

Liz immediately stopped him. She wasn't about to accept any money from him for her part in this. It just seemed wrong.

"No, that's all right," she told him. "I don't have school tonight. I'll just work later than I'd intended."

He knew that pride was important to her, and he wasn't about to argue. "Okay, then why don't I come by later and we can toast your first delivery?" he suggested.

"That sounds good," she responded. "But I'm not sure when I'll get home tonight. Why don't I swing by your place instead when I get done?"

Ethan grinned. It didn't matter who came to whom, as long as they came together. "You talked me into it. It's a deal," he told her.

Edna cleared her throat rather loudly. "I hate

breaking up this forgotten scene out of *Romeo and Juliet*," she announced, "but the hordes are back." The nurse nodded her head toward the door. She had pulled back the curtain just enough to give them a clear view of the returning patients gathering outside. "Looks like they took you at your word when you said to come back in two hours."

Ethan sighed. Time to get back to work. "Let them in, Edna. They've been waiting patiently."

Edna made a dismissive noise at the word *patiently.*

"Ha! Not long enough if you ask me," the nurse grumbled as she unlocked the door again.

As Liz slipped by the older woman on her way out, Edna muttered, "You did good," to her in such a low voice that at first Liz thought she had just imagined it as she tried to sidestep around the returning patients. But as she glanced back, she caught the look on Edna's face and realized that it hadn't been her imagination. She *had* heard the older woman.

Pleased, Liz left the clinic humming to herself. Her feet were barely touching the ground.

It turned out to be another exceedingly long day. The patients who returned to the clinic after Shirley had been taken away seemed to number almost twice as many as there had been initially. Not only that, but there was a steady stream of patients coming in all afternoon.

So much so that that the clinic wound up staying open even longer than it usually did.

At the end of the day, Edna left muttering under her breath that he needed to get a new watch to replace the one he had so he could keep better time.

Ethan heard her even though he pretended not to, but the truth was nothing could have fazed him or wiped the smile from his face. All the patients had been seen, all the crises were averted and he was going to be seeing Liz sometime later tonight. When he came right down to it, that was all that really mattered—especially the last part.

Ethan was home almost an hour when he finally heard the knock on his door. Having just finished with his latest journal entry—he had taken up writing in it again—he closed the book and hurried over to the front door.

Flipping the lock, he threw it open. "It might make things a lot easier if I just give you a key," he declared a second before he realized that the woman on his doorstep wasn't Liz.

Looking as regal as ever, Catherine Van Houghton gave him a distant, puzzled look. "Why in heaven's name would I want a key to this place?" she asked. "It would make more sense if I gave you a key to mine."

"Catherine," he acknowledged numbly, feeling as if he was having some sort of bad dream. "What are you doing here?"

"I asked myself that several times on the way over here," the woman responded. Not waiting for an invitation, she walked in as if it was her right, then shut the door behind her.

Ethan continued to stare at her, trying to figure out what in the world could have possibly prompted this woman to deign to cross his threshold after what she had said to him the last time they had seen one another.

"And what did you answer yourself?" he finally asked when it looked as if she was settling in.

There was no way he was going to allow her to stay, and it wasn't just because Liz was due at any minute now. It was over between Catherine and him, and he didn't want to be a party to any sort of feeble resuscitation attempts intended to bring the corpse that had once been their supposed relationship back to life.

"You'll be happy to know that I have decided to give you another chance. In other words, I'm going to take you back." She looked around the apartment, a distasteful expression on her lips.

"All this supposed noble selflessness of yours has affected your thinking," she declared. "That was why I broke up with you in the first place, so that you could rethink what you've done and get all this nonsense out of your system once and for all."

Catherine looked as if she was going to sit down on the sofa, then apparently decided against it. "Now that you've had time to think, I know you've realized how foolish you were being and have come to your senses." She squared her shoulders, pleased with herself. "I have even convinced my father to let you join his practice the way you were originally supposed to," she declared in a triumphant voice.

When he started to tell her that she needn't have gone to that trouble, Catherine held up her hand. "No need to thank me. Just promise not to act so irrationally again and we can put this unfortunate period behind us."

By the expression on her face, she apparently thought that was the end of it.

The way the woman behaved just took his breath away. But he was in no mood for her games, and he wasn't about to have any part of this.

"Catherine, what are you really doing here?" he asked.

"Haven't you been listening, darling?" Catherine asked, a touch of impatience in her voice. "I *forgive* you. You can come back, and we will just pick up our lives where you willfully dropped them. There won't even be any hard feelings as long as you promise to do what we agreed on."

"*We* never agreed on anything," he reminded the perfectly groomed woman before him. "You were the one who agreed, not me."

A scowl creased her perfect forehead. "Well, someone had to be the logical one, and you were all caught up in the romance of helping the sick and penniless, so I had to do your thinking for you."

"I'm sorry, Catherine. I appreciate you coming all the way here, leaving your ivory tower in order to give me another chance—but I do not want it," he told her flatly.

Shock and then anger flashed in her eyes. "Have you lost your mind?" she shouted.

"On the contrary," he informed her calmly. "I think I finally found it."

Her eyes narrowed, the fury in her tone building. "I want you to know that if I walk out that door, I am *not* coming back."

"I am counting on that," Ethan replied as if

he was trying to get rid of an annoying telemarketer on the phone.

There was disbelief coupled with rage in her eyes, as if Catherine realized that, for the first time in her privileged life, she was being rejected.

For a moment, she didn't speak. And then when she did, her tone bordered on ugly. "You're going to be very sorry!"

"I highly doubt that," he told her honestly.

Enough was enough, Ethan thought as he opened his front door. His indication was clear.

Catherine unleashed a string of highly unflattering curses as she stormed out of his apartment and got into her brand-new Mercedes.

As she started up her car, still viciously cursing at him, his lineage and his patients, Ethan patiently held his tongue. Instead of looking at her, he glanced over her and her car. That was when he thought he caught a glimpse of Liz's car. It was driving away.

His heart froze. Had Liz gotten here while Catherine was unleashing her tirade? Had she heard any of it, particularly the part where Catherine had told him that she forgave him and intended to take him back? He knew very well that Catherine had the kind of voice that carried. She had never been the type to speak softly, because the woman firmly believed that only what she had to say mattered. Everything else was just part of a wall of noise.

A sinking feeling seized him as he watched Liz driving out of his complex and his life. By coming back and carrying on the way she had, Catherine had managed to chase away the best thing that had ever happened to him.

Somehow, he had to make this right before it was too late.

It completely astonished Liz how she could go from feeling as if she was on top of the world one moment down to the absolute depths of despair the very next. But she had.

Eager to see Ethan, she had been about to knock on his door when she heard a woman's voice coming from inside the apartment. She froze.

The second she realized she was listening to Catherine, Ethan's former fiancée, telling him that she was willing to take him back, Liz knew that she had just been fooling herself. How could she have possibly thought that she and Ethan could actually have a life together? Why would he want to be with her when he could be with a beautiful, rich woman of the world who could easily open doors for him, take him anywhere he wanted to go? And they'd had all this time invested together. Why would she ever think he'd choose her?

The only door *she* could open for Ethan was one to a small storage unit stuffed with childhood memorabilia. It definitely was *not* the same thing.

What in the world had she been thinking? Liz silently demanded. It was like telling herself Ethan could be happy with rhinestones after having held a diamond in his hand.

Liz didn't remember driving home. She didn't remember parking her car or subsequently getting out of it. She couldn't even recall placing one foot in front of the other until she had gotten back to her apartment, but somehow, she was there, opening the door and walking inside, feeling as if her insides had been hollowed out using a rusty, jagged carving knife.

It was nice while it lasted, she thought with a deep sigh. But it was time she grew up and realized that they didn't live in a fairy-tale world where the handsome prince chose the scullery maid over the princess. In the real world, he chose the princess who came with a dowry of gold, she thought sadly.

Ethan was just an interlude. A wonderful, wonderful interlude. He was never your endgame, remember that. You still have your work, your goals and, eventually, you'll have that degree.

Numb, exhausted, Liz dropped down onto the sofa. Somehow, the bedroom seemed just too far away for her to walk to.

She could just curl up and sleep here, she told herself. She could—

The doorbell rang, and she jumped. But she remained where she was. She wasn't expecting anyone, and she really wasn't up to being polite right now.

The doorbell rang again. She willed whoever was pressing it to go away.

When she didn't answer the door the third time Ethan rang her doorbell, Ethan doubled up his fist and banged on the door instead.

"C'mon, Liz," he called out. "I know you're in there. I saw your car. Open up the door. Please."

Because the hour was getting late and she didn't want to disturb any of her neighbors, she crossed to the door. Drawing in her breath, she unlocked it. But she didn't open the door very far.

"What do you want, Ethan?" she asked in a voice that sounded as dead as she felt.

He was right, he thought with a pang. Liz *had* overheard Catherine.

"Let me in, Liz," he asked.

"Catherine wouldn't like that," Liz heard herself telling him.

Ethan's brow furrowed in a scowl. It was the first time she had ever seen him look even moderately annoyed. "I don't care what Catherine likes. You're the only one who matters to me, Liz. Now please, let me in."

Stepping back, Liz pulled open the door. "I have no intentions of coming between you and Catherine."

"Good," he responded. "Because there's nothing to come between. Catherine and I have been over for a long time. I told you that," he reminded her.

But Liz was thinking about what she had overheard tonight. "Tell that to Catherine."

"I already did," he answered. "Somehow she had gotten it into her head that despite the fact that she dumped me, this was just a hiatus and she was deciding to call it off. I told her thanks but no thanks. I also told her, in no uncertain terms, to leave."

But Liz shook her head, not sure if she believed him. "I didn't hear that part."

"That's because I'm not as loud as Catherine is when I talk. I want you to read something," he told her, taking from his pocket the journal that had brought them together. "Here," he said.

"Read the last entry. I wrote it just before Catherine came over."

Still very skeptical, Liz looked at the page he indicated. The entry he wrote was in the form of a Yelp review. Next to her name he had written in ten stars—five more than the usual top rating.

Next to the rating, he'd written an explanation: "I am giving Liz ten stars because being with her makes me twice as happy as I ever thought I could possibly be. I don't know what I did to be this lucky, but I hope she never changes her mind."

"Do you mean this?" Liz finally asked quietly, raising her eyes.

"More than you could possibly know," he told her. "Catherine coming over did accomplish one good thing."

"Oh?" Liz braced herself. "And what was that?"

"She made me realize more than ever how very lucky I am to have found someone like you."

"I don't come with an inheritance," Liz pointed out.

"I don't need an inheritance," he answered. "Haven't you heard?" he asked with a smile. "Money can't buy happiness."

"But it can buy peace of mind," Liz countered. And in the long run, she thought, that was important.

"What good is peace of mind without love?" Ethan asked.

"Love?" she echoed.

"Yes, you know," he told her, smiling into her eyes, "that little four-letter word that makes the world go around. You must have heard of it. There're all sorts of songs written about it." He took her hand in his. "As for me, I really believed it was all a myth. And then you came into my life. Suddenly, the sky was bluer, the air was fresher and I could actually hear birds singing in harmony."

Thinking he was making fun of her, Liz tried to pull away, but he wouldn't let her. He captured her other hand as well, holding both of them in his. "Until you came along, I didn't think I actually *could* love, not really. And now that you're here, I don't want to let you go. I certainly don't want to learn how to live without you—because I can't."

She stared at Ethan, convinced she had to be imagining all this. She could feel her pulse quickening. "Are you telling me that you love me?" she asked in disbelief.

"Badly, but yes, that's what I'm trying to tell you." He reached into his pocket. "As you pointed out, I don't have much, but I do have my mother's engagement ring. When she gave it to me, she told me to give it to the woman I couldn't live without once I found her." Taking the ring out of the box, he slipped it on Liz's finger. It was a little loose. He made a mental note to have it sized for her. But right now, he needed to have her say yes. "Well, I found her," he declared. And then he lowered his voice. "Liz Bellamy, will you marry me?"

She searched his face, convinced that for some reason, he was just going through the motions. "Did you give this to Catherine?" she asked.

"No, I didn't," he told her. "Catherine informed me that she expected her ring to be at least five carats. I told her I'd have to save for that," he said wryly. "She was still waiting for it when the engagement was terminated."

He was telling her the truth, Liz thought. She saw sincerity in Ethan's eyes, and the next moment, she was completely undone. "Then it's yes. Oh Lord, yes!" she cried, throwing her arms around his neck.

He grinned at her. "A simple 'yes, Ethan,' will do," he teased just before he kissed her—and sealed both their fates for the rest of their lives.

Epilogue

Nine months later

"I have never seen Ethan looking happier, Mother," Nikki whispered enthusiastically to Maizie.

Nikki's husband, Luke, and their two children were sitting up front in the church's pews that were reserved for the groom's side, but Nikki felt she had to seek her mother out, to thank her and the other two women who had had a hand in orchestrating this happy ending.

"I don't know how you managed it, but you

and the ladies really did it again," Nikki cried.
"Ethan still hasn't a clue that this was all prear-
ranged. I take it that his bride-to-be is equally
in the dark?"

Nikki looked from her mother to Theresa and
Cilia for confirmation.

Cilia's mouth curved. "Like there wasn't a
single match left in the world to light up," she
told Maizie's daughter with a wink.

Nikki smiled warmly at the women. "I knew
I could count on you. You did good!" she told
them in a stage whisper.

Theresa nodded, her handkerchief clutched in
her hand, ready to be pressed into use at a moment's notice. She always teared up at weddings.
"We always do," she told Nikki.

"I'd better be getting back to Luke before the
kids start getting restless," Nikki told the trio.
"But I'll see you at the reception."

Maizie nodded. "Count on it." She turned to
her friends as Nikki made her way back to the
front of the church.

Liz's mother, Ruth, had already been by—
twice—to express her gratitude, putting them
in an even better mood than they already were.

"Well, ladies," Maizie said to her friends,
"looks like we've done it again."

"Was there ever any doubt?" Cilia asked.

Maizie shook her head, happy to have brought yet another couple together. "No, none whatsoever."

"Does it ever bother you?" Theresa suddenly asked her friends. When they looked at her quizzically, she explained, "That the principals in these little arrangements don't even suspect what's going on?"

"Not at all," Maizie answered without hesitation. "It's part of the challenge. And part of the fun." Maizie looked at her two cohorts in matchmaking. "Don't you think so?"

"Absolutely," Theresa answered.

"What she said," Cilia agreed, nodding.

Maizie's smile widened. "I thought so."

"You look absolutely beautiful," Ruth enthused, circling Liz as she did a little last-minute—although entirely unnecessary—fussing with her daughter's veil. "I wish your father could be here to see you," she added wistfully.

Liz knew that her mother was referring to Howard, who had become more than a father to her over the years they had together. "He is, Mom," she assured Ruth. "I can feel it."

Ruth abruptly stopped fussing as she heard the organ music beginning.

"That's our cue," Liz said.

But Ruth remained where she was. Liz looked at her mother with confusion.

"Are you sure you don't feel funny having me walk you down the aisle?" Ruth asked. "Because if you do, then I can—"

Liz squeezed her mother's hand. "No, I don't feel funny. I wouldn't have it any other way," she assured her.

Ruth took a deep breath. "Then here we go."

It was a short distance from the back room to the rear of the church, but it seemed to feel as if it was longer.

The moment Liz and her mother came through the church's double doors, everyone inside the church rose. Their attention was riveted on the bride.

As was Ethan's. Ethan was convinced that he had never seen a more beautiful sight than the vision that was approaching him in slow, measured steps.

His smile widened with each step Liz took that brought her closer to him.

Everything, he thought, had been leading him up to this moment.

To this woman.

"Glad you could make it," Ethan whispered to Liz when she finally was at his side.

"Me, too," Liz answered just before they both turned toward the priest, waiting for him to say the words that would officially unite them in the eyes of the law.

They were already united that way in their souls.

* * * * *

MILLS & BOON

Coming next month

CINDERELLA'S NEW YORK FLING
Cara Colter

The sales assistant, Meredith, swept up all the clothes and left them.

"I feel like Cinderella," Jessica said, sinking into the chair beside him. The dress hitched up on a slender leg. He tried not to look. Failing in that, he tried not to be obvious about looking.

"But it's just about midnight. The glass slipper falls off, and I see what it all costs. I probably can't even afford one thing from here."

Jamie looked at his watch so she wouldn't see the pleasure in his eyes that he was going to play a part in her fairytale.

Not the prince part, of course. Though something about seeing her in all those clothes could tempt any man to play that role, even one as cynical about fairytales as him.

Meredith came back. She held out a piece of paper to Jessica.

Jessica took it, looked at it, and blinked. "Oh," she said. "It's so much less than I expected. Still, I don't need two skirts. So, I should probably take out the pencil-line one and keep the navy slacks."

Meredith snatched the paper back from her. "I forgot to add our preferred customer discount."

Jessica took back the paper with the adjusted price. Her mouth fell open with shocked surprise.

"Alright," she cried, beaming, "I'll take it all!"

As Meredith handled the transaction – giving the one

bill to Jessica and putting the real amount on Jamie's credit card, Jamie realized this was probably the most duplicitous thing he had ever done. But Jessica was absolutely radiant.

"I'll pay you back, of course. The insurance representative said I'll have some money by this afternoon."

How could something feel both so very wrong and so very right at the same time?

When they left the store, Jessica was wearing the brand new sundress. Jamie couldn't help but notice that, in a city where no one paid any attention to anyone else, Jessica was receiving subtle – and deeply appreciative glances – from the men of New York.

A man on a construction site whistled at her. Jamie threw him a warning glance, and then noticed Jessica was blushing as though she had been propositioned.

How could he turn her over to an assistant when it was so complicated? Jessica now looked like a sophisticated woman of the world. But she was the furthest thing from that. He couldn't just cast her out on her own. A still small voice, somewhere in the region of his heart, whispered to him, *admit it, pal, you don't want to.*

Continue reading
CINDERELLA'S NEW YORK FLING
Cara Colter

Available next month
www.millsandboon.co.uk

LET'S TALK
Romance

For exclusive extracts, competitions
and special offers, find us online:

MILLS & BOON

HISTORICAL

Awaken the romance of the past

Escape with historical heroes from time gone by. Whether your passion is for wicked Regency Rakes, muscled Viking warriors or rugged Highlanders, indulge your fantasies and awaken the romance of the past.

MILLS & BOON
MEDICAL
Pulse-Racing Passion

Set your pulse racing with dedicated,
delectable doctors in the high-pressure
world of medicine, where emotions run
high and passion, comfort and love are the
best medicine.

MILLS & BOON

THE HEART OF ROMANCE

A ROMANCE FOR EVERY KIND OF READER

MODERN

Prepare to be swept off your feet by sophisticated, sexy and seductive heroes, in some of the world's most glamourous and romantic locations, where power and passion collide.
8 stories per month.

HISTORICAL

Escape with historical heroes from time gone by. Whether your passion is for wicked Regency Rakes, muscled Vikings or rugged Highlanders, awaken the romance of the past.
6 stories per month.

MEDICAL

Set your pulse racing with dedicated, delectable doctors in the high-pressure world of medicine, where emotions run high and passion, comfort and love are the best medicine.
6 stories per month.

True Love

Celebrate true love with tender stories of heartfelt romance, from the rush of falling in love to the joy a new baby can bring, and a focus on the emotional heart of a relationship.
8 stories per month.

Desire

Indulge in secrets and scandal, intense drama and plenty of sizzle hot action with powerful and passionate heroes who have it all: wealth, status, good looks...everything but the right woman.
6 stories per month.

HEROES

Experience all the excitement of a gripping thriller, with an inter romance at its heart. Resourceful, true-to-life women and strong, fearless men face danger and desire - a killer combination!
8 stories per month.

DARE

Sensual love stories featuring smart, sassy heroines you'd want as best friend, and compelling intense heroes who are worthy of the
4 stories per month.

To see which titles are coming soon, please visit

millsandboon.co.uk/nextmonth